Praise for *The Bamboo Bed*

"*The Bamboo Bed* says more about the Vie[...] all the photographs, interviews, news copy, and t[...] ...y symbolic, extravagant in its tone of parody . . . the [...]sodic text provides a strange landscape without boundary, a front all about one."—*New Republic*

"A brilliant, strange, wondrous performance. . . . The impact of *The Bamboo Bed* comes from its peculiar disjointedness. It is comic surrealism: the sudden shifting between hilarity and outrage; recognizable reality giving way to the symbolic, the mythic, the gothic, the absurd." —*Nation*

"Eastlake brings events on to what seems a single stage, contracting events and circumscribing characters' actions, so that we are left with the brevity and unique logic of a nightmare. . . . A skillful and subtle performance, leaving much to the imagination, while leaving few doubts so far as the real issues and character of the war are concerned." —*Times Literary Supplement*

"Individual scenes light up like a burst of napalm and the raunchy dialog is often mordantly and hysterically funny. War is not only hell, it is downright crazy, Mr. Eastlake says, especially as we practice it in Vietnam, and the grisly perversity of it all can only be endured by throwing reason out the window and letting imagination go wild."—*Publishers Weekly*

"*The Bamboo Bed* approaches the struggle in Vietnam not as a three-dimensional event but as the frighteningly abstract piece of surrealism that we all share on the evening news. Black comedy, myth, shaggy parables of the top secrets of the human heart—these are the literary forms war takes for Eastlake."—*Time*

"This is a very funny novel, but one that catches your laughter up with catharsis, changing the fun into reflection. It is a good novel—a very good novel." —*Library Journal*

"*The Bamboo Bed* is smartly designed . . . characters all talk in kennings, jump about with the elate coolness of Kirk Douglas, and make love in helicopters." —Guy Davenport, *Hudson Review*

WORKS BY WILLIAM EASTLAKE

the
bamboo bed
William Eastlake

Preface by the author

Dalkey Archive Press

Originally published by Simon & Schuster, 1969
Copyright © 1969 by William Eastlake
Preface copyright © 1989 by William Eastlake

First Dalkey Archive edition, 2001

Library of Congress Cataloging-in-Publication Data

Eastlake, William, 1917-1997.
   The bamboo bed / by William Eastlake ; introduction by William
Eastlake.— 1st Dalkey Archive ed.
      p. cm.
   ISBN 1-56478-264-6 (alk. paper)
      1. Vietnamese Conflict, 1961-1975—Fiction.   I. Title.
PS3555.A7 B36 2001
813'.54--dc21   2001028042

Partially funded by grants from the Lannan Foundation, the National Endowment for the Arts, a federal agency, and the Illinois Arts Council, a state agency.

Dalkey Archive Press
www.dalkeyarchive.com

the
bamboo bed

PREFACE

I WROTE this book as a result of going to Vietnam as a correspondent. I went to that war because I felt it was my responsibility as a writer to cover the most historic happening of our time. In the era of the great Civil War between our States, America had the finest writers our country ever produced—Mark Twain, Herman Melville, Walt Whitman—yet they had little to say about the most powerful piece of history in their lifetime. A generation later, Stephen Crane wrote *The Red Badge of Courage,* and two generations later came Margaret Mitchell's best-selling Civil War true romance, *Gone With the Wind.*

I miss very much that the geniuses of the Civil War time remained silent; I regret even more that my own mentors, such as John Steinbeck, in my time did not have a book about a war that divided our country and ended in defeat. I hope that this book might make a small contribution to victory—a victory over those who hang out more flags for another similar war in our time. In any time.

Vietnam was a valuable experience for America. It taught us that there are no winners and everybody loses—the vanquished and the vanquisher. The lesson has not sunk in yet, but I am confident that it will.

An objective nonfiction version of war does not make sense. Because war is chaos. War is insanity in action. Insanity manifest. Only the artist can give form to the weird happenings. I like to think that that is why Carey McWilliams, the editor of *The Nation,* asked me to go to Vietnam as a correspondent for them.

3

If you fear the unconscious, do not read this book. *The Bamboo Bed* is an attempt to explore the workings of the mind when it is set free. The terror of war is a liberator. All that is not said is said. All that is not permitted is permitted. *The Bamboo Bed* is another Mark Twain's *Letters From the Grave*. Much of what Twain wrote was destroyed because it was unacceptable. Now all of what Twain wrote is permitted. We should celebrate this. The artist will make us free. I take small credit for *The Bamboo Bed* when it works. It worked when I listened carefully and allowed the randomness of the unsaid to be said. We should not fear the revelations of army language. Army language is not obscene; it is a futile and faint attempt to protest the obscenity of war. Leo Tolstoy's *War and Peace* ignored, left out, the stuff of war—how soldiers talk. Their language in war is timeless and universal. Even our own Ernest Hemingway, who claimed to be "telling it truly," failed because of his attempts also to reach the Book of the Month Club. But don't condemn Tolstoy and Hemingway. Condemn the mendacity of their time. The lies of omission in their time. War must have a stop. Listen to the soldier. Listen to the dying and the dead. War must have a stop.

In *The Bamboo Bed* I am attempting to accomplish what a painter attempts to see beyond what a photograph shows. All of *The Bamboo Bed* is based on real people, not fiction. Real incidents, not something I made up, yet it is a work of fiction as is the work of an artist who paints a picture that goes beyond what appears to be there to a two-eyed observer. The artist sees the people, sees the incident, with a third eye. A novel of the happenings of war is an attempt to organize the unorganized, to give form and meaning to chaos. An objective view of the war in Vietnam is merely a crowd of statistics. An objective account of a happening is meaningless without the third eye, without the fiction of art. No one saw what Goya, what Rembrandt, what Leonardo saw until these artists showed us the truth beyond the illusions of reality. There were thousands of accounts of whaling before Herman Melville's *Moby-Dick,* yet his fictional account is the only survivor. William Shakespeare's

4

fictional account of a man called Hamlet tells us more about universal and timeless men than any history or factual biography. In *The Bamboo Bed* I could have written what was recorded on a tape recorder, but I wanted to write what was trying to be said by the nurse, by the soldier, by the B-52 bombers, by Agent Orange and all the poisons of war.

When *The Bamboo Bed* was first published, I received a fan letter from a Vietnamese soldier who wanted to translate the book into Vietnamese. I don't know what happened to his project, although this book has been translated into several languages. Both sides should feel a small victory if and when *The Bamboo Bed* makes it into the Vietnamese language. The war will have an ending. Tragedy, black humor, love, and death are comrades in arms.

WILLIAM EASTLAKE
June 1989

1

Madame Dieudonné arose, stark and stripped, in her underground villa at 0600 as was her wont, turned on the shortwave radio and heard the report from Laos that Captain Clancy was dead, then she walked, still naked, to her jewel box, removed a small, black, heavy object, raised it to her head and blew her pretty French brains out. Pas vrai. Not true.

That's the way the papers had it, but they did not get it right. They never do. The newspapers seldom get anything right because they are not creative. Life is an art.

It was true—c'était vrai—that Madame Dieudonné went to the jewel box, removed the gun, but nothing more. Another death did not follow fast upon. The newspapers made a good story. But there is a better one. The truth.

Madame Dieudonné lived in the underground villa. This is very difficult to believe unless you have tried to live on top in Vietnam. It is best not to.

Madame Dieudonné took the black, dark, heavy object from her jewel box and slid it under the golden pillow on her bamboo bed. Then she sat on the edge of the huge circle bed and stared at herself in the ceiling-to-floor curved mirror that reflected all of the bed and thought of all the things that she had not done. We are never long anguished by the things we have done. We are stricken by what we have not done.

She had never told Captain Clancy she loved him because this must be for the books and the movies, certainly not for a war. In a war there cannot be any plans. If you make plans during a war you are lying. It would have been good to lie.

She stared at the naked picture of herself in the great mirror, at the mirror image of a body that had not betrayed her. It was still good. The body of herself that was still firm in all the right places and sloping and undulating and good in all the right places. But a body is for someone else. A body is never for yourself, so that the mirror of herself became a vanity, an indulgence, that was nothing at all because it was mirrored back to no one. Nothing. No man at all.

The power failed now and she went out in the mirror. The reflection, the picture of her naked self disappeared. The VC must have cut the power line to Pleiku. The power failure was good because now she could not see that the captain was not naked beside her. She could not see that he was not here. It is very important to be in bed with someone. A bed is not a bed without two people.

In the black darkness she could see and hear and feel clearly and sharply. She could see and hear and feel with all the sensitivity of the insane. Of the bereft. Of the alone and lost. And now in the bereavement of her mind she felt his arms come around her good and they were good and strong and hard and he swept her backwards good and strong and hard.

It had been a bright and light, almost impossible in the monsoon season, morning seven months past when Clancy had first arrived. Clancy had come in bloody armor. Clancy had come in a tank.

Best not to have him right then. Best to wait till the battle was over. Not the war. Never the war. That would take such an infinity of time that life would be all gone. Several lives, a million, so you cannot be decorous. You must remember that in a war young men come and go. In a war young men come and go and die. The opportunity must be seized. Does that sound too aggressive? Too unfeminine? Too female? Too Madame Dieudonné? Well, that is who she was. Be yourself. Madame Dieudonné was one of a kind. Dieudonné means God-given. I do not know the significance of this. But time will work it out.

Madame Dieudonné said that her lover arrived in armor, a tank. Not quite true. Her lover blossomed in the sky, a gift from the gods. Something like the birds, yet more like an abrupt orange chrysanthemum far up and high and recapitulant too, because as the chute descended among all the other chutes, color-coded for identification, some green and some stripey and some red, it appeared and reappeared in the morning monsoon so that sometimes you saw it and sometimes you could not. A fairy game. A girlhood dream of olden and fairy times, of plumed troops descending in fairy light . . . and then a modern war.

It was an American Search and Destroy Recondo operation to seize and hold the Nu Trang Valley against forward elements of the 27th North Vietnamese Regiment that had already crossed from Cambodia at Dak Mai and were worming their way through Two Corps to seal off the big American base on Tan Sut, then fan out into a flanker position against Saigon.

The reaction to this was all those American people coming down in the middle of Asia. Captain Clancy's A for Alpha Company, 2nd of the 8th. They had been thrown, tossed, into the great green rain forest as a blocking force only three hours before, jammed into C-123s and fed out over the jungles of Nam before you could say General Westmoreland.

And it was not only the abrupt American arrival this precious and light-shattered monsoon morning that amazed Madame Dieudonné. It was their American captain, who not only had a one-inch metal Roman crest riveted to his helmet but a red, white and blue jungle parrot feather stuck there too as a leader point. And something more. A drummer boy arrived, descended in a striped chute and began drumming as a rally point even before his billowing strange flower touched the ground. And if that was not enough, if that was not already a surfeit of madness, an apogee of awful

9

consternation and continued amaze, then the final triumph was the firing of the swimming pool. Soldiers threw some fluid on the pool, lit the pool with a match on the end of a stick, and it glared up over all the rubber plantation to attract the American chutists wherever they might be, from every and any booby trap, pongee stake, rice paddy or old well in which they had fallen. Great gouts of orange flare and black smoke poured above the swimming pool and the crackle of guns as the drummer boy stood by the diving board rolling out a steady tattoo of assembly. Not that Captain Clancy was crazy but that Captain Clancy had what Madame Dieudonné called "panache" or the Vietnamese "tak hi" depending on her mood, or what the British called at Balaclava "pukka" and the Americans at base camp a "weird fucking outfit." The men would follow Clancy over a cliff, into a bottomless abyss. Cheerfully. Anyway with a great deal of style. Style. That's what Clancy had. If you can't win a war with that, then you can't win a war. We will pursue that later.

I will pursue that later is not what Madame Dieudonné thought when she first saw Clancy. But something akin. What did Clancy have besides the plumed helmet and the drummer boy? The ugly proud face. The sword. Yes, he had a sword with which he pointed the men on. What else? This is only the ancient junk of war. The captain had what Madame Dieudonné called something passing strange. Passing strange. Bien étrange. With all the clown costumes and the theater drive, the burning pond, the drummer boy, the flashing sword, the arrival by cloud, there was a gift, a supreme and ascending quality of life. In the inexorable march toward death there was life. The magic man. The magician. Not the taker but the giver of life. Clancy was the soldier magician. The magic man.

And he has arrived here, Madame Dieudonné thought, to bring death? Save the rubber plantation? Save me? Destroy all? Everything? Every person? We shall see. On verra.

The drummer boy at the diving board. Do they have

drummer boys in Nam? Clancy's outfit did. We do know how many drummer boys I saw in Nam. One. How many swords. One. How many Roman helmets. One. Now we will get a hundred letters from ex-soldiers in Nam who drummed, or carried swords and swayed beneath crested Roman helmets.

However, this morning, this day, there was only one Clancy. This was true for Madame Dieudonné. Madame Dieudonné invited Clancy down into the cellar of her villa. The whole house was a cellar.

Clancy ignored her. Clancy was here to do a job. Clancy noticed that she was built well and that somewhere, sometime, someplace, he had known her, and she was built well. He would get back to her later.

The chutists were coming in to the assembly point. The men who dropped from the sky were arriving at the swimming pool bearing their broken, their dead. There were not many dead. The sign of a good outfit is that the dead are kept at a minimum. One dead is not many unless the one is you. Then one becomes an enormous figure.

As the men came in, Clancy had them dig in. Clancy had them form their perimeter around the pool. It was the high ground, the only high ground. Then if the men fell back they would drown in the pool. There was no escape route. That was the way Clancy wanted it. There was a low wall around the pool about ten meters out with grass in between. The grass was so perfect it looked fake. Clancy made his perimeter outside the wall because they were already attracting rockets and mortars that exploded behind walls. A wall was fine in the American Civil War. If there was no wall they built one and called it a breastwork because that's how high walls were. In this war we dig holes and call them shit holes because that's how soldiers talk. All soldiers. All wars. Not nice talk for a lady to hear. War is not nice. War is something else.

As the men came in and Clancy had enough protection for the CP he sent them out again into the jungle of rubber in new fire teams. The old squad after a drop are always missing people. Not all of them are dead. Some, despite the fire in the pool, have missed the rally point and are lost. Some have broken arms and broken legs and broken ankles because they hit down badly. Some are afraid and hiding. Are they the smart ones? We do know that they are the frightened ones. Are they the draft dodgers who were drafted? Or are they the brave who volunteered?

Clancy had no checkoff as they came into the rally point. That would come later, after the battle was won. They came in in ones and twos and threes, hoping it was won. Sometimes they came in in fours and fives and sixes looking for a fight. How do you account for heroism? Because man does not believe in his own death. What about the cowards? The coward believes. They came into the burning pyre, some limping, some hopping, some jumping over the wall.

"What's that?"

"A pool."

"No, that."

"What?"

"That."

"A fucking woman."

"A woman?"

"Yes."

"What's a woman doing in Nam?"

"They got them all over."

"In the middle of a war? In the middle of a fire fight?"

"They live here."

"Yes."

We try, Madame Dieudonné thought.

"Is she a Gook?"

"It's hard to tell."

"Yes."

Very hard to tell, Madame Dieudonné thought, very hard for me when fire drops out of the sky and you are billowed in black smoke and shot at by all sides. When they burn your swimming pool. When a boy stands on the diving board beating a drum. But I will try.

"Captain," she said.

"Later."

"But, Captain," she said, "you can go below where it is safe, where you can direct this from there."

"Later," he said.

Captain Clancy turned and asked, "What's happened to Nathan?"

The drumming had ceased.

"He got zapped."

"Fish him out," Clancy said.

After an interval the drumming continued.

A lieutenant came up and asked, "Shall we push, Captain?"

"Yes."

"They are dug in over there by that seed house."

"Where?"

"There."

"Dig them out," Clancy said.

"We could use a tank."

"We could use an army," Clancy said.

What is this if not an army? Madame Dieudonné wondered. Oh yes, it is a nightmare. A dream. That is what this war is, a bad dream. This too will pass. Ceci aussi va finir. Madame Dieudonné thought this because she was a French colon, a woman who had seen much. Too much?

The lieutenant was back. Had he ever left? "There's our tank, sir."

A thirty-ton tank appeared in the sky. They have planes now that will airlift a house.

The gay yellow parachute that umbrellaed over the tank was as large as a football field. The tank swung back and forth, back and forth, kind of like a precursor and a doom, trying to find its earth. Some place to settle. But it could not stop its pendulum motion. But it must, it must, the lieutenant thought. It must. If the pendulum did not stop, the tank would turn over when it hit. "It must!" the lieutenant said aloud. But it did not, and when the tank hit down in the beginning rubber trees it turned over and lay on its back like a huge helpless turtle in the midst of the small rubber trees.

"I never did like tanks," Clancy said.

Ah, so my hero does not like tanks, Madame Dieudonné thought. That is something to start with. But he does believe in swords and plumes and drummer boys. He must have been fighting for one thousand years, since long ago and far away. He does not like tanks. What about women? We have been around one, two thousand years, too, since long ago and far away.

"Get your pink ass down there, Lieutenant," Clancy said, "and get those Unfriendlies out with pluck."

"And luck."

"Bayonets," Captain Clancy said.

"Okay," the lieutenant said, studying the tactical terrain below. "Okay. Yes."

"Move your pink ass," Clancy said. "Get behind them. Hit them with your flankers wide so you go in big."

"Okay."

"Move your pink ass," the captain said gently. "And stay alive."

"Death before dishonor."

"Yes," the captain said, and he touched the lieutenant as he moved off.

As he moved his pink ass off, Madame Dieudonné thought, this is not a coup de guerre, it is a coup de théâtre. If only the bullets were not real. If only the dead came alive again for the second act. I do not know whether the lieutenant has a derrière rose, but he has a pink face. Red on all the highlights, like a Degas peach. Never shaved yet. We will never know about the derrière rose of the lieutenant but we will know about the captain. All.

Madame Dieudonné was never known for her shyness, never famous for modesty, tact, decorum and all that passes for a lady, even in Nam. You do not control the largest rubber plantation in Viet by games that women play. From an oblique angle and standing slightly above as the captain did—the captain was still above her even though her small feet were planted on a rise—she seemed, in very tight silk and very high black hair, an Oriental toy. Maybe it was a woman in the middle of a battle that did it. She did not belong. She must be not real. The captain would discover all. Later.

Now the jeeps blossomed. The jeeps bloomed out above, along with the other paraphernalia of war. It was the blooming time of war and in the sky. The drop zone was still the rubber nursery where the tank was wrong side up. It was easy to tell the DZ because the young trees were a considerably lighter shade of green from above than the mature rubber trees. It was easy to tell but not easy to hit the bullseye of rubber nursery, with a twenty-knot monsoon drift. So the big and clumsy C1-35s slipped in upwind and gave aerial birth to the gay parachuted junk of war that landed in another country. Cambodia was not far. Some supply landed closer, on Vietnam. Some got in the drop zone. One artillery piece, a 155 howitzer, hit the wrong-side-up tank and lodged there as though it belonged. No veteran was unhappy with the final score of the drop. It was an average day.

The Unfriendlies now commenced an attack to grab all the stuff that fell in the rubber nursery. They wanted more than they had already got. Their attack was blunted, then died for now.

"They're too damn greedy," Clancy said.

A big C-135 swept in right over the villa and released a huge sectioned platform of steel. The great canister took a lucky bounce and made it halfway up the hill before it stopped. Alpha ran down and got it in long pieces and placed it over the pool that had ceased now to burn. They had in twelve minutes constructed a landing zone for the helicopters that would commence tactical resupply.

"Mon Dieu," Madame Dieudonné wondered aloud, "we are again back in the twenty-first century."

The drummer boy that Clancy called Little Nathan sat down. He had been flinging his arms up in the air with great éclat. She liked it. Style. Again style. Now that everyone who was anyone, that is who was still alive, had come home, there was nothing more for Little Nathan to drum about, so he sat down on the perfect grass and wiped one of the sticks on his jungle boot and stuck the tip of the other stick in his mouth and watched the war.

Clancy not only had Little Nathan but all sorts of Vietnamese retainers so that at base camp Clancy moved about like a prince. Clancy had the Vietnamese do everything but fight the war. The Vietnamese would do anything for Clancy but that.

The choppers were coming in now and landing on the swimming pool. Because the rubber trees started at the base of the villa hill and went on to infinity it was the only flat place there was.

The choppers came in with ear-hurting noise like enormous insects from another planet. They came in bringing their hurricane winds and vibrations that shook the foundations of the earth. That's the way it is in Nam, you have the utter and absolute stillness of a primordial, an unrecorded and unwitnessed time—such an awful silence of beauty that is fixed and hushed, such a magnitude of all of time, you cannot breathe.

Then the choppers come.

The world begins.

Man arrives.

And not only that, Madame Dieudonné thought, not only has he arrived but at once departed, as though the only cause for life was to give it, because it was—and she watched them shoot at each other now—as if all the men of the earth were impotent and had arrived at taunting death as some form of fornication.

"You must make it below with me," she said.

"Later."

The choppers using plastic-space-helmeted Blacks for machine gunners touched down, then hurled out the cases of inedible C rations, the myriad parts for unworkable

M16s, the mortar shells that bounced and the blood plasma that burst and dripped into the swimming pool below as though lending it the gift of life. The choppers, having performed their no-mission, hurled themselves away only to rise ten meters and at once crash in a storm of hostile fire and scatter themselves down the slope in a twisted pyre of aluminum scrap with one enormous rotor blade pointing straight up skyward like some shining and final American erection.

Others got away okay—darted off into the monsoon-greening Vietnamese sun as though the hostiles, the Unfriendlies, the 74th North Vietnamese regiment, were using innocent Chinese firecrackers to celebrate the American arrivals and departures.

Beneath the villa the battle flowed up close and then ebbed back into the rubber green. It was not one battle but, like most engagements in Viet, it was many, sometimes separate and distinct, sometimes covert, but always with a seeming divorce and anonymity, without concern or even relationship to what happened in another part of the jungle. In civilian life it is called chaos. In war it is called a battle.

There was one man now in the world who understood the indecipherable code of the chaos below. Clancy. The only man who could untangle in his mind the liquid Sanskrit of the blood below. Clancy.

Madame Dieudonné went below in the villa many times. So did Clancy—below in the jungle. It is fine to give orders from the hill but there is no substitute for contact. You do not gain the love of your men by sitting in a bunker. The men must know that you are sharing their glory and their death. Clancy not only had pluck and luck but another attribute that is God-given. Madame Dieudonné thought him the ugliest and the handsomest man she had ever seen.

Pluck and luck.

Ugly and handsome.

Brave and true.

Little Nathan, the Vietnamese drummer, was a refugee

from our bombers. Every time a village was bombed a few hundred refugees arrived in the villages that were still standing. There were not many still standing in Nam. Those that were not destroyed by the bombers were destroyed by the VC rocketeers. It was the rocketeers and the bombers against the people. The people lost. Little Nathan was a result of the defeat.

Little Nathan went from village to village to find a village that was still standing. That's how he came upon A for Alpha Company, Clancy's outfit. They fed him, then they could not lose him. Every place that Alpha went Little Nathan followed. Alpha became his mother. Clancy, who was the hero of the clan, became his father. They called him Nathan because part of his endless Vietnamese name sounded like that.

Clancy told him, "But, Jesus, boy, you can't fight. Too young."

So Nathan got a drum. Clancy told him, "But, Jesus, boy, if you play that we are dead."

So Little Nathan only played it when their position was already known, or when, like now, Clancy wanted all the boys home.

How can a small, yellow-tan, golden and fine-boned, delicious-eyed Vietnamese child have Clancy for an old man? Alpha for a mother? That is the way the war goes.

They tried to lose him but he would not lose. They tried to discourage him but he would not discourage. As children will in Nam, he learned English, the American army language, quickly and settled down to the only life he knew, to the only parents found—A for Alpha. Captain Clancy. A father found.

"Never leave the perimeter in a fire fight. Stay inside the circle always."

"Yes, sir."

"Do not sir me. Obey me."

"Yes."

"Go and get the drum."

"Yes, sir."

"What did I tell you?"

"Stay inside the circle."

"You are a good boy, Nathan. Tragically there are a million more like you."

"What?"

"Get the drum."

"Why do they say you got the most vicious outfit in Nam?"

"Because they don't . . . Because they have never known . . ." And then Clancy ceased, and then he said, "Get the drum." And then he said, "Never leave the circle. Weave a circle round him thrice for he on honey dew hath fed and drunk the milk of paradise."

"From a book?"

"Yes. With works of art their armies meet and war shall sink beneath their feet."

"An American?"

"No, an Englishman. William Blake. Walt Whitman was the only American poet."

"Is he here?"

"Yes."

"That's nice."

"Yes, it's nice that he came to Nam with us. It's nice that the dead stick around. Nathan?"

"Yes?"

"Never leave the perimeter. Stay in the circle."

"Yes."

"Remember."

Now, on the villa hill, Little Nathan put aside his drumsticks and his drum, then he looked up and saw a helicopter hovering over him in the flak. The Huey seven-place chopper had red lettering on the side which read, THE BAMBOO BED. That was nice. Then he looked over at Madame Dieudonné. She was beautiful. That was nice. She must come with the place. She looked half Vietnamese and half something else.

That was nice. But where was Clancy? Little Nathan remembered the circle. But then he remembered Clancy.

"Come back!" Then Madame Dieudonné caught herself and called to the drummer boy in Vietnamese, "Bai tu! Bai tu!"

But Little Nathan was off to find Clancy. Clancy was missing too long. The thing is, the thing that is important is you can lose parts of something, you can lose parts of A for Alpha Company and survive. But you cannot lose A for Alpha itself and still make it. You cannot lose Clancy. Clancy should take more care of himself.

Nathan looked for the flash of Clancy's sword. Nathan watched for the red, white and blue parrot plume of Clancy's helmet. Little Nathan stumbled down the hill to be with Clancy.

Captain Clancy was performing a cool job in a small war. He moved from fire point to fire point, sometimes using the sword as a scythe or a machete to get through, sometimes as a cane, a walking stick, a pointer-out of hostiles, a remonstrance and a threat, a chastisement and encouragement to A for Alpha, an American and secret weapon against the foe, but always a flashing banner, emblematic of A for Alpha, a scintillant promise and threat.

Clancy rested on his sword. The battle went well. The enemy did not want to fight here. They had not chosen the place. The enemy always wanted to fight the battle of their choosing. If they met stiff resistance here they would withdraw back into Cambodia and cross another day, another place.

Good, because Clancy had other business today. Madame Dieudonné. When he first saw her he knew he had known her with a deep and understanding intimacy since all of time, that the para-drop here in this part of the jungle had been foreordained. Not only that but she was waiting for him to drop. She had been waiting for someone to drop from the sky that was him.

Wait, he told her, staring into the jungle. Wait, not long,

and I will be with you. You will notice that the enemy fire power is increasing, he silently told her, told the jungle. It will steadily go up and up and up until it reaches a crescendo of final despair. It means they are pulling out. Because they are covering their retreat. No, because no army retreats ever. They withdraw, or retire to a better position, but no army ever retreats. No, never!

The volleying now was terrific, mostly small arms and automatic weapons. You could tell our 50s by that slow cyclic rate of fire and you could pick up the Russian 7.4s by the steady zip. The stuff was coming through the trees and pocking into the villa hill so hard that it could have been a monsoon hail that hit the hill, causing it to explode all over, to jump. The hill that jumped.

Little Nathan was stumbling down. He had come to rescue Clancy. He was caught in the middle of the hill when the hail began. There was no cover.

Clancy saw this and stepped from the safety of the rubber jungle into the clearing to draw fire on himself. This was no heroic action. The instant plan was to draw fire away from Nathan who still had a hundred meters to go. Clancy raised something so that it flashed like a heliograph. This was no heroic action because no instant plan can be. It was simply the only way to stop the hail on Nathan who had no cover. Where the hail fell next you dealt with next. But Clancy could draw no fire because they were shooting at everything.

Nathan dissolved. Disappeared on the hill that jumped. Nathan did not exist.

Clancy stuck his sword in a rubber tree and walked up the villa hill toward where something had ceased to be. The hail quit. Quicker than it had started it stopped. When Clancy got to where Nathan had been there was almost nothing. You had to know exactly what you were looking for to notice anything. If Nathan had been wearing a helmet there would have been the remains of something.

Clancy could hear the drum.

Now that the small and deadly quick war was over Clancy made it up to the top of the villa hill.

Clancy could still hear the drum.

There was none of the shooting noise of war now but there was still the music of the drum.

It must be turned off. In no place could he see a drummer.

Clancy went through a dark teak door surrounded by an arch of sandbags. The steps led down into the villa. The drumming continued. Clancy opened several doors but in the rooms there was no drummer. Now he opened a door and she was sitting on the huge oval bamboo bed.

She motioned to him and he lay beside her.

"The noise," he said.

"What?"

"The drum," he said.

"Yes. I hear it too."

Her hand flowed over his chest. It was nice that she heard it too, Clancy thought.

"If we stay here awhile it will go away for both of us," she said.

And he did, and the drumming finally ceased, and the drumming was replaced by the sound of the bamboo.

"That's better, isn't it?" she said.

"Yes," he said in the gentleness of her. "Yes," he said and he knew at once where the drumming had fled. It had gone inside both of them and would remain locked within them forever, along with the sound of the bamboo.

"It is very much better," he said, and then he moved and said, "Oh Christ." Then he said, "The God damn war."

Then she moved both hands quickly down his back lightly and it was quiet. Outside in the huge, terrific silence the Vietnamese jungle waited and watched.

2

SEVEN months later, the seven months after Madame Dieudonné and the captain had met and in a different part of the jungle, she walked naked. She walked naked in the moon. The moon, a saffron cut. The moon a voyager out of Laos by way of Burma and Darjeeling. She walks naked because she is lost. And we cannot give her a zap. We cannot give her a burst from the M16s because she is our captain's bride.

The same seven months later and in a darker part of the jungle and below a ridge called Red Boy which Clancy had just contested with pluck but not with luck, and within a shadowing groove of bamboo, our captain lay dying. Am I living or dead? I do not know. Where am I? the captain thought. What am I doing here? How did I get here? What was that noise? That harp, no, it was a guitar. Are the Indians playing guitars now? All I remember is that I was with Custer's Seventh Cavalry riding toward the Little Big Horn and we were struck by the Indians. After we crossed the Rosebud we made it to Ridge Red Boy and then we were hit. No. I must have my wars confused. That was another time, another place. Other Indians. Ridge Red Boy rings a bell though. Why?

Captain Clancy looked around. What am I doing in this bamboo bed? Bamboo? How did I get so far from home? From the hills of home? Oh, I remember. I remember fighting down the Street Without Joy, crossing the Perfume River, storming the citadel of Hue, getting hit and entering the Palace of Perfect Peace. Then what country is this? On the Perfume River. But where does the Perfume River go? I can see the Palace of Perfect Peace. It must be in some country. Or is it? I could be dead. But I just heard a guitar and I just heard what could be a noisy bird, or a helicopter. In what country would there be a noisy bird, a guitar, a helicopter and the Palace of Perfect Peace? You're dead. Yes, dead, Clancy told himself. Dead. But listen to the guitar. I hear a chopper coming in now, somewhere over there on Ridge Red Boy now. They will learn nothing. My friend Mike will learn absolutely nothing from the dead.

The grave-registration chopper came in low over the remains of Clancy's outfit. Everyone on Ridge Red Boy to Mike seemed very dead. They were quiet as lambs. Sometimes you could only see what looked like smoke coming up from a fire but it was only ground fog. Everyone with Clancy was dead. All the Alpha Company. It was the biggest thing since Custer. Mike, who called himself a correspondent, had to watch himself. You tended to take the side of the Indians. You got to remember that this is not the Little Big Horn. This is Vietnam. Vietnam. Vietnam. They all died in Vietnam. A long way from home. What were the Americans doing here? The same thing they were doing in Indian Country. In Sioux Territory. They were protecting Americans. They were protecting Americans from the Red Hordes. God Help Clancy.

You could tell here from above how Clancy blundered. Clancy blundered by being in Vietnam. That's a speech. The chopper circled now low over the dead battle. Clancy had blundered by not holding the ridge. Clancy had blundered by being forced into a valley, a declivity in the hills. It was the classic American blunder in Vietnam of giving the Indians the cover. The enemy was fighting from the protection of the jungle. You couldn't see them. Americans love the open. Americans do not trust the jungle. The first thing the Americans did in America was clear a forest and plant the cities.

Concentrate on the battle below. Do not always take the side of the Indians. You could see here clearly from above how Clancy blew it. In the part of the highlands of Vietnam near the Cambodia-Laos bunch-up there is no true open country. Everything is in patches. You could see where Clancy's point squad had made contact with the enemy. You could see, you could tell, by all the shit of war, where Clancy had made, where Clancy had tried to make, his first stand on the ridge and then allowed his perimeter to be bent by the hostiles attacking down the ridge. Then Clancy's final regrouping in the draw where all the bodies were. Clancy should have held that ridge at all costs. If you must fight in the open fight high. Then the only way the enemy can kill you is with arching fire. Mortar fire. You can dig in against mortar fire. When they force you in the valley you are duck soup. They can hit you with everything from above. From the way the bodies lie Clancy had mounted three counterattacks to get the ridge back that he had too early conceded. The attacks were not in concert. He did not hit them all at once. There should have been more American bodies on the ridge. Clancy should have paid any price to get back the ridge. The ridge was the only opportunity. The valley was death. Ah, but the valley is comfortable. The hill is tough. And the men are all given out and dragging ass, tired and leaking blood. See where they stumbled up and where shot down. See where they failed. See where they tried again and again and again. Where they were shot down. See the paths of bright they made with their blood. See Clancy pointing them on with his sword. War is kind. See Clancy pointing them on with his sword. See Clancy pointing them on up the ridge. Once more into the breach. Once more, men, for God and Country and Alpha. I blew the ridge. Get it back. Get it back. Get it back for Clancy. Go Weintraub! Go Dumphries! Go Clinton! Get that fucksucker back! I need it. Now Oliphant! Now Stapleton, Marshall, Smith! Get me the fucksucker back! I will lead this charge. Every man behind me. Where has every young man gone? Why is that native killing me? Why Weintraub? Why Clinton? Why Oliphant? All dead. The valley is beautiful, warm, and in this season of Vietnam soft in the monsoon wet. Contemplative, withdrawn, silent and now bepatched, bequilted with all of the dead, alive with scarlet color, gay with the dead.

The helicopter that carried Mike made one more big circle to see if it would pick up ground fire, then came in and hit down in the middle of Clancy's dead with a smooth chonk noise.

The grave-registration people got out first. They ejected in the manner of all soldiers from an alighting chopper, jumping out before it quite touched the ground, then running as fast as they could go to escape the giant wind. When they got to the perimeter of Alpha's dead they stopped abruptly as though they had come to a cliff and then they came back slowly, picking their way among Alpha's dead, embarrassed and wondering what to do about all this. The lieutenant got out and told the body people not to touch any of the bodies until the army photographers had shot all the positions in which they had fallen. This was important, he said, so Intelligence could tell how the battle was lost. Or won, he said. We are not here to draw conclusions right now. The lieutenant was very young and had red hair. The grave-registration people just stood now quiet among the dead, holding their bags in which they would place the dead, folded over their arms like waiters.

The army photographers alighted now holding their cameras at high port like weapons, and began to shoot away at the dead almost at random, but they began at the concentric of the perimeter and worked outward in ever widening waves of shooting so that there was a method to their shots. The young lieutenant kept telling them not to touch. The photographers kept having trouble with the angle of repose in which many of the Alpha bodies lay. They had not fallen so that the army photographers could shoot them properly. It was important that they be shot so Intelligence could tell the direction they were pointing when they were hit, how many bodies had jammed guns, how many bodies ran out of ammo. What was the configuration of each body in relation to the configuration of the neighbor body, and then to the configuration of the immediate group of bodies in which the body rests. What relation does said group of bodies have to neighbor groups? To all groups? Bodies should be photographed in such a way so that patterns of final action of dead are clear and manifest to establish Alpha's response, if possible, to loss of ridge. Do bodies' configurations show aggressive or regressive response to ridge objective? Where body position of men and commissioned officers? Does body position of noncommissioned officers manifest immediate body group leadership? Neighbor body group leadership? Photographer should manifest if possible commissioned officer's response to command situation. Does command officer placement of body manifest command presence? Lack of same? Does placement of commissioned officer's body manifest battle plan? Lack of same? Find Clancy. Photographers should photograph all mutilations. Does Captain Clancy's body show normal kill? Planned mutilation? Do commissioned officers' bodies show more mutilation than ear men? When battle situation became negative did ear men attempt to throw away ears? Hide ears? Display ears?

"Don't touch," the lieutenant said.

Mike was examining the bodies. He had never seen it so bad.

"Don't touch," the lieutenant said.

"What's this about ears?" Mike said.

"Ears?" the lieutenant said.

"Yes."

"You must mean years," the lieutenant said. "We have some five-year men, some ten-year men."

"I see them," Mike said.

"I wouldn't write about it if I were you," the lieutenant said.

"You'd pull my credentials?"

"Yes."

"I'll have a look-see," Mike said.

"Don't touch," the lieutenant said.

Mike leaned over a soft-faced boy whose M16 had jammed. The boy body had never shaved. He was that young. The boy had something stuck in his mouth.

"Jesus," Mike said.

The young lieutenant knelt down alongside the correspondent now.

"You see how bad the enemy can be."

"Yes," Mike said. "Why has it got a condom on it?"

"Because Alpha Company was traveling through Jungle swamp. There's an organism that gets in the penis opening and travels up to the liver. The condom protects the penis."

Mike made a movement to remove it.

"Don't touch," the lieutenant said.

"Why don't you bag him?"

"Intelligence wants pictures."

"Bag all of them," Mike said, "and let's get them out of here."

"It won't be long," the lieutenant said.

"If I report this you'll lift my credentials?"

"I don't know what the brass will do," the lieutenant said. "I do know the people at home can't take it."

"They might stop your war," Mike said.

"They don't understand guerrilla war," the lieutenant said.

"You're tough," Mike said.

"Listen." The lieutenant touched the correspondent.

"Don't touch," Mike said.

"Listen," the lieutenant said, "it makes me sick. I hope it always makes me sick."

Mike stood up. There was an odor in the jungle now from the bodies that Mike had not noticed when the chopper rotor was turning. Now the chopper was dead. It was very quiet in the jungle.

"How did Clancy get into this?"

"He asked for it," the lieutenant said.

"I heard different."

"You heard wrong," the lieutenant said.

"I heard he was ordered out here."

"He ordered himself out. Clancy's an old ear collector. Alpha Company always had that reputation. Clancy's an old ear collector."

When the lieutenant became angry his white skin that could not tolerate the sun became red like his hair. His red hair was clipped short under his green helmet and when the young lieutenant became angry his white skin matched the hair.

"Clancy wanted to provoke the VC, Victor Charlie. Clancy wanted to collect more ears."

"I don't believe that."

The lieutenant kicked something with his boot.

"Why not scalps?" the correspondent said.

"Because they're too difficult to take. Did you ever try to take a scalp?"

"No."

"It's difficult," the lieutenant said.

"What makes you think Alpha Company asked for this?"

"Because Clancy could have made it up the hill," the lieutenant said, pointing. "But he stayed down here on the narrow ridge hoping Charlie would hit him, you see," the lieutenant said carefully. "Look. It's only a hundred more meters up the ridge to the top of the hill. That makes a perfect defense up there, you can see that. And Clancy knew Charlie could see that too and he wouldn't hit. That's why Clancy stayed down here. Clancy wanted Charlie to try to take him."

"A full battalion?"

"Clancy didn't know Charlie had a full battalion."

"How do you know that?"

"We had contact with his RTO man. Before radio went dead. Clancy guessed the Unfriendlies as maybe an overstrength company."

"Unfriendlies?"

"NVA. North Vietnamese Army. Clancy knew that. They are quite good." The lieutenant almost mused now, looking over the dead, reflective, and sad.

"We got a man alive here, lieutenant," someone called.

The jungle had been most quiet and everyone had been moving through the bodies with caution, almost soundlessly, so that the announcement was abrupt, peremptory and rude, almost uncalled for.

"Don't touch," the lieutenant said. The lieutenant raised his arm for a medic and moved toward the call sinuously winding through the bodies with a snakelike silent grace. The man who called, the man who made the discovery, was a body man, one of the grave-registration people. He had been standing gently with his bag over one arm waiting patiently for the others to finish when he noticed a movement where there should have been none.

"Don't touch," the lieutenant said, standing over the alive. "See what you can do," he said to the medic.

Each of the American dead had received a bullet through the head, carefully administered to each soldier by the enemy after they had overrun the position, to make absolutely certain that each was dead. The soldier who was alive had received his bullet too, but it had been deflected by the helmet and you could see when the medic removed the helmet from the head of the young Mexican soldier that it had only torn through the very black, very thick hair and lodged in the head bone. The soldier was dying of natural causes of battle. You could see this when the medic removed the boy Mexican's shirt which he did skillfully now with a knife. The boy had been sprayed with hostile machine-gun fire, eight bullets entering the boy Mexican's olive-colored body just above the pelvis. The boy with the olive body in the American olive-colored jungle uniform was cut in half. But he lived for now, taking in sudden gusts of air terrifically as though each were his last.

"Nothing can be done," the medic said without saying

anything. The medic's hands were just frozen over the body, not moving to succor, just antic and motionless like a stalled marionette.

"Water?" the lieutenant asked.

The medic shook his head no.

"If he's going to go it could make it easier," the lieutenant said. "He seems to be looking at us for water."

The medic shook his head okay. Nothing would make any difference.

When one of the photographers tried to give the boy Mexican water from his canteen the water would not run in the mouth; it just poured down over the Mexican's chin and down his chest till it reached his belly and mixed with the blood that was there.

"I think the son of a bitch is dead," one of the army photographers who was not pouring the water said.

"No," one of the body men said. "Let me try it."

"That's enough," the medic said, letting the body down. "I think he's dead now."

"How could the son of a bitch last so long when he was cut in half?"

"We have funny things like this all the time," the medic said. "Another funny thing is I've seen guys dead without a mark on them."

"Concussion? But there's always a little blood from the ears or something, isn't there?"

"No, I've seen them dead without any reason at all," the medic said, wiping clean the face of the Mexican boy with the water the Mexican could not drink. "If you look good at the guys around here I bet you'll find at least one that doesn't have a mark on him that's dead. It's funny. Some guys will die without any reason at all and some guys will live without any reason at all." The medic looked perplexed. Then the medic allowed the boy's head to rest on his smashed helmet. "You'll find some guys with just that one bullet in the head given by the Unfriendlies after they overran Alpha."

"Some guys will play dead," the army photographer said, "hoping to pass for dead among the dead."

"They don't get away with it though too much," the medic said. But the medic was not listening to himself. He was still perplexed that the Mexican boy could have lived so long when he was cut in half. "It's funny, that's all," the medic said.

"You want them to die?"

"I don't want them to suffer," the medic said.

"There's another live one over here," someone called.

"Don't touch," the lieutenant said.

But no one moved. There was a hiatus in the movement in the jungle, as though, Mike thought, no one here wanted to be deceived again, no one wanted to be taken in by another illusion. The problem was that Alpha was all dead. You could tell that with a glance. Anyone could see that they were ready to be photographed and placed in bags. It wasn't planned for anyone to come back to life. It made all the dead seem too much like people. The dead should stay dead.

"Maybe this one's real," someone said.

That started a drift toward the caller.

"Don't touch," the lieutenant said.

Mike got there early. It was a Negro. It did not seem as though the boy was hit. He was lying in a bed of bamboo. He looked comfortable. The Negro boy had a beginning half-smile on his face, but the smile was frozen. The eyes too were immobile. The Negro boy's eyes looked up, past the correspondent and on up to the hole at the top of the jungle canopy. There were two elongated fronds that crossed way up there at the apex of the canopy. Maybe that's what he was looking at. Maybe he was staring at nothing. The Negro boy said something but nothing came out. His lips moved and words seemed to be forming but nothing came out. Maybe he was saying, Mike thought, that he had come a long way since he was dragged up with the rats in the ghetto. He had never been close to white people before, excepting relief workers. Now he had joined the club. In death do us join.

The young Negro stopped breathing. The white medic was on top of the Negro boy like a lover. In one sudden deft movement the white medic was down on the bed of bamboo with his white arms around the black boy, his white lips to the black lips, breathing in white life to black death. The Negro lover did not respond. It was too late. The white boy was late. The eyes were all shut. Then abruptly the young Negro's chest began to heave. The eyes opened. But not to life, Mike thought, but to outrage, a kind of wild surmise and amaze at all this. As though he had gone to death in some kind of mute acceptance of no life and now come back to this, the lover's embrace, the lover lips of the white medic.

The white medic ceased now, withdrew his lips from the young Negro's and tried to catch the erratic breathing of the Negro in his hand to give it a life rhythm. He was astraddle the boy now, up from the bamboo bed and administering a regular beat with his hands to the young Negro's chest.

"Ah," the Negro said.

"Ah," the white boy said.

"Ah ah ah," they both said.

Now the medic allowed the boy beneath to breathe on his own.

"Ah," the lieutenant said.

"Ah-h-h-h-h," everyone said.

Now the jungle made sounds. The awful silence had given way to the noises that usually accompany an American motion picture. The cry of gaudy birds seemed fake. The complaints of small animals, distant, remote, like some sound track that had blurred, some other mix for a different cinema, so that you not only expected that the next reel would announce the mistake, that this war would have to start all over again, but that the whole damn thing would be thrown out with whoever was responsible for this disaster here at Ridge Red Boy, this unacceptable nightmare, this horror, this unmentionable destruction of Clancy and all his men. But more, the correspondent thought, this is the finis, the end of man in this clearing, this opening in the jungle, the end of humankind itself and the planet earth on which it abides. And ah, the correspondent thought—and ah—. He found himself doing it too now, celebrating the rebirth, the resurrection of the black man and the rebirth and resurrection after the crucifixion of maybe humankind itself. And ah, he reflected, they, Alpha Company, the ear hunters, and maybe not ah, because all of Alpha Company were standing in for us, surrogate, and all of us are collectors of ears.

"Will he make it?" the young lieutenant said.

The medic looked perplexed. It was his favorite and especial expression. Then he went down in the bamboo bed in lover attitude to listen to the heart.

"No," he said from the black heart. "No."

"No?"

"Because," the medic said from the black heart. "No. Because they were supposed to be all dead here and we needed body room in the chopper and there was no room for my shit."

"Blood plasma?"

"We didn't bring any," the medic said.

"Can he talk?"

"Yes." The medic passed a white hand in front of the black face. The black eyes did not follow it.

"Ask him what happened to Clancy's body. Clancy is missing."

The medic made a gentle movement with his hands along the throat of the Negro and whispered to him with lover closeness, "What happened to the captain?"

"He dead."

"Where is the body?"

"The RTO man," the Negro pronounced slowly.

"Appelfinger carried him off," the medic said to the lieutenant.

"Can you give the boy some morphine?" the lieutenant said to the medic.

"I don't like his heart."

"Risky?"

"Yes."

"Can he talk more?"

"I don't think it would be good," the medic said.

"All right, keep him quiet," the lieutenant said.

"They was so nice," the Negro said.

"I said keep him quiet," the lieutenant said. And the lieutenant thought, war is so nice. Looking over all the dead he thought ROTC was never like this, and he thought in this war everything is permitted so that there is nothing to be forgiven. And he thought about the ears that Clancy took and he thought a man can read and read and read and think and think and still be a villain and he thought there are no villains, there are only wars. And he said, "If the photographers are finished put the men into the bags."

And then there was that jungle silence again, this awful and stern admonition and threat of the retribution of Asia to white trespassers. But that is metaphysical, the lieutenant thought, and it is only the VC you have to fear. More, it is only yourself you have to fear. It is only Clancy you have to fear. But Clancy is dead.

"When you find pieces of body," the lieutenant said, "try to match them and put the matched pieces into one separate bag. Remember a man has only two arms and two legs and one head each. I don't want to find two heads in one bag."

And the lieutenant thought, Clancy is dead but the crimes that Clancy did live after him. Custer too. Custer liked to destroy the villages and shoot up the natives too. Listen to this, the lieutenant told Captain Clancy silently, what you did in the villages is not new. Collecting ears is not new. Listen, Clancy, to Lieutenant James D. Connors describing the massacre of the Indians after the battle of Sand Creek. "The next day I did not see a body of a man, woman or Indian child that was not scalped by us, and in many instances the bodies were mutilated in the most horrible manner. Men's, women's and children's private parts cut out. I saw one of our men who had cut out a woman's private parts and had them for exhibition on a stick. Some of our men wore them in their hats." I don't think you can top that, Clancy. I don't think war has come very far since then. I don't think your ears can top that, Clancy. I don't think what the Unfriendlies did here today can top that either.

"What's happening, Lieutenant?" Mike said.

"Happening?" the lieutenant said. "I was thinking."

"This man is dead," the medic said, pointing to the Negro.

"Bag him," the lieutenant said.

"What were you thinking?" the correspondent said.

"That this makes me sick. Awful sick."

"Have you ever seen it this bad?"

"No, I have never seen it this bad," the lieutenant said, spacing his words as though the correspondent Mike were taking each separate word down. "No, I have never seen it this bad in my whole life. I have never seen it this bad. No, I have never seen it this bad. Is that what you want me to say?"

"Take it easy," Mike said.

"Okay," the lieutenant said. "I'm sorry." And then the lieutenant heard something. It was the sound of a mortar shell dropping into a mortar tube in the jungle. It was the sound the lieutenant had heard too many times before, then the poof as the enemy mortar came out of the tube, then the whine as it traveled to their perimeter. The symphony. The music of Vietnam. Incoming! The lieutenant hollered as loud as he could make it, "Incoming!"

Incoming? Where? Who? Why? The shell hit their helicopter and it all exploded in a towering orange hot pillar of fire in the jungle.

"Pull the bodies around you, men, and try to dig in! Use the bodies as a perimeter!" the lieutenant hollered. Then the lieutenant said quietly to the correspondent, "I'm sorry I got you into this."

"You didn't," Mike said.

"I'll try to get Search and Rescue on the radio."

"You do that," Mike said.

3

—————————

Hᴀ, ha, ha, Clancy said, gently, quietly. They are in trouble. The Ghoulies got it. I hope Mike did not go in with the Ghoulies. My friend Mike was sent out here to relieve me of command. He pretends to be a newspaper reporter. That's all right. He would probably make a good one. How did I know about Mike—what Mike was up to? Madame Dieudonné. Madame Dieudonné is my whore, my French whore. And she's not French. She's got a cover too. She's Vietnamese, and she's not a whore. She's a businesswoman. That's all right because every American in Nam has a cover. We are all pretending to do one thing and working something else. There goes the Bamboo Bed, Captain Knightbridge and Nurse Janine—Tarzan and Jane. I hope they screw themselves to death. No, I don't. I hope they have a bright and happy life.

The 379th Search and Rescue copter, the Bamboo Bed, dazzled up in the Vietnamese sun, aerial and bright. There was no one at the controls.

"You're sure it's all right?" she said.

"Perfectly all right," he said.

Now the copter, the Bamboo Bed, fell off abruptly, not like a huge bird but more a dancing, vivid butterfly. It fell and then seemed to hit some invisible bottom in the vast luminous nimbus of the aqueous Asian sky before it again, the Bamboo Bed, the helicopter, plumed upward in capricious and insubstantial glints and flashes as though not powered by some idiot engine but magic and gossamer-impelled, feckless and light.

"Look," she said with her hand on him beneath his hard belly.

"Yes."

The woman and the man were tangled in fantastic attitudes on the rear seat, lying beneath the silent, hard and black vanadium-steel M60 machine gun.

"Which way do you want to go now?"

"Any way you want."

"This way," she said and she went down down down and he went up up up until the Bamboo Bed paused its jerking gyrations in abrupt amaze, just hanging there in the hushed, indifferent infinity, inflexible and calm, as though just discovering the planet beneath in stilled and prayerful consternation before it, the gay copter, moved again in sudden antic bursts, the wild and fairy movements of the helicopter, the Bamboo Bed, still butterflylike, peremptory and mad. Now it was still.

"You like it this way?"

"Yes," he said.

"More?"

"Yes," he said. "More."

"Tell me when you are going to come. We will come together."

"Yes."

It is, he thought, this sex in the sky and above a battle, it is, he thought, something such as the communion of war. We all come together. Those that come together rum a dum dum together. You all come, you heah? This is your President speaking and I want you all to come to the war. Hear me now. You all listen. I see you all over there in the corner trying to dodge the draft. Listen to me now. I want you all to come.

The helicopter slipped awfully to the starboard and in the same quick instant took four machine-gun bursts on the fleeing side so that the ground fire, hard and straight, rising from the somber innocent steady jungle forest beneath flew harmlessly past the darting butterfly.

"Shall I stop?"

"No."

"Not for the war?"

"It's a dirty war."

"But somebody has to do it."

"More?"

"Yes."

"Somebody has to do it."

And they did it in the helicopter, the Bamboo Bed, that sailed and jerked vivid and mothlike in the Vietnamese sun. The sun had beaten the green foliage of the abiding endless Asian jungle below into a sharp glinting emerald enamel on top; beneath, the color fled down in paler hues through four canopies until the bottom leaves were yellow in the dark. On top the forest was a hard plastic marine green. Vietnam in the sun. The Bamboo Bed still twirled, kitelike in the aqueous blue. The mist, arising from the jungle perfect green, arose to give the sky a gentle watery tint, oceanic and serene.

Oliver and Elgar were WASPs that did not sting. They were pacifists fighting a war. They belonged in the same outfit as the helicopter, the Bamboo Bed. The same outfit as nurse Janine Bliss and Captain Knightbridge who were up in the terrible and tropic, gay blue green yonder now. The outfit was the forward element of the 379th Special Task Force Search and Rescue. They were pacifists in fact rather than theory because Oliver and Elgar simply never killed anybody. They did not have pink berets or green shoes or any other clown costume to make them look militant, to scare the enemy, to make the enemy laugh.

Oliver and Elgar made the enemy cry. They looked like small American farmers who had had a bad year. Too much rain. They wore their green military jungle uniforms like bloomers. They billowed out in all the wrong places. They wore their pointy peaked baseball-like military caps canted to the side instead of the front so they each looked like half of Napoleon.

Oliver and Elgar were supposed to be listening to the radio. That was their job, to find out whether anybody wanted to be Searched and Rescued, Rescued and Searched. Instead they were looking up at the rescue copter, the Bamboo Bed, to where Tarzan and Jane had gone to get away from it all. Oliver and Elgar called themselves Space Cadets. They called the leaders of the Space Cadets Tarzan and Jane because they all lived in the jungle like monkeys and Tarzan and Jane talked to them. The 379th had lived in the jungle of the Pleiku Plateau so long they felt like apes. They looked like apes. They acted like apes. They took on the mentality of apes. They took on so much the mentality of apes that they no longer believed in killing as men do, as men will, as men should. Oliver and Elgar no longer believed in war. They had become completely uncivilized. They no longer wanted to kill their own kind.

"Golly gee," Oliver said, "if we ever get caught not wanting to kill our own kind we'll be in trouble with the United States Army."

"Of which we are members of."

"Yes."

"We'll be in trouble with everybody."

"Of which we are members of."

"Don't keep saying of which we are members of."

"Don't you feel like a member any more?"

"No."

"You've been in the jungle too long."

"Yes."

"You want out."

"Golly gee," Oliver said, "what's going to happen to us when they find out we want out of humankind?"

"They will be sore as hell. They will put us in a cage for not killing our own kind. It will say on the sign under our cage in the Brooklyn Zoo, HOMO SAPS WHO DON'T KILL OUR OWN KIND. GENUS UNKNOWN."

Oliver kept saying Golly gee because he had been in the jungle so long that sometimes he forgot how to talk army obscenity. This does not yet happen to everyone but it happens, and it happened to Oliver. It was beginning to happen to Elgar. It may have been happening to Oliver and Elgar because they were WASPs to start with—White Anglo-Saxon Protestants. WASPs who did no hurt. They had pinched white faces and English blue eyes as very blue as the blue field with the white stars in the American flag. The canopy of jungle that hid the sun from their faces by making their faces whiter seemed to make their eyes bluer. The more they lived in the jungle the more they looked like the WASPs they were. Wasper and Waspier. WASPs who did not sting. From Troy, New York.

Oliver and Elgar who used to be from Troy, New York, stared at each other in the filtering soft green-blue light of the forest. Who used to be from Troy, New York, and now felt more part of this place.

"I heard on the radio transmitter this morning that Clancy's outfit got wiped out," Oliver said.

"You mean all killed? Not Clancy too?"

"We reckon."

"Did you report this to Captain Knightbridge?"

"No."

"That's supposed to be our job."

"I didn't want to make him feel bad," Oliver said.

"Our job is to report what we hear on the transmitter."

"I didn't want to make the captain feel bad," Oliver said.

"How is Search and Rescue going to rescue people if you don't report who needs to be rescued?"

"They don't need to be rescued."

"Explain. Explain."

"They're all dead," Oliver said.

Captain Knightbridge and the beautiful nurse lieutenant were still up there someplace in the nothing of space having the nothing of sex. Not quite true. It is true that they were having sex and that they were not making love. But sex is not to be dismissed entirely or altogether. There is something to be said for sex entirely and of itself. Ask any good psychiatrist. Ask anyone who feels his way around in this world. Making love is better though. Making love is better because you can have a real bamboo bed on R and R in Thailand. Rest and Recreation in Thailand. There is no rest and no recreation on Rest and Recreation. It's all Sex and Sex. Rest and Recreation is S and S. That is the way with the army, they have taken to lying about everything.

Be that as it may, the beautiful lieutenant and the captain had gone up in the Bamboo Bed to make love. You cannot make love in the jungle, there are too many ants. At least it's true in the jungles of Vietnam. All of Vietnam is a jungle. Do not worry about the VC, the Unfriendlies. It is the beautiful and awful jungle that watches. It is the terrible, magnificent forest that waits.

But making love in a bamboo bed is the best. And they knew the best. A bamboo bed is the language and the touch of Asia. The Bamboo Bed in the sky is where life begins, from where life is rescued. The bamboo bed on the ground, in the jungle, is where life ends. The bamboo bed is the celebration of life and at once the bamboo bed is the down floor of the jungle forest where fine fellows die. Just like that. A queer thing. In the willowing bamboo life is like that. A queer thing.

"Did you hear something?"

"Listen."

"Something on the radio?"

"Listen," Captain Knightbridge said.

4

THE body people, the grave-registration people, were stranded now up on Clancy's ridge, Ridge Red Boy, the ridge where Clancy had failed. They were building a fort or revetment around themselves with all the bodies they had come there to collect. The enemy were throwing all kinds of things, mortars and rockets, light and heavy machine-gun fire and small-arms fire, flame and anti-personnel weaponry, phosphorus and smoke and all kinds of grenades, grenades that exploded on contact and in the air, grenades that you could throw back and grenades that exploded if you tried, grenades that just sat there and looked at you while you tried to figure out what to do. They are the worst kind, Mike thought.

The tall red-haired lieutenant who had never seen it quite so bad was keeping his head. If you can keep your royal head while all around you are losing theirs, then you must be sleeping with the queen, Mike thought. Mike had all sorts of quick crazy thoughts in the first few seconds after they were hit by the North Vietnamese Regular Army. I am here. They are firing at me. What am I doing here? Why did I come here?

Where is the red-haired lieutenant? Dead? No, that's him ordering the dead. Telling his people to arrange the dead for defense. Captain Clancy's company is still fighting a holding action. Clancy always said never say die.

The lieutenant was busy in the thick of the incoming, going around from body to body checking the weapons to find those M16 rifles that had jammed. When he found a jammed rifle he would give a cry of delight because it meant he had found some ammo. There were plenty of the dead soldiers' rifles that had run out of ammo. The soldiers' rifles that had jammed not only had the ammo that was still left in the clip but also the full clips that had not been fired yet. So the lieutenant was matching the ammo to the good rifles. Sometimes he would clear a jammed gun if it was not too bad. The red-haired lieutenant would bring the gun over to Mike's hole and work on it. The most common failure of the American rifle is that it fires too fast. A soldier can fire in one minute far more shells than he can carry, and after two hundred rounds the weapon begins to cook off the shells prematurely, causing a jam. Or through excess firepower the chamber builds up carbon, sticking the shell so that the extractor cannot pull it out. It tears the rim of the shell. The M16, Mike thought, is a fine weapon for the movies, but it's not much of a gun for a war. The outside of the weapon is made of fiber glass and it looks like a toy. The lieutenant was surrounded by a pile of children's toys and he seemed to be examining them with delight and clearing the malfunctions like a small boy. The lieutenant had somehow lost his helmet so that each time an incoming shell hit close his red hair would stand on end from the concussion. Mike had wanted to see some close combat. Was this close enough? Close enough for now. Close enough forever, Amen.

The lieutenant was crawling now, distributing his cleared weapons to the grave-registration people. Had they come to register their own graves? The lieutenant handed them a weapon furtively as though it were a passport to hell, actually because he was on his belly and so were they, looking out on the exploding jungle like furtive animals, rabbits who were trapped with no way out, the red showing in their eyes, somber and scared. The lieutenant told each of them to hold their fire until he gave the command and meanwhile to gather all the rocks within reach. Rocks? Sometimes the lieutenant would give the orders to a dead man; the grave-registration people hugged the ground so tightly and were so awfully silent it was difficult to tell, but the dead always refused the weapon whilst the graves people always reached out a hand to receive it—that was a good way to tell the dead from the soon dead. Rocks? Defend yourself in any way you can, the lieutenant shouted to each separately. As soon as their barrage lifts they'll come at us. When your ammo's gone use your rifle as a club. Kick them in the balls. Gouge their eyes out and take their weapon and turn it against them. In absolutely no circumstances are you to withdraw. Do you understand? Are you reading me loud and clear? Die here! I will kill any man who moves back. And then he would slap each of them on their rear with the palm of his hand and repeat, "Good man, good luck," before he crawled on to the next, bearing an M16 toy.

The lieutenant was back with Mike now and he crawled into Mike's depression. What Clancy's men had had time to dig, you could not call holes. This lieutenant was still without his helmet and the red hair was all down over his very deepset blue eyes. He appeared collected, calm and thoughtful, almost joyful that he was busy busy busy and maybe joyful that life at the ending was this abruptly simple, that the enemy had dictated the end. That he was in command at the Alamo. That there was no way out. That each man does the very best he can in his spot. All of life you retreat a little, Mike thought. Always there is a way out, some way around so that when you finally get it you are moving backward.

The lieutenant winked at Mike. A shell exploded very close and the lieutenant said, "Is it like the movies?" And Mike tried to answer but he could not. He only forced a smile back, but the lieutenant was already talking to his RTO man, and the radio man told him he could make no contact with Search and Rescue, with the Bamboo Bed.

"Keep trying," the lieutenant said, and then he told the radio man to keep his ass down. "They will always try to place a mortar round in on our radio if they can," the lieutenant told Mike. As though, Mike thought, he were at a cocktail party and the lieutenant were telling him they were all uninvited guests. Mike still couldn't say anything. The words would come out later. And they did too; as the lieutenant moved away Mike hollered at him, "You cheerful son of a bitch. You cheerful war-loving redheaded son of a bitch."

"What?" the radio man said.

"Keep trying," Mike said to the RTO man.

The lieutenant was crawling, scouting the perimeter to see if there was some way out. Certainly they could withdraw to a better position than this. If Captain Clancy could not hold this position then who could? Another thought the lieutenant had. Somehow he must discourage the enemy from attacking at all. But how? He could call in an air strike, but radio can't contact shit. If some plane or chopper would overfly the position they could relay the message on to base. If. If. If. The lieutenant told himself if only Clancy hadn't started a war. Hey, look over there, the lieutenant told himself. Is it an antimissile missile? No, it's the Bamboo Bed.

The chopper made a sudden sweep in low, curving in like a bird. It picked up hostile ground fire and curved away again and up.

"Can you read me?"

"Positive."

"Will you relay message?"

"Positive."

"This is Operation Ghoulie. We need gunships. Will you relay this and maintain contact? We are surrounded."

"Positive. Over and out."

"Screw Clancy," the radio man said. "Over and out."

"What's that?" the lieutenant said, crawling up to the RTO man.

"I say fuck everyone that got us into this, sir."

"I understand, soldier," the lieutenant said quietly. "I understand, but that will be all."

"Yes, sir."

46

Mike crawled into their depression now. The mortars were still incoming and now a great shower of bamboo, muck, monkeys, stones, mahogany and sharp shrapnel burst terrifically close and then again and then again until all of the jungle came upside down and commingled in one violent roar, one explosion fantastically joined to the next so that all war was happening at once and here in a phantasmagoria of such bright noise that it was soundless.

"Why don't they hit us?" Mike said. "Why don't they attack? What are they waiting for?"

"Death."

"What?"

"They are in no hurry to take us," the lieutenant said. "They got a big reception when they took Clancy. When they took Clancy they took a lot of dead themselves. But they will come."

"When?"

"In good time."

"I think you're all dead," Mike said, and then Mike shouted. "I think all you Ghoulies are dead. All dead, dead. What are you doing out here with your bags and your cameras, your cameras and your bags? You're collecting for the dead. The dead are collecting for the dead."

"Shut up," the lieutenant said.

"I'm sorry," Mike said.

"They will come in good time," the lieutenant said quietly. "Can you get anything on the radio?" he said to his RTO.

"No."

"The enemy will come before our relief does," the lieutenant said.

"Yes," the radio boy said. "On our overfly I was in contact with base. Everyone is engaged in Operation Lucky Strike."

"What happened to Hammer Stroke?"

"Canceled."

"Daffodil?"

"That was canceled too. There is a total commitment of everything in Two Corps to Butcher Stroke."

"Butcher Stroke?"

"Yes."

"Then we will get no relief."

"Positive," the butcher boy, the Ghoulie boy, the radio man said.

Wait, Mike thought. I was right, they are all dead. All these Ghoulies are dead. What am I doing here? Am I dead? Then Mike heard the ear-shattering explosions and he judged that he was not dead.

"What was Daffodil?" Mike asked.

"That was an operation south of Danang on the Bon Hai River to clear out the VC infrastructure. It means you are forced to burn out many villages."

"I don't like Daffodil."

"None of us do," the lieutenant said. "Are you getting hold of yourself now?"

"Yes, I think so," Mike said. "I know who you are now."

"Who are we?"

"The dead," Mike said.

The lieutenant crawled away from Mike, propping up the dead as he went. The thing to do was to make the dead look like the living and the living look like the dead. The living would exchange roles with the dead; that way the VC would still be fighting the dead. Victor Charlie would waste his ammo killing people he had already killed. Clancy fights on. Clancy might pull this off yet. It was Clancy's second chance.

Crawling like a crab, the lieutenant told each of his men to behave like the dead, to remain inert and without movement and to prop up the dead in a fighting position, to drape their bodies that would not work on a gun that would not work, facing toward the enemy, placing the bodies on the rise, they themselves to remain in the depressions. Each time the dead were hit they were to be placed again in fighting position. The lieutenant noticed that the monsoon jungle fog was moving in, and this would help.

Everything will help, the lieutenant thought. We have already lost so we cannot lose. Clancy already blew this one. I do not like the way my men look. Did you see their faces? Each man I crawl to gives me the same look of implacable hatred. The reptilian stare. Something has happened to all of their eyes. Their eyes flick at me redshot and slitted. I expect their tongues to dart out. They want to crawl into holes like giant lizards. They blame me. They don't blame Clancy. They don't blame the dead for not having triumphed, they blame me. I got them here. I cannot get them out. It is not my job to get them out. They know that. It is my job to bury them. It is my job to bury everyone. Bury them at Con Thien, at Khe San, at Vo Dat, at Try An. I have got a job to do and I try to do it. But the burial squad should not bury themselves. Why not? You cannot collect people as long as I have collected people without knowing, almost hoping—anyway you have got to have some justification for being alive. That justification is that some day in this war someone will collect you. You sound like a ghoul. That is why we call ourselves the Ghoulies. We thought of it before someone else did. That seems to make it better. I am bored with the job. I would like someone to collect me for a change. See how they feel about it then. If that is true, why in Christ's name are you going around preparing a defense? Because even the dead do not want to die. The correspondent is right. We are dead. We will never get out of this trap alive. But he did not mean it that way. He meant only the dead would collect the dead. Little does he know. That I have a plan.

The red-haired lieutenant had each of these thoughts between the terrific burst of each mortar shell. The red-haired lieutenant's plan was this: If the enemy will not come to you, then why don't you go to the enemy? There was nothing else to do. He would need help. He touched the man alongside him. The man was dead. It was one of Clancy's men. Clancy's men were no good. Clancy's men were no good to him now. He pulled on another man's leg. He was a good man. He was alive. The good man looked back at the lieu-

49

5

Above G for Ghoulie who had gone in to bury A for Alpha, the Bamboo Bed, the Search and Rescue helicopter, did not move like a bumblebee or a bird, but in phantasmagoric bobbling now as though thrown up from below by some inept juggler who was missing, some painted-faced conjurer who had tried to keep three or five bright baubles in the air and had fumbled all but this. The Bamboo Bed was the only object in the air, the only and counterfeit illusion left, all else lay busted on the stage below.

"And it's not that I don't want to fight," Captain Knightbridge said. "It's because I have already fought."

"Captain Clancy does it. Colonel Yvor does it."

"And they do it well."

"What's stopping you?"

"I did it too well," Knightbridge said. "I killed too well."

"Do you still want the drink?"

"Yes."

She poured him something from a thermos into a clean empty C-ration can that once held salmon. The thermos tinkled even above the whack of the rotor. It tinkled like diamonds.

"Can you still taste the salmon?"

"Yes."

"Is it okay?"

"It's okay. It's fine," he said.

"What's that down there?"

"A fire fight."

"What's the red smoke?"

"Trouble."

Knightbridge put on the headset earphones, switched on the FM. With the lip mike stalked in front he looked like a spaceman.

"I am receiving you, G for Ghoulie," he said. Then he waited and said, "Positive." Then again, "Positive," and then he waited again, listening to the Negro sergeant whose second platoon of Ghoulie Company, the grave-registration outfit, the Fourth of the Seventh, was in great trouble below. Then Knightbridge said, "Positive," and switched off the set.

"We're going to try for a pickup," he said to Nurse Janine. "Drink all of this drink," Knightbridge said, passing the salmon C-ration can with whiskey to her. "All of it. Tighten your seat belt until it hurts. Lean yourself forward into a minimum target. Drink it all. We will try for a pickup. G for Ghoulie is being overrun. They are dying."

"The wounded?"

"No, Ghoulie. Ghoulie's perimeter is being overrun. Charlie is chopping them up. Ghoulie is dying."

"But you were going for a gun ship."

"They can't make it and Medivac can't make it. They just lost a medic chopper in a pickup attempt."

"All right," she said. "Do it. Do it."

"Drink it up."

She drank it up and buckled up till it hurt. "All right, do it. Do it," she said.

The ship shuddered, air shaking under full awful power, and then leaped down in a fantastic swoop, terrific and down. The copter hurtled and whirled in the Asian sky above the fire fight, danced and skittered in elusive spurts against the unseen pursuit below, because you could not see what it was avoiding, what it was attempting to flee, the copter seemed an insane exotic bird of another country, unknown, unsung, unsinging, an avian and phoenix that fell drunken through the green-glass Asian sky in panic motion, in wild and uncontrolled child bursts of hide and seek.

He and she, the man and the woman, the lieutenant and the captain, sealed inside, encapsulated in the bird being shot by the hunters in the forest below, were tensed, expectant of death, but there is something in motion that is confused with life, that becomes ignorance of death.

"Yes," Knightbridge said, "the sons of bitches," and he allowed the copter to flare up and away in a tremulous sailing sweep from the fire below that had remarked thirty-four perfect hits in the starboard side of the Bamboo Bed. The captain allowed the copter to flee up until it became a speck, a spark in the purpling monsoon cloud from the fires beneath. Now he forced the copter to big circle, then to big circle again in the purple monsoon before he forced her down, down, abruptly like a hawk that has folded its wings or a busted buzzard shot and plummeting down straight and down down and down and down until at one hundred meters it went wingspread to glide and then to hit into the jungle trees touch touch touch touch because the captain was bringing her into stricken Ghoulie Company at ground zero at one hundred knots to avoid those thirty-four perfect holes on the starboard side this time. The theory being they do not hit what they do not have angle or time to see. The theory being that you must brush the trees to slow her down this time. This time the cut treetops flew up in a steady swift line of jungle confetti. This time the Bamboo Bed bucked and yawed in the heavy sea of tree. This time she crackled into the bamboo at letdown, flinging the stalks skyward, a mad reaper of bamboo. Until this time she fled into the final elephant grass and settled in the midst of Ghoulie— the small rear stabilizer blade still twirling gaily to celebrate God knows what. The big huge main rotor turning turning big and huge, slow, sad, its somber shadow covering all of bleeding, burning perimeter Red Boy.

Now the black sergeant popped up from a grass-camouflaged foxhole like a trick game and popped over to the copter in almost one trick sudden movement, stuck his head into the flung-open door, his jaws again working in almost the same abrupt movement.

"You got to get out now," he hollered. "Now! Charlie just brought up rockets. Lift ass now!"

"The wounded?"

"Lift ass now!"

"The wounded?"

"All right," the Negro said quietly and reached in and touched the captain's shoulder, and then he turned and made an arm movement toward the mist-shrouded edge of perimeter Ghoulie. "All right." And there was a movement in the hot burning mist of Ghoulie, shadows carrying shadows.

"All right." The Negro leaned in to see who had come to join the dying and the dead and winked.

"Rough?" Knightbridge leaned at the Negro.

"Yes," the Negro said. "Charlie thinks he can take us."

"Can he?"

"No."

"Why?"

"I'll get them out."

"How?"

"I'll get them out," the Negro said.

"Your mission?"

"To check out Clancy's Alpha Company," the Negro said.

"Accomplished?"

"Charlie accomplished," the Negro said.

"Get them all?"

"Yes."

"You had body count?"

"Yes."

"Clancy?"

"Him too," the black soldier said. "We presume." The Negro named Pike looked around the cockpit in a kind of strange surmise. "Yes, we presumed that." And then his voice trembling off, "Yes, that is what we presume."

"Clancy?"

"Yes. But no body, and no body for his RTO man, Appel-finger."

"You can get your boys out?"

"Yes."

Janine had gotten out of the other side of the ship and she and Mike were helping Ghoulie men stack something alongside the Bamboo Bed before they lifted them gently in.

From the controls Knightbridge turned up more revs. The black soldier Pike still had his head inside as though the paper-thin aluminum shell of the Bamboo Bed might have some magic against the rain of death outside. Now Sergeant Pike stared out the port window and said, "When you lift ass out you're in trouble." And then he pointed to the still-burning Medivac chopper that was burning in surprise gusts as though amazed at her own death. The very black jet fuel smoke and the green flame pennanted up gently in the elephant grass and then without cause burst into a wild towering tall rage of light and darkness, the fierce fire lashing the monsoon in quick and gaudy light, the darkness of black-green smoke beneath spreading in solemn dirge through the quiet bamboo.

"I'll get them out," the black Pike said.

"The saddle?"

"Yes," Pike said, pointing to the U in the ridge. "I'll get them out that saddle. If I can hold Charlie till dark."

"How's your ammo?"

"Plenty. Too much. We got a para drop from Base Tam Ky. It's too much. Before we pull out we're going to have to blow, burn or bury."

"Don't bury. Charlie's cute."

"We'll burn," Pike said.

"Try to filter your boys out before you hit Charlie. Don't hit Charlie," the captain said, "unless you have to."

"I won't," Pike said. "I know Charlie."

But no one knew Charlie. Charlie did not know himself. Charlie's own mother did not know him. Charlie was the great unknown because Charlie was the enemy, the Unfriendly, the villain of the piece. Charlie took it well because Charlie had an enemy too—us.

"The wounded are inboard," Pike said. "Lift ass off."

Janine and Mike got back in the front and buckled up. The ship had taken on eighteen new holes but they would not affect liftoff. The wounded would affect liftoff because LZ Red Boy was only eighteen meters circumference and the pure jungle went up thirty meters all around so the Bamboo Bed would have to rise vertically and slowly so every Unfriendly in Two Corps would get a shot at the Bamboo Bed.

"We'll have a squad hold you down," Sergeant Pike said. "So you can get full power and bounce ass off."

"Okay."

"Don't give her full power until you hear my mortars and M6os plaster the shit out of Charlie to keep him pinned down. "I'll give you red smoke."

"I want out," the wounded red-haired lieutenant on the rear floor of the chopper kept repeating. Part of his left hip had been blown off and he kept repeating "I want out."

"You're no good to us no more," Pike said.

"I'm not turning over command."

"Yes, you are," Pike said.

"Pike?"

"Yes, sir?" the black sergeant said.

"Help me."

"You're no good to us no more."

"Pike?"

"Yes, sir?"

"Fuck you," the lieutenant said.

"He's awfully bad," Pike, the black sergeant said. "He's my buddy. You take him out. I'll bring the rest. Ready? Go, baby, go! Like now!"

The door was slammed, the red smoke canisters were released and a squad of men crawled up and grabbed the runners of the Bamboo Bed. The machine guns started, then the mortars, so that the Bamboo Bed rose in a deadly field of green, red and black smoke, the Medivac chopper burning trails of black and green, the canisters of red smoke that billowed up in a fountain of bright blood mixed with emerald and black so with the orange muzzle blast from the machine guns and with the blue bursting mortar shells outside the perimeter you had to hold your breath to see or hear or even feel anything and so they rose up and up slow slow in the plume of death, slow slow in the giant and pulsing fire, until Knightbridge noticed a dangling leg; when the ship weaved you could see the leg fling out below. One of the soldiers had not let go of the undercarriage in time and now it was too late. The Bamboo Bed was too high. Knightbridge let her down. They were almost outside and away. Now they would have to go back down into burning Red Boy. They would have to rise from the dead once more. She came down gently, released her dangling man lightly, started back up softly, but steadily, then got hit bad and fell off to her port side and stood at this crazy angle long and painful seconds until the Bamboo Bed recovered and began her awkward climb straight up.

"Wow!"

They were out.

"God damn!"

They were away.

"I want out."

They were safe.

"I am not going to turn over my command."

They were high and safe and away from the blinding fire fight below.

Now all of the wounded in the rear were quiet. The wounded were so quiet that no one wanted to look for fear they had become dead.

6

AFTER the red-haired lieutenant was Medivacked out by the Bamboo Bed the black sergeant Pike was in command of G for Ghoulie Company. G for Ghoulie would have no time to bury A for Alpha. G for Ghoulie were being buried themselves by mortar shells. By rockets. By recoilless cannon. Black Pike figured the best thing to do was surrender the outfit before the B52s came to rescue them with bombs and buried them all alive. Black Pike had always wanted to surrender a bunch of white guys anyway. There is no greater honor on this earth to a black man than to hand white men to yellow men for killing. Black Pike had led the Detroit race riots. Black Pike had been captured by the whites, racing through the night with a fiery burning torch on his way to burn down the Ford Motor Corporation at River Rouge.

"Caught this nigger redhanded hightailing it for Henry's place with a torch."

In court they could prove nothing. In court the American Civil Liberties Union defended Pike, proved the Constitution gives every man the right to bear torches.

Black Pike waited for his chance. Now his chance had come. Get Whitey. There is no stronger bond. The bond of suffering. The bond that binds people of color the whole world over. The bond of pain.

Black Pike looked at each of the soldiers under his command in the glare of the mortar bursts. He wanted to make certain they were all white. They were still white okay. All white. Pike's plan was this: to take out his white flag from his rear pocket and walk toward the yellow men and say to them, Take them all. Do with them what you will. I wash my hands.

Pike had come prepared for this. The army does not allow a soldier to carry anything white in the field. Black Pike had purchased a large white silk handkerchief from a whore in Da Nang.

Sergeant Pike touched the handkerchief. It was still there.

Pike had played the game. The game is this—everyone in the army is equal. The interdependency in the common great death is the big equalizer. Each individual is bound to all of humankind in the fraternity of blood that flows out. The army will not tolerate any racist nonsense. That is the army game. The game Pike played.

The red-haired lieutenant whose name was Peterbilt had fouled up the game. At 0800 and beneath a rocket-fragmented wild banana tree that Pike watched now, the lieutenant had heard an incoming mortar round and dropped on black Pike to cover him and got his own ass shot off. Wow! It was no longer a game. The red-haired lieutenant named Peterbilt played for keeps. It had started many months before the incident at the wild banana tree. They were close. The lieutenant and the sergeant were very close. Before the incident here at Clancy's A for Alpha they had buried men under at Chon Long, An Keh. They had buried them at Dan Hue, Dak To and everywhere in Nam. And it was not only Peterbilt who ruined the game. All the whites were guilty. There was not a God damn white guy in the outfit who was not a human being. Whitey had become people. This outfit has robbed me of everything I have lived for. The sons of bitches. Everything I planned my whole life for. The white bastards. Not all white people, but this gang are no good. No God damn good at all. They ruined everything. A man can't live. A man has nothing to live for if he can't hate. Still, there are the people on the outside to hate.

"Sarge?"

"There are the people on the outside," Pike said.

"What?"

The remains of G for Ghoulie had fallen back on Pike's bunker. There were seven of them. Seven Whiteys left. Soon there would be none.

"Sarge, there's a lull."

"I can hear. I can feel," Pike said.

"Sarge, we could cut ass out."

"There are the people on the outside," Pike said.

"Pike has blown."

"No," Pike said taking something from his rear pocket and wiping his face. Peterbilt's blood from his face. His blown ass blood. "No. That's what Charlie wants. He will cut you down like rice. Everyone hold their fire. That's an order. Let Charlie make his move. How many rounds for the M60?"

"Three belts."

"Hold your fire until Charlie is at thirty meters, then cut Charlie down like corn. Check your elevation. Your weapon travels up. You been chopping bamboo."

"Sarge?"

"Yes?"

"You going to get us out?"

So this was Whitey.

There was a big jungle silence. All of the jungle waited.

"Sarge," Billy Crike said from the M60, "you guys cut ass. I'll cover your withdrawal."

So this was Whitey.

"Who will cover you?" Pike said.

"I'm only one ass."

"I will make that decision," Pike said.

Yes, Pike thought, I will make all decisions. I am the black god. But I don't want to play god. I don't want to play anything any more. In combat that is the one problem, the problem of remaining alive. The problem of being a survivor, the embarrassment of living, the guilt of being alive. Now that Peterbilt was dead Pike could become the only survivor. Peterbilt is not dead. He only got his ass shot off. He will live. Yes, but many will die because Captain Clancy could not successfully defend this position here on Ridge Red Boy. Was Clancy the same soldier that shot at me in Detroit? No matter. Are some of these seven white soldiers under my command here now my enemies in Detroit? No matter. If they were not then they will be next time. The riots next time. The only people who did not shoot at me in Detroit and who will not shoot at me in the riots next time are the people in the Bamboo Bed, Search and Rescue. But in any reckoning they are crazy. There is no hope for the Black in Whitey's America save insanity. As long as General Sanity prevails and General Principle and General Respect for General Law and Order, General Whitey's law and General Whitey's order, there will always be General Sanity in overall command. You black sons of bitches have got to learn respect for the law and the order. If you don't like a law you change it. Beg Whitey to change it.

"Sarge?"

"Yes?"

"Are you going to get us out?"

"Yes."

"How?"

"I will beg the enemy to stop shooting."

"That's pretty good. Sarge?"

"Yes?"

"Why are the Unfriendlies so quiet?"

"They are regrouping for an assault. They are not being circumspect as much as cautious. They know they can take us."

"Sarge?"

"Yes."

"Do you have a hard on for society?"

"Yes. Every soldier does."

"They got us into this."

"Yes."

"Not Clancy when he blew A for Alpha?"

"Yes. Clancy too."

"Sarge, maybe we won't get out of this. I'm sorry you're different."

"What in the hell do you want to say, Tommy?"

"That I never noticed that you were different before."

"Oh?"

"That until 0600 when we got pinned down here you were a buddy. Now you're playing a game. We been together seven months. I never noticed you were black before because you never noticed we were white."

"We were playing a game."

"Were we, Sarge?"

"I think so, Tommy. I don't know. I want you to keep your eyes on that bamboo at forty meters. When you see a movement at the top of the cover I want you to touch me. Don't explain but touch me. Then hold up the number of fingers giving the separate movements, then point out each one silently."

"Positive."

The jungle waited. The sweat dripped. It was all very silent.

"Tommy, if I get you out and if I were to move my family in next to you in the States how would you act?"

"I don't know."

"How would Lieutenant Peterbilt act?"

"Help you move in."

"The rest of the outfit?"

"Help you move in your shit."

"And if the neighbors objected?"

"Fight."

"But you don't know, Tommy, what you would do?"

Tommy Travis stroked his weapon, his M79 grenade launcher, a weapon he had retrieved from one of Alpha's dead. Now he loosened his helmet strap against concussion and said, "I don't know. Because I have been in Nam long enough to know that no one knows. Everyone knows how they would like to behave, but no one knows how they will behave."

"I will get you out," Pike said.

Tommy touched Pike sharply, then held up in front of Pike's heavy-helmeted face four fingers, shook them to emphasize the number, then pointed into the bamboo four times.

Pike leaned forward in the low, palm-lined bunker and said in a big whisper, "Hold your weapons. Charlie is moving laterally to draw fire. They are trying to get us to expose our position."

Now Pike touched the M79 man on the shoulder.

"Over there at the base of the breadfruit tree. Notice the yellow spot. Zero your weapon one meter high and two clicks south and give them one round when I touch your shoulder. That is their CP."

There was still the clack clack clacking of the bamboo and the gentle movement high up. Pike knew the location of the enemy command post because a fire base had been established below the breadfruit tree by the Unfriendlies to shoot up our chopper when they Medivacked Peterbilt out. Pike signaled Tommy for one round by touching his shoulder that held the grenade launcher. Then Pike raised his binoculars up and focused them below the dangling breadfruit. There was a rush of the explosion in the bunker and the breadfruit tree came down.

"Good boy, Tommy," Pike said. Then he said to everyone, and returning to the heavy whisper, "We will not get cover darkness till 1800. We will have to keep them off balance or they will take us. The first monsoon creep we get we will crawl out and engage them. Now we wait for the ground fog. I want each of you to pass me your weapon and I will check it. When you pass me your weapons tell me how many full clips you have. Break the weapon before you pass it to me and I will reassemble. Clear?"

"Seven clips."

"Five."

"Eight clips."

"Three."

"Nine."

"One."

"Take these four," Pike said to the man who had said one. The jungle was silent.

You have to know the jungle, Pike thought. Understand it. You cannot hate it. You have got to learn how to take advantage of the opportunities it presents. The jungle is cruel, hot, wet, stupid, smart, cunning, quiet.

"She is beginning to ground fog," Pike said. "In three minutes we move out. This is no attempt to take them, only to spoil them. To get them to change the plan. We have got to stall their attack until 1800. Clear?"

I said I would get you out, Pike thought. But I did not say how. You could go out in a bag and you could go out as Charlie's prisoner. The black man and the yellow man are soul brothers. The black man and the yellow man have suffered from the white man, the Clancy man, a long time now. Clancy got Alpha into this mess to kill niggers. To kill niggers and Mexicans and Gooks. To kill me.

Every man in Nam on both sides wonders what it would be like to be taken prisoner. Then he knows. Unless you want prisoners for Intelligence you kill them. You figure the other side, the Unfriendlies, do the same thing. Sad. But war is sad. War is shit. War is fear. I am afraid. I am afraid of the niggers, the Mexicans and the Gooks. I am afraid of myself. I will join the apes. I will become the black Tarzan and get myself a bamboo bed and fuck the world.

"I want each of you," black Pike said, "to maintain three meters' separation. When we hit Charlie, use your knife. Charlie will be surprised to meet you in the elephant grass. Charlie thinks he's got us. Charlie will say, What the hell is happening here in the elephant grass? and then Charlie will be dead. We will not kill enough of them to make a dent, but enough of Charlie to stall his attack. No guns. Leave your guns here. Questions?"

"Yes. Why?"

"Why what?"

"We leave our guns here?"

"Because," Pike said, "this is not a television show or an old movie. I will not be leading you with a sword. I will be crawling on my ass. We will stay on the ridge. The Clancy men blew the ridge and charged to get it back. We will do the opposite."

"To be different?"

"To save our ass," Pike said. "There are seven of us. There are a million of them. Move out. Follow me."

The seven moved forward in a fan. When they got to the tall dense sharp elephant grass Charlie was there. Charlie was not expecting. There were sudden animal noises, then the jungle was abruptly silent again. The terrible silence. When they were all back in the bunker again excepting one, Pike counted them. Pike could see Arnold had not made it, but he counted them twice hoping he would get the magic seven. He got six. He got six twice.

"Who didn't show back?" Pike said.

"Fucking Arnold."

"I will go get him," Pike said.

Someone touched Pike and said, "No."

Pike shook off the touch and slithered out toward the elephant grass.

What they don't understand, Pike thought, what they will never know is that war is kind. What they don't know is that Fucking Arnold is my soul brother. They don't understand that a man can't help being born the color he is born. That a man has no control over being born white. That I got Arnold into this and I will get Arnold out. White or green. Black or red. They don't understand that black is not a Whitey trick. Wait.

Pike paused on the edge of the elephant grass.

What they do not understand, what no white man knows

65

is how many people I am. I can kill Arnold. I can save Arnold. It's up to Whitey. I can surrender Arnold. I can rescue Arnold. It's all up to Whitey.

Where is Arnold now?

Hiding.

Do not hide from me, Arnold. I have come to take you back. I am your sergeant.

Pike parted the elephant grass and slithered more. You can tell where the soldiers are in Nam because it is where the birds are not. Birds flee when soldiers enter. Pike touched the body of an Unfriendly, an NVA soldier. You can always tell where the fighting is in Nam because it is where our Allies are not. The South Vietnamese soldier flees when fighting enters. But it was true about birds and it was helpful to know, to avoid ambush.

Where is Arnold?

Hiding.

I am your sergeant.

Pike touched something sticky.

Pike turned it over.

It was Arnold.

Arnold had killed himself.

Arnold had committed suicide.

With his own knife.

Arnold had been ordered into the elephant grass to kill Gooks and gone into the elephant grass and killed himself.

"I will take you back with me, Arnold," Pike whispered. "I will take you back to the bunker and give you a decent burial."

No, I will bury you here. Pike removed his entrenching tool and buried Arnold. Arnold was small and slight and from New York City, but he did not bury easily. No one does in the Pleiku plateau of Nam. The soil is red and spongy and tough and makes it difficult to plow the rice in the paddies and bury Arnold. Pike scraped away at the red, tough dirt without raising his body, only his arms, which is difficult in the red sun, the red burning sun of Nam.

"Fucking Arnold," Pike whispered. "Fucking Arnold, rest in peace."

Pike was back in the bunker.

"Did they get Arnold?"

"Did they get Arnold, Sarge?"

"I did," black Pike said.

"Explain."

"Who do you think got us out here?"

"The war."

"I did."

"Bullshit."

"Who do you think ordered Arnold out there? I did."

"The war."

"No. It was me," Pike said.

"Arnold took his chances."

"Arnold killed himself," Pike said.

The six survivors stared at each other. They looked at each other to keep from looking at themselves.

"I don't understand it," Pike said. "I don't understand it because I understand it too well. Does that make sense?"

"Yes, Sergeant. It's best not to think about it."

"Thanks," Pike said. "I been thinking too much. Tommy, get your ass down or you'll draw fire."

"What time is sunset?"

"1800 hours," Pike said. Pike checked his watch and then stared at the sun. "Eleven minutes."

"And we cut ass out?"

"Yes, you do," Pike said.

"All of us?"

"No. I will cover you," Pike said.

"Then we can cover you when you leapfrog us."

"No," Pike said. "There is no place to hide between here and the Ridge saddle. No protection. You got to keep moving until you get away."

Pike took out his handkerchief and wiped his face, his big white handkerchief he had bought from a whore in Da Nang, and wiped his black face. It still contained Peterbilt's blood.

"Like I said," Pike said, "for the black man there is no greater satisfaction—"

"Yes?"

"If a man can't—"

"Yes?"

"Make it himself, then he must see someone else—"

"Say it, Sergeant."

"Make it," Sergeant Pike said. And then he said, "Cut ass out. It's 1800. That's an order."

The men ran for the gap in the hill, hopping, as soldiers will, like big-assed birds. But in the tropics the jungle sun sinks quickly and they were only faint ghosts now. Pike started his cover fire over the heads of his men. His boys. His Whiteys. Now Pike drew very heavy enemy reaction on himself. Two great mortar shells exploded inside of his bunker at once and the tropic sun sank quickly and the bamboo in the night went clack clack clack and the elephant grass cling cling cling and then all the world went absolutely and deadly silent.

7

Aɴᴅ here, and naked on the balcony of the Suranwangse Hotel and in Dak Sut, and after slamming in and darting out with the body of black Pike in the Bamboo Bed, Knightbridge stared out unseeing at the sighting moon slanting up, the torrid moon, palm-eclipsed, coconut-tangled, effulgent, rising terrific. He was silent.

"Just hold me," she said.

"I said it was Clancy," he said.

"Just hold me."

"But that he hadn't asked for it."

"Tighter."

"But that both sides—because, you see, it's a guerrilla war."

"Not now."

"That it's not only Clancy—"

"Not now," she said. "Tighter."

And that was all she remembered, all she remembered except something hard, and the terrific slanting sighting moon in an explosion of stabbing lights and flashes, and then her body descending in soft quietude to a gentle pulsing and unutterable calm.

The Asiatic sun was up at six but Janine was already turning back the bed on which they had not slept. They had slept on the balcony, on the rattan bamboo bed with which they were both marked, both temporarily but fiercely welted, branded by the Vietnamese bamboo bed. She fetched her green raw-silk mandarin dress, covering her pink nakedness with the slick cool green glow, and went out with Knight-bridge.

"When is Mike . . . ?"

"Now."

"Not next year, not next month, but now," Knightbridge said.

"I told him what had happened. I never thought he would keep insisting."

"I'll see him."

"No. Don't be a damn fool, K," Janine said, touching him. "He won't listen because he never does. He doesn't get paid to listen." Janine paused. "I'd rather you didn't." Her hair flashed a heliograph, a harsh red-gold in the steady tropic sun. "I'll meet him in the park."

"Yes," Knightbridge said, and then he laughed and then he said, "I'll be at the sidewalk café."

"I'll take you there."

"I can make it all right," Knightbridge said.

Janine crossed by herself to the park and sat in front of the white elephant and watched Knightbridge dissolve in the tropic steam and hushed heat, and lost now in the explosion of gaudy Dak Sut color, and Janine thought it will be all right because he has got to learn to remember as I have to learn to forget. And Mike . . .

Mike came up and sat down on the bench across from the white elephant and next to Janine.

"So you're assigned to Intelligence now?" Janine said to Mike.

"I didn't want to see you to talk about that," Mike said.

"And now you will have to find Clancy?"

"If he's alive. But I didn't want to talk about that."

"I don't like to do this to you, Mike. You and Knight-bridge, you and K. You've got a lot in common."

"Yes," Mike said, looking at her. Then Mike looked across at the white elephant and then at the apes in the next great prison cage. The apes were amusing themselves by thinking and staring at the elephant. The elephant stared back and thought too. Mike's mind was a blank now but he said, "What does he do that I couldn't do?"

"You are hurt," she said.

"If he was transferred to Search and Rescue it can't be anything good."

"You're being petulant," she said.

"What does he do in bed that I don't do?"

"I have hurt you," she said.

"If K gets killed do you think I'll still be around?"

"You don't have to say anything like that."

Mike leaned back away from the elephant. "I guess not," Mike said. "I guess I don't have to say anything at all. I am a W.I.A., I shouldn't talk. I shouldn't say anything until I get fixed up."

"A Wounded in Action," she said. "What kind of action?"

"The worst kind," Mike said.

"You'll recover," she said. "Time. You know, damn it, I am very sorry," she said.

Mike looked at the apes. He seemed to be consulting the apes.

"The damn war should keep me occupied," he said. "Looking for Clancy."

"Is he alive?"

"Yes," Mike said. "We had a faint contact with his RTO man, the boy who got him out."

"What do you expect to find out from Clancy?"

"The secret of the war," Mike said.

"Who did what to who and why?"

"Yes," Mike said, looking through her now to the cage. "Exactly like that. Something like that. I'd better get my junk together."

"Yes," she said. And then she said, "I'm sorry, Mike." And then she said again, "I'm sorry, Mike," and she meant it.

Knightbridge was sitting in the outdoor café of the Suranwangse Hotel watching Janine in the park across the teeming street talking with Mike. Knightbridge was listening to, but not hearing, the cowboy and the Indian who had just walked up. The cowboy and the Indian were named Bethany Quinn and Peter Scott. They were types, Knightbridge thought. They were both types who wander Asia looking for The Message. The youth who have not found The Word in America. Peter's hair was longer than Bethany's. They had been to India, they must have been to India, and they must have studied Zen in Japan. Now they were here to stop the war. Flower Power. There's nothing wrong with that, Knightbridge thought. We have tried everything else. Despite the fact that Peter was an Indian, Peter wore rimless Benjamin Franklin glasses, mandarin beads and a huge dome-shaped cowboy hat. But there was something in Peter's eyes, a kind of hardness, that told Knightbridge that one time Peter was a soldier, and there was something in those eyes too that said he had fled. Bethany must have picked him up. She looked like the type that collected casualties, all of life's wounded. Her hair was braided like an Indian's and her eyes were small and quick and blue. The blue-eyed Indian. Last night on this terrace they had said they were from San Francisco. San Francisco Indians.

"Do you mind?"

"No. Sit down," Knightbridge said.

"Sit down, Peter," Bethany said.

Peter untangled himself from his great guitar and sat down on the iron chair and tilted his dome hat back and stared at Knightbridge for some message.

"Not today," Knightbridge said.

Knightbridge looked across at Janine sitting with Mike. They were both gesticulating now in the park as Rotarians will, or children. They were separated by the thronged street and an omnipresent Asian haze redolent of orchids and the high stench of sweet piss. They were separated too by something Bethany was saying.

"Look," Bethany said. "Once Peter was a soldier. Now we are going to stop the war."

Knightbridge watched over the street between the elephant and the apes to Janine in the park. Janine wore green, a study in green, so that she was almost in camouflage within the exotic flora of the zoo. Mike was in suntans, a highlight and emergent in the hot palette of Asia.

"You don't believe we can stop the war?" Bethany said.

"Of course you can," Knightbridge said. "Of course." And he looked at her quick eyes and down at her fringed suede jacket that had a large button sign that said I HAVE A DREAM. "With that sign you can do anything," Knightbridge said.

"Is that your girl over there with that man in the zoo?"

"Yes."

"Is that her husband?"

"Never that."

"Can I help?"

"No, you cannot help."

"I am very big on problems that are not my own."

"I know."

"I am very large on people's problems, but this war is a toughy."

"Yes, it is."

"I could sit on my small ass in Santa Barbara," Bethany said.

"San Francisco?"

"No one wants to admit they're from Santa Barbara," Bethany said. "I found Peter here and together we are somebody."

"Alone you are . . . ?"

"Nobody. Haven't you discovered that yet? I hope you're not buying that Zen meemoo."

"Zen?"

"Yes," Bethany said. "I have been through all that and come out here."

"This is where you come out? In a war?"

"Yes," Bethany said. "What can I do to help? We know about Ridge Red Boy."

Peter stared at Knightbridge for The Answer.

"I do not have the answer," Knightbridge said. "I do not have any of the answers."

"We are moral people. Does that shock you?" Bethany said.

"It should," Knightbridge said. And then Knightbridge said, "Where did you get that sign, that button sign, you're wearing, I HAVE A DREAM?"

"Berkeley."

"Not Santa Barbara?"

"No, Berkeley. They God damn are not going to take Berkeley away from us, are they, Peter?"

Peter continued to stare at Knightbridge and it was a disembodied stare, as though it were the dead searching. But this boy could not have been on that ridge, Knightbridge told himself. He could not have been on that ridge because he is here and no one who was there can be here. It is that simple. Ridge Red Boy was the great simplifier. But Peter continued to stare and Knightbridge looked over into the zoo at Janine and Mike where something was happening and then back here where nothing at all was happening except Peter's eyes. They were big and black and they stared at him under that dome hat and Knightbridge wondered where he had seen, felt, that stare before and he remembered it was on Ridge Red Boy, but he was not on Red Boy now. No one was.

And Bethany was saying to him with the dense seriousness of the very young, "It's all we have left, the dream, but it's all that matters, it's all we need. It might save us. Can I help?"

"Help? Yes, if you could—"

Bethany snapped her fingers in front of Peter's eyes and something happened and Knightbridge stood up and tried to make his way across the street against the riot, against the river of Asia. Now he came up in back of Janine on the park bench, kissed her on the ear and said, "I want to have you, Janine. Now."

"All right, K. Mike just left."

"That's good."

"We'd better let them make up the room first, K."

"Why?"

"Respectability. We owe them the appearance anyway."

"Yes," Knightbridge said, sitting down. "It's their world. What did he say?"

"Mike said it would be my own fucking funeral."

"Yes," Knightbridge said, touching her.

"Later," she said. "Later."

Bethany and Peter came up now and Bethany said, "Peter is a virgin. That's why he wears that guitar, to protect himself from women. Play something, Peter. Play 'This Land.'"

Peter Scott played "This Land."

"Do you dig?" Bethany said.

"What?" Knightbridge said.

"Do you like it?"

"Yes."

"Peter is not really a virgin," Bethany said. "I screw him all the time. If you know how, it's easy to get by that guitar to the real Peter. What do you think of that? I screw him in broad daylight."

"Yes."

"There's nothing wrong with that," Bethany said. "That's what I learned at Berkeley. I mean, in effect, frankly, the normal drive is there, isn't it? When you're hungry you don't go behind a bush and eat. That's why Peter and I do it in broad daylight."

"Broad daylight?"

"In effect."

"You either do it in broad daylight or you don't do it in broad daylight," Janine said.

"I like your cool," Bethany said, and then she said, "Play something more, Peter."

Peter started to play "This Land" and Bethany said, "Not again. Play 'The Big Rock Candy Mountain,' Peter." And Peter did.

When Peter finished Bethany said, "We are on our way to the front to give flowers to the troops. Flower Power. You don't think we could allow Asia to go down the drain, do you?"

"Oh, no," Knightbridge said.

"I've got news for you. I think we should allow Asia to go down the drain," Bethany said.

"I bet you have something important to do right now," Knightbridge said.

"Nothing more important than helping you," Bethany said. "I'm sure if we could get your problem out in the open and kick it around—but I feel I'm meeting resistance. Resistance is most frequently disguised hostility."

"Disguised?" Janine said.

"Yes, you are a coolie," Bethany said. "I like that. And what I like about you, Mr. Knightbridge," Bethany said, "when I act like a child you treat me like an adult. You give me straight answers. I sure wish I could help you with your problem, Captain Knightbridge."

"I sure wish you could too, Bethany," Knightbridge said.

"Shall I have Peter play something?"

"Not now."

Bethany grabbed Peter by the guitar and they twanged off. On the terrace of the Suranwangse Hotel they walked into the arms of Mike. Mike stopped them and made Peter a proposition and Bethany said to Mike, "What makes you think he would be interested in your Clancy mission? Do we look like loonybirds who can't keep our pants zipped? Oh no, oh no, oh no. If you have a mission do it yourself. Personally we have more important things to do. Peter and I are people too."

"No one said you weren't people," Mike said. "That's why I'm giving Peter this mission. I believe Peter here is especially fitted for it."

"Don't try to butter Peter's ass," Bethany said. "Peter is mine. I found him first. If you want to butter someone's ass don't butter Peter's. Did you know that Peter is in trouble?"

"Yes."

"Did you know that man's role is naturally aggressive and that this accounts for sex?"

"No."

"That it accounts for war too?"

"No."

"That it accounts for art? Art is a male thing. War is a male thing. Did you know . . . ?"

"No."

"Did you know that Hitler tried to paint pictures, Napoleon tried to write a novel?"

"No."

"Show me a soldier who is not a failure," Bethany said.

"Well, I would have thought—"

"Don't think," Bethany said. "Thinking is not a male thing. When a man thinks he comes up with a war. Thinking is a female thing."

"And she comes up with a baby?"

"A baby is better than a body," Bethany said.

"Why doesn't Peter talk?"

"Because Peter has stopped talking and thinking too," Bethany said.

"You think if he thinks then he will go back?"

"Any male would."

"That that is the way out?"

"Yes," Bethany said. "You were on Clancy's Red Boy?"

"Yes." And then Mike said, "I only want to help."

"You can't help by spying."

"We don't spy on anybody," Mike said. "Not anybody who doesn't want to be spied on."

"I'll just leave that hanging right there," Bethany said, and she and Peter wandered off down the thronged street, Peter with his wild and solemn eyes, those lost soldier eyes searching the Asian pavement now.

They look innocent enough, don't they? Mike told himself watching them move off. Innocent as hell. But Peter is a deserter from Clancy's outfit. Peter is a deserter disguised as a guitar. Disguised as a cowboy, and she is the Indian. The cowboy and the Indian. The deserter and the Indian. Did you notice the button Bethany had on her jerkin? It said I HAVE A DREAM. I hope she never loses it. I hope that with everything she will see in Viet, the dream will always be there. Never say die. Peter was with Clancy's outfit, but Peter deserted before Red Boy. Why? One thing is certain, you can't desert Clancy. I found that out a long time ago. Peter will go back. Peter could lead me back. But Clancy could be dying. Never say dead.

Mike walked off.

"Shall we go up now?" Knightbridge said, watching Mike go.

"Yes, now," Janine said. "Now."

ing lasts too long. The VC break contact to fight another day, another place, another way. Here outside Dak Sut in the straight and flat rice paddy broken every thousand hectares by wind-screening and boundary-demarking acacia trees there was a reconnaissance outfit from the Eighth Cav pinned down by small arms and mortar fire. Mike did not take cover. Maybe the VC would understand his situation and withhold fire. The VC would understand a busted and blown-apart heart when they saw one. They would realize too that he was looking for Clancy. They had probably suffered many shot-up hearts. And they must all be looking for Clancy. Everyone is. They would withhold fire. What the VC did not know with all their busted hearts was that he was with Army Intelligence, that he was sent to relieve Clancy of command. He was late. The VC had already relieved Clancy. This correspondent business was to deceive the brass. The brass would be careful what they told to Intelligence. A reporter was a harmless nut, all of them, a harmless nuisance who could be controlled by the threat of lifting his credentials if he told something he should not tell. It had worked splendidly. The bad part was that Mike did not know now who he was. The fine line between two people he was not had become one person he was not. Clancy was to blame. Janine was to blame. Knightbridge and his 379th Search and Rescue was certainly to blame. Here you have a simple war going on and then an outfit in a Bamboo Bed decide to be neutral. Janine behaves like a woman. Clancy behaves like a man. The bad part is that war is kind. War is a dirty mess that covers it all over with dirt that becomes flamboyant and gay —vivid jungle that is beautiful. War is thoughtful, considerate, far-thinking, murderous, and it hurts, and war is the revelation. War opens the curtain on us all and shows us what we are not. What Clancy was not. I remember well what Clancy was not. Why was the army removing Clancy? Because although at all times there seems to be no order in army chaos sometimes they do make a tentative gesture toward life.

Clancy and I were boys together. We were Indians together. That is, we went to the same private broken boarding
school for boys who were not. Boys from broken homes. Prettyfields, Somerset County, Liberty Corners, New Jersey. Ha!
A wicked place, a kind place, a broken place. Many times it
was there that we played at being Indians that we were not.
Now we are playing good guys. Because we are here. Because
we wanted . . . ?

"No one loves us," the American colonel from the Eighth
Cav said. The tanks had formed a circle defense perimeter
against the hostiles and Mike walked in. Mike recognized
the colonel who was talking. It was Yvor. They had taken
two prisoners and their tanks were still drawing fire from a
close village. It looked as though they had gotten a schoolteacher and a farm boy. You never know what you will pick
up in a fire fight in Nam.

"No one loves us," the colonel named Yvor said.

The Vietcong schoolteacher and the farm boy lay at their
feet like broken dummies. They had their hands tied behind
their backs and sugar sacks were tented and tucked over their
heads. Soon the schoolteacher and the farm boy would be
dead. They were VC but they did not look like the armed
villains you read about in *The New York Times* or *Paris
Match*. They were naked except for black pants. Their bodies looked starved and hunted. The schoolteacher kept holding his breath under his sugar sack against the bullets that
would hit him.

"I'll be fucked if I can do it," the American captain said.
"I do not know how much longer my men can do it."

"The Vietnamese smile. They love us in the daytime and
shoot at us at night," Colonel Yvor said.

The chaplain came up, evangelical. "You gentlemen are
invited to the services at 1600."

"What the fuck for?" the captain said.

"Our Lord," the chaplain said.

"Your lord can kiss my—"

"You better leave," the colonel said to the chaplain.

"Yes, kiss off," the captain said.

The chaplain dissolved into the elephant grass.

"Our good captain wants to shoot them all," the colonel said.

"The chaplains or the VC?" Mike asked.

"All. Everyone," the colonel said.

"I bring them in here and the recon turns them loose," the captain said.

"We send them for Intelligence."

"But afterwards."

"Afterwards is difficult," the colonel said.

"Shit."

The Vietcong schoolteacher groaned under his hood and the interpreter told him to shut up.

"It disturbs the captain's thinking," the colonel said.

"Sir?"

"Yes, captain?"

"How much longer?"

The colonel did not say anything. The colonel looked down at the schoolteacher tied up in the bag. But the colonel did not say anything. The schoolteacher looked like a CARE package that had been broken. The colonel still did not say anything.

"Sir?"

"Can I say something in front of the press?"

"You can try."

"With the colonel's permission."

"Shove it," the colonel said.

The captain was silent.

"Go ahead, Captain. This correspondent here works for a newspaper."

"For God and country," the captain said.

"Whose God and whose country?" the captain said.

The colonel said, "He doesn't know where he stands."

"In a rice paddy over a schoolteacher," Mike said.

"Shit," the captain said.

The radio man requested artillery for Bravo Company. The colonel was given binoculars, a sergeant held them before his eyes. After he had looked at a distant bridge, a far village, and carefully at a close grove of trees, he said, "Seven rounds." The artillery was concealed in the trees.

The sergeant handed the binoculars back to the colonel's driver and the tied sack groaned.

"The village?"

The colonel nodded yes, that it was the village, and then he nodded no, that he did not like it.

"Shit," the captain said. Now the captain mused silently and then he said, "The chaplain had no business up here."

"Correct," the colonel said.

The captain said the words "Jesus Christ," and then he thought about the whole situation more carefully and said the word "shit" again as though this word were ultimate and supreme, and the cannon repeated it again, firing into the village where the people were, again and again and again as the schoolteacher groaned and the interrogator tried to shut him up and the lights went out—that is, Mike suddenly realized that all around was dark and they gathered up the sacks of Asian prisoners and walked back into the night.

"Yes, no one loves us," the colonel repeated.

Going back in the darkness Mike asked the colonel about Clancy.

"I don't remember a Clancy," the colonel said.

"Yes, you do."

"Clancy wanted love," the colonel said.

"Doesn't everyone?"

"No," the colonel said. The colonel thought about this as the jeep slid down the dirt wall to avoid the VC mines. "Let's say, for Christ's sake," the colonel said, "that Clancy went about getting love in a peculiar way."

"Clancy was a peculiar person."

"Positive," the colonel said.

"I've got to find him."
"I thought he was dead."
"No."
"It would be better if he were dead," the colonel said.

9

THE great B52 bombers were on their way to stop the war. The great B52 bombers were on their way to eliminate Clancy. They had been ordered in by Colonel Yvor, not exactly to eliminate Clancy but that is what is exactly happening, Clancy thought. The bombs dropped. Colonel Yvor had probably ordered them in to save an outfit. When all else fails you eliminate everything. The bombs dropped. There is nothing like a good bombing to solve everything. Save something by eliminating everything. Colonel Yvor is no fool. Clancy had escaped. With luck some of the bombs might hit me. Colonel Yvor is no fool. Another thing, Clancy thought, another thing. While you are thinking these crazy thoughts, what about Mike? Mike was sent out to remove me. Tell Clancy to go home. Clancy is spoiling the war. Clancy is giving the war a bad reputation. If Mike got there to Ridge Red Boy he got there too late. I had already done my job and left. I did the best I could. It was the first one I lost. Sorry, Mike.

What is that noise? The bombs dropping? No, I mean the other noise. It sounds like a guitar. Isn't that something, to play a guitar while the bombs are dropping? What will our great generals in their awful wisdom think of next?

The American bomber crew were doing nicely above Clancy too. They had just begun to serve martinis.

"With or without?"

"With or without what?"

"Ice."

"Of course I want ice."

"I mean do you want me to shake it in the shaker or put it in your glass?"

"Shake it in the shaker."

"I don't like this," the commander of the B52 said. "Some poor devils may be killed down there."

"I assure you," the captain said, "no poor devils are getting killed down there."

"Promise?"

"Scout's honor."

"Then shake mine in the shaker too," the commander said.

The dying Clancy was making this conversation up as he felt the bombs hitting.

Wham!

Something from the B52 dropped close.

Wham!

The spiders would lose their hold on the trees.

Wham!

Our Father . . .

Wham!

Who art in the B52 . . .

Wham!

A string of bombs was laid neatly alongside somewhere near where Clancy lay and they went off Wham! Wham! Wham! and Clancy held onto a mahogany tree as a boy hangs on in the tunnel of love and he could feel the scorpions and the spiders coming down. Clancy brushed them off. Clancy thought about the young boy medic named Oliphant who was hit by hostile machine-gun fire during the last assault that overran Clancy's A for Alpha on Ridge Red Boy. The boy medic, Oliphant, who as the long stream of bullets went into him kept trying to brush them off. Clancy did not like to think about this. The bombing ended now but the guitar continued.

We have got one long fine war, Clancy thought. I guess this is the way a war ends. What happened to Mike? What happened to Search and Rescue with their Bamboo Bed?

Clancy looked around him at the shattered, bloodied bamboo. I got one. I hope everyone listening to me has got a bamboo bed of their own.

Then Clancy was silent, very silent. But he had never said anything. His throat wound would not let him speak. His eyes spoke.

The captain and the lieutenant, Knightbridge and Bliss, had quit Dak Sut and were back looking for Clancy, back at the 379th Search and Rescue. Mike, who had lost his girl, lost Janine, was down there someplace in the aqueous, gaudy green Vietnam jungle below looking for Clancy. The United States Army was looking for Clancy. The world. The Bamboo Bed was wandering off someplace over Vietnam. The Bamboo Bed without anyone at the controls had skittered off sideways to Laos or Cambodia. Laos and Cambodia are not far. Burma is not far. They could have been over Burma. To be over Cambodia during this part of the war was illegal. The prince there made a fuss about it. So they could have been over Burma when they were actually over Cambodia. But whether they were over Cambodia or not they must be very careful about getting over into the front seat, back to the controls. Don't rock the boat. She might crash right in the prince's lap. Get caught red-handed.

"Be careful," she said.

"I will," he said, and he moved slyly, trying not to let the Bamboo Bed know he was moving so the thing would not crash.

I did not mean to call you a thing, he said to himself. The captain said to the Bamboo Bed. Just keep steady a bit and everyone will make it out all right. No, I did not mean to call you a thing. We were just making a little something in your back seat because your front seats are bucket and separate. Now if you will just let me get over your armored ass, then we will have a good look for Clancy.

The front seats were armor-plated on the back sides with hard compacted fiber glass that absorbed bullets or anything the Unfriendlies chose to throw in that direction. No, I did not mean to call you a thing. Just be quiet and don't lurch until I get my hands on your controls. That's a good baby.

"Be careful," she said from the rear seat.

"What do you mean, they're all dead?" Elgar said.

"I mean," Oliver said, watching the bushes for the enemy and seeing only the small red Laotian tanagers, birds that shot like bullets, "I mean Captain Clancy's Alpha Company is no longer of this world. They have all gone the way of Big Chief Many Feathers, George Armstrong Custer and Tom Mix."

"What else is new?"

"Captain Clancy planted the first American flag above the citadel of Hue across the Perfume River atop the Palace of Perfect Peace."

"But it's not supposed to be an American war."

"As a symbol of something."

"Is that good?"

"Clancy lost his head."

"Literally or figuratively?"

"Every way. Both."

"What do we do now?"

"Pick up the pieces."

"Are there any?"

"Private Appelfinger of Alpha Company still lives."

"How you know?"

"I got a call from him on the transmitter. If you find Appelfinger you find Clancy."

"The army newspaper has got Ridge Red Boy pegged as a victory."

"That makes sense."

The two WASPs, Oliver and Elgar, stared around the jungle at what God had wrought. Stared at the other insects. There were bright red, white and golden flies that gemmed the black-green fronds. There was the dreadful heat that seemed substantial, that had the quality of liquid, a hot and gaseous substance that was not only palpable and alive, but inescapable, so that the monsoon rain forest became a prison, a burning cell that covered all you could see, all the green fire of existence.

"What we have got to do," Elgar said, "is stop cremating ourselves. Sitting here and listening to the war radio."

"The calls for help are very depressing."

"Particularly when they always call Search and Rescue when it's too late."

"After they have lost the battle."

"They should call us before they start one."

"We would advise against it."

"That way they wouldn't have a war."

"Sad. Sad."

"Let us get back to our radio."

"Captain Knightbridge and Janine could be in trouble."

"What kind of trouble?"

"I don't know," Oliver said. "These things take time."

"Time is shit."

"War is shit."

"Golly gee, how would you know?"

"I've just got a hunch," Oliver said.

"I've got a hunch," Knightbridge said, "that we're over Cambodia."

How in the hell the captain can tell, Nurse Janine thought, because to her, to anyone, it all looked the same. To her, to anyone, it was all an attempt, a conspiracy by the forever endless forest and the concealing monsoon to hide the awful beauty and the terrible poverty of Asia, because, she thought . . . and then she thought and said, "We could have been killed."

"Yes," Knightbridge said from the controls.

The naked lieutenant was still in the back seat and still with her hard round ass and firm tits and all beneath the terrific whack whack of the rotor blades. Yes, the naked lieutenant thought, and they fight down there because they are not man enough to do what we're doing up here. "You agree?"

Knightbridge pointed to his ear that he could not hear above the giant noise of the jet engine, the rotor blades.

The lieutenant crawled in the front, her tits touching the top of the turning turret turntable, the solid white ass, white sloping shoulders all very white, white, almost a blue in the torrid Vietnamese sun up here above the monsoon. Her hair was a natural wild red and her eyes a big natural green, her lips and mouth full and wide and titillating, the better to kiss you with, her thighs and hips lithe and strong and quick, the better to . . .

"What?" he said.

She leaned over in the aerial greenhouse, the hard Vietnamese sun-hit solarium of the cockpit.

"Are you okay?"

"Still alive," he said.

"Where are we?"

"Above the monsoon."

Now there was a break in the weather beneath, but more, they had been driving through the thick substance of the monsoon and safe, they were borne by it and secure, now they came out over the precipice of cloud and the space fell off way way down to the insecure planet, the awful distance to the bottom of the infinite, precipitous and far.

The captain pointed to a fire fight.

All of Asia was ablaze in spots and from all the way up here you could see it burn. And from all the way up here you could see something shimmer.

A villa with a pool on top.

"Madame Dieudonné's villa."

"Who is she?"

"Clancy's girl."

"Then you know where you are?"

"Near the Cambodian border."

"What's that over there?"

"Rubber, rubber, rubber. It goes on for a million miles."

"Why?"

"I don't know."

"Is it to make junk? I would sooner walk," she said, "than use their God damn cars. And flying, that's for the birds."

"I didn't do it," he said.

"I know you didn't," she said, touching him. "Who planted all that rubber way out here?"

"The French."

"And now that the French have gone, who has got the rubber?"

"The French have not gone, only the French army has gone. All the other French are here still."

"Why didn't the French civilians leave with the French Army?"

"Because they knew we were arriving."

"Why are we flying naked over Vietnam?"

"Because the men are always looking for Tarzan and Jane in the jungle. I believe that Sergeant Batcheck must have some kind of merit badges that he passes out to his Boy Scouts that catch us in flagrante."

"What's that mean?"

"I don't know, but it's all I learned at West Point," Captain Knightbridge said.

"Then use it, boy."

"I will."

"Screw up a storm."

"Yes."

"I can't believe you learned that at West Point."

"No, it was a hobby."

"A serious hobby."

"Yes. When you get out of West Point you don't even know what to do with your pecker."

"I do," she said, and she touched him.

"Excepting to point it at the enemy."

"And?"

"And get it blown off, I guess. Who knows? I don't know. They might even run."

"I wouldn't run," she said.

"You big brave girl." And he moved over and petted her tits as he would lambs. Sweet lambs.

"Why did you join the army?" she said.

"I didn't. I simply went to West Point because that is where my father wanted to go."

"Why don't you fight?"

"Because I'm not angry at anyone."

"Didn't West Point train you?"

He was silent.

"Where are we?" Janine said.

"In the sun. Naked above the monsoon and in the sun. Above the war, naked in the sun."

"Where are we?" Elgar said.

"We are not lost, and we are not crazy. You see, we are acting out our role as soldiers. The Task Force, everybody here, is playing soldier, playing being crazy, but we know we are acting, but when you are playing a role and don't know it, then you are really crazy and lost. But *we* are not lost," Oliver said. "We are in the jungle but someplace only a few hundred meters from the base camp. We are not lost."

"I will tell you this," Elgar said. "That if Captain Knightbridge finds out that we are lost he will think we are piss-poor soldiers."

"Oh, he knows that already."

"That we are lost?"

"That we are piss-poor soldiers."

"Are you lost too?" Elgar said to a man who moved in the monsoon.

"It's Captain Knightbridge's friend Mike," Oliver said. "The man who is trying to get lost as a correspondent."

"I'm not trying to get lost as a correspondent," Mike said. "It simply helps me when you are trying to find out something not to be with Intelligence. Did Knightbridge tell you?"

"Maybe he did and maybe we divined it on our own," Elgar said. "It's a crazy war."

"Knightbridge can be a son of a bitch," Mike said.

"What was that?"

"Knightbridge steals things," Mike said.

"You're not making sense," Elgar said, moving up to Mike in the bamboo with Oliver.

"Yes, join the war," Oliver said. Oliver cut off a piece of bamboo with his jackknife and waved it over his head like a missing banner.

"Rally round the flag, boys," Oliver said.

"Hold it," Mike said. "Hold everything. I want to talk to you."

They all sat down on the bamboo with Oliver's bamboo flag between them.

"What do you want to talk to us about?" Elgar said.

"Clancy."

"He's dead," Oliver said.

A shot whistled over their heads.

"We have reason to believe he's alive," Mike said.

"Simply because we got a pickup from his RTO man," Oliver said.

"More than that," Mike said.

"Simply because Appelfinger, the RTO man we got a pickup from, was Clancy's buddy."

"It's more than that," Mike said.

"Was it that shot?"

"We don't know," Mike said.

"Was it that Appelfinger left Ridge Red Boy with Clancy's body?"

"We're not certain it was a body," Mike said.

Elgar cut another stick of bamboo and he stuck it in the ground between them as though to establish their position, to fly out more flags.

"Why are you so interested in Clancy?" Oliver said. "There are so many people missing."

"I've got a message for him," Mike said. "And we must

piece together what happened, how it happened and why it happened."

"And this is the biggest thing since Custer," Oliver said.

"And find out who is to blame," Mike said.

"We know," Oliver said. "You were going to court-martial Clancy." Oliver pulled his bamboo flag out of the aqueous ooze of Vietnam. "We all know that."

"Knightbridge can be a son of a bitch," Mike said.

"No, it's simply that Clancy has friends," Oliver said. "Don't you know this war is so damn complicated that we have to divide it between the Friendly and the Unfriendly? Clancy was a Friendly."

"I know. That's why I'm hanging around here," Mike said.

"That won't do any good," Oliver said, taking his bamboo banner out of the ground and waving it over all their heads. "We are lost."

"I'm still concerned about who fired that shot," Mike said. "They had observation on us. They never fired again. It could have been a warning."

"Then why don't you take it?" Elgar said.

"Come. Follow me. I'll get you out of here," Mike said.

"Back to our base?"

"Yes," Mike said.

"You will stay with us there?"

"No."

"Why?" Oliver waved the bamboo flag above their heads.

"Because I feel like an Unfriendly here," Mike said.

"But you're going to see Tarzan?"

"Yes. Tarzan and Jane," Mike said.

10

How did Clancy get to Ridge Red Boy? By way of Prettyfields. You get to Ridge Red Boy through the battlefields of Prettyfields. Don't be cute, Mike told himself. Just sit down here in the monsoon and try to remember one day at Prettyfields. What about the day we massacred the Boy Scouts? The day Clancy did not get that first medal he ever got. When the Boy Scouts like locusts or aphids in early June covered the New Jersey countryside in a green swath, peering out from underneath their wide campaign hats and above their green kerchiefs with that fast and facile grin. Our visiting Boy Scouts arrived in early June from East Orange and set up their camp on Rye Hill. They were led by a tall and bony character in short pants called Mr. Tuferino and he had an assistant in identical short pants and whistle named Mr. Pepperpound. They were both blown-up enlargements of the miniature boys, even to the kerchief, campaign hat and merit badge.

Mr. Tuferino was standing towering above Little Clancy at the exit to the Boy Scout tent. The yellow fly flapped in the quick Somerset County wind and Mr. Tuferino blew on his whistle. Little Clancy pulled on Mr. Tuferino's tall leather shoe.

"Listen to me."

But Mr. Tuferino blew again on his whistle, again and again and again.

"Listen," Little Clancy said, still pulling.

The huge and bony giant tilted his campaign hat and

stared down at Little Clancy but raised his whistle again. Mr. Tuferino was not only very big but he was also very large on war. Mr. Tuferino had Mr. Pepperpound drill the boys every morning before they got up. I mean the Scouts were all too sleepy to know whether the order had been squads right or squads left, dress right or dress left, and so they marched, wandered around like small lost doves or earthbound pigeons searching for a crumb. That is until Mr. Tuferino got there from his morning coffee, when he maneuvered them like ants.

"Be prepared, Mr. Pepperpound. Be prepared." Mr. Tuferino was always brisk and pleased with himself.

"He's giving them good military discipline," I said.

"Maybe," Little Clancy said.

"I can tell," I said, "that if he ordered them over a cliff the Scouts would do it."

"We could take them at their own game," Little Clancy said. "In battle, then burn down their camp and send them back to East Orange where they came from, those that survive. But first," Little Clancy said, "we got to learn how to be an army of soldiers."

Little Clancy broke us up into armies, then divided us into divisions, regiments, battalions, companies, but when he got down to companies there wasn't anyone left, so he said, "We will all just fight under me. But first we got to learn how to be soldiers, how to beat those ants. Discipline."

He gave me the job of drilling us like we had seen the Boy Scouts do. We weren't very good at squads right and squads left, and when he gave "To the rear, march!" it was like in a Charlie Chaplin movie.

"I'm about fed up," Little Clancy said. "Stop scratching, Mike, and listen to me. We will never defeat the Boy Scouts, not if you don't watch Mr. Tuferino carefully and see what he does, and when he's out there on the parade ground he doesn't scratch himself, Mike."

"Yes, sir," I said.

"I'm worried," Little Clancy said. "They are returning

to East Orange in a month and I don't think my men will be in shape for a year."

"Ten years," I said.

"Mike," Little Clancy said, "what do you think 'To the rear, march' means? Why is it that when Mr. Pepperpound says it they all do not do it and when Tuferino raises his eyebrow they do it?"

Little Clancy spread out his maps beneath the royal oak.

"We are right here," Little Clancy said, smudging the map. "And they are over here," Little Clancy said, moving his paw, "camped on Rye Hill. Now if we cross down here at the Dead River at midnight we could fall upon them at dawn."

"Where's dawn?" I said.

Eddie Markowitz laughed and Little Clancy said, "Don't laugh, Eddie. What do you think 'To the rear, march' means?"

"Banging into each other," Eddie Markowitz said.

"That's right," Little Clancy said. "We are going to win their war. The way I see it," Little Clancy said, "we'll have to wait until they're going through the Dead River Woods and then fall upon them from ambush."

"Where's that?" I said.

Little Clancy pounded on me, got me down and twisted my nose. "That's where it is," Little Clancy said. Then he got up and stuck his thumb through his other fingers in a fist. "That's what's left of Mike's nose. Anybody else want to know where dawn is? Anyone else don't know where ambush is located?" Clancy hunched down again over his maps. "We got to think like Indians," he said, pointing to the woods. "Mr. Pepperpound will be in the lead up here, then the band back here, then the troops in green. That's pretty good camouflage, but you'll know them by their snot-noses. We'll be behind every tree. Is that clear, men?"

"Our strength is as the strength of ten because our hearts are pure," I said.

"Something like that," Little Clancy said. "And tire irons and broken bottles and slingshots."

"There is a tree," I said, "in the middle of the Dead River Woods, right where they'll have to come down the path. It's shaped like a big Y, and if we could get enough inner tubes linked together we could make a sling and shoot something at them."

"No," Little Clancy said. "I've got it. What about shooting Mr. Tuferino at his Boy Scouts?"

The plan was abandoned because we couldn't find enough inner tubes or because we couldn't find Mr. Tuferino, or better, because we wanted to come from ambush like Indians from behind every tree.

"Without cavalry," Kazaluski said, "we could be lost." This was a prejudice with Kazaluski. One of his ancestors had come over a long time ago, while Washington was at Valley Forge. But everybody here had ancestors, some kind of parents, forefathers, with a background and such, not as fancy as Kazaluski's but enough to have come from someone of flesh and blood and bone. That is, everyone but Little Clancy who was maneuvering us in the Dead River Woods. We knew that Little Clancy had vaguely come from some place in the Midwest, but no one visited him and no letters were received or sent. It was as though he had suddenly appeared as an apparition from nowhere and was going no place.

The next day we made plans for the ambush by going over the field. Clancy guessed the distance from the Rye Hill Boy Scout encampment to the Dead River Woods at three miles. Kazaluski, Clancy's executive officer, reckoned it would take the Boy Scouts twenty-five minutes to arrive at our ambush.

We were going past the Boy Scout encampment now and they were listening to a lecture by Mr. Tuferino. Mr. Tuferino towered over his green-suited and kerchiefed charges with controlled resolution as though it were a quiet day in East Orange.

"Good evening, Mr. Tuferino," Little Clancy said.

"Get away," Mr. Tuferino said.

"Have no fear," Little Clancy said quietly as we disappeared over Rye Hill. We straggled down into the South Field with Little Clancy leading. When we got into the Dead River Woods Little Clancy said, "How long did that take to get from there to here?"

"Twenty minutes," I said.

"We will have a mounted Prettyfields soldier on Rye Hill," Little Clancy said. "As soon as the Boy Scouts leave he will set a signal fire."

"With what?"

"With a Boy Scout tent," Clancy said. "Then we will know down here we can expect the Boy Scouts soon. Line up in back of the trees," Little Clancy said.

"You can't line up in back of the trees," I said.

"Try," Little Clancy said.

We all scattered in back of the trees.

"That's perfect," Little Clancy said. "I can't see a thing. Now I see something coming down Rye Hill."

"It's Chief Eaton," I said. Chief Eaton was the headmaster of Prettyfields School.

"Everybody stay where you are," Little Clancy said. "He's coming straight down the path. He'll fall over the trip wire and spoil our war."

"Or start another," I said.

"I'll go out and turn him around," Little Clancy said.

"Good evening, Little Clancy. I'm going down by the river if I can get by you."

"Did you know there were Indians down there?" Little Clancy said.

"Little Clancy," Chief Eaton said abruptly, turning and retreating, "don't kill the Boy Scouts."

"Yes, Chief," Little Clancy said quietly, and then raising his voice, "It's all clear, men."

We walked back past the Boy Scouts the day before the battle. Mr. Tuferino was standing spare and alone in front of the scoutmaster's tent watching the sun disappear, tragic, except that Mr. Tuferino had on short pants. All his soldiers were asleep or bedded down. A lantern flitted here and there and sometimes a flashlight lanced the half light. But there was no prospect of doom. Tonight was like any other night away from East Orange.

We didn't sleep much that night, the night before we killed the Boy Scouts. We all got together in the attic to look at maps over a candle. It wasn't exactly the attic, it was a space behind the wall in the Green Hall where there was an entrance to get at the pipes beneath the sloping eaves.

"What you got to keep in mind," Little Clancy said, holding onto the cold-water pipe, "is that when their cavalry comes in sight—"

"They got no cavalry," I said.

"Like I said," Little Clancy said, "when their cavalry dashes—"

"I'll give you the cavalry," I said, "if you'll give me airplanes."

Little Clancy let go of the pipe and slid over.

"Now where were we?" I said.

"Listen," Little Clancy said, holding the roll of maps to his mouth like a flute, "if a man had the eagerness of the Boy Scouts and was going someplace, think what he could do."

"The Boy Scouts are organized," I said.

"They're organized, Mike, to tie knots."

"If they're so harmless, Little Clancy, then why are we going to ambush them tomorrow?"

"To teach them," Little Clancy said, "that we love them too."

When we got down to the woods the next day Little Clancy said, "Watch for the signal. When you see us burning one of their tents you will know they are on the march. Another thing," Little Clancy said, "Mr. Pepperpound always leads his troops way up ahead or else he brings up the rear. Either way we can drive a wedge between him and his troops. Without a leader his troops will be lost."

"Do we take any prisoners?" I said.

"Kill them all," Little Clancy said. "We've got a five-day march back to our boats through hostile country."

"You said you burned our boats," I said. "To keep us from retreating."

"I mean it's a five-day march back to where the boats were," Little Clancy said.

"It seems to me," I said, "we could hold some of their high chiefs and princes for money. We could get a lot of gold and joolery that way."

"No," Little Clancy said. "Boy Scouts come from middle-class families."

"Nothing will quite become them so much in this life as their leaving it?" I said.

"That's right, Mike. Listen to what Mike says and do as I do," Little Clancy said. "Stick around, Mike, and you can write my speeches."

"Look! The signal! The tent is burning," I said.

"That means they're on the march," Little Clancy said. "I want you to ignore their artillery and their wagon trains."

"They're crossing the oak field," I said.

"All right. Behind the trees," Little Clancy said. "And remember and don't raid their baggage trains."

"There's nothing in it anyway," I said, "except merit badges and knots."

"Remember," Little Clancy said, "we drive a wedge between Mr. Pepperpound and the men, make them leaderless."

We could hear the noise of the Boy Scouts now, their mess kits rattling, their band was quiet except for the drummer boys tapping out the step, and it wasn't Mr. Pepperpound who was marching with the troops, it was Mr. Tuferino. Mr. Tuferino hove into sight now all by himself in the lead, the neatly accoutered troops following to a perfect beat. When Mr. Tuferino passed my tree he must have been all of twenty feet ahead and when we fell upon them Tuferino was still there ahead. Someone threw a loop around Mr. Tuferino and tied him to a tree Indian fashion. The

East Orange Boy Scouts beat a retreat to the safety of the river. They had no weapons except how to build a fire and mental hygiene, none of which was handy now. We were armed with everything. I got in a lot of good licks before I got lost, then came upon Mr. Tuferino tied to the tree. Little Clancy was undoing the rope.

"What happened, Mr. Tuferino?" Little Clancy said. Then he saw me and said, "Mike and I were going fishing when we heard all the noise. That's a tough gang that hangs out in Liberty Corners. You must have run into them. Do you know what one of them said to me the other day, Mr. Tuferino? He said, 'I hate Boy Scouts.'"

"So do I," Mr. Tuferino said.

"What did you say?" Little Clancy said.

"I said," Mr. Tuferino said, "I think you had something to do with this."

"You don't believe me," Little Clancy said. "Ask Mike. Isn't there a bunch of boys, Mike, in Liberty Corners who hate Boy Scouts?"

"I believe so," I said without lying.

"You see," Little Clancy said. "It's lucky I came along. You wait right here, Mr. Tuferino. I'll see what I can do to save what's left of your boys. Stay with him, Mike."

"Yes, sir."

"Wait!" Mr. Tuferino said.

"I won't be more than five minutes," Little Clancy said and he took off faster than I could move. Later, when Little Clancy got his medal, I always wondered about Mr. Tuferino's "Wait!" Not that he wanted to get all his Boy Scouts killed but maybe that he wanted things to go a little farther than they did. The world will never know. We were alone together there by the fallen ropes and the big tree.

"What is your name?" Mr. Tuferino said.

"Mike McAdams, sir."

"The other boy, does he have any real name? Anything in the records besides Little Clancy?"

"Not that I know of, sir. We call him Iron Man. I think his first name is William."

"Does he have a mother, father, anyone who visits him?"

"He must have had a mother some time or other," I said.

"No, I don't believe so," Mr. Tuferino said. "I certainly don't agree. Of no woman born."

"What?"

"You certainly have to hand it to him though," Mr. Tuferino said. "He certainly takes the cake."

"All clear," Little Clancy said, arriving back. "My men beat them off."

"Your men beat them off" Mr. Tuferino said.

"Yes, sir," Little Clancy said.

Later that month, after the Boy Scouts had long since departed for East Orange, the medal for Little Clancy arrived, his first but not last medal. It seems they were always giving medals for everything in those days. This one had been voted by the All-Council of the Boy Scouts and recommended by Mr. Tuferino. Why? Everyone knew. It was perfectly plain to everyone but me because I was the only one who heard Mr. Tuferino holler at Little Clancy, "Wait!" Maybe I'm reading things into it, but I'm not reading anything into what Chief Eaton did about it when he got Little Clancy in the office in the guise of awarding him the medal. We all waited. We all waited because we wondered, wondered why Chief Eaton didn't award Clancy the medal when we all lined up on the grass for reveille and retreat, when they raised and pulled down the flag. Little Clancy told us that night what happened. When Clancy went in the office Chief Eaton was sitting there examining the medal.

"Do you know what this says?" Chief Eaton said, not looking up.

"No, sir."

"It says for outstanding bravery. Do you believe that, Little Clancy?"

"No, sir."

"Did you start it?"

"What, sir?"

Chief Eaton fingered Little Clancy's gold medal. "Melt this thing down and it'll be worth about five dollars."

There was a big silence.

"You didn't rescue any Boy Scouts, Little Clancy."

"Yes, sir."

"You admit it. Then maybe you do deserve a medal. I was going to drop this medal in the wastebasket and make you pick it out, but you admit it. What do you admit, Little Clancy? Did you start the whole thing?"

"I don't—"

"And you know I didn't either. You knew I didn't like having Boy Scouts pushed off on me either, and every summer too, and you thought you could get around me now by being honest, even honest. Look, I'm going to have to drop the medal in the wastebasket and make you pick it out because that's the way things are done in this world."

"Yes, sir."

"There it is." Mr. Eaton dropped the medal into the wastebasket. "There it is. Get it."

But Clancy never did. Never took the medal.

Never did?

No, not then, Mike told himself.

11

From his CP tent Knightbridge made contact with Appelfinger, Clancy's buddy, on the radio, and then it went dead. Before his radio went dead Appelfinger had tried to give his position but Appelfinger did not know where he was.

Knightbridge pushed back the radio and there was Mike.

"Any luck?" Mike said.

"We found Clancy."

"Where?"

"We don't know."

"Where is that?"

"Near Appelfinger, his RTO man. But Appelfinger doesn't know where he is."

"I don't know where I am either," Mike said. "That is, just when I think I got things sorted out it goes dead again."

"Colonel Yvor knows."

"I know," Mike said.

"You know everything."

"Yes," Mike said. "I know everything and everything always adds up to nothing."

"Sit down."

"No."

"If you still feel that way why did you come?"

"Because there is one thing I don't know."

"Janine?"

"That I know," Mike said.

"I wish you would sit ass down."

"Why don't you and Colonel Yvor make a better pretense of looking for Clancy?"

"You think we should put on a better act?"

"Yes."

"You are talking about the whole war now," Knightbridge said.

"I would like to isolate Clancy."

"You can't."

"The more I know the more I do not know."

"That's right."

"If I could start at one point and end at another point. Who ordered Clancy out there?"

"No one."

"When did Clancy die?"

"He is still alive."

"Yvor ordered him out, didn't he?"

"There is someone over Yvor."

"If Clancy is not dead now, he is dying."

"We hope."

"Say that again."

"A man should not suffer."

"Let's try an overfly."

"You want to go up in that?"

Mike stared out through the opening of the tent. The monsoon was thick and shifting as in a dream, but solid and palpable too as in a wall, so that when the wall of foam moved away you knew it would soon move back. Now it moved into the tent but only halfway so that Mike abruptly felt invisible and Knightbridge felt exposed.

"Clancy and I grew up together," Mike said. "We were dragged up together in the same busted home. It was a place called Prettyfields. They sent boys there from problem homes or no homes. It was called Prettyfields," Mike said. "The Episcopal Church. They taught us how to get along without parents."

"How?"

"They gave up," Mike said.

"And then the army."

"Yes," Mike said from the monsoon. "Because out there they don't know what they want. On the outside it's a game."

"Then a game is what they want."

"Yes," Mike said. "Women."

Knightbridge heard the voice rising out of the monsoon, removed and detached as though it were disembodied. The voice could have been arriving by some remote and yet-to-be-invented gadget, something that was relayed now only off satellites but soon off people so that life itself would become confused and obsolete.

"Women," Mike said.

"And after Prettyfields?"

"I told you," Mike said. "The God damned army. And then Ridge Red Boy. I still can't get out of that perimeter. All those dead. All the American dead."

"Why don't you go and see Janine?"

"But Clancy wasn't there. In the perimeter everyone was there but Clancy."

"And his RTO."

"Yes."

"And where was Colonel Yvor? With Mai Li. And where was my good friend K? He was with Janine." Mike now had taken to asking and answering all the questions. "And where was I? I was looking for Clancy to kick his ass out of the service."

"Why don't you see Janine?" Knightbridge said.

"Janine?"

"It's always good to talk to a woman."

"I don't know how to talk to a woman."

"No one does," Knightbridge said. "But being with them—"

"Woman . . . woman." Mike's voice seemed to have an idea now. "Woman? What about Madame Dieudonné? He could maybe . . . He could have maybe made it there to the underground villa."

"Too far," Knightbridge said.

"Maybe it was me," Mike said, his voice coming up with another idea. "Maybe Clancy knew that he had had it, that it was only maybe a question of days, hours, minutes, before I found him. We used to play a game at Prettyfields called Hare and Hounds. You have to catch a boy if you are a hound, and touch him three times and say 'You are dead.' Maybe Clancy could feel that touch. Maybe he knew he was about to be caught up with. He could feel that touch and he could hear me saying 'Clancy, Clancy, you are dead.' "

"Maybe Janine could—"

"And it was not only that threat but the threat of being a civilian, being lost again, and that's maybe why they wanted him removed, because he was trying too hard in a no-war. That is, growing up in Prettyfields he never quite understood the language on the outside and so he thought they meant fight when they said fight. And later they said no-holds-barred and he thought they meant that too. Never having been a civilian, never having been outside an institution, he did not know that we had never been told that people did not mean what they say."

"Yes."

"But what I want to make absolutely clear," Mike said from the mist of the monsoon, "what I have got to get out is that I was chasing Clancy way back there when in Prettyfields we had this game of Hare and Hounds and I was chasing him, chasing Little Clancy, and he was always just ahead. It was as though he were letting me get that close on purpose so that he could bound away to another hiding place. And it went on that way all day and into the darkness and on the following day I sat back of him in class and I reached forward to touch him and he turned and pointed at me with it."

"What?"

"A knife."

"A knife?"

"Yes, but it seemed like a sword."

"Did you touch him three times?"

"No. But maybe that's what I was going to do now. Maybe that's why I took this job."

"So you could touch him three times?"

"Yes."

"Something else now has touched him three times."

"Don't you think with luck we could take off and find a break in the weather?"

"I can't even see you," Knightbridge said.

"I'm sure Clancy has forgotten the game. I don't think he felt he was about to feel my touch," Mike said, "but I will never forget that damn sword."

"We will never know," Knightbridge said. "Why don't you see Janine?"

"Clancy, Clancy, you are dead," Mike said from the monsoon. "Janine? Janine? Why Janine?"

"You were very close," Knightbridge said. "Very close. Maybe she can help. We can't move now and you are destroying yourself by going over this. You are still playing Hare and Hounds and we are grounded. We can't look."

"Janine. Janine wouldn't want to see anyone from Prettyfields," Mike said.

"Why don't you try?"

"I tried. Remember? I lost."

Janine could hear them talking. Janine tried to keep from hearing what they were saying and then at once she was trying to hear everything they were saying.

Now they were talking about Clancy.

Now they were trying to get Colonel Yvor on the radio.

Prettyfields again.

What in the hell was Prettyfields? A woman can't screw Prettyfields.

If a man wants to find out about a man he should go to a woman. Mike should see Madame Dieudonné.

Men are only interested in getting to the top of another hill.

He wants to touch Clancy three times because men never cease to be children.

Now they are going to fight. K keeps telling Mike they can't go up in this monsoon and play Hare and Hounds.

"Why don't you go fuck yourself?" Mike said.

"That's no way to talk, Janine thought. Their story will never get in the *Woman's Home Companion*. They will have to clean that part up. Why do men have to use that word all the time? Because they are not getting any. Poor Mike. And the five hundred thousand other boys that are here.

Now they have got Colonel Yvor on the radio. Now Mike is mad as hell with Colonel Yvor.

Mike hates everybody.

Mike's not getting any.

Everything's not sex, Janine thought. Don't try to make everything sex. I have got an oversexed mind. No, not mind.

"Fly," she said to the gilded tropic fly lighting on another fly on the ridge pole of her jungle tent. "Vietnamese fly," she said, "the gilded fly doth lecher in my sight." All is not sex. Mike wants to find out what makes this war go round. Who caused Ridge Red Boy. Who caused the death of everyone in A for Alpha. All those men. Boys. Children. Those young, young men. War? No. Mike wants a more specific answer than that. Mike has come all the road from Prettyfields to find out. The answer lies in Clancy.

Does it?

Now Mike is giving Colonel Yvor hell on the radio.

Yvor is not talking.

Doesn't Mike realize that Colonel Yvor is a colonel?

Mike doesn't give a damn.

Doesn't Mike realize Colonel Yvor gave his arms for his country?

Mike still doesn't give a damn. What have you done lately?

No, Mike didn't say that, "Fly. Go right on screwing." What he said was you ordered Clancy out there without any support, without any escape route.

Now Colonel Yvor said quietly, so quietly it could only

be heard two tents away and through a driving monsoon. "Correspondent or Captain or whatever you are, why don't you take your investigation, roll it up neatly and shove it up your ass? Why don't you?"

"Because there is going to be a court-martial. You."

"Oh. Oh?"

"Can you help me?"

"Oh?"

"Can you help me, Colonel?"

"Yes."

There was a burst of fire.

"I am under attack."

"Are you certain, Colonel, it was not your sergeant Billy Joe who fired that burst?"

"I am under attack," the colonel repeated. "Over and out."

And all of us are, Janine thought. By the boys from Prettyfields. Prettyfields. What a strange name for a man like Clancy to come from. I came from Kansas. From what frangipani vine do you come, Fly? We talk to insects because in a jungle in Nam there is no one else. What animal is Clancy talking to?

Mike is talking to K. Mike is off the radio now.

"We have got to get our ass up there."

There was a silence.

I suppose they do, Janine thought. I suppose they have to get their manly asses up there and crash in the monsoon to prove they are manly asses. Two more less men in the world. Mike was a fine man. The problem with Mike was that he was not here. A man must be here. They are both fine men, but K was here. Try having a man some time when he is not here. A man must be here.

Now Mike is leaving. He is going to take out through the jungle on his own. By foot. I must talk to him. No, talking to him now wouldn't do any good. He is crazy to see Clancy before Clancy goes. He is crazy. No, it is what this situation does to people. I can do nothing to stop him because a man will not listen to a woman who is done with him. I could not do any good. A woman should be allowed to have two men. They could keep two men happy nicely. But men are competitive, acquisitive, possessive. Wonderful. And necessary to a woman. But they will not share. They want all or nothing. I could share.

"You won't get a hundred meters before you are zapped by the VC," Knightbridge said to Mike.

"Or a Friendly? And I mean by that, as impossible as the enemy is to find, as phantom and as fleeting, as God damn nowhere when you shoot they are still there someplace and marked in those black pajamas or stark monkey-naked and wearing nothing but the cheekbone-to-cheekbone grin, yet you still know God damn well they are the Unfriendlies."

"Do you?"

"And you know they are not the only ones who are going to shoot you in the fucking back."

And there they go again, Janine thought. Substituting the word for the act. It's an old army survival device. And she let her eyes wander, her green eyes wander over the fly and past the spider to all the army survival devices, the Atabrine and the Halazone and the morphine and the endless rolls of bandages and splints and tape—all these and other survival devices, but the best survival device was death. It could be true for Clancy. It could be true for any other and all other people who had anything to do with the end of A for Alpha.

Love is the greatest survival device. It is the best. Love is the long-time ecstasy. Death is short but very sweet in the jungle. An escape route.

When you are surrounded on all sides and there is no direction to turn, when there is no love, you accept death. That is what happened to A for Alpha. There is no mystery. There was no conspiracy. There was no plot.

Janine half-rose on her army cot, brushing back the streaming red hair from her green-eyed face. She would tell Mike right now. She would tell him what caused the death of A for Alpha.

It would save Clancy. Clancy could live again.

It would save Yvor.

It would save Knightbridge.

It would save Mike from himself.

It would save everyone.

Everyone could go home and live happily ever after. She would no longer have to have sex at ten thousand feet to prove anything. Everything would be proved. Love approves of everything. Love is doing things to each other that each other loves doing.

Wait. What did I say that was going to solve everything? What was going to stop Mike from touching Clancy and saying "You are dead" and then closing Clancy's eyes?

It was this. Janine looked up and along the ridge pole and out into the solid green wall behind which all the Unfriendlies hid and said, "When you are screwed in every way, when there is no concern and no direction to turn, when there is no love, then you accept death."

Bullshit.

That was Colonel Yvor speaking.

And you know they are not the only ones who are going to shoot you in the fucking back.

That was Mike.

We screw at ten thousand feet with full pack and set a record.

That was K.

It was a man's jungle. It was a jungle of pride. A proud jungle. And there was no hope. Nothing. Nothing. Nothing.

Janine relaxed back in the bed. It was a man's jungle. A jungle of man. They want to confront each other. Confrontation. Confrontation. Confrontation in the bright and dark jungle. A jungle of men. But there was Madame Dieudonné.

There is Madame Dieudonné, Janine thought, watching with green eyes the yellow slope of tent merge and become lost in the monsoon. She could not see her own bright splash and long scatter of red hair beneath the tent with a red cross that tilted down. There is still Madame Dieudonné and there is still a Captain Clancy. There is still something to become. There is still something in this nothing of a jungle they have not touched.

They? Who is They? Who is They who have not yet touched something that is beautiful? So you have not solved anything. You have only met another mystery here in the dark and bright jungle. They?

Janine walked across the wet tent platform and raised back the tent fly and looked up at the no sun. Standing there wet in the wet with her green eyes and green army fatigues that clung to her all over like a Vietnamese leech. And there seemed to be the cold withdrawing of blood too as she listened to the no confrontation in the next tent that seemed to have no wall.

"I can't see," Knightbridge said evenly, in cold army language, "I can't see how it makes one small fucking iota of difference what happened at Red Boy."

"Not one fucking iota?"

"That's right. Not one fucking iota."

Janine wondered what iota meant.

She wondered what fucking meant. She wondered what anything meant. In a jungle where words become meaningless you wonder what everything means.

"Because it happens all the time," Knightbridge said. "Red Boy."

"Yes."

"But I understand your concern. I fucking well do. Clancy."

"Yes," Mike said.

"But—"

"But shit."

"I didn't say that," Knightbridge said.

"Where were *you*? I understand you made contact with A for Alpha on an overfly," Mike said.

"That was G for Ghoulie Company. You know that. You were there."

"No contact before G for Ghoulie?"

"None. Scratch that. Yes and no."

"Wow," Mike said. "Fucking wow."

"We had a weak signal from his RTO, Appelfinger. It was meaningless."

"I understand that Clancy guessed the Unfriendlies, the NVA, battalion as a company."

"That was Search and Destroy that made that radio contact. We are Search and Rescue. Remember?"

There was a silence.

"Meaningless. You said you picked up something that was meaningless. What was meaningless?"

" 'They.' "

"What does 'They' mean?"

"That's all we got. That word 'They' was repeated twice and then the message blurred."

"They? Fuck me," Mike said.

"That's how I felt too," Knightbridge said.

They, Janine thought up at the no sun. That's where I got that word. K told me. That's where I got that word. I remember now. But that does not help, does it? We are right back to where everything began. They?

"They" is everyone with whom we have no contact. "They" is all the people who speak another language. Your son, your daughter. Your lover. "They" is everyone who is very close and receding, fading away, until they are lost. Until they become "They."

Bullshit.

Shoot you in the fucking back.

Screw at ten thousand feet.

But what was blurred in the radio contact? What did not come through? Janine raised the tent flap higher to see something in the jungle she could not see. To reveal something that was invisible, impalpable and inchoate, but it was there and moving like a giant soft hand, a gentle presence, and almost palpable now through all the shot and all the blood and busted bones and broken hopes and dreams on Red Boy. I see. I see. I see, she said to what she did not see, at what she could not see, ever, but only feel, which was at once more, but fading until she stood again naked in an alien jungle. One million miles from home.

"As I said," Knightbridge said, "you leave this perimeter and you are dead."

"I am touched by your concern," Mike said.

"Janine did what she had to do."

"I suppose Clancy did what he had to do?"

"Yes," Knightbridge said.

Again that deathless, that jungle-awful silence. The jungle listening and tentative. Janine too.

"I could give you a few men," Knightbridge said.

"Your clowns?"

"They function."

"They function?" Mike was standing now outside the sagging CP tent, the sagging jungle, the moving monsoon. The darkness.

"How?" Mike said.

"The way we can."

"Sure," Mike said, turning, and his one canvas combat boot stuck in the ooze. "The way we can. Of course."

"I can give you a small foot patrol. You can make it to Red Boy, but there is nothing there."

"There is nothing here," Mike said. "I can make it better alone."

"No man . . ." And then Knightbridge caught himself sounding like the professor at the Point and ceased.

"Where are those civilians down? Appelfinger? Colonel Yvor?"

"Someplace between the Ban Kin and the Phong."

"Great," Mike said, sucking off in the ooze. "That's an accurate fix. Find them and then Clancy. Easy."

"It's as accurate a fix as you'll ever get," Knightbridge said, "in this war. That's what they call this. A war."

But Mike was already lost. Disappeared in the jungle that watched and listened and waited.

Janine let the tent flap drop. The tent with the red cross. Then she flung herself on the bed and cried.

Knightbridge heard her but he did not know what to do. Men never do, Janine thought. Ah, men. Ah, war.

But she still cried. The quiet jungle watching. The bamboo moved once—clack. And then twice—clack and clack. Knightbridge heard her still crying but he did not hear.

12

Now that I have got all the self-pity out of my system, Mike thought, I can get back to Clancy. All I have to do to end Clancy's agony is touch him three times and after each touch say one word and it all adds up to You Are Dead. And then Clancy can get up again and run like new. Except that it's not Little Clancy now. It's not a game now. It's Big Clancy now. It's a war now. All the games of our youth have led us to the war of our death.

Mike fell down. He fell down again and got up by pulling on the bamboo. That was nice. Alone in a swamp in Nam. Lost in the Viet morass. Banyan trees with endless exposed, contorted roots with abrupt knee angles so the sagging and mournful trees might, like some prehistoric and unknown animal-vegetable, balance themselves and walk away. Where to?

Where to? I must get to Clancy. To get to Clancy I must get back to Madame Dieudonné. Why didn't Janine tell me that? Janine must have known that. What every woman knows. Janine won't tell me anything any longer. Not now. I figured it all out by myself. Smart chap. Lost in a swamp in Nam. No, not lost. I've got my two-way wrist video-radio.

"Have you got your two-way wrist video-radio, Crip?"

"Yes, Little Clancy."

"Then pick up the Indians."

I don't have a two-way video-radio but I've got this wrist compass now. I hope Big Clancy will settle for that.

When I left Knightbridge's perimeter I was bearing north

northwest. I picked up this banyan swamp okay and now I've got to bear two clicks east. In about four kilometers I should pick up the plantation. The world of rubber. The world of Madame Dieudonné.

Madame Dieudonné watched Mike coming through the sun, through the perfect and militant-soldier row on row of rubber.

Madame Dieudonné hoped it was Clancy. She somehow hoped that the truth on the Laos radio was not true. There had been no Red Boy. All the soldiers that had been knocked down would get up again and live happily ever after. I have a dream. I have a need. I have a hurt. What other woman in the world has seen her dead one come back? Now I am the luckiest, the most fortunate, fortunate human being that ever lived. I am one of those select ones that has been chosen. Now he comes. The Vietnamese say—they do not understand —everyone says that I am the most fortunate woman in the world because I have the second-largest rubber plantation in the world. They do not know that it does not work now. Nothing works now. They do not know that all of the money in the world is nothing. They do not know that all of the piastres, all of the francs and dollars and lira and marks that rubber buys, is nothing. After Red Boy everything is nothing. It must be Clancy now against that sun because it cannot be someone else. It would be too unkind. War is kind. You cannot substitute someone for someone else. No one else can be him. We have had a knowing now for a thousand years. Maybe more. Since time. We have had a knowing past bliss, past loss. And he will not die. He will not certainly die on Red Boy. Le Garçon Rouge. You cannot move a great hand and knock everyone down on one ridge. Like toy soldiers. There is no soft hand moving across this jungle, this Asia, saying, "Come with me, my pretty ones. Pretty one." Prettyfields. Prettyfields. Pretty Fields. Mon capitain, what did that mean? This is no place to continue a game. No time. The stakes are too high. So high. But you come. Out of the sun. I dare not kiss you because I have fear. I have fear that it is not you. A trick. A trick like the Laotian radio saying you were dead. All dead on Garcon Rouge. Not true. I do not run to kiss you because I have all joy. I have an ecstasy mingled with fear. That is what you said about combat. It is an ecstasy mixed with a great fear. That when the ecstasy becomes bigger than the fear you have the heroes and the medals and the death. But you are alive in the sun. True. And the radio and the newspapers and the generals are great liars telling the great lie. They sit around large tables seriously telling serious lies to a serious old man who has gone to sleep. But you are the truth. In the sun and alive. That is the truth.

The truth is too serious, too precious, too awfully precious to be knocked down on Ridge Red Boy. The truth is bigger than serious old men sitting around large tables. The truth is you, you blossoming out of the sun that first day, after such a time, blooming out of the sky that first day after all of eternity. Such an endless time. Time has no stop but time must have a beginning and you were the beginning, and it will not end now, ever.

I do not come to you because I am patient. I do not go to you because you will come to me. Like that first day. The first day that ever was. Will be.

Mike could see the villa now. It looked wounded. All of the surface of the villa had been blackened with napalm, torn by artillery and rockets. Both sides had done their best to finish it off. Close by the villa hill the rubber trees had all been knocked down. Both sides do not like a redoubt. Both sides are suspicious of something that is not theirs. But both sides would have to dig a little deeper. The villa was still there, underneath. The surface was unwell. What do you mean, unwell? It looks like the pictures of Verdun after the First World War. It looks like what was left over after they built a freeway through Albuquerque. Things are trying to stand that cannot stand. All of the bomb holes made by the great bombers are filled to the brim with black water with something that looks like cinders floating and bits of hand. Unwell? Great bulldozers have pushed with tank treads two meters wide myriad roads that lead to nowhere and come back to where they started, so that it looks like a Pacific Palisades housing development that failed and was falling tired into the sea, bankrupt and forlorn and rotting and blasted in the last fighting flurry of man, a last and final stab and cut to leave his mark and quit. Unwell? But man is doing quite well, thank you. Wait until you see what we have knocked down in another part of the forest.

"Wait one little fucking minute," Mike said holding up his hand. "Stop shooting at me!" Mike flopped down and felt a sting as though something had bitten him. Wait one fucking minute until you find out which side I am on. Or doesn't that make any difference? You bastards. Whoever you are. You motherfuckers whoever you are, you don't speak English too well. You don't speak Army too well either. You speak bullets. You speak bullets all too God damn well.

Mike tried to worm his way deeper into the hard red earth to escape the people who spoke bullets, who peppered their hard, lead words straight at him, and he tried to worm his way into the earth a little more, a little more, to escape the crude one-sided killing conversation. How does a mole worm his way a little deeper into the earth? I must watch better next time. I will become a trained observer of moles. An expert. The world authority. I will write a book. I will get an enormous money advance against future staggering royalties and go home and live happily ever after. Fuck Clancy. I won't even have to write the book after this exhibition of moling. They will erect a monument here to the human worm. The greatest mole that ever lived. The mole that did not find Clancy. Fuck Clancy. So great will be my moling fame that people will take me on faith. If I say I found Clancy they will believe. God, that sting is getting worse.

Don't worry, Clancy, I am still with you.

The American Army is still after you.

The game is not over.

Yes, it is, Clancy. I want to help. God, can you believe I want to help? Can't you see how it can help if we can find out all that happened in another part of the forest? Your part of the jungle?

Who put you there and why? All those boys. All of A for Alpha. Gone. If we can see clearly your part of the picture, then all the puzzle picture will begin to fit. Then we will see maybe what we are doing ten thousand miles from home, trying to worm a little deeper and getting stung. Jesus, it hurts now and it is getting hot. Remember, Clancy, when we used to get stung we put mud on it? Mud won't help this one. This is a son of a bitch of a Vietnamese bee. Probably born in the States. No matter which side fired it. They steal everything here, Clancy. Everybody steals everything. Knightbridge stole Janine. To screw at ten thousand feet. Imagine that.

The bullets still flew like bees above Mike's head. Fast hard bees.

Stop shooting. Please stop shooting. I have only come to pay a call on Madame Dieudonné. I don't like the reception. She does not receive well. I will just drop my card and leave. I will not stand on formality. Pretend I never called. No, just say Mike called. Do not bother to return the call. Jesus, it hurts. How will I ever get out of here? I feel unwell.

When Mike next opened his eyes after he was hit by something, someone was standing over him telling him to be someone else.

Someone wanted him to be Clancy.

When you are hit by something and go out and then come to, you refuse to believe that any interval of time has taken place.

Mike woke up in heaven. Heaven in Nam is defined as the farthest distance from a war you can get. Heaven is a bamboo bed in an underground villa.

It is a beautiful woman standing over you in a place that is not a hospital. A hospital is still a war.

A beautiful woman who looks Vietnamese.

"I came here," Mike said, "to find something out about the captain."

The beautiful woman who looked Vietnamese did not say anything. She did not say anything because she was crazy. No, it is not that, Mike thought. It's that she is stunned, she is shocked that I am not somebody else.

"I am sorry," Mike said. But it's too late, Mike thought. It is too late not to be someone else. She must have built up a lot of hope seeing an American coming through the rubber in the sun. Against the sun all Americans look alike. In Asia Americans look alike any place. We are all look-alikes. But not Clancy.

"Can you tell me," he said up to the face of Madame Dieudonné, "can you tell me what happened before Ridge Red Boy?"

The face was gone. It was replaced by another face. It was not a very good face. It was an all right face. It was the face of Madame's son Etienne. It was a simpleminded face.

"You should not have walked out of the jungle alone. Everyone shoots at people who are alone."

Good. I will keep that thought, Mike thought.

"You have been hit-ted by a concussion grenade, but soon you will be very all right. Maman will never be all right."

"You mean I can't speak to her?"

"No one can," Etienne said. "She is alone."

"Alone? But then can you . . . ?"

"Yes," Etienne said. "Because I hear many voices."

"Great."

"I have many talkings."

"You learned."

"I have not learn-ed. I know," Etienne said. The face over Mike was flat, insistent, unremitting and fixed. "I know the captain was evil."

"Evil?"

"Yes. Before the evil Maman and myself were living in a great happiness. The happiness of ourselves."

"The happiness of ourselves?"

"Yes," the flat face over him said, and there was something feminine in that boy face, but all men in Asia . . . But he is supposed to be French. Wasn't she French, Madame Dieudonné?

"The happiness of yourselves."

"Yes. Maman and I. My mozzaire. Before this evil. Before the captain sent me off to Cambodia."

"Why Cambodia?"

"Because it is someplace that is not here. Someplace where Maman is not. The captain made this place a place where God is not."

"A place where God is not?"

"Yes. Her he prostituted. He made her do many things. Strange acts. Many times. Bad. Bad. Evil."

The face floated away now and then returned recapitulant and twisted as though it were the same and wrong picture slide returning to a magic lantern, the operator fumbling and inept.

"Vraiment. Vraiment," the face above him said.

"You knew?"

"Because I watch-ed."

"You watched?"

"I watch-ed them naked through a secret mirror."

"Cambodia?"

"No one ever goes to Cambodia," Etienne said. "Cambodia is where everyone goes but no one arrives."

"You listened?"

"I was hearing through the ears of the Buddha." Etienne pointed over the bamboo bed to a flatulent, grinning green enigma in jade.

"Bastard."

"But you would like to see what I saw."

"Yes."

"And hear what I heard."

"Yes. No, I don't give a damn."

"Because you want to believe in the captain. In the evil,

124

you want to believe. I will make you look in the mirror of yourself. The American mirror."

"Let's stick to Clancy."

"Because you do not want to inward look. Inward see."

"You son of a bitch."

"There is this enormous pretending. The Clancy search. You are for yourself searching."

"Go away."

"Captain Clancy—"

"Go ahead."

"Evil. He would not ever this bamboo bed leave."

"I will." `

Mike looked around at all the mirrors, all the crazy mirrors, there seemed to be no certain one, all the crazy mirrors such as in a funhouse, and the one Buddha. There was only one Buddha and it was at once silly and grave, and now it was listening too. The Buddha silly and grave and listening.

"And this Captain Clancy," the face above him continued, "Your Clancy. The Magic Man."

"You're a voyeur."

"No. Because—" The voice in the face ceased. "No, because she is something that is mine. If you can understand that. Clancy is something that is yours. You can understand that. Maman is something that is mine."

"But I don't give a damn."

"No one does," the voice above said. "She did not. Before she was alone she did not."

"And now?"

"Still not," Etienne said.

There was a long steady quiet. Mike moved and the bamboo bed ee-eeked.

"Before this," Mike said, "before this did he ever . . . the bamboo . . . did he ever mention Red Boy?"

"A red boy?"

"Ridge Red Boy."

"Yes."

"Ah now," Mike said. "Ah now." But again the face was

gone. Again the disappearing Red Boy. So maybe the whole thing was a mirror trick. All done with mirrors. Maybe Red Boy was a mirror trick, something that never happened. No, it happened. It very much happened all right. Red Boy.

The face was back. Maybe it never left. Maybe it was the concussion grenade that still had him floating. Still had the face floating in and out. But it was better now since Etienne said yes to Red Boy. I know now I will leave this bamboo bed. This one.

"He said," Etienne said, "that was where to which they were going. On the day of our dead."

"The day of our dead?"

"Yes."

"Whatever that means."

"We have a day when we celebrate our dead, that is the day that Captain Clancy left for Red Boy so we all knew that we would never again see him or ever see anyone who was with him. Because it was the day of the dead, and now you must convince Maman that he is dead, that nothing can happen to bring him from the dead back."

"I will talk to her but I cannot convince her of something that I do not know myself."

"Tell her he left for Red Boy on the day of the dead."

"You have already told her everything idiotic."

"The day of the dead is not idiotic. It is a fact. Nothing can it stop."

"Captain Clancy is alive," Mike said.

"This you know?"

"This we suspect."

"When he arrived there was no graciousness, no tact. That he simply took Maman to the bamboo bed and there did it. While the fighting in the rubber was still going on. That he did not to us himself introduce."

Mike got up and sat on the edge of the bed. His head was clearing now. He could see okay. This boy was hysterical. This boy was in love with his mother. We are all in love with our mothers. But we let them live a life. He cannot let his live a life. He has a problem. But it is his problem. It is not my problem. It sure must have been Clancy's problem. I bet he gave Clancy a bad time. I do not think I can get much out of this boy. I do not think I can much out of him get.

"It was the day of our dead."

"I know," Mike said. "Red Boy. The day of our dead it was."

"You me mock?"

"You're God damn right I do," Mike said. "I came up here to get some information and you tell me all your God damn mother problem. Fuck your mother, and don't tell me that's what Clancy he was doing. I know that." Mike paused. "I am sorry. The language I used about your mother."

"She is a whore," Etienne said.

"She was, she is," Mike said carefully from the edge of the bamboo bed, "she is okay. Clancy is in love of her with. Is that clear to you? She is very much decent. She is decent very much. If that is not clear I will the shit out of you beat." Mike stared past Etienne and into the Buddha that listened, past the Buddha that listened and into the mirror that watched. It watched all of the bamboo bed, all of Etienne and all of Mike. "I do not threatening prefer. It is the grenade concussion speaking. I do things to people sometimes and that's bad. It is the war. I do things to people but I never threaten people. Never. I apologize to myself. As for you, Etienne, go fuck yourself. Let me put that in non-army language. Let others do what others need to do. It is called love. It is called compassion. It is called tolerance."

"But I—" Etienne said.

"I know you cannot do what I have proposed that you do. We must cancel that project." What was the project? I am confused. Confuse-ed. The mirrors, the crazy mirrors and the crazy Buddha have confuse-ed me. And the smile of the Buddha, the incense, the perfume here. This room. It is a room of a performance. It is a stage design-ed for someone to perform. I must go. I must leave the stage. I must arise from the bamboo bed.

"Etienne."

"Yes, sir?"

"Etienne, adieu."

"Yes, sir."

Why is he sirring me? Have I buffaloed him? Did something I said work? What did I say? I must rally my forces. I must once more into the breach. Maybe I can take Red Boy.

"Etienne, what did you mean when you said Clancy left for Ridge Red Boy on the day of our dead?"

"Because it was the day of fifteen years since my papa—"

"Dien Bien Phu?"

"—left," Etienne said.

That would be about correct, but not relevant, Mike thought.

"And why do you sir me? Was it because I reminded—?"

"Of my fazzer you reminded me."

"A French officer?"

"Colonel."

Probably relevant and correct. Where do I go now? Where does anyone go now from the day of our dead?

They go home.

They go to Dien Bien Phu.

They go to Ridge Red Boy.

I will go see Madame Dieudonné. No, I will not go see her because she is alone. We are all alone excepting me, because I am the hunter. No hunter is alone. There is always another hunter in the jungle. There is always another phantom hunter shadowing. A shadow shadowing shadows. In Nam it is true. A hunter is not alone. Madame Dieudonné is alone. God help her in Nam. God help her and all the other women who are alone, anywhere.

The hunter arose from the bamboo bed, went to a black teak door and walked out into the mahogany jungle.

But first he must traverse an endless plantation of perfect rubber. The rubber that stretched. The rubber that stretched from Cambodia the infinite distance to the China Sea. The rubber that leaned to see the hunter go.

They say the jungle is your friend in Vietnam. There are only two precautions you must take with the jungle in Nam. One, they say you must never be in the jungle at night, and two, you must never be in the jungle in the daytime. That is what they say about the jungle in Nam. They seem to know. They know.

The hunter bent north away from the China Sea and soon he quit the perfect rubber of Madame Dieudonné and was in the jumbled jungle, the jumbled jungle of mahogany and teak. Did you know that teak is valuable? That it is protected by a law? They protect trees.

Did you know that Peter Scott, of Peter and Bethany, is an army man? A deserter. Did you know that he, Peter, when he quit the American Army, joined the VC?

The hunter knew.

Did you know that Peter was one, one of the American ones who joined the VC, who got in a fire fight with an American patrol, and they thought they had killed Peter, but Peter was not easily killed? Peter finally deserted the VC as he had finally deserted the Americans. Peter deserted everyone, and is now wandering around Vietnam in the disguise of a guitar. There are others, but Peter is one.

The hunter knew.

Peter is one who tried the VC. That failed utterly. There was no song for Peter in an army. Switching sides does not help. There is no song for Peter anywhere. Peter had gone into Vista and switched to the Peace Corps, then he switched to a university but decided it had nothing. Then he switched to another university that had nothing and was promptly drafted for all his pains. Peter was always switching, searching for a way out of his pain. The way out of the IBM machine. Peter had found no more in the VC than he found in the universities that had nothing.

Prettyfields, Mike the hunter thought. Prettyfields.

Mike sat down on a knee of banyan tree and thought. The VC were a lousy front, a lousy cover for Peter. Bethany, Peter's Bethany, has a lousy cover. Bethany is exactly what she says she is. That is never a good cover.

Does Clancy have a good cover? the hunter thought. Yes, Clancy has a splendid cover. Death.

What about me? Mike the hunter got up and walked off in the direction he had carefully planned that would lead to the solution. The direction that led to the solution was a morass of tight-together bamboo and depthless slimy viscous black liquid and great and ominous and sinister trees that leaned forward over the miasma and waited and watched, waiting and watched the hunter. The man with a gun. The man without a cover.

Me, Mike thought. Everyone who, everything that, watches me, that's my cover. It's not a bad cover. It's a pretty big cover.

Mike sloshed forward in the black solution and through the straight slender tight bamboo.

The jungle cover.

13

CAPTAIN Knightbridge of Search and Rescue Special Forward Task Force Three Seven Nine got into West Point in the manner of Edgar Allan Poe and Whistler, who both did time there. Captain Knightbridge survived West Point and lived to go to Vietnam where he would soon die. That is, at this time he believed the war would last forever and the luck could not hold. Captain Knightbridge, unlike Edgar Allan Poe, was not a poet. Unlike Whistler, he was not a painter.

"What the hell is he then?"

"Head of Search and Rescue."

"Our leader."

"Yes. Our leader."

"God help the poor son of a bitch."

The man who wanted God to help Captain Knightbridge was named Speedy, alias Ha Phut Hem Sing. You see, the poor soul was an Asian, a Vietnamese, not a red-blooded American like you and me.

"Do you trust him?"

"Sure."

"I mean a guy who's been in the Vietcong?"

"That's the best kind."

"You mean they fight?"

"That's right."

"I bet if the VC catch him they cut off his balls."

"That's his problem."

"I bet he'd miss them though."

"I guess so. Wouldn't you?"

"No, not Speedy's. I got a pair of my own to fight for."

"To have and to hold."

"That's right."

"You kill me, Batcheck."

"One day I will," Batcheck said.

Batcheck said this because Batcheck was the chopper pilot who flew like a crazy man for Search and Rescue. He might kill them all. A strange way to behave, because he was a poet, a poet chopper pilot who did not go to West Point like Edgar Allan Poe and Captain Knightbridge.

"Make sense."

"The war doesn't make sense."

"All right. A crazy poet chopper pilot makes sense."

"Like the war."

"Yes."

Then there was Ozz. Ozz was Batcheck's copilot. Osgood Allen. The secret dream of Ozz, and he dreamed it many times, was that Batcheck was killed and he became the pilot. When Ozz became the pilot he planned to fly to Katmandu and declare himself neutral. He had other dreams too. The favorite one was that when he became the lone pilot he would win the war and get decorated like a cake.

"He has all the dreams of men without responsibility. I believe Ozz once read a book called *God Is My Co-Pilot*, and suffered from confusion of identity. I believe all his dreams are wet."

The man who believed all his buddy's dreams were wet was Disraeli Pond, the port gunner, who, under the influence of his namesake's victory over the Arabs, shot up everything in the jungle for a week. Disraeli's dreams also dwelt in marble halls, and he wondered ofttimes and aloud, back from a mission, what Lord Byron would have done. Once at Phan Rang Disraeli went on a diet of rice and vinegar because that's what Byron did, and Batcheck said that when Disraeli died they would find Missolonghi engraved on his heart.

Lavender, the purple Negro and starboard gunner for Search and Rescue, who wore gold teeth and a pink scarf, had taken his Peace Corps training for Peru and then was shipped off to the army by an IBM machine. Lavender still believed in Peace, and even when the Vietcong threw rice at his plane, candlesticks, palm trees, elephant tusks, mangoes, French horns and boxes of condoms as the chopper lifted off and struggled over the early morning jungle, Lavender merely looked down at the Unfriendlies with his peaceful golden grin and shot the shit out of them from his flying machine, his pink scarf aflash on his purple body, the green wind strong, as millions of Vietnamese girl hearts cheered.

Then there were Oliver and Elgar.

The rest of our side in the LZ in the jungle were Ho Chi Minh, Karl Marx and the Naked Chinaman. They all had unpronounceable Vietnamese names and were called these famous names because Ho Chi Minh looked like Ho Chi Minh, Karl Marx talked politics, and the Naked Chinaman wore no clothes. They were the Asian representatives at Special Task Force 379, the Forward Element, Search and Rescue, under the illustrious Captain Knightbridge. The Asian representatives with the American unit were there to see that no harm came to the civilians, that no stray villages were bombed, that no Vietnamese girls were raped without written consent, signed by a notary. You'd think they'd be a bunch of crooks, but they were puritanical because they were all Vietcong, and don't let this alarm you. On their time off all the Vietnamese are Vietcong, because at this stage in the war no one had the slightest idea which side would win, so everyone played both sides against the Americans. Most of the South Vietnamese generals on our side carried Vietcong cards in case of an emergency, a defeat. The Prime Minister of South Vietnam carried a card too, not out of expediency but because he believed in the cause. He believed in everything.

The Asian representatives to Task Force 379 were also good at fixing the helicopter, the Bamboo Bed, when no one else could. They were also good at filling in for any of the American machine gunners when one was shot up or when one, before a dangerous mission, was faking the clap. Except for Karl Marx, who never filled in for a machine gunner because he was against killing on principle.

"But we haven't hit anybody lately."

"I know, but you could," Karl Marx said. "Anyway, I don't think he's got the clap."

The Asian representatives were also good at talking about Dien Bien Phu where they finally beat the ass off the French. Ho Chi Minh who was there never let anyone forget it and railed on about all the gory details like an American Legionnaire at a bar in Tampa.

"Lay off, will you?"

"You should realize what you're up against," Ho Chi Minh said. "That you Americans, like the French, are mortal."

"They could get it right here in this LZ in the jungle," Speedy said. "Our Dien Bien Phu."

"Yes," Ho Chi Minh said.

"I don't think we'll get it like the French did. We got too much bullshit going for us," Ozz said.

"We could still get it. Right, Speedy?"

"Right," Speedy said.

Nurse Jane was shacked up at the edge of the clearing with Tarzan. That is, each morning the men watched Second Lieutenant Janine Bliss, ruined by Knightbridge, emerge from her tent and commune with the monkeys.

"Coo coo coo," Nurse Jane said.

"Ha ha ha," the monkeys answered.

"Come back in here," Knightbridge said.

"Is that an order?"

"I think so."

"Ha ha ha," the monkeys said.

This morning was a typical monsoon Vietnamese day. Nurse Jane was off scampering in the forest with her friends the monkeys. Our allies were conferring with the Vietcong.

The men were jerking off and Knightbridge was sulking in his tent with a bottle of Old Crow.

"Come back, Nurse Jane," the captain said.

"Hung over?" Batcheck said to Knightbridge.

"No," Captain Knightbridge said. "And I resent your imagination, Batcheck. That's what comes of your being a poet. I have no liquor. Lieutenant Bliss is occupied, as are the men, and the Asians are repairing the houses in the village. I have been flying cover for the remains of Ghoulie. Five got out. Pike stuck and bought a farm. I got his body out. Anything new on Captain Clancy?"

"No, sir."

"You've been in the jungle too long, Batcheck."

"Yes, sir."

"How many more months do you have to go over here?"

"Three."

"How many times shot down?"

"Four."

"Come back at five."

"Five?"

"Five o'clock; 1700 hours," Captain Knightbridge said. "There's a mission."

"Yes, sir," Batcheck said and fled the tent.

"Why I love Nurse Jane," Ozz wrote. "I love Nurse Jane because in the first mortar attack when everyone was scared shitless Nurse Jane held my hand, and when Mike and now the civilians, Peter and Bethany, were lost in the jungle the first thing Nurse Jane said was, 'Let's go.' "

Peter and Bethany had been first spotted over in Eye Corps near Con Thien, giving out flowers to the First Marine Division. But the Marines did not provoke. They sent Peter and Bethany back to the rear where they sat at a crossroad and all their flowers spoiled. Next Peter and Bethany showed up outside Pleiku which is a long way south of Con Thien. This time they had a new bunch of flowers and this time they were handing them to the Fourth Armored Division and this time Peter got a good punch in the nose.

"You never know when you'll run into luck," Bethany said.

By now Army was very much concerned with two unarmed civilians wandering around Vietnam giving out flowers during a war. Division traced Peter and Bethany to the point on the Plateau Du Kontum where Peter got his bust in the nose, then Army lost them, could not find them, asked Task Force Search and Rescue to have a look. Army figured Peter and Bethany probably went on to Con Thien or Pleiku. Actually Peter and Bethany carried their flowers over the Meng Yeng Pass hoping to get to An Khe and got lost.

"There's no point in carrying the flowers now," Bethany said.

"Yes."

"I'm cold and hungry," Bethany said. "Do you have any more C rations we stole from the Marines?"

"No."

"Do you have the blankets we stole from the army?"

"We didn't steal them, we borrowed them."

Peter sat down on the only rock in Meng Yeng Pass but he couldn't see out. They were lost in the glittering green jewelry of the jungle.

"The trip is over."

"That's right."

"I feel awful."

"Play something on the guitar."

"I feel awful. I don't want to play anything. I don't want to play any more games."

"It was fun."

"No, it wasn't. I got a bust in the jaw."

"You simply gave the Marines some flowers."

"Well, we're lost too," Peter said, stepping off the only rock in Meng Yeng Pass. "The trip is over. I can't get high enough to see out."

"High enough?"

"Yes, Bethany. If only I could see out. This is a jewel-box trap. Green emeralds in the trees, attar fire and topaz, the diamonds of light and the rings and ropes of endless frangipani necklaces in the rich-bitch jungle."

"If you could get high enough . . ."

"If I could get high enough."

"A tree, Peter. Climb a tree."

"But it looks so slippery and wet."

"You could see out and get help if you get high enough, Peter."

"I'll try," Peter said and he handed his guitar to Bethany. Bethany dropped it. "Everything is so hot and wet," Bethany said.

"It's a long way down," Peter said, looking.

"Can you see?"

"Yes."

"What do you see?"

"I see a hunter." And then there was a shot and Peter fell all the way down—down, hitting a branch, stopping and then falling some more, breaking through and falling until Peter struck the ground with a solid thump, the way it sounds when a good player hits the heart of the instrument with the heel of his hand for a deep percussion effect.

"You're not dead, Peter!"

"You're not watching, Lavender."

Lavender and Batcheck, Disraeli and Ozz and Captain Knightbridge, going fast as the chopper could go.

"How can we lose the war," Batcheck said, "when we can see everything?"

"We can manage," Knightbridge said.

"I can't see a damn thing," Lavender said, "except the tops of the trees."

"We're over Meng Yeng Pass," Disraeli said.

"Bring her down low," Knightbridge said. "There's a hole in the canopies."

"But they were on the ground. A person can't fall up, sir."

"That's right," Knightbridge said. "Take her home."

"Going to abandon them to the tigers?"

"Yes."

"Why?"

"We are low on fuel."

"Oh, I better get my ass home," Batcheck said, tilting the ship fast and away.

"Shall we have another look?"

"Low on fuel."

"Home?"

"Home."

"Who shot you, Peter?"

"The man with the gun."

"Who was that?"

"The hunter."

"Everyone in Nam is a hunter, Peter."

"This man," Peter said carefully, "was the hunter."

"What did he say?"

"He didn't say, he shot."

"Poor Peter."

A man was standing over them now. Mike.

"Hello," Mike said.

"He's come to say he's sorry he shot you, Peter."

"I'm here to say you shoot at anything that moves," Mike said.

"But Peter is only a civilian," Bethany said.

"No, he's not a civilian," Mike said.

"He is now."

"You don't become a civilian by saying you are a civilian," Mike said looking down at Peter.

"Oh, yes you do," Bethany said. "You can become anything you want."

"Look," Mike said. "I don't give a damn. And I am not looking for Peter. I only shot him because he was in a tree. I only shot before I was shot. There are hundreds of Peters wandering around in Nam."

"You have got that problem solved?"

"We solve it by ignoring it," Mike said.

"You cannot ignore Peter," Bethany said. "You cannot ignore a whole generation."

My God, Mike thought, she is going to make a speech. I have ignored a whole generation. This is not a lost generation. This is the ignored generation. The generation that is used by old people to kill young people. The generation that is kept fighting a war in nowhere so there will not be a revolution somewhere. I could write a speech. Do I believe the speech? Everyone believes the speech. Everyone believes everything and feels nothing.

Mike was down alongside Peter now, putting a patch on Peter from his first-aid kit.

"He's in shock now," Mike said. "But he feels nothing. It will not begin to hurt till later. Now he feels nothing."

"You're still looking for Clancy?"

"Yes," Mike said, but not looking up at Bethany from his patch job. "Yes." Mike had Peter's leg stretched out like an inner tube.

"Do you want to know something?"

"No," Mike said.

Mike could feel Bethany pouncing around in the jungle above him. Moving there in the jungle above him and around him like a cat, feline and soft and quick.

"That Clancy was a collector," Bethany said.

"I told you I didn't want to know anything," Mike said.

"That we know where Clancy is."

"What?" Mike said laying aside his patch. "Where?"

"Hell," Bethany said.

Mike went back to his patch. He could write that speech too.

"Do you like being a hunter?"

Mike went on with his patch. Peter was so soft that nothing stuck to him.

"Do you like being a hunter?"

"I just work here," Mike said. And then Mike remembered

her generation was the generation that was ignored and said, "Clancy and I grew up together. You just don't let things happen to people you love. Do you understand?"

"Yes," Bethany said.

Love. That was a word Mike thought he would never use to describe what went on between him and Clancy, but I guess it was a good enough word. It was a word that covered everything. They use the word hate a lot now, and they kill a lot now. What about love? That was a word that everyone feared more than they feared the VC. It is damn strange when you can fear love more than you fear the enemy. But one in investigation must not investigate too much. There must be an army regulation against it. You can hate Clancy. In the army that would be permitted. You cannot be indifferent to the son of a bitch. Never. And you cannot love him because the army is above love.

"Did you see Clancy?"

"No, but I feel him close by," Bethany said.

"Not good enough in this jungle," Mike said.

"Did you know Peter was in Clancy's outfit?"

Mike turned toward Bethany now.

"Peter left—decided to become a civilian, before Ridge Red Boy."

"It was a good time," Mike said.

"Because Clancy wouldn't let him go on Red Boy. That's why Peter became a civilian when he found that out. When Clancy told him he couldn't go on Red Boy."

"Couldn't get killed?"

"Yes," Bethany said. "And no. It was because Peter had long hair. That he looked too much like Custer. Clancy didn't want to risk that happening again."

"He could have ordered him to cut it off."

"Clancy doesn't operate that way. Peter says Clancy never ordered anyone to do anything."

"I can't believe that's why he saved Peter. Long hair."

"No one can," Bethany said. "Clancy was strange."

"Yes," Mike said. Mike rose. "You're God damn right," he

said. "Strange." Then he touched Peter with his boot. "I think the patch will work. Stay right here till I get a chopper out."

"Where are you going?" And Bethany wondered where a hunter went.

"I'll keep moving."

"You'll never find Clancy that way."

"I don't know," Mike said. "I can't sit."

So, Bethany thought, a hunter is someone who cannot sit. "Good luck," she said.

"I will need more luck than I will get," Mike said, and he was gone someplace into the jungle. The jungle that was noplace, Bethany thought, and she stared down at Peter's patch.

Although I am young, Bethany thought, I believe that people will still be searching when I am old. That that is what life is and means, a search, a hunt for something that is never found. And that is good because if it was found, then life would have no meaning. Bethany thought this as she stared down at Peter's patch. The patched Peter. Now she thought she could hear God. The jungle. The great green god. Bethany had it then almost clear, but at once it fled and she was left surrounded now with only the jungle presence, the soundless throb of seething silence, a caterwaul, a scream of quietude that mounted to a crescendo of the final tomb, the bamboo shroud and the slitted opening above to the monsoon of no sky, the jungle life with no death, with eternal life which is at once eternal death because, she thought—listen—and it was fled again, that which she had come so far to find was flash. Illusion and great green flash.

"Look," she said to Peter, "the hunter is gone. The hunted rest and the great green god—listen. But you cannot listen. But that is all right because—and listen. I will listen for all that cannot." And she looked down at the patched Peter and sobbed and the jungle forest stood intolerant and vast as jungles will, endless and serene and waiting and hushed. So her small cry was swallowed in silence. Lost.

"Where's my guitar?"

"Here's your guitar, Peter."

And the dying Clancy heard somewhere out there in the awful blackness of the green-black jungle something like angels tripping on tight wires, some sounds like soft vivid flowers opening against a chrome drum, but somewhere distant out there in the jungle night, far and faint.

14

THERE goes that God damn guitar again, Clancy thought. Well anyway I have established that it's not a harp. That I'm not dead. I have established that I am not dead. Where in hell did Appelfinger go? Where is Search and Rescue? How do you expect them to find you under a three-canopy jungle? Impossible. If I could only crawl far enough to get to a clearing. Then when I got to the clearing, to have enough strength to signal effectively. In a whole lonely life a man cannot signal effectively. How do you expect a wounded man dying in the jungle to make it? Search and Rescue could find those people playing the guitar. They are making enough noise. Anyway those people must be mobile and they must be trying to make contact. If the Bamboo Bed can find them, maybe they will find me. If Appelfinger is still around he will find the people playing the guitar, then we can all get together and have a ball.

Clancy touched his bleeding throat.

A funeral. But I have something important to tell. I could such a tale unfold. Why don't they listen? Can't Search and Rescue hear that guitar?

"Ho Chi Minh and the Naked Chinaman are smoking pot in the village. Anybody in Search and Rescue want to go?" Ozz said.

"Supposing something goes wrong with the Bamboo Bed? They shouldn't smoke pot."

"Then maybe we'd have to fix it ourselves."

"The white man," Disraeli said, "will never learn to fix anything as mysterious as a jet turbine or a multipitch 4X rotor. It takes the blindness of the East. Asiatics who don't understand the complexities, the factor of the impossible. The white man can manufacture them but the limit of Western knowledge ends there. Anyway I wouldn't go up in a chopper a white man fixed. Will you go to help the Gooks smoke pot?"

"I object to the terminology."

"The Asian representatives."

"I might."

"If you can tear yourself away from Letters from the Grave."

"Letters from the Earth. Don't make it worse than it is."

"Who sent you that?"

"Mother."

"You must have a cheerful fucking mother."

"Ma does all right," Disraeli said.

"Do you suppose those two civilians we didn't rescue today were on pot?"

"The two civilians we didn't rescue today? What about Clancy's A for Alpha we didn't rescue yesterday?"

"But they weren't giving flowers away to the Marines."

"But Clancy's outfit gave their lives for a Vietnam they never heard of."

"That's all right because everyone is doing it."

"True," Batcheck said. "Let me think about that. No, it's not true," Batcheck said. "Only poor stupid sons of bitches that let themselves get drafted, like you and me."

"Batcheck, I still refuse to believe you haven't got good stuff in you. You drive that chopper like a kite," Disraeli said.

"Thank you, Dizzy," Batcheck said. "I always knew you were crazy."

"Let's go and help the Chinaman smoke pot."

Captain Knightbridge in his command-post tent was poised over a map carefully measuring the distances on a tactical map of the Plateau Du Kontum to see if the two people could have got from Ban Dan, where they were spotted by the 17th at 1800 hours, to Meng Yeng Pass where they spotted the hole in the jungle canopy at 0600 hours. Yes, the flower people could have been at Meng Yeng Pass. They could have made it easily. But the chopper was not ready. Captain Knightbridge could see Karl Marx working on the main rotor of the Bamboo Bed from his command-post tent. Still it did not make any difference whether the Bamboo Bed was ready. The flower people could rot. You could winch a soldier down through a hole in the canopy right into a Vietcong trap. It had already happened once. Karl Marx had warned them. Karl Marx had said you make that pickup on Dragon Mountain and Vietcong kill you for sure. The VC had blown the shit out of the Bamboo Bed that day at Dragon Mountain on the fake pickup. Still this could be Karl Marx's way of getting in good with the Americans. Building up the confidence of the Americans in Karl Marx until the day, the big day, when Karl Marx would lead the Americans to their Dien Bien Phu, their big defeat. The same could be said for Ho Chi Minh and the Naked Chinaman. After you had been in this country for a year you don't trust any Asian. After you have been in Vietnam two months you want to kill them all, three months and you regret that you didn't. Four months and they kill you. Knightbridge told himself he would have to watch this kind of thinking. Now he watched Karl Marx adjust the rotors on the Bamboo Bed. Karl Marx could sabotage the chopper but Knightbridge made him fly. Knightbridge never told him when. Karl Marx would never know when he was committing suicide.

Knightbridge watched Nurse Janine cut across the perimeter. Knightbridge wondered how any outfit got along without a woman. Without women men turn into beasts. Without women men will finally kill any man that moves. Every gesture is a threat. Madness. That is why the Americans declared every town in Vietnam off limits. The army too. The military sets up whorehouses for the men close to base camp. Whores are not women. Vietnamese whores are the tears of women. If a soldier went to town and met a woman he would be lost to the service. Was everyone in Search and Rescue lost to the service? No, because Search and Rescue was a shit outfit to begin with. They picked up all the damage that the military had done. All the mistakes the army had made. The dying and the dead. But the VC shot at them too because they wore an American uniform in the Bamboo Bed. The VC did not understand subtle distinctions. The VC did not understand what beautiful people Special Task Forces 379 Search and Rescue were. The Bamboo Bed should have a sign writ on it—ALL SIDES BRING US YOUR SICK, YOUR WOUNDED AND YOUR DEAD. THE BAMBOO BED. Then both sides would war against it. Both enemies would borrow ammunition from each other. AK47s, Russian tanks, Molotov grenades and Chinese firecrackers would be exchanged for Ford halftracks, M15s and Tums for the Tummy. Both sides would bring down the Bamboo Bed. There's nothing that bothers enemies more than a third party. Like two people screwing desperately in a hot room. The maid appears suddenly bearing a towel. The flag of the Bamboo Bed.

Knightbridge studied the map again for the lost Clancy. Everyone was lost since that asshole Johnson took over. This is no way to think about the President of the United States of America. The Commander in Chief. Hail to the Chief. Johnson became President of the United States of America because a lunatic shot Kennedy. So the destiny of the great planet Earth was decided by the moon. Of such chance stuff is life on this world made.

Destiny flings condoms, earth, Chinese firecrackers. Knightbridge must concentrate on the map. A West Pointer must never concern himself with politics. The first law of the jungle. The Point points the way.

Nurse Janine was coming back across the perimeter now toward the close jungle. Knightbridge mused, You Jane, me Tarzan. That was the way the men saw it. Knightbridge called her Lieutenant which she was, and treated her like a whore which she was not. Lieutenant, we will screw at 0600 with full pack. Be sure to take your pill, it's dangerous up here. We might have a private. What would all the good neighbors say if we had an enlisted man for a baby? Screw it! She's a good girl. A fine woman, and I shouldn't treat her like a whore. Still, there's so little time, so damn little time, but I've got to watch it. Still, maybe all women want to be treated like whores. I must be going crazy. I've been in the jungle too long. Too long in the jungle with Winken, Blinken and Nod, with Oliver and Elgar, with Speedy and Ozz, with Batcheck, Dizzy and Lavender, with Ho Chi Minh, the Naked Chinaman, Karl Marx. And these are the Asians who are not trying to kill me. All the rest are after me. Picture a naked man being chased by seventy-eight million Asians. That's me. Now staring over a terrain map of Vietnam in a command tent in a clearing in the jungle outside of Dong Sut surrounded by hostiles, embattled by Friendlies with the Bamboo Bed the only escape route left and that's being torn apart by an Asian representative named Karl Marx. The Point never tells you what to do in a situation like this. The Point never told us anything. The Point tells you who's on first. West Point is great on sports. Sandhurst, St. Cyr, the French too. Battles are lost on the playing fields of children.

I got to get hold of myself. I have a mission to perform. Many missions. Where are Batcheck, Disraeli and Ozz? How goes the Bamboo Bed?

Knightbridge picked up the transmitter telephone and it was dead. He was greeted only with a hum and then some voices in Vietnamese giving the American position in VC code to Hanoi. Knightbridge hung up the receiver and looked out again at Karl Marx working on the Bamboo Bed.

Karl Marx, whose name was Nam Phat Do, replaced another socket in the Pittsburgh snap-on wrench. Nam Phat Do appreciated neatness. He had all of the sockets arranged in a tray with the neatness of diamonds in a jewel box.

"How's it coming?" Captain Knightbridge wanted to know.

"Okay," Karl Marx said.

"How soon?"

"Could be an hour."

"Sure?"

"Could be days."

"No."

"Could be weeks," Karl Marx said.

Karl Marx, alias Nam Phat Do, like mechanics the whole world over, was a sadist. He enjoyed the power his knowledge over the mysteries of machinery gave him over ordinary people.

"Could take months," Karl Marx said, "if we have to send back to the Philippines for a part. Why don't you go and keep Nurse Jane happy?"

"Listen," Captain Knightbridge said, "her name is Lieutenant Bliss."

"Yes, sir."

"What does communism have to offer the Asian?"

"I'll have to think about that."

"Think about that and stop thinking about Nurse Jane."

"Lieutenant Bliss."

"Touché," Knightbridge said.

"What does capitalism have to offer America?" Nam Phat Do said.

"This thing you're working on."

"How much it cost?"

"A half a million," Captain Knightbridge said.

"Piastres?"

"Dollars."

"Ask for your money back."

"All sales are final."

"Then I'll see if I can fix her up."

"Where's Batcheck?"

"The village."

"Disraeli? Lavender? Osgood? Oliver and Elgar?"

"The village."

"Why don't you ever go to the village?"

"Because I am a dedicated man," Karl Marx said.

"Is Ho Chi Minh dedicated?"

"Yes."

"The Naked Chinaman?"

"They are both dedicated in their way."

"I'm sorry not using their proper names but I find Vietnamese difficult."

"That's all right."

"I admire the way you people speak English."

"We're dedicated."

"I hope you're dedicated to the right side."

"I hope so too," Karl Marx said, tapping the rotor with his wrench. "I hope we win."

"Who?"

"Those that win."

"You mean you hope the side that wins wins? Well, now that that's cleared up you can get back to work."

"If you'll let me."

"One thing more. Where does Ho Chi Minh stand?"

"He's still fighting the battle of Dien Bien Phu."

"Was he really there?"

"Yes."

"Why does he have to fight it all over again here?"

"Because that's the way the world is," Karl Marx said. "People never learn."

"You get that thing fixed," Captain Knightbridge said, "or Americans kill you for sure."

Captain Knightbridge went over to Nurse Jane's tent which bore a sign with the medical Red Cross and the name Lieutenant Janine Bliss. Knightbridge opened the flap and said, "I see everyone hasn't gone to the village."

"Yes, sir," Janine said.

Knightbridge wanted to tell her that the bullets were real. That although everyone involved in the war was a clown or insane there were some who got into it because it happened to be their business—like himself. But it was her business too.

She had gone to an army school too. While he was learning how to make people come apart she was learning how to make people grow back together again. She was born in Kansas City to a Marine captain. She never forgave either of them, Kansas City or the Marine captain. She had a brother close to her own age who came over very early in this war and who got his testes blown off. She still used that same word, testes, even though now she knew they were his balls. Her brother had only been in Vietnam two days when it happened. She was very close to her brother. Janine was absolutely certain that if there was somewhere where men were being blown apart a woman should be there to put them back together again.

Knightbridge looked at her green eyes, her red hair. He and she were both professional soldiers. Maybe they knew something that no one else knew, understood things that no one else understood. How could you have a war without professionals? They could not have started this war without them. They had to have a few people who already were trained in the art, people who already were proficient in blowing people up, and others who could try and put people back together again. Without professionals there could never be a war. No one would ever dare start one. God bless West Point.

"I was just thinking," Knightbridge said, "that nothing you learn at West Point applies to a war. You'd think they would have at least dropped a hint. After all, I was there for four years."

"Four years without women would teach you something," Janine said.

"There's one man, only one, that's trying to help," Knightbridge said, taking off his helmet and sitting on it next to the bed. Janine was lying on the bed, a canvas cot. She was in jungle fatigues. She had those green eyes too, and very red hair and she had her hands clasped in back of her head, relaxed, tired and beautiful.

"This one man who is trying to help, who got Clancy into

the Red Boy trap, is Colonel Yvor," Knightbridge said. "He's head of our TAOR, Tactical Area Of Responsibility. He arrives by command jeep, flags screaming from all fenders. They let him out. He looks around, gets back in the jeep and says, 'Bullshit.' They drive away all flags flying. He hollers back at us, 'Bullshit, Knightbridge, it's all bullshit.' That's all he ever says. He is gone."

"You didn't come here to tell me that."

"And the fact that he doesn't have any arms. I don't mean weapons, I mean elbows and hands and things—Colonel Yvor doesn't have any arms. Very militant. It's amazing how much more clean-cut, more military a man looks without elbows and hands and things sticking out, how much more a straight line you get without the military carelessness of hands and arms."

"How did he lose them?"

"He may have had them removed. No one knows. And then one day it occurred to me how big-chested Colonel Yvor was, as though he had those arms folded across his chest in an attitude of prayer. That maybe they were in a cast in this attitude of prayer. No one has the courage to ask the colonel. You just don't ask a person, let alone a bird colonel, 'What happened to your arms? You don't seem to have any."

"The mystery—"

"But then I can hear him saying, Bullshit, Knightbridge. Bullshit."

"That's all?"

"One day after he looked around and before he left with flags flying on his jeep, he chucked me under the chin and said, 'Vietcong kill you for sure.' "

"How could he chuck you under the chin if he doesn't have arms?"

"That's the way it felt. I swear that's the way it was, like a cold finger, a knife on my throat, when he said 'Vietcong kill you for sure, Knightbridge.' "

"That's all?"

"That's absolutely all," Knightbridge said, rising.

"Kiss me."

"Later," he said and quit the tent.

I don't know, Janine thought when Knightbridge was gone, K's probably right in leaving this tent. The army can't stop their war just because a girl feels horny. They can't rush out with a white flag and say, Look here, fellows, now we're going to have some sex. They can't and they won't. The fact that I work sixteen hours a day patching them up makes no difference. They've got to have war twenty-four hours. That's fine with me. Most of the time I'm too tired for sex. But not always. Most of the time I'm too aware of the army discipline, the regulations, but not always. Most of the time I'm too aware that I was brought up a Christian, but not always. Most of the time I'm too aware of how lousy my figure looks in army fatigues—just about always. I would like to put on a dress again. I would like to be a woman again. Instead of raping people, I would like to be raped. "That's a terrible thing to say," she said, and then she picked up a book entitled *Battles of Battambang*, tossed it aside and said "Shit!," picked up another entitled *Richer by Asia* and began to read, staring into the book with her green eyes, her red hair above a white white face, the hair beginning to stir now in the monsoon wind out of Laos across the Vietnam highlands and into the tent.

15

Dɪsʀᴀᴇʟɪ Pond never used his whole name, because it sounded too much like a place. He wanted to make his first name his last because then he would sound Jewish. Ozz didn't know whether Diz wanted to sound Jewish because Pond wanted to renounce his culture or what.

"Or what," Dizzy said.

"I maybe suspect you are not embracing Israel as much as rejecting America. Or what," Ozz said.

"It's got nothing to do with or what," Disraeli said.

"Is it because the Jews are cleaning up on the Arabs now and you want to identify with them because we ain't doing any good against the Vietcong?"

"How can you use 'ain't' and 'identify' in the same sentence?"

"Is it because we don't talk good enough for you, Dizzy?" Ozz said.

"You talk good enough sometimes," Disraeli said.

"How come you got a name like Disraeli if you're not Jewish already?"

"Because my progenitors were English," Disraeli said. "One of my brothers is named Gordon because of Gordon of Khartoum. My great grandfather was given the name Disraeli because Disraeli was the famous prime minister of England at the time. He's the one that got the Suez Canal for the British, so I got that."

"The name or the Suez Canal?"

"What does progenitor mean?" Ho Chi Minh said putting down his pipe.

"Where you come from."

"I come from Hanoi," Ho said.

"Canton," the Naked Chinaman said.

Ho actually came from Kuk Ho just outside of Hanoi but Hanoi sounded like number one, which is the best, Cheap Charlie or number ten is the worst. The Naked Chinaman was about number five, not because he came from Canton but because he hadn't been in on Dien Bien Phu. If you didn't help beat the shit out of the French you were lucky to rise above number nine. Some said he rose to number five because he kissed ass, but this was not true. It was simply that, like the American Army, the Vietcong used the buddy system. Like Batcheck and Ozz, Disraeli and Lavender, Tarzan and Jane, Oliver and Elgar, the VC had buddies too. Like Boy Scouts it kept people from getting lost in the jungle. And when you were dead there was someone to mourn you, someone to care, to sort the scalps, the blooded money, and to wedge your aluminum dog tag between your front teeth with your name and number so they knew who you were, so that your body would not get lost and your soul was at last free to soar up wildly into the fucked-up blue yonder. That's what buddies are for.

Ho Chi Minh and the Naked Chinaman joined the Vietcong when they were fifteen and, through daring exploits, self-sacrifice, dedication and good connections, rose rapidly in the ranks until they got busted for smoking opium. The stories you hear about the Vietcong hopped up with drugs, charging the Americans, are not true. The Vietcong are Communists, and, like all other religious people, they are puritanical. No booze or drugs. Women in moderation. The Tarzan and Jane gambit would be a hanging offense. They'd be stoned by the Red Guards, then made to walk to Peking in sackcloth and ashes. No, Ho Chi Minh and the Naked Chinaman were simply buddies hooked on junk who were assigned to cover Search and Rescue by the VC, but were not trusted by the VC. They were on probation. They were not even told where a tunnel was that right now and for the last two weeks was being dug under the outer perimeter of the Americans at Search and Rescue. The Americans didn't know where it was either, but they weren't supposed to. Some of the Americans suspected, heard strange noises at night, but they thought it must be Tarzan and Jane going at it.

Coneybeare and Weatherwax didn't know about it either, and they were the American soldiers assigned to the village to oversee RD (Revolutionary Development). They were in charge of the native village PFs (Popular Forces), training them in LTO (Local Tactical Operations) to resist the VC (the only Asians who would fight). Coneybeare and Weatherwax were buddies who had signed on for another tour in Vietnam. When their year here was up they had gone back to the States to the town of Amityville in Illinois where their homes were. Before they went back to Amityville Weatherwax and Coneybeare had no intention of coming back to Vietnam ever. But Coneybeare and Weatherwax came back to the jungles of Asia to shoot and be shot at rather than stay in the land of the free and the home of the brave. Why? Coneybeare and Weatherwax could not answer.

"It's simply because," Batcheck said, "no one in the States gives a damn about the Vietnamese war. They want to forget it. Anyway, you're supposed to win a war. You remind them that it's still going on. You're supposed to win a war or get killed. You guys didn't do either. America has always won all the wars. What were you guys up to? What did you say the name of your jerkwater was?" Batcheck asked.

"Amityville."

"The girls of Amityville were afraid of you," Ozz said, "because you killed people. You were afraid of the girls because you didn't know how to talk to children no more."

"Any more."

"Yes," Ozz said. "Here you know something about everything. There you know nothing about nothing. Here you're somebody, a big fucking white hero striding through the jungle leading all those zipperheads, killing all those Gooks. In the States you mow the lawn."

"In the States they got riots," Lavender said. "Who would I be there?"

"Here our fucking hearts go out to you, Lavender," Batcheck said.

"Thank you," Lavender said.

"But that's not the point," Batcheck said. "The point here is we're not discussing your God damn Negro problem, Lavender. We're discussing their fucking white problem."

"That's true," Lavender said.

"The point is that's our country. If Weatherwax and Coneybeare can't make it back there who the hell can?"

"Now you're talking," Lavender said.

"I get fed up with your talk," Disraeli said. "I can make it back there."

"Listen to him," Ho Chi Minh said. "Listen to him."

"Let's not," Batcheck said. "Let's listen to what Weatherwax and Coneybeare have to say."

"In their defense," Ozz said.

"We don't have to defend ourselves," Weatherwax and Coneybeare said.

"Who will tell us why in the fucking Jesus Christ you signed up for another tour in this shit hole?"

"Coneybeare."

"All right," Coneybeare said, "I'll tell you. The answer is we don't know."

"Don't know?"

"We don't know."

"Listen to him," Ho Chi Minh said. "Listen to him."

"Listen to the transmitter," Batcheck said. "SOS."

"What's it say, Batcheck? What's it say?"

"Somebody down in the jungle."

"Who? Where?"

"It's dead."

"Why?"

156

"Because transmission went dead. Maybe he's dead."

"Who?"

"Let's fly ass out there and find out," Batcheck said.

The radio man for all-killed A for Alpha Company was not dead. He had only begun to live. He had just thrown his transmitter into the Song Phong River. The young man's name was PFC Charles Appelfinger, serial number 7241089, late of Alpha Company, Second of the Eighth, and now a free man. Charles Appelfinger had deserted Alpha Company when they were pinned down in a fire fight on Ridge Red Boy between Chan Ho and Kup Sin. PFC Charles Appelfinger, 7241089, had been well indoctrinated by the army and Alpha on what to do if captured and many other things, but they had not told him what to do if he got involved in a losing fire fight on Ridge Red Boy. They did tell him proudly that the American soldier thought for himself and that's what gave the American soldier a big advantage over the Gooks who had all the thinking done for them in Hanoi. Captain Clancy had said when Victor Charlie, the VC's, leader, gets killed Charlie doesn't know what to do. When I get killed I know every man jack of you will know how to think for yourselves. When Captain Clancy was hit Appelfinger maybe thought, I better save my own ass.

Clancy was Appelfinger's buddy and if Clancy was killed Appelfinger wouldn't have anything to live for. I mean Appelfinger wouldn't have anything to die for. For the NVA had caught Clancy's outfit in a box and they wouldn't let go until anyone even vaguely associated with Clancy was dead. This was bad news for the Eighth Cav (Better Than the Best). It was bad news for Clancy's buddy, Appelfinger. How could a private have a captain for a buddy? Our army in Asia is democratic as hell. But not that democratic. The thing was that Clancy didn't know that Appelfinger was his buddy. Appelfinger had latched onto Clancy unbeknownst to Clancy. Clancy was not an ordinary American captain like anybody else. When Major Fairlie of the Eighth Cavalry said,

I've never read a book in my life and will beat the shit out of anyone who has, Captain Clancy said, I've read every book ever printed and will beat the shit out of anyone who hasn't. That was Clancy. The gauntlet was down. They didn't fight. They never do. But Clancy had declared himself. He had admitted in front of all the officers in the officers' bar that he read books. A capital crime. A hanging offense. As people drifted away from Clancy Appelfinger drifted toward him until they met. Bump, they met that night in the jungle darkness.

"Who's that?"

"It's me, Appelfinger."

"Oh?"

"I read books too."

"Better watch out. American Army kill you for sure."

"Have they got you?"

"Yes, they got me. They got me leading a fucked-up outfit on a mission that doesn't have a chance."

"Decoy?"

"That's right. We're supposed to decoy two battalions of North Vietnamese regulars out of the hills onto Ridge Red Boy."

"Is this bait the only way they can get them out?"

"I guess it is."

"It was nice knowing you, sir."

"It was nice knowing you, son."

The plan was a perfect success. The NVA was sucked out of the hills and hit by the Third of the Ninth. The Americans had been looking for this bunch for a long time and now they had got them. The bait had worked. The Americans sealed up the ravines to the hills and put Arvin and Rok blocking forces at both ends of the valley. It was only a matter of time before they had a complete victory. The only bad part was, and this was never mentioned in army circles, the only bad part was the bait had been eaten. Before the Third of the Ninth got there the enemy had already polished off Alpha and were picking their teeth with Chinese toothpicks when the rescue force arrived. When the rescue force arrived there was nothing to rescue. Dead Alpha Company, the bad part, could have been a source of embarrassment to the United States Army, excepting they chose to ignore it. The Army is not so dumb as you think. The Army concentrated on the good part. The American people at home concentrated on the good part too. The American people at home are not so dumb as you think either. Pretty good stuff there too.

"Nevertheless," Private Appelfinger said as he threw A for Alpha's transmitter into the Song Phong River, "it won't work." When Appelfinger said it would not work he was not referring to the radio. He was talking about his act of cowardice. The dead remember. You think that you can join the American army and take off when it gets rough. Well, you can't, because the dead remember. The dead talk back, and they cannot be contradicted. You can call a living person a liar but not a dead man. And people listen to the dead with respect. Whether you're for the war or against the war, whether you believe we should be in Vietnam or out of Vietnam, you still see the nobility of the dead. Whether the dead are victims or heroes, they are very much okay, and they talk.

As Appelfinger sat alone beside the Song Phong River the dead told him this: "It's okay, Appy. Any one of us would like to be in your shoes."

"No."

"Don't you think we would have run if we'd had the chance?"

"No."

"We know you wanted to stay and help, Appy. It was your legs that took you off."

"Fuck you!" Appelfinger said to the silent river, the quiet jungle. "Fuck you! Fuck you! Fuck you!"

"You depended on us and we depended on you, but our perimeter was busted, Appy. They were pouring through and you are very young, Appy. Mama loves you."

"No."

"So long. It was nice knowing you."

"No."

"See you in church."

"No."

"See you in the whorehouse."

"No," Appelfinger told the wild boar, the hidden listening monkeys. "No, I won't see you anyplace. No one will ever see you anyplace."

"Correct."

"What you guys don't understand, I stayed as long as I could."

"Sure, Appy."

"I bet you don't know how I got out."

"No."

"I took a gun from one of their dead."

"Correct."

"Crawled out among them and began firing at you."

"Wow."

"Over your heads. You remember one of the Gooks stood up and hollered 'Imperialists go home or Liberation Army kill you for sure'? That was me. After that I fell back and away into the jungle. But I never left our perimeter until I saw him get it. I never left our perimeter until Clancy was hit. I wanted to get the man who shot Clancy."

"Sure, Appy."

"I'll get him too."

"Sure."

"The Gook who shot Clancy."

"Sure."

"Fuck you! Fuck you! Fuck you!" Appelfinger told the silent stream, the quiet jungle.

"Let's go," Appelfinger told himself. "Goodbye," Appelfinger said to the radio transmitter whose antenna still stuck out of the water like the showing mast of a sunken ship. "I've carried that God damn squawker all over Vietnam." PFC Charles Appelfinger had been the RTO, the radio man for Alpha. "I like that had been, used to be," Appelfinger said. "Now I'm a free man. I'm alive too." They used to call him Appy, that man up ahead with the antenna sticking out of his ass. The Martian. The coward. "No," Appelfinger told himself, "they never said that at all. Coward, I mean. They always counted on me and I counted on them. Oh boy. But that's all right because I'm still alive. If a man's not alive he's nothing. What about all those people who never went to war? What about them? What about those people who say we got to stay here? They're not here. What about them? Where are they? Where are you? It's my ass that's getting shot off. It's my buddies who get killed. Yes. Where was I? What happened to that AK47 I took from the VC dead guy? What did I do with that? What do I want it for? I'm going to kill the man who killed Clancy. No, I'm not. I said I would. To hell with that. Clancy can look after himself. No, he can't. Who cares? No one cares. I care. Coward cares. The man with the antenna sticking out of his ass. The Martian, Appelfinger. The man who took off like a big-assed bird. And to think of it," Appelfinger said, "what did I do with that AK47? That Chinese gun I took from the enemy dead to fire at the Americans? I must have left it where I threw the radio into the river."

Appelfinger went back and got the enemy AK47 weapon. Then Appelfinger began to run. He ran and he ran and he ran. He was not running toward anything but away from something so the idea was not to run in any particular direction but the idea was to keep going, to keep moving, to run and run and run past all recovering past thinking. The thinking is what is bad. The running is what is good. Appelfinger ran past all understanding, past all comprehension, past the old battlefield, the old bivouac area, the LZ, the landing zone, where they had arrived, the battlefield of the fire fight where his comrades had departed, where his buddies left him. That's right. They took off. Death is the easy way out. It takes courage to live. Death is the final refuge of the coward. Only the brave flee. Only the coward stands. The important

16

The great Asian night of jungle rose around Clancy towering and grand, making man minuscule and intruder, lost and soundless. Clancy heard the voices of Bethany and Peter, sibilant and faint in the darkness of the rain forest. Ridge Red Boy rattled back their impotent talk until now the forest stood alone and silent again in the enormous weight of silence, the utter stillness of the close dead on Ridge Red Boy.

Who goes there? Clancy wondered.

A holy man and an Indian? No, it's two Indians.

I thought we killed all the Indians. No, this time the Indians killed us.

If they are Indians they are American Indians. Because they are white. Two white people from the States. How could they get here? Who would want them? Where are they going and how will they get out? They probably got here the same way you did and they will get out the same way you will. In a bag.

Clancy raised his hand.

"Look, Peter," Bethany said.

Peter leaned over Clancy and examined him carefully. Clancy was lost in the camouflage of fronds and yellow flowers and spattered blood. Someone seemed to have brought the blood there in a sprinkling can and waved it over the jungle still life until it dripped.

Clancy stared at Peter. Clancy's eyes were rigid and fixed in concern and absolute disbelief.

And then as the sun glinted, Bethany, for the first time, saw death. Bethany saw the death of Clancy. All the bright spatters of Clancy's blood.

She shrieked. The jungle shrieked back.

"Run! We've got to find help. Run!" She grabbed Peter and they fell. "Run!"

They got up now and ran full panic through the jungle until the jungle caught them and threw them down hard. The whole jungle is a vein of vines to catch people who run. They ran and got caught and thrown down again and again and again until they hit the river and there was no place to run and Bethany saw the radio, its antenna sticking up out of the Song Phong River.

"If we can find the man who goes with that radio we can call help for the dying man. The dying man all in blood."

But instead they ran. They turned from the river and ran into the weave and snarl of the fantastic jungle without purpose, without direction.

They ran until Bethany stumbled on something. Bethany propped it up.

"Appelfinger," Peter said.

"Positive," Private Appelfinger said, turning his head.

"We found Clancy."

"Alive?"

"Yes," Peter said. "Can you salvage the radio?"

"No."

"Even if we hang it out to dry?"

"No."

"Even if we take it apart and hang it out to dry? Clancy is bad."

Appelfinger watched the fading monsoon moving in and out like a gentle woman.

"If we hang the radio out good," Appelfinger said.

"Then that's exactly what we'll do," Bethany said.

"What happened?" Peter said.

"Our position on Ridge Red Boy was overrun by the

enemy," Appelfinger said. "Everyone in Alpha Company was killed excepting me. I pretended to be dead."

"Clancy?"

"I'll kill the man who killed Clancy."

"That won't help," Bethany said.

"Yes, it will."

"No, it won't."

"Who knows what will help him, Bethany?" Peter said.

"I know the dead don't know, don't care, don't listen."

"Who knows, Bethany, whether the dead listen?" Peter said.

"I know those guys do," Appelfinger said. "They hear every God damn thing. I counted on them and they counted on me."

"And they're dead."

"Yes."

"Do you hear that, Bethany?" Peter said. "Do you hear that? Can't you see it?"

"No."

"I see it perfectly," Peter said. "He counted on them and they counted on him."

"If we're going to retrieve the radio we'll be under enemy observation. Let me show you how to work this Chinese gun," Appelfinger said.

"No," Peter said, but Appelfinger ignored him.

"Give me your hand."

Peter gave Appelfinger his hand and Appelfinger placed Peter's hand on the weapon. "You put a round in the firing chamber by pulling here and releasing suddenly. Now the weapon is capable of firing thirty-two rounds, a full clip. Do not let the fact that it's a foreign weapon panic you. Notice the similarity of this AK47 to our own M16. The safety is further forward. Up here is safe. Down is fire, to the right is fully automatic, to the left semi-automatic. The clip insertion is identical to our own weapon except you tap it with the palm of your hand like this, until you feel it bottom in the chamber. Notice the quick tap. Also notice we have another full clip taped to the end of the inserted clip. This enables us to fire a double clip by a simple reverse motion. Are you ready to fire?"

"Yes," Peter said.

"Stand."

Peter stood.

Appelfinger said, "Eighth Cav, better than the best. The Second of the Ninth. Second Platoon, Alpha Company. Take this, you yellow sons of a bitches! Fire!"

"I can't any more," Peter said.

"Pull the trigger."

"I can't," Peter said.

"I understand," Appelfinger said.

"I don't understand," Peter said.

"I understand," Bethany said.

"We better move out of here," Appelfinger said.

"Can I carry the gun?"

"No, I'll carry the gun," Appelfinger said.

"Before A for Alpha was all dead did you get off a call for help?"

"Yes, but it didn't do any good," Appelfinger said.

"Why?"

"Because Search and Rescue in this TAOR is a fucked-up outfit."

"What's that mean?" Bethany said. "Is that good?"

"No, it isn't, Bethany," Peter said.

"They say," Bethany said, "that Peter deserted the army. That is not true. America deserted Peter. What was that shot? Are they trying to kill us?"

"Yes," Appelfinger said.

The Bamboo Bed of Search and Rescue was making it across the top of the jungle as fast as it could go to the rescue. The Bamboo Bed was doing one hundred and fifty, which seems fifteen hundred miles an hour when you are only a foot over the jungle. The Bamboo Bed was filled with Batcheck and Ozz, Lavender and Dizzy, Weatherwax and Coneybeare, Oliver and Elgar. They were all leaning tentatively forward as though this would get them more speed. Like the rest of the army they did not know where they were going but they were going there fast.

"Return to base." It was Captain Knightbridge on radio calling them back.

"Just when we were having some fun," Disraeli said.

"How do we know it's Knightbridge?" Ozz said. "It could be VC."

"Identify yourself," Batcheck said into the mike.

"A very good idea," Captain Knightbridge said. "The VCs could cut into our wavelength. How do I identify myself?"

"How does he identify himself?" Batcheck asked everyone in the Bamboo Bed.

"Tell him the Americans are shitheads and see what his reaction is."

"I can't see what his reaction is," Batcheck said. "We're not on video."

"Try it anyway," Elgar said.

"Give it a try," Weatherwax said.

"The Americans are shit."

"Shitheads," Coneybeare said.

"The Americans are shitheads," Batcheck said.

"That's interesting," Knightbridge said.

"What did he say?"

"He said it was interesting."

"That got him."

"No, I think it's interesting myself," Coneybeare said.

"Ask him who's winning the war."

"Who's winning the war?"

"We are."

"Who's we?"

"The VC."

"We got him."

"No, you haven't," Ozz said. "Everybody says that to confuse us. Ask him why he said that."

"Why did you say that?"

"I'm pissed off."

"What did he say?" Disraeli said.

"He said he was pissed off."

"Why?"

"Why are you pissed off?"

"Because of your stupid questions," Knightbridge said.

"What's a good question?"

"Who's leading the American League."

"Who's leading the American League?"

"I don't know."

"Who's leading the National League?"

"I don't know that either."

"Hey, guys," Batcheck announced to everyone in the Bamboo Bed, "this guy's an American. He doesn't know a fucking thing. Captain Knightbridge, sir, we'll be right home."

17

Aн yes, Clancy knew the funny part, but ah yes, there is a bad part. The bad part is that we have not seen our brothers die, and unless you have failed everyone utterly you have not truly suffered. How can you know the terror and the majesty of the Asian jungle if you have not known the towering darkness of its despair? And what measures do we have to send boys to quick death in strange forests? What license? We are all intimate strangers met in a jungle near Red Boy, and soon we die.

The good part is concern and comradeship in the wild joy of life followed by death. Followed by Colonel Yvor.

Captain Knightbridge wanted all the boys in Search and Rescue to come home so they could look for, so they could rescue, their leader, Colonel Yvor. Colonel Yvor was down in the mountains someplace south of Dak To, probably near Clancy. Find Yvor and you find Clancy. Don't find Clancy, Clancy knows. Find Clancy.

Colonel Yvor had wakened that morning to the feeling of his Vietnamese child bride playing with his cock.

"Stop playing with my Yo-Yo, Child Bride."

"You big Cheap Charlie, you buy me nothing else to play with. You number ten."

"Bring the radio over here, Child Bride. That sounds like Knightbridge on the transmitter."

"Good morning, Colonel Yvor."

"Bullshit, Knightbridge. Bullshit."

"No fix on the flower people yet."

"Good."

"One contact with Alpha Company. All dead."

"Good."

"Why do you say that, sir?"

"Because it's bullshit."

"Why do you say that?"

"Because you made contact. You don't contact the dead. What happened to Clancy?"

"I guess Captain Clancy is dead."

"Don't guess. Make sure the son of a bitch is dead. This is the biggest thing since Custer."

"But . . ."

"Because that's the story we gave out. Whole brave Alpha Company dies in trap sprung by Eighth Cav. Sources close to Colonel Yvor revealed today enemy in full flight, one thousand Unfriendlies already dead. Captain Knightbridge of Search and Rescue turned to this reporter and said, 'This is the most fantastic sight I've ever seen.' "

"But . . ."

"No buts, Knightbridge. We don't want to make the whole press God damn liars, do we? So this is what we do, we dummy up, understand? I feel as lousy about losing all of Alpha Company as you do, but General Westmoreland's going to award them all the Iron Cross with Oak Leaf Clusters posthumously, and we'll do whatever else we can for them. I've seen a lot of men die, Knightbridge, and very few go out the way they did. It's a rare opportunity to be remembered the way Custer is remembered, and that's not something we toss out lightly the way Lincoln did with that other thing at Gettysburg."

"You big bullshit," the child bride said.

"You put a hold on everything you say, Knightbridge, particularly the ear thing, and I'll hop out there in an H13 chopper and cover you. Over and out."

"But, sir . . ."

"Didn't I tell you war is shit, Knightbridge? One day

you'll listen. One day you'll get what you didn't get at the Point."

Mai Li, the child bride, put the mike back on the transmitter.

"Thank you, Mai Li," Colonel Yvor said. "You're God damn good to me."

"Mai Li play with Yo-Yo?"

"No. Now we fight with VC."

"VC kill you for sure," the child bride said.

"Put a cigar in my mouth, light it and then dress me."

"What kind of cigar? Same same?"

"Same same."

"What kind of clothes?"

"Same same," Colonel Yvor said.

In ten minutes more Colonel Yvor was at 200 meters in the glass-bubble helicopter with the same cigar. His pilot was Billy Joe Sitwell from Sapola, Georgia, and each time Colonel Yvor wanted the cigar removed from his face so that he could breathe he would make a supersonic whine that only Sergeant Billy Joe could hear, and Billy Joe would remove the cigar from Colonel Yvor's face. Billy Joe could hear Colonel Yvor's supersonic whine because he owned a spotted German shorthair in Sapola, Georgia, who used the same supersonic whine every time he wanted the door opened or something done for him because, of course, the German shorthair, like Colonel Yvor, didn't have any arms either. No dogs do.

"Billy Joe, I like the way you lift the cigar out of my mouth. You don't pull it or jerk it out like Mai Li."

"Thank you, sir."

"Still, she's only fourteen."

"Yes, sir."

"She'll learn."

"She sure will, sir."

"Billy Joe, where the hell are we going?"

171

"We have a recon check on the flower people and Appel-finger. We might pick up Clancy."

"But we might pick up his friend Mike," Colonel Yvor said.

"Yes, we could, sir."

"That would not be good, Billy."

"Shall we turn back, sir?"

"No, go ahead, Billy."

"Shall I pop the cigar back in your mouth?"

"No, I want to talk some more, Billy Joe. It's a beautiful Vietnamese day, isn't it?"

"It sure is, sir."

"Billy Joe, why do you wear that Confederate flag in your buttonhole?"

"I don't know, sir."

"Billy Joe, what are you doing in this war?"

"Driving the chopper."

"Answer me."

"Stopping the Communists."

Colonel Yvor thought about this while watching the green monsoon sky above the dark jungle below.

"Very well, Billy Joe, you may place the cigar in my mouth."

Billy Joe put it there in the manner that he would insert a pacifier in the mouth of babies and sucklings. Billy Joe loved Colonel Yvor. Billy Joe loved the army, loved the war, loved the VC who made it all possible. Billy Joe hated the South Vietnamese army allies, Arvin, because they would not fight, hated the American Marines because they fought too much and made the army look bad. Hated the new army Chinook two-rotor helicopter because it dragged its ass at takeoff, hated the weather in Vietnam. There is no monsoon season, there is only one monsoon and it lasts all year. Billy Joe also hated his American South. He loved Negroes and after the war wanted to marry one and live in Paris, France, where they understood. The South did not understand. Pretended not to, the God damn hypocrites. Loved Lavender and hoped he returned the affection. Loved Colonel Yvor's child bride, Mai Li, and wanted to go to bed with her, would marry her too because he didn't like white girls, but Colonel Yvor had thought of it first. The thing to do was get rid of Colonel Yvor. Are you crazy or something? Colonel Yvor is the war. Without Colonel Yvor the Communists would be in Saigon now, maybe even Kansas City or New York City, New York. Can't tell. Don't know. Couldn't take a chance. To know the strength, the power, the glory of Colonel Yvor you had to be with him in the monsoon dark over the jungles of Vietnam on a Search and Rescue, then you would know that Colonel Yvor was kind of God searching us out down there in the jungle of doubt, uncertainty and despair, rescuing us all from the jungle of darkness and doom.

Now Billy Joe detected Colonel Yvor's supersonic whine and removed the cigar from his lips.

"Take her up, Billy Joe," Colonel Yvor said. "I want to see more."

"We'll pick up enemy ground fire if we go up, sir."

"I want to see more," Colonel Yvor said.

"I don't want to get you killed."

"If I get killed you will have Mai Li all to yourself."

"But you're the war."

"If I'm the war, take us up so I can see what's happening to me."

"Positive."

"Negative, Billy Joe. I still can't see. Take her up to one thousand."

"We are, sir."

"Take her up to two thousand."

"How's that?"

"Negative. Try seven."

"What?"

"Try four."

"Okay?"

"Five."

"That's about it, sir."

"There's a hole in the clouds about three clicks northeast. Swoop down through and hold at one."

"Positive."

"I said hold at one."

"Sorry, sir."

"I've got a fix on a fire fight."

"Where?"

"Two clicks south southwest."

"Positive."

"Billy Joe, rig up my gun."

"Positive."

Billy Joe locked Colonel Yvor's door open and then swung up the M6o machine gun, then secured the weapon, cocked it, put it off safe and on fire, then fired one burst to clear the weapon, then picked up the string that was tied to the trigger and had a button at the end, and placed the button in Colonel Yvor's mouth between his teeth, and the good colonel who was the war all by himself yanked back his head and the gun went bang bang bang. Actually it was an M6o with a high cyclic rate of fire close to a thousand rounds a minute, so it made its long bangs too close together. It was like the tearing noise of a great thickness of cloth going at a steady and quick rip. The volley tore into a covey of neutral passing ravens flying with the monsoon over Pleiku Pass, but the jungle below that came up abruptly while the pilot was fiddling with the gun was not neutral as people claim jungles are; this one beneath in Vietnam was ominous, wet and dark, filled with disasters and death, brimming with the poison of darts, booby traps that draw and quarter, castrate and decapitate, ants as large as saucers that move in armies, deadfalls filled with sharp pongee stakes, rotting fish, malaria, hepatitis, dead and dying soldiers from both sides, heroes, cowards, deserters, sadists, masochists, busted bugles, M79s and malfunctioning Browning machine guns, two hundred tons of inedible shit called C rations, four stranded USO troops, abandoned Patton tanks and rusting American amtracks blown skyward by our own B52s in a successful saturation symposium near Dak Sut, fourteen dead Negro troopers in pink scarves and green berets caught in an NVA crossfire and lying at the bottom of the Bien Tien draw staring up with no eyes at the no sun. Opium caravans using aged arthritic Burmese elephants being dive-bombed and mortared by both sides. The glare of mahogany, teak, banyan, flambeau, rubber and bong trees all dripping a sweet-smelling syrupy piss on the red earth that looks like old blood. That's what the jungle is. That's what the jungle hides. That's what the H13 bubble chopper containing Colonel Yvor and Billy Joe was crashing into now.

Up up came the ground fire from heavy automatic weapons. Down down came the chopper.

"Bring her up, Billy."

"Can't, sir."

"Bring her up, William."

"Now, sir."

"Bring her up, Billy."

"Got her."

"Good, Billy."

Colonel Yvor was talking through the string and the button in his teeth. The string was threaded through the firing grip of the M60 so that it would not tangle on the way to his mouth.

"Get me in position so I can kick ass on Charlie, Billy."

Billy tilted the bubble, slanted the chopper so much to starboard that Colonel Yvor was pointing almost straight down. Colonel Yvor yanked off a burst with his head, a long burst so that there was a straight taut stream of red rope from the glass-glinting fishbowl chopper to the rubber and teak or from the rubber and teak to the glass-glinting fishbowl chopper. At a distance the tightrope of fire could be going either way. Death could be coming up or down, around or sideways, crisscross or smack between the eyes or coming down through your helmet head or straight up through your armored ass.

"Kick her glass ass to starboard, Billy, so I can kick ass on Charlie's flank."

"Yes, sir."

"Now, Billy."

"Yes, sir."

"I said now, Billy. And get her glass ass to starboard."

"She's power-locked, sir, turning out very low RPMs. If I maneuver we'll crash."

"Then let her crash, but kick her glass ass to starboard first."

"I can't do that, sir."

"Then talk to her, Billy."

"The colonel wants you to behave."

"That's an order, Billy."

"That's an order," Sergeant Billy Joe said to the glass-bottomed bowl. "Order of Colonel Yvor."

The fishbowl coughed, then dropped, then recovered, then slowly now began turning out maximum RPMs.

Billy flipped the chopper rudely on its starboard side and Colonel Yvor yanked back on his head that held the button tied to the string that was fastened to the trigger that activated the gun that sprayed the jungle with enough lead for all wars everywhere, enough firepower for all enemies anyplace, any time, anywhere they may try to hide.

Below and behind a fallen mahogany log in the Vietnamese jungle, hiding from Colonel Yvor's fire hose of lead that sprayed all around them, were Peter, Bethany and Appelfinger. And Appelfinger was firing the Chinese AK47 at the glass-bottomed chopper and hitting it good.

"We're losing altitude, sir."

"Not yet, Billy."

"We're hit bad."

"Not yet, Billy. I have not yet finished firing."

"We are going down."

"Not yet, Billy," Colonel Yvor said.

*   *   *

"Why are you shooting at them?" Bethany wanted to know.

"Because they are shooting at us," Appelfinger said.

"Who is shooting at whom?" Peter wanted to know.

"Everyone is shooting at each other, Peter," Bethany said.

"Why?"

"War."

"I mean, why are you shooting at the same side?"

"Let him shoot, Peter," Bethany said. "Don't bother him."

But Peter had to know, and between clips he pulled on Appelfinger's leg.

"Why are you shooting at the same side?"

"A good question," Bethany said.

"Because it's Colonel Yvor, can't you see?"

"No," Peter said.

"They've gone," Appelfinger said. "But they will be back."

"Why have they gone and why will they be back?"

"Because their gun probably jammed," Appelfinger said. "You see, they're hovering over there out of our range. When they get it cleared they'll be back."

"Why will they be back?"

"Because it's Colonel Yvor."

"Why does he shoot at you?"

"Because he's Colonel Yvor."

"Why do you shoot at Colonel Yvor?"

"War."

"I am not crazy."

"That's true," Bethany said. "Peter is not crazy."

"Because," Appelfinger said, laying the stock of the Chinese AK47 against the mahogany log, "because Yvor is the war."

"Oh?"

"Yes. That's why Clancy was sent out on that suicide patrol as bait to get the Chinese to come out of the hills. Colonel Yvor knew that Clancy knew all about him."

"Knew all about him?"

"About his being the war. There aren't many possibles, a

few on each side. You don't think this war goes on by itself, do you?"

"Yes."

"Well, it doesn't. And throwing a few flowers around is not going to help. We've got to get the man who killed Clancy. Colonel Yvor for one."

"Clancy?"

"Yes, and if Alpha collected ears I bet Yvor does something worse. I admit Clancy read books but I bet many people on both sides read books. It's just that they keep it a secret. The awful thing is that not one of them offered to help Clancy. They were scared. They joined in the witch hunt themselves. Well, they were scared. I was scared too, but I was Clancy's buddy. A man's got to have a buddy that he can depend on and I was Clancy's buddy. I've got to kill the man who killed Clancy. Colonel Yvor pinned that ear rap and that reading rap on Clancy because he knew that Clancy knew."

"About his being the war?"

"Yes. And something more too."

"Well."

"Well nothing," Appelfinger said, picking up his Chinese gun, inserting a clip, throwing in a shell, then cocking the piece. "You think spreading flowers is going to stop the war?"

"I don't think killing Captain Clancy kept the war going and I don't think killing Colonel Yvor will stop the war," Peter said. "Even if there's something more. What more is there? I don't think you know. Clancy knew, but you don't know."

"Ye of little faith," Appelfinger said.

"The thing is . . ."

"The thing is," Colonel Yvor said as Sergeant Billy Joe tried to clear the weapon, "we've got to stay here out of range until we're ready to kick ass."

Billy Joe swung the M6o, pointed the muzzle at himself,

inserted a cleaning rod and pounded at the jammed round, at the same time maneuvering the chopper.

"Quite a trick," Colonel Yvor said. "I'm going to put you in for the Croix de Guerre, Billy."

"Sir, are you keeping this war going?"

"Could one man keep the war going?"

"He could try."

"I simply want to kick ass on those people down there."

"How do you know they're not Friendlies?"

"Would Friendlies fire back?"

"I would."

"You're an exceptional person, Billy," Colonel Yvor said. "How are you doing, Billy?"

"I'm not doing so good."

"We better call for a gun ship, Billy. Still I'd like to finish this job myself."

"I bet you would."

"What's that?"

"I'm not doing no good," Billy said.

"None of us are, Billy," Colonel Yvor said. "This war's a mess. We should straighten it out. I'd like to bomb Peking."

"I bet you would."

"I heard you that time, Billy. I don't have a good image, do I?"

"Beautiful."

"Would I look better with arms?"

"Beauty is in the eye of the beholder," Sergeant Billy Joe said.

"Where did you get that from, Sergeant? Lavender? Batcheck? Disraeli? Ozz? Who is the poet? Knightbridge? Nurse Jane?"

"Batcheck."

"Batcheck? There must be a new school of poetry since I was a boy."

"When I was young and twenty . . ."

"Billy!"

"Yes, sir."

"We don't recite poetry when our gun is jammed and we are being fired upon."

"Yes, sir."

"How are you coming?"

"I think I got it, sir."

"Watch the chopper."

Billy put both hands back on the controls.

"All right. Now test-fire the gun."

"It's pointing straight at me, sir."

"Swing her to full port and fire."

"It still don't want to do no good, sir."

"God damn it," Colonel Yvor said, pounding the gun with both hands. "God damn it, God damn it, God damn it."

The gun fired.

"Hitting it with both hands done the trick."

"I didn't, Billy."

"It seemed that way," Billy said.

"We assume hands, Billy, then we extrapolate from an illusion."

"I bet that's it. What did you say?" Billy Joe said.

"I said we better wait a minute before we go in."

"Why?"

"Figure out a plan," Colonel Yvor said.

"I had a German shorthair once called Simon."

"What's that got to do with it?"

"Simon would stay out of range of a porcupine or skunk, but just out of range, darting around out there, then Simon would roll over. You see, when a porcupine or a skunk roll over they are helpless. Then Simon would dart in and finish them. All they had to do was imitate Simon and they were done for."

"Did the porcupines roll over for Simon?"

"No. But I think Simon had a good idea."

"If the enemy did all the things they should do we would have finished them off a long time ago, Billy."

"Why don't they, sir?"

"They're not very bright, Billy. Why don't you exchange the rear M60 for this one?"

"Why didn't we think of that before?"

"We're not very bright either, Billy."

As Billy Joe exchanged the guns, reaching around with one arm, Colonel Yvor said, "What would Simon say if we darted in frontally and took them in one bite?"

"Simon would say they got a Chinese 7.62 light machine gun or an AK47."

"Sounds like an AK47."

"That's what Simon would say too," Billy Joe said.

"We will try a frontal assault," Colonel Yvor said. "We will go straight at them without maneuver, cut them right down the middle, blast them where they don't anticipate, until we see the whites of their eyes."

"What do we do then, sir?"

"Keep right on going. Are you ready?"

"Ready, sir."

"It seems to me," Bethany said, "if they knew we were Friendlies they would not attack. How can you have a war if you don't have sides?"

"That problem has caused Colonel Yvor many sleepless nights too," Appelfinger said. "But Colonel Yvor will figure a way around it."

"If only we could show him we're Friendlies."

"Everyone alive in the jungle is an enemy," Appelfinger said.

"Can't he see you're an American soldier?"

"I lost my shit," Appelfinger said.

"How?" Peter said.

"I kind of threw it away."

"Why?"

"So I could pass as a VC."

"Well, you're still passing," Peter said. "Congratulations."

"We must think of something."

"Why doesn't Peter," Bethany said, "sit on this mahogany

log in full view and play the guitar? That way, in effect, no one could shoot at us."

"That way, in effect," Appelfinger said, "Peter would be shot full of holes."

"Why?"

"Because Colonel Yvor might not appreciate the guitar."

"But you don't know."

"Not for certain. If Peter wants to take the chance . . ."

"I don't want to take the chance," Peter said.

"In effect," Bethany said, "Peter is a deserter."

"Yes," Peter said.

But Peter had the courage of his cowardice. Peter did not know this but he had come to Vietnam to desert life. Peter gathered up his guitar and sat on the mahogany log, waiting for the enemy to hit, in the clearing in the jungle, a long way from home. Peter had come to Vietnam to die as many did, because death is the great problem solver. Many appear in dispatches as heroes, but they are all looking, as Peter was looking, for the great solution. When death comes the great solution is in the form of small people in black pajamas and strange-shaped straw hats. In the States the great solution comes in the shape of cigarettes, LSD, heroin and 300-horse-power automobiles. In Vietnam it is all quite simple.

"I don't mind sitting on this mahogany log and playing my guitar," Peter said.

"I'm not going to let you kill yourself, Peter," Bethany said.

"You no longer believe in the power of love?"

"Not here."

"Well, I still believe in it. Certainly no one can shoot at a man sitting in the middle of a jungle playing a guitar on a mahogany log."

"Can I say something?" Appelfinger said.

"Yes."

"Colonel Yvor can shoot at a man in the middle of a jungle playing a mahogany guitar."

"That isn't what Peter said. Peter said, in effect, no one

can shoot at a man alone in the middle of the jungle demonstrating love."

"Colonel Yvor can," Appelfinger said.

"A deserter alone in the middle of a jungle playing a guitar?"

"Colonel Yvor will."

"How about you?"

"Yes, I could."

"Is that what war does to you?"

"Yes, it does."

"But this is love."

"Love could be a VC trick."

"Explain yourself."

"All the bar girls in Saigon are VC."

"Peter's an American."

"Still could be fake love." Appelfinger touched Bethany with his AK47. "Your flowers are fake love."

"Maybe he's got a point, Bethany."

"No, he hasn't, Peter."

"If you both want to sit on the log and get the shit shot out of you go ahead," Appelfinger said.

"Maybe he's got a point, Bethany."

"If he had a point, Peter, he wouldn't be out here in the jungle himself."

"Drafted."

"But the jungle."

"Orders."

"You don't have to do everything you're told. In effect, a person still has free will."

"In effect, yes," Appelfinger said. "But not in the army."

"If you won't sit on that log, Peter, I will."

"Good boy," Appelfinger said.

"War is a very sobering experience," Peter said.

"War is only an extension of the middle-class hangup, Peter. You know that," Bethany said.

"Yes."

"I didn't know that," Appelfinger said.

"It's not something you can get out of books," Bethany said. "You have to come from upper middle-class parents like Peter and I did. You have to suffer that experience to know that life can open up like a flower."

"Okay, let's get the damn thing over with."

"Peter, Peter," Bethany said. "You're not the same old Peter."

"Peter, Peter," Appelfinger said. "Here comes Colonel Yvor."

"Okay, Billy Joe, let's kick ass on those VC," Colonel Yvor said.

"Positive."

"Take her up, full power at one hundred meters, then turn starboard, then I'll kick ass."

"Positive."

"Look, Billy, they got a VC decoy sitting on the log playing a guitar."

"Full beard."

"What won't they think of next?"

"VC get you for sure," Billy Joe said.

"Maybe we shouldn't go in, Billy."

"Why, sir?"

"They want us to."

"That's true. They're sucking us."

"It's a trap, Billy."

"Why don't we land, sir, someplace else and take them from the rear?"

"You're a genius, Billy."

"Not really, sir."

"And a modest one."

"Thank you, sir."

"I'll get you the Maltese Cross."

"Where's an LZ, sir?"

"There is no landing zone here, Billy. We'll have to blast one."

"Negative. If we blast one we'll give away our LZ."

"We'll blast several, Billy. That way they won't know which one is it."

"Positive."

"And radio Knightbridge at Search and Rescue to get all his kids' asses out here. Bring the Bamboo Bed. If they won't come for us tell him we think we have spotted one of Clancy's boys."

"Positive."

18

A VIETNAMESE child found a helmet. With a helmet you can play war. The American soldiers were playing children too. Both sides play children. Come, we will all be children in death. The peasants are not children. The Vietnamese peasant is a rice-paddy-working adult. Children cannot cope with him. You destroy what you do not, cannot, understand. Children laugh and cry to see such things. A Vietnamese child found a dead helmet. With a helmet you can play war.

Jungle up there, Clancy thought, don't stand so straight, so admonitory and silent, so superior, aloof, so all unseeing and calm. Jungle, uncommitted, reserved, distant, incipient and wise and patient for children. A child who found the dead helmet. A helmet of the dead.

What's that explosion?

"They're blasting several LZs to fool us," Appelfinger said. "They must think we're kids. But it will only draw VC. We better get out of here. I'll radio Search and Rescue."

"With what?"

"That's right," Appelfinger said. "I've got to get that radio. I threw the radio in the Phong."

"If you had the radio you could tell Yvor to call off his attack."

"I could tell Yvor Clancy is still alive, that Clancy is somewhere in the area. But maybe Yvor doesn't want to hear that."

"That why you threw the radio in the river?" Peter said.

"We better get out of here," Appelfinger said.

"Still running?"

"We will get that radio," Appelfinger said.

"Why did you change your mind, Appelfinger?"

"Because I believe in evolution," Appelfinger said. "Change."

"The fact that Alpha Company had an evolutionist as a radio man may change the whole course of the world."

"And a deserter," Appelfinger said, looking at Peter.

"Peter did not desert. It's just that he looked too much like Custer," Bethany said. "Clancy did not want American history to repeat itself."

"But it did."

"That was not Peter's fault."

"Yes, Peter does look like Custer," Appelfinger said, staring at Peter. "But so does Clancy. And everyone on our side looked like Custer when those Indians overran Alpha. Except me."

"Because you took off."

"Because I am an evolutionist. I believe history can be changed."

"Isn't that self-serving?"

"Maybe," Appelfinger said, thinking. "I will get back to you. But I don't think Peter quit because Clancy said he looked like Custer."

"Why then?"

"I said I would get back to you," Appelfinger said. "But now you can tell me what this button sign means you got pinned on you—I HAVE A DREAM. What is the dream?"

"America."

"Oh God!"

"The dream," Bethany said. "What was Alpha fighting for?"

"Our fucking life, that's what for."

"What I'm trying to do," Bethany said to Appelfinger, "what I'm trying to do is save you. If I can get you to talk, then you won't blow up and burst. Peter burst. I am trying to put Peter back together again now. Tell me what happened in your own language."

"Fuck you."

"Tell me what happened on Red Boy."

"Alpha Company," Appelfinger said, "was surrounded the night before. We knew they would try to take us in the morning so we kept them under mortar attack all night with the two mortars and the two hundred mortar rounds we had left. The idea was to keep them off balance and to make them think we were at full strength. Just before dawn, or maybe it was beginning dawn, that first Vietnamese yellow-red light, Clancy told everyone to have a mad minute."

"Mad minute?"

"That's when the whole outfit fires everything they got at the VC. It makes you feel better. I got off five clips. Everything is so absolutely silent in the jungle, but you know they're out there, maybe three, four hundred of them, getting ready to take you, so when Clancy said prepare to fire a mad minute it felt awful good."

"Could you see them?" Bethany asked.

"You never do," Appelfinger said. "But it sure felt good to live for one minute."

"Did you have that much ammunition? I mean that you could afford to fire into the jungle wildly for one minute?"

"Yes. We had a flare-drop resupply that night at 2000. Victor Charlie didn't get much. Most of it fell in our perimeter."

"Who is Victor Charlie?"

"VC. Victor Charlie is our radio call for Vietcong. Like all our companies are called A Alpha, B Bravo and C Charlie."

"Calling your own C companies Charlie and the enemy Charlie too, doesn't that confuse things?"

"No, because you say Charlie Company. You know that's us. They're just called Charlie."

"You say that part of your ammo flare-drop that night fell to Victor Charlie. Can he use our ammunition in his guns?"

"No. Just some of the mortar shells, but Charlie saves it all, figuring he will overrun our perimeter in the morning. Then he uses the guns of our dead guys. That's really why our guys are killed, because they've run out of ammo."

"I hear, too, our guns jam."

"That's the M16. Yes, it does. But not if you keep it very clean. And not if you don't try to get off too many rounds and burn it up."

"How fast will our rifles fire?"

"Seven hundred a minute."

"How does that compare with the heavy machine gun?"

"Six hundred."

"How did they come at you?"

"First they hit with mortars and rockets, pretty big stuff."

"How do they carry that big stuff in the jungle? How much does a rocket weigh?"

"Almost a hundred pounds, about ninety. The rocket launcher maybe another ten. It's just a tin tube. Two men carry the rocket on a bamboo sling between them."

"What about a mortar gun?"

"That's heavy as hell, but it breaks down and is divided up."

"Could you see them?"

"Not yet. They were coming at us from the trees into the bamboo and then the elephant grass. We should have cut that tall grass down, enlarged our field of fire, but we didn't have time. Then I saw a bunch of them. They were the first ones I ever saw good. They were moving from the trees into the bamboo, not charging us like in the movies, but moving like they were looking for maybe a place to sleep or have a picnic."

"Picnic?"

"That's why I didn't shoot, because I thought they might be looking for a table, and then I was shooting and they were going down, but not going down like human beings but like in some kind of game you buy at a store for children and they were kind of surprised when they were hit, like this was not in the game. And the good part is it's like TV, that is, nobody is getting killed. People are going down and things like that but nobody's really dead, no blood or things like that, that wouldn't be allowed on TV—the blood comes later and nobody dies until the guy next to you gets killed."

"Then you believe?"

"No no no, not at once, because it's too early in the fire fight and you need him and everybody needs everybody and if it could happen to him it could happen to anybody. Do you understand? No, no, no," Appelfinger said quietly and to himself, "it was too early and too late and you can't do this because I am one of yourself and this can't happen, shouldn't happen to us because I am one of yourself, and leastwise not to an American."

"How does it feel when you know you're going to die?"

"Caught."

"Where?"

"In the balls."

"That doesn't tell me anything."

"You been lied to. That's how it feels."

"And so you . . ."

"Run. But not before you think where. Because you can run into the wrong part of the bamboo."

"The others?"

"Dead."

"All?"

"Maybe three or four made it out."

"Where are they?"

"Who knows?" Appelfinger said.

"But you saw the man who killed Clancy?"

"Yes."

"Who?"

"Like I said," Appelfinger said, "it was just starting that piss-red and yellow Vietnamese dawn when they hit us."

"Hadn't we better move?"

"No," Appelfinger said. "I want Yvor to land first so he

won't get observation on the direction we take. Where was I?"

"The man who killed Clancy."

"All of us," Appelfinger said. "The whole damn company. Yes, before they hit us I'd been on the radio the whole damn night trying to get help from the dragon ships, but help does not come easy in a monsoon. You'd think with all those helicopters, airplanes, tanks, amtracks and rubber bands that forty-fifty billion a year can buy you'd just have to press a button and the VC would run. But the jungle is on their side. The jungle is on their side and all the junk we got is no match for the jungle. Our tanks get lost in it. Our brains get malaria in it, and from up above you can't see nothing in it. That was true the day Charlie hit Alpha. Our own side couldn't find us. I gave them a fix on our position as good as I could but they couldn't find us. From up there the jungle looks the same all over. We tried releasing smoke bombs to show them our perimeter but they were green. Green was the only color we had left. We had a smoke canister marked red but it shot out green. Green smoke against the green jungle. Green against green. Some girl at the factory, I guess, was thinking about her date, not thinking about the labeling job, so it shot out green.

"First it was the gun ship that couldn't find us. Later on it was everyone who couldn't find us, but first it was the gun ship that couldn't find us. A gun ship is a chopper that carries rockets. Like I said, resupply had found us that night by the light of the fire fight, but when it got light no one could find us. Then a dragon ship found us. I don't know how he found us. A dragon ship is a C47 converted to a gun ship. Anyway it came over and fired at everyone without any discrimination. It shot at both sides regardless of grade, rank or serial number, regardless of race, creed or color. The shells just rained down from above. Most of them burst in the tree canopy and didn't do any harm, but it kept the VC from attacking for about ten minutes, as long as they were there, and then the dragon ship went home and the VC took us."

191

"Do you have a guilt about escaping alive?"

"I guess so."

"Would it have done any good for you to have stayed?"

"No."

"Do they scalp us?"

"No."

"Do they kill the wounded?"

"Sometimes."

"I understand that some of our gentlemen collect ears."

"Ears?"

"Ears."

"No."

"You sure?"

"Only some that I know of."

"Why?"

"To have something to show," Appelfinger said, and then Appelfinger said, "Follow me."

"Where are we going?"

"To find the radio."

"Why don't you follow the trail?"

"They booby-trap the trails."

"Do we do that too?"

"No. We ambush."

"Like Indians."

"Yes."

In this part of the jungle it was about four canopy. That is, there were four layers of growth searching for the sun. The top canopy was at about thirty meters and each succeeding layer graduated down until they were crawling under one meter in a tangle of vines. If they had a machete it would have been easier, but not much. If Peter had not been a deserter it might have been easier, but not much, it was so dark down here. Peter came last and followed the noise ahead.

"How do you fight here?" Bethany said.

Appelfinger paused. "We manage."

"Where there's a war there's a way," Bethany said. "But how do you manage—?"

"Yes?"

"How do you manage to get through this stuff? Do you know where you're going?"

"Yes."

"How?"

"Experience."

"But how can you tell direction? It must be as dark for you as it is for me."

"Yes."

"Then how can you tell?"

"I will tell you all the secrets when I find out which side you're on."

"Love."

"I don't know whether I trust love," Appelfinger said.

"Did you see the man who killed Clancy?"

"Yes." Appelfinger turned. "We had maybe seven men left. It was maybe their fourth assault. They had overrun about two-thirds of the perimeter."

"Seven men out of—?"

"One three two."

"One hundred and thirty-two?"

"Yes. Clancy rose like a rock. More like a fallen log that has been hit at one end and it starts up for a half-second in the act of going someplace else, and Clancy hollered, 'Everybody alive make for the bamboo!' "

"That's when you ran?"

"No. I froze. That's when Clancy got hit by one of our own M79s held by a Chinaman."

"How do you know it wasn't Colonel Yvor who killed Clancy?"

"Because Colonel Yvor is on our side."

"Who's on whose side?" Peter said.

"Shut up," Appelfinger said. "I got plenty of problems."

"Yes, you do," Peter said.

"Then let's get our asses out of here and locate the radio," Appelfinger said, and he began to untangle all the tangle that lay ahead because he did not choose to follow the cleared path that had death in it.

Yes, Clancy thought, hearing the movement close, in getting through the jungle in Vietnam there is always a point where you want to lie down and hide and let the war go ahead without you. The war gets on surprisingly well without you as a matter of fact. You reach a point where you believe that the war could get on without anyone. As though it had a momentum of its own, as though the war were sentient and alive, although born of men it now has a life separate, unremitting, without meaning, purposeless, without direction, feckless, willful and mad. And it hurts. And those people out there are crawling into a trap.

19

"**I** would like to try for a pickup once more," Mike said.

"No," Knightbridge said. "We are closed in now." And Knightbridge looked out in the weather. "You said you knew exactly where they were. We have been there twice."

"They moved," Mike said. "I told them to stick and they moved."

"Peter Scott, the deserter, and Bethany, the girl. I guess they don't want to be found. Peter would be shot."

"The army doesn't shoot anybody anymore," Mike said. "Peter is a quiet one. Army simply wants Peter to talk."

"About Clancy?"

"Yes."

"Peter was not on Red Boy."

"That's what we want to talk about," Mike said. "But they moved. I told them I would be back for a pickup but they moved."

"Are they okay?"

"I plinked him. Superficial. He was in a tree. The trees are for the Unfriendlies. I should have told him that."

"The messages we never receive . . ."

"What's that?"

"They moved. If Clancy would move we'd have a better chance at him."

"Yes, it would be good if Clancy would move," Mike said. "Can you get Colonel Yvor on that thing?"

"No. Yvor has broken contact."

"That son of a bitch."

Knightbridge leaned forward on the radio and looked up at Mike. "Did you talk to Madame Dieudonné?"

"No. I talked to her son."

"Idiot."

"Yes," Mike said.

"You should have talked to Madame Dieudonné."

"She is alone," Mike said.

Knightbridge thought about this, staring at the radio. He repeated the word "alone" and then tried the radio again, but there was nothing.

"I will go over to Colonel Yvor's CP and see what I can find out," Mike said.

"You will find Mai Li."

"Is she alone?"

"Mai Li will never be alone," Knightbridge said. "She is not built that way."

"I've got to keep moving," Mike said.

"You better," Knightbridge said. "They are digging a tunnel under this place."

"How do you know?"

"Yvor got a tip."

"Do the VC trust Yvor?"

"It could be that the VC are arrogant. It could be that they don't give a damn whether we know that they are digging a tunnel or not, as long as we don't know where the tunnel is. That way they can drive us crazy."

"Crazy?"

"Yes," Knightbridge said. "It is the latest thing in this war. The new weapon."

"Does it work?"

"Excellently," Knightbridge said running his hands through his hair. "It works beautifully."

"I will stick if I can help."

"No," Knightbridge said looking up at Mike. "You keep moving."

"It's all I can do," Mike said from the tent flap.

196

"Yes," Knightbridge said. "It's all anyone can do now, keep moving." Then he paused and said, "Did you speak to Janine?" But Mike was already gone.

Yes, Knightbridge thought, they always . . . But they never . . . Because they . . . And then he thought—They. That damn word "They" again. I would like to receive that part of Clancy's message that was blurred. Maybe he is still sending the message. The message that will never be picked up. We are all a result of messages that are never received. Who is this man standing here? A Vietnamese. That's right. I sent for him. Why did I send for him? Because I am about to be blown up.

"Ho Chi Minh."

"Yes, sir."

"Why don't you help the boys look for that tunnel?"

"What tunnel?"

"The one the VC are digging under our camp."

"Is that so?"

"Yes."

"How do you know?"

"We got a tip."

"Interesting."

"We thought so."

"Why didn't the VC tell me?" Ho said.

"The VC don't trust you."

"The VC don't trust anybody," Ho Chi Minh said.

"On your way out will you tell Lieutenant Bliss I want to see her?"

"What about?"

"You don't ask the captain what about," Captain Knightbridge said.

"I just did."

"But it's not done in the American Army."

"I'm not in the American Army."

"You're attached."

"Not very," Ho Chi Minh said.

"Go out and help my boys find the tunnel."

"How?"

"We're rodding the area and we've got a ground-listening electronic D.S. in the supply tent."

"What does D.S. mean?"

"I don't know," Captain Knightbridge said.

"Any luck with it?"

"So far we've picked up some jungle gophers burrowing under the mess tent and a couple fornicating in the village."

"Couple?"

"Two people," the captain said, holding up two fingers.

"Very interesting," Ho Chi Minh said slowly, thinking about it.

"Yes."

"Very sensitive."

"Yes," Knightbridge said. "To everything but VC."

"How did Yvor ever get in the army without arms?" Ho said.

"He had them when he came in. There's a regulation about that."

"Interesting."

"They say that he lost one arm in Korea, the other one maybe at Can Tho. Some say he hasn't lost them at all."

"I'm sorry I asked."

"That's all right."

"Care for a drink?" Ho said.

"Help yourself," Knightbridge said.

Ho Chi Minh poured himself a drinking glass full of Knightbridge's Gordon gin. "Looks like water."

"Yes."

"You sure you won't join me?"

"No," Knightbridge said.

"What about Clancy?"

"What about him?"

"What's his secret?"

"We'll find out."

"In the end."

"Yes," Knightbridge said.

Ho Chi Minh set the glass of Gordon's gin on the camp table and studied it. There was a long silence and then Ho Chi Minh said, "We had the same problem at Dien Bien Phu."

"No, you didn't."

"Why so aggressive, Captain?"

"Because you didn't have any problem at Dien Bien Phu. You're just trying to work that battle into this."

"I'm sorry about that," Ho said.

"You're sure the VC didn't tell you where the tunnel is?"

"No." Ho Chi Minh stared at the gin and then at Knightbridge. "They don't tell me anything," he said.

"Sad."

"Yes," he said.

"I'm sorry."

"There's nothing you can do about it," Ho Chi Minh said. "I made my bed and I'll lie in it."

"Interesting."

"Have some."

"Thank you, no," Knightbridge said.

"We generally let the Gordon convoys get through," Ho said.

"What do you prefer?"

"Scotch."

"I've noticed the Scotch convoys haven't been getting through at all here."

They both stared at the glass.

"Trouble?"

"I'm worried about A for Alpha we lost," Knightbridge said.

"It happens."

"Yes."

"Any survivors?"

"Appelfinger."

"Good man?"

"No. Yes."

"I'm also worried about those civilians." Captain Knightbridge picked up the empty glass and examined it. "Tell me about Dien Bien Phu."

"You got the same situation here at Con Ky. Here at Con Ky you've set up a base to interdict our main Laos-Cambodia supply trail."

"It's only a small Search and Rescue base."

"That's what you think."

"You know more about it than General Westmoreland?"

"Generals seem to suffer from a general malaise," Ho said. "Do you mind?"

"Help yourself."

"Gordon's. Gordon of Khartoum?"

"I don't think so. You seem to be quite a student."

"I was at Dien Bien Phu."

"I thought I told you to send in Lieutenant Bliss."

"Nurse Jane?"

"Lieutenant Bliss."

"Same same," Ho said. "And I wasn't just a coolie at Dien Bien Phu, not just an ammunition bearer."

"What were you, Ho?"

Ho measured out a half-glass carefully, exactly. "Wouldn't you like to know?"

"Yes."

"I don't like to talk about it."

"Send in Lieutenant Bliss on your way out."

"Artillery captain," Ho said.

"Where trained?"

"Hanoi."

"What position?"

"F.O."

"Forward Observer."

"Yes," Ho said. "My brain is being ginwashed."

"Captain seems a high rank for a forward observer."

"I speak French. I could mingle with the French so that I was just more than just an ordinary F.O."

"And now you speak English."

"Yes."

"How much do they pay you?"

"Who?"

"The enemy."

"My dear Captain Knightbridge, I have great difficulty remembering who the enemy is."

"Ho?"

"Yes."

"What mistake did the French Army make?"

"Arriving."

"Ho, the Americans are not going to leave."

"Shall I send in Lieutenant Bliss?"

"Yes."

"Before I go," Ho said, "the French were good soldiers. Their general, de Tassigny, was not winning but he was not losing. You do not understand what a great triumph this was, not winning and not losing. So de Tassigny was fired. He was finally replaced by Navarre. When General Navarre stepped off the plane in Saigon he said, "Victory is like a woman. Victory belongs only to those who know how to take her." Everyone knew then that France had lost the war. Dien Bien Phu was only a question of where and what time. Then General Navarre—"

"With an abrupt insight into himself," Knightbridge said.

"Decided to resign," Ho said. "And then with French logic he decided to stay on."

"French logic."

"He would try to understand us," Ho said. "That is the genius of the British. They don't try to understand anyone."

"Get to Dien Bien Phu."

"You will get to Dien Bien Phu soon enough," Ho said. "Shall I send in Lieutenant Bliss?"

"Yes."

"Shall I take the bottle?"

"No."

"You're confusing me."

"That is because I have arrived," Captain Knightbridge said. Captain Knightbridge watched Captain Ho Chi Minh,

Forward Observer, leave, late F.O. of Nguyen Giap's North Vietnamese Army and now observing us, Knightbridge thought. Best to fire him. No, best to keep him close. You can't fire him anyway. He was appointed as our Asia observer. He was appointed by himself probably. Ho appointed Ho. Ho took the bottle. That's all right. What my men can't find sober he may find drunk. The VC tunnel. I wonder if the VC tunnel under us exists. I wonder if this country exists. I wonder if Ho was really at Dien Bien Phu. I guess so. Everyone was there.

"Good morning, Lieutenant Bliss. How are you this fine morning? Isn't it a fine morning to have a tunnel dug under you and be in the Bamboo Bed and set a world record by doing it at five thousand feet and then break that record while the whole world stands agog by doing it at ten thousand feet in the Bamboo Bed?"

"Agog?"

"Yes. The war must have some meaning even if it's an obscenity."

"Why don't you resign your commission?"

"Because we are all dependent on each other. Because the soldier can't resign his commission because he ain't got one. The soldier is stuck here. I will stick." Knightbridge picked up the empty glass. "I would rather be a victim than an executioner. Because the world is being run by the military and you can't leave the world to those sons of bitches. Because I don't know how to do anything else. Because you can't abandon the Bamboo Bed, Search and Rescue. Soon the whole world will need to be rescued. Someone has got to be around to do it. Because I don't know how to do anything else. I said that."

"Yes, you did."

"Why don't you resign your commission, Lieutenant Bliss?"

"Because being a man . . . that is, your being a man . . . Then soon, and it is only a question of time—and soon—before you too will shoot at anything that moves. That's the way men are—afraid. Afraid of anything that moves. And everything you said before is—is—"

"Bullshit?"

"No, not that. Not that word. Not Colonel Yvor's word. But soon—"

"The flower people?"

"Yes. The only ones that admit their fear. Their fear of anything that moves."

"I'll get them on the radio." Knightbridge turned it on.

"They haven't got one."

"If they're so damn sensitive," Knightbridge said, "we should be able to pick them up anyway."

"If they're not already busy killing people," Lieutenant Bliss said. "That's why I don't resign my commission. Everyone is up to it. Even after they've forgotten what the fighting is about both sides will shoot at anything that moves because it moves, and anyplace in the world, and that's why a woman has to be here."

"The Bamboo Bed. Yes," Knightbridge said. "Sit down. You're all wrought up. What do you think of my idea?"

"To do it at ten thousand feet?"

"Yes."

"All right."

"Because it's not killing people," Knightbridge said. "Would you believe I didn't have any of this?" Knightbridge said, holding up the empty glass.

"Yes. Because you don't need it to get your ideas."

"What are we going to do about those poor bastards down in the jungle? I can't even get Yvor on this thing." Knightbridge touched the radio. Then Knightbridge said, "Did you hear that?"

"No."

"The radio. It sounded like Appelfinger."

20

P<small>ETER</small> and Bethany, Appelfinger and
God had finally got into the clearing in the forest alongside
the Song Phong where old Appelfinger had chucked in the
radio transmitter. God was with them, Bethany knew, because they had gotten through the terrible jungle without
incident.

"This will be good for your book, Peter."

"What book?"

"Your book 'God Is Missing.' "

"I don't have an ending."

"You will, Peter."

"Yes," Peter said. "The ending will come soon."

"I don't like to hear you talk like that, Peter."

They had emerged into a small clearing on the Song
Phong River where all the trees bent over, stared into the
darkling jungle stream with serious intent, sinister and sad.
The abrupt butterflies darted in the jungle fog as though
bringing capricious telegrams announcing the birth of millions more. The epiphytes and parasites grabbed the trees
for dear life and way up huge orchids bloomed in secret
splendor. Down below on the fog-strewn jungle floor Appelfinger fished the radio out of the Phong and set up quick
shop.

"I don't like to hear you talk like that, Peter," Bethany
repeated. "Because you had such a good start on the book."

"You mean the part where Clancy missed a man and said,
'Who is missing?' "

"Then you said—"

"God is missing, Captain."

"And he said—"

"You've blown your mind."

"And you said—"

"Look around, Captain."

There was a great noise here in this jungle now.

"What's that?"

"An elephant," Appelfinger said.

"What are you going to do about it?"

"There's not much anyone can do about an elephant."

"Why don't you shoot the elephant?" Bethany whispered to Appelfinger.

"Because," Appelfinger said, "I don't believe in shooting animals."

"You shoot people."

"That's different," Appelfinger said.

"Listen to Appelfinger," Peter said. "He's quite a philosopher if you pay attention."

The elephant stood staring at them, at the far end of the clearing in the forest. It might be an elephant that had escaped from the opium smugglers from Burma who got in a fire fight with the Chinese in Laos. The Chinese in Laos really live in Thailand. They are the part of the Chinese army that was defeated in China and did not escape to Formosa. They make their living as bandits. This business takes them all over Southeast Asia. But the elephant at the edge of the forest staring at them with eyes whose reports he did not believe and ears whose reports he would not listen to did not have any marks of captivity. It was a wild elephant. It had never seen people before close up. The elephant had heard people fighting and seen people running, but it had never got close enough to really see them. People looked like strange fish to the elephant, four legs, two eyes and two ears and one head just like elephants except they stand on their rear legs and use their front legs for fighting in an upright position. People appear to fight all the time. People fight each other.

People are born with a gun. The elephant had never seen a human being without a gun. People fart through their guns and their farting kills other people at whom their farting is directed.

This elephant standing here had been to every country in this part of Southeast Asia: Vietnam, where he was standing now, Cambodia, Laos, which were close, and Burma, India and China, which were not far. This elephant did not know one country from another country. That does not mean that the figment of United States of America does not exist. It only means that in Asia America is a figment in men's minds. This elephant ate figments every morning. Figments are delicious. Figments should not be seen or heard but eaten. But to kill other people over figments that don't exist was to this elephant the height of something or other. Another thing that was the height of something or other to this elephant was something he could make neither hide nor hair of. The person that he could not make hide nor hair of was Captain Clancy. He had seen the Iron Man dying all by himself and wondered why he did not get in touch . . . but I am anthropomorphizing. And a lot of other dirty things, Appelfinger thought.

Appelfinger had the radio telephone almost all apart and Appelfinger did not have an instruction book to put it back together again. Maybe that's what bothers the elephant, Appelfinger thought. He sees me hopelessly entangled in a mantrap, hopelessly lost and wandering about in the last part, the bad part, of the twentieth century. What was the good part? The good part was the early part of the twentieth century, when Teddy Roosevelt charged straight up San Juan Hill. Since then it's all been downhill. But the elephant doesn't know this. The elephant doesn't know we're all crazy. The elephant believes this to be the normal lot of man. He believes that I enjoy taking this radio telephone apart without an instruction book and not being able to put it together again. But I will fool him because I have that within which passeth show, I will hoist him on his own petard. Which is quite a trick with an elephant, being as heavy as they are.

As heavy as they like to think themselves to be. I will get it back in the order in which it was because I will, I will, I will. Tom the Bootblack. Phil the Fiddler. Paddle Your Own Canoe. Sink or Swim. Do or Die. Survive or Perish. From Canal Boy to President. I will I will I will.

"We know you will, Private Appelfinger," Bethany said. "I never thought for a second that you would not get the radio telephone back in the order it was."

"Thanks."

"Not at all. Even Peter who is a deserter never doubted that you would succeed."

"What has my being a deserter got to do with it?" Peter said.

"I was thinking," Appelfinger said, "that the elephant is still here."

"Why doesn't he go about his business?"

"His business is us."

"Do they eat people?"

"They eat figments," Appelfinger said.

"Do they eat people?"

"No, they don't like people."

"Why?"

"Because people fart lethally."

"Is that what you have been thinking about?"

"Yes."

"Why haven't you been thinking about how to put that thing back together again the way it was?"

"Everybody's got a different idea about the way it was," Appelfinger said. "It's like history. Like Clancy said, history is a record of people committing suicide. I personally believe history to be a religion. I have evidence."

"Don't interrupt your work to give the evidence now."

"Yes," Appelfinger said, tendering transistors tenderly from leaf to leaf. "It's like those Chinamen who work on the Bamboo Bed. They never saw a helicopter until the day before yesterday and yet, and yet, this is the interesting part." Appelfinger placed a rheostat on a frond for emphasis because that's where the rheostat belonged in Appelfinger's order of things. "The interesting part is the Bamboo Bed works like a dream. If that's not religion then I wouldn't know religion if I saw it." Appelfinger placed his hand above his face like a visor to demonstrate. "Like seeing that elephant. Jesus, he's some elephant."

"Is he still there?"

"He sure is. I want to get back to my theory."

"Hurry. Hurry with the radio," Bethany said.

"If no one minds I'd like to get back to the elephant," Peter said. "What do you see?"

"Hurry," Bethany said.

"I mean—and now I'm addressing my question to Appelfinger—do you see this as a sign that the enemy who knocked you off, the rest of your company off, a sign that the enemy still are in the area? The VC use elephants, don't they?"

"No."

"Don't just say no."

"No, sir."

"I mean the newspapers say the Vietcong use them for pack animals."

"That's what the newspapers say. The newspapers are figments. Now just watch me put this bugass back together again."

"Hurry. Hurry. Someone is dying," Bethany said.

The one-eared Chinaman stood against the rubber tree watching the elephant. His name was Cho Lin. His home was Peking. His regiment was the 319th. Like the Americans, it was not Cho Lin's country either. Like Captain Knightbridge, Captain Cho Lin was a professional soldier. While Captain Knightbridge was going to West Point, Captain Cho Lin went to the staff college in Leningrad. While Clancy, Knightbridge and Yvor were fighting in Korea, so was Cho Lin, on the other side. The thing that surprised Cho Lin was that the Americans would come so far, all the way around the world, so that he could get a shot at them. Cho Lin appreciated the fact that all he had to do was step out his back door and there were the Americans. Then all he had to do was blast away. It was nice for the Americans to come all this way for the recreation of the Chinese. Every China person that's born alive, and there are close to a billion of them, is brought up to hate Americans. They all hate together. There is a togetherness in their hatred. Hate! Hate! Hate! Now all together, Hate! Hate! Hate! You back there with a fly on your head in the third row, what's your name?

"Cho Lin."

"Why aren't you hating today?"

"Not feeling well."

"I want all of you," the Chinese cadre instructor said, "to hate one individual. To hate everyone is to hate no one."

After the instructor let that truth sink in he said, "Now who do you hate?"

"John D. Rockefeller."

"You?"

"Henry Ford."

"You?"

"J. P. Morgan."

"You?"

"Fu Manchu."

"Who's Fu Manchu?"

"The only American I know."

China is a big country. China is the biggest country in the world outside Russia. We'll soon fix that, the cadre instructor said. The instructor fixed many other things too that Chairman Mao thought needed fixing, and soon little Cho Lin was in the Red Guards. The nice thing about the Red Guards was that you could go around breaking things all day and no one would stop you. The middle class were the enemy. One fine day they looked all over Canton for some middle class, but they couldn't find any. The middle class are more sought after in China than the Communists in the United States. Cho Lin heard of a Communist who lived not far from Syracuse, New York.

"But we are not interested in Communists in America,"

the instructor said. "We're interested in finding middle class in China."

"Let's just go out and beat up on anybody," Cho Lin said. "Else what are Red Guards for?"

But no matter how much fun you have there comes a time when you have to pay the piper. Cho Lin was sent off to Vietnam.

"Why?"

"Because the Red Guard is smashing too much stuff in China. Go to Vietnam and smash things."

"But the Chinese are not supposed to be in Vietnam."

"We're not supposed to be in India either."

So Cho Lin went to fight in Vietnam because the Chinese are not supposed to be in India. If you think the logic is far-fetched then you have never read the little red book. The red book is the Chinese Bible. No Bibles are supposed to make sense.

The first thing that Cho Lin did when he got to Vietnam was to try to kill Clancy. Captain William D. (Iron Man) Clancy, A for Alpha Company, Second of the Eighth. It had not been easy. Clancy's outfit had fought terrifically. Now Cho Lin was following an elephant out of curiosity. They do not have elephants in China. Anyway Cho Lin had never seen one. The North Vietnamese Army does not use them. Cho Lin was attached to the NVA to make things legal. Clancy was saving the world from communism. Cho Lin was saving the world from capitalism. Clancy's mother saved string, his father, old newspapers. Cho Lin's mother and father saved cats that fell in the Wai Pe Canal.

Everyone saves something or someone because they are attached to something, Cho Lin said to himself stupidly as he watched the elephant. My, aren't they strange beasts? Cho Lin thought, looking at the Americans. I must get the rest of my outfit and kill them.

"I thought I saw someone standing at the edge of the clearing," Peter said.

"Felt someone," Bethany said.

"Yes, I felt there was someone there watching us," Peter said.

"The elephant is still there," Appelfinger said. "It wasn't the elephant?"

"No, it wasn't the elephant," Peter said.

"Captain Clancy?"

"No."

"You sure it wasn't Clancy?"

"It was an Oriental," Peter said. "I could fee—I could smell him," Peter said.

"Peter is very large at extrasensory perception," Bethany said.

"No, it was smell," Peter said.

"What was the man doing here?"

"Figuring out a way to kill us."

"Why else would a man be watching us?" Appelfinger said.

"The world has come a long way," Bethany said, "when the only reason a man looks at you for is to figure out a way to kill you."

"A long way," Appelfinger agreed.

"How long will it take to dry out the radio?"

"We'll see," Appelfinger said, looking around at all the plants and trees he had festooned with chrome pieces from the radio so that it looked like Christmastime, all the trees bedecked, bejeweled. "We'll see." Appelfinger placed his hands on his hips and stared around at his work. "I hope it's all dry and back together again before that man gets back with his buddies."

"Or before Colonel Yvor gets here. And what about your Captain Clancy?"

"Yes," Appelfinger said.

"Why are they firing now?"

"Because they are counter-evolutionary."

"What's that mean?"

"Because we exist," Appelfinger said

21

APPELFINGER was firing back at the Unfriendlies to protect his drying radio that was draped on the trees. To protect his radio must be it, he told himself, because he had long since died with Alpha Company. All the rest of his life would be not life. All of his life now must be dedicated to a cause. What cause? Finding Clancy. After the battle he had left Clancy propped up against a tree and he had gone to the river to get water for Clancy. When he got back with the water Clancy was gone. The Gooks must have got Clancy. The Gooks giveth and the Gooks taketh away. But why didn't the Unfriendlies booby-trap Clancy's body and get me too when I went back to get Clancy? They could have killed him silently with a knife and propped his body up so that he looked real against the tree, then they booby-trap the body and when I touch Clancy we both blow up in all the colors of the American flag. That's an old trick of the Unfriendlies. It usually works beautifully. Maybe Victor Charlie is losing his touch. Maybe Charlie doesn't know his way around any more.

Appelfinger gave Charlie a short burst in the direction of the jungle. Maybe the enemy had other uses for Captain Clancy. Maybe Clancy just got up and walked away. Maybe Clancy by now walked right out of the war. People will do that. But where do they go? The jungle is no place to be alone in. Vietnam is no place to be alone in. You can spot a white guy a mile away. Maybe Clancy will join the Gooks. Clancy would be the last man to join the Gooks. Clancy was my buddy. I would never have a buddy that would join the Gooks. Why not? What have the Gooks ever done to you that you would not join them? Plenty. If you're a revolutionist like you claim to be, it seems to me you would join the Gooks. I said I was an evolutionist, wise guy, Appelfinger told himself. Evolutionist. Well, it still seems to me if you were an evolutionist you would join the Gooks even more. Why? Because evolutionists believe in everybody being happy so that the race can survive. Not necessarily, Appelfinger said, and he gave the Unfriendlies another short burst. Evolutionists believe that Gooks are just as good as anybody else. You are no better than a Gook, Appelfinger. That's very true, Appelfinger said. I never said I was better than a Gook. Then why are you shooting at the Gooks, Appelfinger? Because they shot at me. I am no better than a Gook but a Gook is no better than me. Remember that, if you ever talk to yourself again. A Gook is no better than an Appelfinger. Evolution can be carried too far. Evolution must have a stop. If I thought when I got into evolution it would make a Gook better than an Appelfinger I would never have gotten into evolution.

Appelfinger fired another short burst, this time against evolution. But now that you've been an evolutionist for so long you'll find there is no other way to turn. There are many paths to heaven even if there is no heaven. That's true. And on the path you have chosen I do not believe there is any turning back. That is true. And given this truth, who is going to start evolution? Is everyone going to arrive at evolution at once and say, all at the same time, I'm not going to kill any more Gooks? I guess not. Then why don't you stop killing Gooks? It's their country. I know it's their country. Then why don't you stop killing Gooks? Because . . . because . . . Appelfinger looked over at the black-green hill of jungle. Because you don't understand evolution. Maybe I understand it too well. No, you don't, Appelfinger said. In my kind of evolution there is nothing against killing Gooks, right? No, there is only one true evolution, there cannot be different kinds of evolution to suit each person. You either have evolution and recognize the truth or you have no evolution at all. I believe that, Appelfinger said. Then stop shooting Gooks. Let me think about that, Appelfinger said.

"Why do you talk to yourself?" Peter said.

Appelfinger looked at the deserter and wondered where he came from. Then he saw the girl and wondered where she came from. Then he remembered and said, "Please don't interrupt me."

Where was I when—where were we? I had just promised to stop shooting at the Gooks. No, I hadn't promised to stop shooting at the Gooks at all. Yes, you did. I said I would think about it, Appelfinger said. Then think about this. Where is the moral center you always talk about? How can you have evolution without a moral center? How can you have anything without it? You can't, Appelfinger said. You always said evolution was good. You always said that if you did not interfere with evolution, evolution would do its best to see that the human species survives. It always has. Yes, it always has, Appelfinger agreed. You always said that if it wasn't for evolution we wouldn't be here. Yes, I always said that, Appelfinger said. Then get off your ass, Appelfinger said, and stop shooting Gooks. Go find Clancy. Clancy is dead. You don't know that. He was almost dead when I propped him against the tree. Maybe you went back to the wrong tree after you went and got the water. No, it was the same tree. Maybe he wandered off. No, the Unfriendlies got Clancy. Maybe you don't want to find Clancy. Maybe I don't. Then there was more in your relationship with Clancy than met the eye, more than met your own eye. Maybe there was, Appelfinger. If Clancy was a son of a bitch, then that's okay, but he was my son of a bitch. Okay, but let me alone now. I'm surrounded by Unfriendlies.

"You must feel threatened," Peter said, "talking to yourself like that."

"I sure am threatened," Appelfinger said. "I am threatened by a whole Gook army." Appelfinger gave them a burst.

"Do you know what your problem is?" Peter said.

"Yes. The Gook Army."

"No," Peter said, "they're not shooting at you now."

"Then they're sneaking up on us."

"You feel threatened, surrounded and cut off?"

"Yes."

"Paranoid," Peter said.

"For Christ's sake, I'm a soldier. We're in Vietnam getting the shit kicked out of us."

"That's right, Peter," Bethany said.

"I think there's something more," Peter said.

"No, a war is enough, Peter," Bethany said. "War would account for his behavior certainly, Peter."

"You're taking his side."

"Everyone's shooting at him, Peter."

Peter strummed his guitar.

"Will you please stop playing that God damn thing in the time of war?" Appelfinger said.

"It's always the time of war," Peter said. "If I waited till it wasn't the time of war I would never play."

"But not in the middle of a fire fight. Please."

"But not in the middle of a fire fight. He's right, Peter. Please."

"Then the song would never be heard in the land."

"That just suits me shitting fine," Appelfinger said. "Is everybody else happy?" And then Appelfinger grabbed himself so that he would not grab the deserter and tear him apart.

Doesn't the idiot realize the Unfriendlies would as soon kill him as look at him? He is one of those people who march in a peace march back home that you read about in the *Stars and Stripes,* a person that does not exist, a person that was dreamed up to get us excited about the war and kill more Gooks, a person that is so unpatriotic that it will take maybe a hundred years and fifty books to prove that he was right, a person that doesn't believe in anything, not even evolution. "Do you believe in evolution?"

"I believe you did something wrong with Clancy."

Fucking Jesus to Betsy, Appelfinger thought, I pick these people up out of the jungle, try to give them another chance in life, and the first chance they get they screw me. "What do you mean, done something with Clancy? How do you know I did anything with Clancy?"

"Because you talked in your fight. Between bursts at the Unfriendlies you talked."

"Well, I didn't say I did anything wrong with Clancy."

"You left him all alone."

"But I was going back."

"But did you?"

"I went back to a mahogany tree with mahogany blood."

"Don't move now," Bethany said in a different tone, "but I think I see an Unfriendly."

"Where?"

"On top of that banyan tree." Bethany pointed. "Can't you see him, Peter? Sense him, I mean?"

"I feel something inimical," Peter said.

"I spot the bastard," Appelfinger said and he raised his automatic rifle, but he only fired off one single alone shot that echoed big and sudden in the green jungle of the Vietnam highlands, and out of the top of the tallest tree there came down a body as though it had been thrown down for an offering. Appelfinger set the gun back on automatic fire. "What were you saying?" Appelfinger said.

"You mean you can kill a person and go right back to normal again?" Bethany said.

"It makes me feel good," Appelfinger said. "If I go a whole day without killing nobody I can't sleep at night."

"Your conscience bothers you?"

"I just don't feel right," Appelfinger said. "I remember I went a whole week once without killing nobody. I was ready for the psycho ward. It's the same with all the guys."

"What are you afraid of?" Peter said.

"People like you. Peacemakers. Draft card burners. Deserters."

"Why?"

"Because you make us feel like criminals."

"Why don't you kill us then? Why do you just kill the Unfriendlies?"

"Because you know very well you can't kill the Friendlies. That way you wouldn't have a war, you'd just have a lot of chaos. If you got a war you got to have rules. You got to have Friendlies and Unfriendlies, the white guys and the Gooks. They shoot at every white guy they see, we shoot at all the Gooks. I am ready to go home the day after tomorrow."

"Why not today?"

"I've got things to do. When they start a war they can't stop it any time they want."

"You mean you got to get revenge because they wiped out your outfit?"

"Maybe."

"You get to like it over here?"

"Maybe."

"After all this killing it will seem awful dull back home."

"Maybe."

"What did you do with Clancy? And before that?"

"I'm not going to answer that."

"Peter is on your side," Bethany said. "Peter is trying to stop the war."

"People like you never do any good for your own side," Appelfinger said.

"Peter is middle class. What more do you want?" Bethany said. "Peter's father is vice-president of something. He's probably vice-president of something that makes napalm. How middle class can you get? How American do you want Peter to be?"

"Just don't mention Clancy no more," Appelfinger said.

Peter strummed the guitar. An enemy shot went off and

217

a bullet went through the fronds above them with a zip noise.

"Go ahead, play," Appelfinger said. "You be the bait. I'll pick up the sniper."

"I never thought when I began this trip," Peter said, "that I would be the bait to pick up the sniper."

"Play something, Peter."

Peter strummed.

"Play a protest song, Peter."

Peter strummed.

"Play 'This Land Was Made for You and Me.' "

"It wasn't," Peter said.

"Play 'Where Have All the Young Girls Gone?' "

"Gone with young men every one," Peter said.

"Where have all the young men gone?"

"Gone for soldiers every one."

"Where have all the soldiers gone?"

"Gone to graveyards every one."

"Play something cheerful," Appelfinger said.

"Is the radio dry yet?"

"No," Appelfinger said, staring up at the bejeweled forest. "You can't hurry a war."

Now a bullet clipped in and took out the top ornament that was shaped and glittered like a star.

"They have arrived."

22

COLONEL Yvor and Billy Joe had hurriedly landed their two-man H13 bubble chopper downstream near the Bon Hiem River. They had hurriedly blasted two fake LZs which had slowly fooled no one. But that's the way it is in war, you do the things you have to do and hope to survive. If you don't do anything to fool the enemy and you get it, then you tell yourself, What a damn fool I was not to try it. Try what? Like screwing the general's daughter to get a promotion. Like blasting three fake LZs before the real one.

When they got on the ground Billy Joe took the string out of Colonel Yvor's mouth and asked him what directions we want to go and Colonel Yvor looked at the ground and said, "What are those holes?"

"Elephant tracks."

"Was Clancy interested in elephants?"

"I don't know, sir."

"Can you start this chopper again?"

"I think so."

"If you can't, VC kill you for sure."

"If we could catch the enemy using elephants, sir, it could account for a lot."

"Such as, Billy Joe?"

"Such as the reason why we're winning." Billy Joe gestured with Colonel Yvor's cigar. "Because they got elephants and we got tanks."

"Can a tank get around in the jungle, Billy?"

"No, sir." Billy thought. "But we got choppers."

"Can you see anything in the jungle from upstairs, Billy?"

"No, sir." Billy thought. "But we got—we got the will to win."

"Sure you have, Billy," Colonel Yvor said. "Sure you have. But we need some kind of equipment that works in this country. Let's find ourselves an elephant."

"Right now, sir?"

"Put the cigar back in my mouth, Billy, and I'll have a think."

And this is what Colonel Yvor thought. Elephants are out. Elephants are out because that would mean we had lost the war. That would mean we had lost faith in the future. America is nothing without faith in the twenty-first century. It is better to lose the war than to lose faith. Elephants are all right in their place, but the elephant's place is about fourth century, about fourth century B.C. Better to lose the war than to admit the future was a mistake. The enemy has not got one single solitary airplane down here, not one small tank yet. What has the enemy got? Balls? We got those too. Elephants? Not much help. Ho Chi Minh? We got a Ho Chi Minh working for Search and Rescue. Communism? We got Karl Marx. In our great and considered desperation we have even invented people. Love? We have screwed everyone in Vietnam. Love? We love each other. Love? Don't keep harping on that. They go around killing everybody, don't they? They just killed Alpha Company, didn't they?

"Yes. sir. They sure did that very thing."

"That boy running out on Alpha didn't help."

"No, sir, that sure did not help."

"I did not kill Alpha, Billy Joe. I had to get those Chinks out of the hills."

"Positive."

"The American people did not kill Alpha."

"Negative."

"You know, Billy Joe, after a war is all over writers sit down and come up with the God damnedest things."

"It makes me laugh."

"Blame innocent people."

"It makes me laugh."

"Who killed Alpha?"

"No one did, sir."

"No one?"

"Alpha was an accident."

"Accident?"

"Alpha was bait, sir. A worm."

"A worm?"

"Yes, sir. You don't feel sorry every time you have to kill a piece of bait, do you?"

"Yes."

"Sir, I've been helped an awful lot by Norman Vincent Peale."

"You have, Billy?"

"Yes, sir. He found out that you can ventilate, lump, then drop."

"He did?"

"Yes, sir. He found out that you first ventilate all the problems out of your system, then you put them in a lump on the table, look at them until you see they're not important, and then while they're still in a lump you drop them."

"But first you must be stupid."

"Kind of."

"That lets me out."

"You have pride, sir."

"Positive."

Billy Joe looked around the bubble chopper as though searching for some way to let pride out, but he could find no opening except where the machine gun was.

"Sir, did you ever pray?"

"Negative."

"Sir, you don't have a Man Upstairs?"

"Negative."

"Boy, sir, you sure are in trouble, sir."

"Positive. Billy Joe, what are we doing here?"

"Waiting for you to finish thinking, sir."

"I've finished."

"All done?"

"Except this. Captain Knightbridge is getting away with murder, Billy. Captain Knightbridge is getting away with murder because he hasn't murdered anyone. He's hiding behind Search and Rescue. He thinks he's rescuing the world. Well, God damn it, when they finish that tunnel under his camp and blow him to hell he'll have another think coming."

"He sure will, sir."

"He killed Alpha as much as anybody."

"He sure did, sir."

"Why do you say that?"

"Because you did, sir."

"Good enough, Billy. You're a good boy."

But Colonel Yvor did not think Billy Joe was very bright. Billy Joe was a typical collector of ears. Why do some American soldiers collect ears? Because they are scared. Because it is difficult to take a scalp. Because they are punishing the people who sent them here. They are saying, Lookit, Mother, look what you did to me. They want to make it impossible to turn back. They collect ears because they are brought up in a religion that teaches—Colonel Yvor made his silent supersonic whine and Billy Joe removed the cigar.

"Pride but not decency."

"Yes, sir."

"Faith but not confidence."

"Yes, sir."

"Self-love rather than self-respect."

"What's that, sir?"

"I was trying to figure out why you collect VC ears, Billy."

"But I don't, sir."

"Good boy, Billy. Let's follow the elephant tracks."

"Sir, don't you believe in collecting ears?"

"No."

"Sir, didn't it make you bitter to lose your dependages?"

"Dependages?"

"Arms."

"No."

"Sir, why do you fight the war?"

"It's all I know, Billy. What would I do on the outside?"

"Not much."

"Let's follow those elephant tracks, Billy."

"The way I see it," Bethany said, "I don't see much to Search and Rescue if they can't search and rescue anybody." Bethany thought about this, watching Appelfinger dry the radio. "Peter and I have been lost for a week now," Bethany said. "I wish that elephant would stop staring at us."

"We are not lost," Peter said, "if an elephant knows where we are."

"No, an elephant is not important," Bethany said. "But your Colonel Yvor knows where we are," Bethany said to Appelfinger.

"He knows where we are," Appelfinger said, "but he doesn't know who we are. That's why Colonel Yvor was shooting at us. That's the whole confusion of this war. Nobody knows who anybody else is. Your God is missing and no one cares. "Yes," Appelfinger said sadly. Appelfinger leaned forward on his rifle and looked around at the clearing in the jungle. It looked like the place where death would come. It looked like the place where his company, A for Alpha, the Second of the Eighth, commanded by Captain W. B. Clancy, got it. The same silent, awesome clearing in the jungle where death always comes. The bad part about all clearing in the jungle in Vietnam is that you got no observation outside the perimeter. The clearing itself has always got a rubble of down jungle that keeps you from getting a clear field of fire, then the elephant grass starts and then the bamboo, then the forest. So that the enemy has always got a perfect cover out of which to kill you, a clearing in the jungle anyplace in Asia is a place where you wait for death to come.

"I'd like to clear ass out of this exposed fucker," Appelfinger said reverting to army language, "but . . ."

"But your radio is drying," Peter said.

"Yes. About this extrasensory perception you got—" Appelfinger looked out over the flash hider of his Chinese gun and into the utter green darkness of the fantastic forest. "Can you—tell me, can you talk to the dead? To Clancy?"

"Yes."

"What does he say?"

"Nothing," Peter said.

"Nothing?"

"That is a quality of the dead," Peter said.

"Clancy will talk."

"Don't hold your breath," Peter said.

"Clancy will talk."

"Only through you now," Peter said.

Appelfinger felt it would be no longer fruitful to pursue this subject with Flower Power. Extrasensory perception may exist all right, Appelfinger thought, but Peter does not. His friend Bethany almost exists but not quite. Not quite, because I do not want to screw her. A man out here in the jungle for ten months and you see a girl and don't want to screw her, something is wrong. I guess the bad part is it's an American girl. Somehow you don't want to have anything to do with them. Appelfinger stared out into the jungle trying to forget all the bad parts. When a man doesn't have too much longer to live, when he is being hit by the Friendlies as well as the enemies, he better try to think about the good part.

"Do you believe," Appelfinger said over his Chinese flash cover, "do you believe that to be understood is to be found out?"

"I believe you must have been a tremendous asset to our infantry company in a fire fight," Peter said.

"I was only the radio man," Appelfinger said. "I was your contact with the outside world."

"Gave you a chance to think?"

"Yes," Appelfinger said. "And remember, to be a good infantryman you not only have got to be able to shoot the enemy but you got to learn how to shoot the shit too."

"Then Peter would not be a good soldier," Bethany said. "Peter must think a long time before Peter says anything. I'm glad Peter deserted."

"Do you know what else I believe in?"

"I said I'm glad Peter deserted."

"I believe that if everyone, every soldier—" Appelfinger pointed his Chinese gun at the jungle. "Let me say first that every soldier hears death ticking off inside him."

"Yes."

"Not only every soldier," Appelfinger said, "but every male human being. Not every female human being. They don't hear death ticking off inside them because they feel life ticking inside them. Like Nurse Jane. A female would rather fuck than fight."

"True," Peter said.

"Very crude," Bethany said.

"Yes," Appelfinger said. "Women are very crude."

"I mean you're crude, Appelfinger."

"Yes, but I'm not crude enough," Appelfinger said. "You see, women have found a way out because of this life ticking off inside them. But males, no. Screwing is not enough for a man. It helps, yes. Things would be much worse without it, but just screwing for a man is a poor substitute for the ecstasy of war. That's the point I want to make about evolution. When man was primitive as hell maybe two, three million years ago, he could do as he God damn pleased just like the apes. Now it's different, but man is not different, so he kills people because that's the only thing society permits him to do outside of being a mature person. I recommend dirty sex. I recommend that because it's more ecstasy than killing people or being a mature person. We got to find a substitute for war."

"But, Dr. Appelfinger—"

"But nonsense," Appelfinger said. "Have you got a substitute for war? Have you got something that will stop that clock of death?"

"Yes."

"I know you have," Appelfinger said. "But everyone cannot be a vagabond, smoke hashish, dress up like Indians, become voluntary criminals."

"Okay," Peter said. "But we are not sitting in a café. We are in the middle of a jungle about to be killed by both sides. I suggest we do something about it."

"We don't want peace. It's too fucking dull and it won't stop the ticking. Maybe nothing will except the Bamboo Bed."

"The Bamboo Bed?"

"Yes, the Bamboo Bed. No one knows what goes on inside that Bamboo Bed. No one can fix it except Karl Marx, Ho Chi Minh and the Naked Chinaman, and even they don't know how. It's a religion maybe. And it only works by performing some rite, and when Tarzan and Jane are naked and doing acrobatics inside the Bamboo Bed at ten thousand feet you can imagine what it's like."

"Sounds exciting."

"That's what I mean," Appelfinger said.

"But it could crash."

"That's what I mean," Appelfinger said. "It's a good substitute for war. Then instead of having everybody in Search and Destroy you'd have everybody in Search and Rescue."

"It's too simplistic."

"Then you don't know the Bamboo Bed," Appelfinger said.

"That was a shot. Tell us what to do."

"Get your ass down," Appelfinger said.

The elephant was amazed because what the elephant observed was that three groups of people were firing at each other. There are only supposed to be two. How can you have a war when there are three? If you have a winner and a loser what happens to the third party? Soon there were four.

Most people who have fought in Vietnam will tell you

that most contacts are made by small groups and that most contacts are accidental. God damn true, the elephant thought, but this is the first time I've ever seen four groups of them going at it hammer and tongs.

The way the accident happened was this, and like all accidents there was delinquency involved. They were all in Vietnam, they were all curious. None of them ran from a fight, which means there were no South Vietnamese troops involved in this one. When I say they were all curious I mean they were all scared. Not only scared that they would miss something, but scared too that something would happen that would finally affect them.

Cho Lin brought a squad of NVA down to hit Appelfinger's outfit (this is the second time in the last few days he had hit Appelfinger's outfit. This time he would try to polish off the remains). While Cho Lin was hitting Appelfinger, up come Colonel Yvor and Billy Joe and tear into all of them.

"Go back and get the M60 out of the bubble chopper, Billy Joe, and don't forget my button and string."

Billy Joe ran back and got the M60 machine gun off the side of the chopper, but in the confusion of being shot at he forgot Colonel Yvor's button and string.

"God damn, Billy Joe, go back and get my button and string."

So while Billy Joe ran back through the fire fight to get the button and string, Colonel Yvor just sat there and watched the elephant. "That elephant must think we're a bunch of fucking fools," Colonel Yvor said.

23

Come enter here, all you white man, black man, yellow man, thief. Clancy's bright blood beckoned to everyone. Come enter the forest of tropic and dark thoughts, of purple and black dreams, of innocence and ruthless silence. The forest, a high, splendid green sag, closing around all in deadly gay noose, dappled, ubiquitous and hushed. A friend of all the Unfriendlies.

The jungle, capricious, indifferent, the candescent forest stood rank on rank and rose tier on tier abruptly now, ominous, concerned. The low fronds closed webbed platoons around all, the trees in green army strength formed a camouflaged terror of no retreat, the vines tangled out to catch any man that moved, fell, stumbled or died in the green trap.

"Here we are, Billy Joe, going along as nice as you please, following a phony elephant."

"A phony elephant, sir?"

"A phony elephant in a fake war, Billy."

"I tell you, sir, the dead are real."

"Only the dead are real, Billy. Imagine ringing in a fake elephant on us."

"Imagine that, sir."

"What would your Norman Vincent Peale think of that, Billy?"

"He would try to think of something positive."

"Something positive about an elephant?"

"Yes, sir."

"Tell me something positive about the war."

"If God be for us who can be against us?"

"Get down," Yvor said, laying an impalpable hand on Billy. "I heard something on our left flank. We are walking straight into an ambush. We will stay here in the bamboo and make them commit themselves. Now what were you saying, Billy?"

"If God be with us who can be against us?"

Colonel Yvor put his mouth right next to Billy's ear and whispered, "Bullshit."

"I can do all things through Christ who strengtheneth me."

"Knock it off, Billy," Yvor whispered. "Listen. The whole world is following a fake elephant, Billy. The whole world is walking into an ambush. The ambush is right here—Vietnam. Everybody says they're looking for Clancy. You believe that, Billy? Don't. Nobody gives a good God damn about Clancy."

"Yes, sir."

"Clancy took his chance in the jungle just like anybody else."

"Yes, sir."

"That's the way the bullet bounces, Billy."

"Yes, sir."

"I want to get back to Mai Li just as much as Clancy wanted to get back to his Madame Dieudonné, back to his God damn books. Everybody says Clancy and Christ."

"Do they?"

"Yes."

"I never heard anybody."

"Sure they do, Billy. Clancy and Christ. It sounds like a law firm, doesn't it?"

"Yes, sir."

"Every war's got one, Billy. They're trying to pin this one on me."

"I hadn't heard."

"You will, Billy. You will. Do you hear them now?"

"It sounds like they're setting up an ambush."

"They want to suck in all of us they can, Billy. They used

what was left of Clancy's outfit for bait—Appelfinger. Appelfinger picked up two civilians, then us, then Search and Rescue. Now they are going to eat us all up including the bait."

"What was used to bait them out of the hills will be used to bait us out of the towns."

"Yes, you are beginning to catch on, Billy."

"I never did get to know Clancy too well."

"I did, Billy."

"He was a swell guy."

"He was an agitator, Billy."

"Yes, I hear Captain Clancy screwed up a terrible storm with Madame Dieudonné—the ear thing—and he read books too. Well, I read Norman Vincent Peale."

"The army understands that, Billy."

"I reckon it's swell of you to take me into your confidence, sir. When you could be talking to generals."

"Generals talk bullshit."

"That's good to know."

"I found that knowledge valuable, Billy. It saved my life many times."

"How do we get out of here, sir?"

"Maybe we don't, Billy. Why don't you take and put a cigar in my mouth, Billy, so I can think?"

Billy Joe fished into Colonel Yvor's rucksack, which contained a box of thirty Marsh Wheelings and fifty Optimos. That was all the rucksack contained. That was all the supplies Colonel Yvor carried.

"Marsh Wheeling or Optimo, sir?"

"Optimo."

Billy popped an Optimo in Colonel Yvor's mouth and watched for the results.

Colonel Yvor looked around at the jungle canopy. They were in a second-growth section of the forest. A place that had been cleared for an LZ maybe a year ago. The jungle was coming back to its climax phase. It grew while you watched. The jungle growing back was like the VC. Like

Victor Charlie replacing itself after it had been wiped out. The thing to do would be to find a different code name for the VC than Victor Charlie. The name Victor Charlie was bad for the morale. The fact that the VC come back as fast as the jungle was bad for the morale too. There was no way to stop the jungle from coming back. The tactical situation here is probably this: The people who killed Clancy had pursued the remains of Clancy's outfit. Appelfinger went to a clearing in the jungle. Instead of wiping him out they are ambushing his relief. That was probably Appelfinger I was firing at from the chopper. Everybody makes mistakes. Yvor made his supersonic whine and Sergeant Billy Joe removed his cigar.

"That was probably our own men we were shooting at," Yvor announced.

"I was thinking the same thing," Billy Joe said. "But then I thought further and I thought everybody makes mistakes. You can't have success, sir, unless you're willing to risk failure."

"Yes, Billy."

"And then I thought further and I remembered that Norman Vincent Peale and his wife brought God into a working partnership in all their problems and activities."

"That was nice."

"That way it made failure seem better."

"Yes. Billy, do you realize you're smoking my cigar?"

"Imagine that."

"Billy, do you realize you're discussing Norman Vincent Peale in the middle of a Vietcong ambush?"

"I realize that, sir. I always fall back on him when I'm in trouble."

"Why don't you fall back on me?"

"Because our situation is hopeless."

"Yes. They have got us surrounded on all sides. Set up the machine gun. Did you bring my button and string?"

"Yes, sir."

While Billy Joe set up the M60 Colonel Yvor looked over

the terrain for a field of fire. I wonder what happened to my cigar. No matter. Search and Rescue. I wonder what the hell happened to Search and Rescue. The Bamboo Bed. What a bunch of fuck-ups Knightbridge has got. How do they expect to win the war by fighting it the way they don't fight. I wonder what happened to my bubble chopper. The VC have probably got it and are in fake contact with Knightbridge trying to get him to make a pickup on them. If his West Point training had any influence on him he will probably try the pickup. I worked myself up through the ranks. I would be just as happy in the ranks as I am as a colonel. Bullshit.

"Are you ready, Billy?"

"Yes, sir."

"How many rounds you got in the bandoliers?"

"Four hundred."

"Good. Now, Billy, as soon as we engage the enemy I want you to take off."

"How am I going to do that?"

"I can work the trigger with the string from the trigger to my mouth. If I have to change the trajectory of the weapon I can do it with my foot."

"I mean how can I leave you all alone?"

"Easy, Billy. I can fight this war all by myself."

"I believe you could, sir."

"Let me try it, Billy."

"What do you want me to do?"

"Check out Clancy."

"Check out Clancy?"

"Yes."

Billy weighed the bandoliers of M60 machine-gun ammunition in his arms, the huge snakes of ammo clung all over him, involuted, parasitic, as though it grew, belonged to him, almost with movement, dull, glittering, pythonlike and alive. Billy began to undrape the heavy snakes of ammunition.

"I don't feel natural without this."

"Ammo is your blanket, Billy. It's like my cigar."

"Do you need your cigar, sir?"

"Yes."

"I need ammo too. I couldn't live long without ammo."

"Live long enough to find out what the enemy's up to, Billy."

"You think I'll find out if I follow the elephant?"

"Yes."

"Do you want the cigar in your mouth or the machine gun—I mean the button?"

"The button."

"Are we under observation, sir?"

"Negative. But they know we're in the area. They think they have our TAOR cut off. I will identify our position to them with a few bursts. That should cover your withdrawal. Backtrack and check out the bubble chopper. Then get to Appelfinger."

"And the elephant."

"Same same."

"But, sir, how are you going to withdraw, sir?"

"This is how I am going to die, Billy."

"You got it all planned. You set up a base of fire here to suck the enemy in, meanwhile; meanwhile Appelfinger, the civilians and myself will escape in the bubble chopper?"

"Yes."

"No."

"That's an order, Billy."

"I can't leave you here to be killed."

"Somebody's got to be the bait, Billy."

"Why not me?"

"You're more mobile. This whole operation will abort. We minimize the opportunity of success unless I stick."

"That's army talk."

"It's the only talk we got, Billy."

"What about Mai Li?"

"Take care of her."

"No."

"You don't say no to a full bird colonel."

"I can't take care of her, sir."

"You'll learn."

"I'd rather stick."

"She'll teach you, Billy."

"I'd better stick here."

"I thought of it first."

"You're pulling rank now."

"That's right," Colonel Yvor said.

"Then I'll stick," Sergeant Billy Joe said, redraping the python, the endless alive skein of ammunition, back around himself where it belonged. Where it felt good.

"You want to be a hero, Billy?"

"I don't want to be a deserter."

"You'd rather be a Clancy?"

"Yes."

"You're not afraid of Mai Li?"

"That's part of it. Everything is part of it. In my part of Georgia we don't do what you want me to do. We don't let people get killed for us."

"Jesus Christ and Clancy got killed for us, Billy."

"That's just in books."

Colonel Yvor wondered how he could think so long without his cigar. Maybe his thinking was suffering. Maybe my thinking isn't being maximized or some such army bullshit. Colonel Yvor looked around at all the silent, staring, waiting, patient canopy of stupid horror called jungle in war and said, "I don't think in your part of Georgia, Billy, people have imaginations. They don't know what it's like to be hit."

"Yes, sir, they do."

"There's none of me left, Billy." Colonel Yvor watched the waving bamboo. "The ending is not going to get much."

"Then you're going to stick?"

"Yes, sir, Billy."

"You got me in this mess and now you'll get me out?"

"I got everybody in this mess and I'll get one man out."

"Everybody?"

"The whole world."

"You must think you're awful important."

"Yes."

"I'll be quick, sir. I'll get radio and get you out."

"If you can find radio."

"Appelfinger's got radio."

"The bottom of the Song Phong."

"He must have retrieved it by now."

"Then it's hanging up in the jungle to dry."

"I'll take our bubble chopper back from those Gooks and radio for gun ships."

"No, you'll follow orders."

"Then somehow, sir, I'll get the Bamboo Bed. I'll get Search and Rescue."

"Search and Rescue? The Bamboo Bed? Billy, put the button in my mouth and cut out."

Billy put the button that was tied to the string that led to the M16 into Colonel Yvor's mouth and the Colonel watched him unwind the ammunition and arrange it carefully so that it would feed properly into the breech mechanism of the weapon. Then Billy Joe kissed his colonel on the forehead and was gone.

Then Colonel Yvor began to curse quietly. He was not only cursing for Captain Clancy. He was cursing, he told himself, for Billy Joe and all the Captain Clancys who were long dead. He was cursing for Mai Li and even the Bamboo Bed Search and Rescue. Search and Rescue were not even in the war. Cry for them anyway. Search and Rescue were fuck-ups. Yes, the Bamboo Bed, Search and Rescue, were no God damn good. All the more, Colonel Yvor advised himself, all the more. . . .

24

Captain Knightbridge stared at the sign that delimited their perimeter. Search and Rescue. He wondered who would not be rescued next. Not only Captain Clancy but a whole long list of the people they had not rescued could be photocopied and filed so that even with microfilm miniaturization it would still extend halfway around the world. The Bamboo Bed had not rescued Clancy and it had not rescued Knightbridge himself. That was a good start on the people Search and Rescue had not rescued. Those civilians out there in the jungle with Appelfinger must be singing now, "How many years must a man . . ." because those are the kind of civilians they were. How many years must a man go to the Academy before they get the Point? Something like that. But there are many civilians in the jungle we have not rescued. The jungle of the world. Jesus, you are being profound today. I wish this radio would tell me something. I wish this radio would tell me anything. It could tell me where the tunnel is the VC are digging under our camp.

The thing about the tunnel the VC are digging under us is that it shows the VC don't trust us. They don't believe that Search and Rescue means what it says. Do you know who believes that Search and Rescue means what it says? No one. No one at all. If no one at all believes what it says how can you expect the enemy to believe it? Because the enemy should have faith. That's the truth for the day, Captain Knightbridge thought.

Why should the enemy take us on faith? Why should anyone take anything on faith? Because we're Americans?

"Explain yourself, buddy."

"Captain."

"Captain, sir."

"I don't have to explain anything. I'm a captain in the
United States Army and I don't have to make sense."

"I'm your superior."

"There are no superiors."

"I got to explain to you that you been had."

"What are you talking to yourself about?" Lieutenant Bliss
said.

"Sit down, Jane," Knightbridge said. "I'm trying to get
a position on some people out there and no luck."

"How many down?"

"Five now, I think. Yvor's gone in."

"Ho Chi Minh says he's got a lead on the tunnel," Lavender said.

"When are they going to blow us up?"

"That's not the right question to ask," Disraeli said.

"I'm getting God damn tired," Knightbridge said. "I'm
getting God damn tired being tactful about finding out when
I'm going to be killed."

"We have got to be patient," Oliver said. "The electronic-
detection device is still picking up those people screwing in
the village."

"Still?"

"Well, it's probably a different couple now," Elgar said.

"I guess all we can be sure of, certain of," Knightbridge
said, "is that they are a VC couple and not our gallant South
Vietnamese allies."

"Because?"

"You know because."

"Because," Batcheck said, "our South Vietnamese allies
can't even jerk off in style. We will go and look for the
tunnel."

"Yes."

"What is the moral of that?" Janine said, watching them go. "Maybe it's what my father always said."

"Your Marine captain father?"

"Yes," Janine said. "That the Marines are impotent, that they were always charging up hills to prove they were not impotent. But when they got to the top of the hill they were still impotent. Or dead."

"There must be a point there someplace," Knightbridge said.

"Daddy always said—"

"Your Marine daddy."

"Daddy always said the Marines are the American Mamelukes. The Mamelukes were the warrior group from the Ukraine who ruled Egypt for four hundred years."

"I know. I went to the Point for four hundred years."

"Daddy said the Mamelukes—"

"The Egyptian Marines."

"Were homosexuals."

"Yes." Knightbridge touched the radio.

"When they weren't fighting they were buggering each other."

"Your father must have been popular in the Marines."

"Daddy said the American Marines were never quite like that."

"As any Marine will tell you," Knightbridge said.

"Daddy said it was all the Marines could do to get to the top of that hill. That they did not even have the courage of their perversions."

"I still say your captain father must have been popular in the Marines."

"Daddy said he was not trying to win a popularity contest. That he was in the Marines by mistake. That there was no way out. Being in the Marines was like being in the Egyptian Mamelukes, no way out. Anyway, charging up to the top of that hill was all he knew how to do."

"Ah, now we're getting someplace," Knightbridge said. "We are all where we are because of a mistake. But what I want to know is how did the Mameluke Marines screw Egypt for four hundred years without screwing women? How did they make kids? Where did the young Mameluke Marines come from for four hundred years?"

"The Mamelukes bought slave boys in the Ukraine."

"And the American Marines?"

"Daddy was drafted."

"It's probably cheaper that way," Knightbridge said. "I'm about to give up on this thing. I don't know why Appelfinger doesn't contact me."

"What about Colonel Yvor?"

"Yvor lost his ship to Victor Charlie. He and Billy Joe wandered away from their bubble chopper and Charlie found it. The first thing Charlie did was call me for a pickup. Charlie wants to blast the Bamboo Bed."

"Doesn't everyone?"

"Yes."

"How did Billy and the Colonel wander away from their chopper?"

"Meanwhile the VC are digging a tunnel under our camp to blow us up when they get around to it. A typical day in Vietnam. But now I'm not complaining, Ma." Knightbridge removed the batteries from the radio. "Ma, I sure do love it here in Vietnam waiting with all these sweet Marines waiting to be blowed up. They sure are real nice to me, Ma. In a way you might say too nice. I don't want to conclude on too awful a sour note, Ma, and so, like our awful good Colonel says, we are winning the war. Colonel Yvor says, 'Like I told you fifty soldiers yesterday, I tell you ten soldiers left today, we are winning the war.' "

Knightbridge blew inside the set where the batteries had been.

"Let's go to bed," Janine said.

"You said Ho Chi Minh had a lead on the tunnel?"

"He said tomorrow the VC would tell him where the tunnel is."

"They're always telling him that."

"Let's go to bed," Janine said.

Knightbridge put the batteries back. "Not in the middle of the day. There's a regulation against it. Anyway—" Knightbridge stared at the set—"anyway I want to try to make contact."

"Why don't you get the boys to work the set?"

"The boys are searching for that tunnel," Knightbridge said.

Actually, the boys were sitting in a bar in the village, a bar run by Vietnamese children. The tunnel began, originated, in the back room of the bar so as they sat in the bar it was necessary for the VC to come by them with the dirt they removed from the tunnel and throw it in the street.

"See what the boys in the back room will have," Batcheck said.

"We are supposed to be looking for the tunnel," Disraeli said.

"I hear," Ozz said, "that they got a mission for us."

Lavender, his gold teeth all afire, said, "There's a reporter here wants to speak to us. I think he's with Intelligence."

"Intelligence?" Batcheck said.

"Yes," Lavender said. "A for Alpha killed was the biggest thing since Custer. He wants to talk to survivors."

"There ain't any," Ozz said.

A man entered the Children's Bar. It was Mike McAdams.

"Where is your commander?" Mike said.

"Tarzan? He's with Jane."

"Where else?" Mike said. "Who are those people passing through here carrying out dirt?"

"VC."

"Why the dirt?"

"They're digging a tunnel under our camp," Batcheck said.

"What for?"

"To blow us up."

"Why don't you stop them?"

"They'd only dig another," Ozz said.

"Yes," Disraeli said, "and you don't want to discourage people."

"No."

"It can give them all kinds of emotional problems."

"Yes."

"It's hard enough to get these Viet people to do any kind of work at all," Weatherwax and Coneybeare said. "When they get started on something, a project of their own, it's best not to stop them."

"The truth is," Batcheck said, "and no bullshit, the truth is this is a fake tunnel the Viet are digging here. It doesn't go under our camp. It doesn't go anyplace. They're digging the real one someplace else. They know we got electronic detection. This tunnel is being dug to confuse us."

"What about Alpha Company?"

"What about it?"

"It's the biggest single loss our side has had in the war. How did they get it?"

"They were bait."

"What does that mean?"

"They bring the Chinamen out of the hills. Bait."

"But they're not supposed to be annihilated."

"No, that was a mistake. Something went wrong."

"What went wrong?"

"We made a mistake."

"What was the mistake?"

"Leaving home."

Mike sat down. This is what he came ten thousand miles to find out? This was why he had left home?

"There was Captain Clancy," he said.

"Yes, sir, there was," Ozz said. "In many ways Clancy was a stupid man."

"How?"

"Like getting killed and all."

"But isn't that why you go to war?"

"No. That's why you do not go to war," Coneybeare said. "Anybody can come over here and get killed like Clancy did."

241

"I disagree," Weatherwax said.

"Why?" Mike wanted to know.

"You want to know too much," Ozz said. "That's why we joined the army, to get away from people like you. You remind me of my father."

"My father was quite black," Lavender said. "I'll go along with everything Ozz said. I'll go along with anything. I don't want to fight."

"What you doing here then?" Mike said.

"I'm with Search and Rescue. Everything I got is tied up in the Bamboo Bed."

"Everything?"

"Yes, man."

"What do you know about Clancy?" Mike said. What happened on Hill 904? What happened on Ridge Red Boy?

"904 and Red Boy are different."

"I know," Mike said, "but 904 led to Red Boy. What do you know about Clancy?"

Lavender looked at Batcheck, waiting for Batcheck to translate what Mike had just said. This man who called himself Mike McAdams was something else. He was going to find out about Clancy and give away the whole secret of the war. Or was he here to expose Tarzan and Jane? Maybe to discover who was digging the tunnel and where the tunnel was going. If he was here to expose Tarzan and Jane, then everything was quite simple. They would kick ass on him. Because that would mean that he was against the four fucking freedoms. Below the jungle, within the jungle, above and beyond the jungle, Tarzan and Jane had thought of everything and everyone loved them for it. On the other hand if it's for Clancy, then he's dead. I mean this Mike McAdams is dead.

Batcheck looked at Mike thoughtfully. "It's not that Lavender does not understand your question about Clancy. It's simply that Lavender grew up with black people. As a matter of fact his parents were black."

"Positive."

"Lavender," Batcheck told Mike carefully, "believes all white people to be crazy, so he is very much at ease with all white people. Particularly soldiers. But not Intelligence officers."

"And poets?"

"How did you know?"

"I guessed," Mike said.

"I am in the unique position," Batcheck said, counting on his fingers, "of being white and a soldier too, but a poet as well, and if all this doesn't cement our relationship I can kick ass on Lavender because I'm his commanding sergeant as well."

"That's about right," Lavender said.

"Now, speaking for Lavender and myself and everybody, what the hell are you doing here?"

"That's about right," Lavender said.

"You're not supposed to say that again," Batcheck said to Lavender. "I asked this man a question."

"I'm sorry," Lavender said.

"What am I doing here?" Mike McAdams said. "I told you I'm here to find out about Clancy."

"Ask the enemy."

"That's not good enough."

"You want us to give away the secret of the war?"

"Yes."

"Then I guess you'll have to find Clancy. But while you're here would you like to see what's going on in our TAOR?"

"Yes, I would," Mike said.

"We have got some people down in the jungle, but we can't get radio contact."

"Who?"

"Appelfinger. He's the remains of Captain Clancy's Alpha Company. Then the remains of Colonel Yvor are down in the jungle."

"I know about Colonel Yvor," Mike said. "What's the secret?"

"Colonel Yvor knows the secret."

"Does Appelfinger know it?"

"Probably."

"I would like to see Appelfinger," Mike McAdams said.

"Appelfinger is not seeing anyone at the moment," Batcheck said.

"Who else is down in the jungle?"

"Everyone."

"Who is down in your Tactical Area of Responsibility?"

"Two civilians, a boy and a girl."

"What was their objective?"

"Love."

"Crazy."

"Yes."

"We are probably the only sane people left," Batcheck said. Batcheck paused and looked around at the others for confirmations of this truth. The soldiers all agreed, shaking their heads yes. They were probably the only sane people left. Disraeli and Ozz and Coneybeare and Weatherwax kept pounding on the big table of the Children's Bar and Grill and Secondhand Whorehouse. Ozz kept saying, "They're nuts, all nuts," and Disraeli repeated, "You've got to keep those Arabs running. It's the only way out."

"Wait," Batcheck said. "Don't tear this place apart. The Children's Bar and Grill and Secondhand Whorehouse is a respectable place."

"Why is it called that?" Mike said.

"Because that's its name," Batcheck said. "Why don't you let us show you around? Where would you like to start? The Bamboo Bed?"

"The tunnel."

"This is a fake tunnel," Batcheck said. "They won't tell us where the real tunnel is. They won't even tell Ho Chi Minh, Karl Marx or the Naked Chinaman. Our Asian observers. They're supposed to keep us from bombing a village without proper papers."

"Where do you get proper papers to bomb a village?"

"Channels."

"What channels?"

"That's part of the secret."

"What have you got to show me?"

"Just about everything's secret now," Batcheck said.

"The bridge," Ozz said. "The one we sold to the VC. Show him the bridge."

"The bridge you sold to the VC?"

"It was our extra bridge we had coming into the town," Batcheck said. "There were two so we sold one. It was extra."

"Redundant."

"Yes," Ozz said. "So much so everyone was afraid to cross it."

"That's true," Weatherwax said. "It took three men to guard it day and night so we sold it to the VC."

"How much?"

"Three thousand piastres. Half in military scrip."

"What do they do with military scrip?"

"Smoke it."

"What do they do with the bridge?"

"Right now they want to sell it back to us."

"Why?"

"So they can blow it up."

"What for?"

"Because they've got a Tactical Area of Responsibility too."

"Why didn't they think of that before?"

"Because it was a good deal. Where else can you buy a bridge for three thousand piastres? Most countries won't even take piastres hardly now."

"But now they realize it was a mistake?"

"The VC, Charlie, fucks up like anybody else," Batcheck said.

"Quite as much?"

"That's the way the war's going at the moment," Batcheck said. Then Batcheck said, "I hear you want to court-martial Clancy."

There was a silence.

"Do you want to see our bridge or not?"

"I thought you said it was redundant."

"We've discovered it's not as redundant as we first thought," Ozz said. "With a little work it will be like new. Just some burned timbers from the French days."

"Yes. The French had troubles with that damn bridge too," Batcheck said.

"I am on my way to Hill 904," Mike said. "904 is where Clancy made it good, where he won all the medals before he bought a farm on Ridge Red Boy. Hill 904 is where he might try to go back to if he were dying. We stopped here to take on fuel for my chopper."

"Do you want to see Captain Knightbridge, Tarzan and Jane?"

"No," Mike said.

"I hear you and Knightbridge used to be buddies."

"Yes," Mike said. Mike reached for his Japanese tape recorder.

"Did you have that tape set turned on?"

"Yes."

"If we'd known that we'd have tried to sound better," Disraeli said.

25

HILL 904 was a big son of a bitch. It was called 904 because it was 904 meters high. Hill 904 was a tough son of a bitch. Almost every American unit in the highlands had tried to take it. Some had succeeded, some had failed, some had taken it many times at great cost. Other times the Unfriendlies had given it to the Americans. They'd killed all the Americans they cared to kill that day and pulled out. But one fine day the Unfriendlies decided to hold Hill 904. It was the same day the Americans decided to take it. So uphill the Americans went. The Unfriendlies, being in a magnificent position on top of Hill 904, killed all the Americans in sight. You would have thought, Captain Knightbridge thought, that the Americans would have learned from the British at Bunker Hill. The British lost the flower of their army trying to take Bunker Hill from the Americans. The Americans just sat there on the hill and killed every British flower in sight. On Hill 904 it was the Americans that were the cut flowers. On Hill 904 it was the Americans who had all the latest, most modern equipment against some farmers, dug in on a hill. Up the Hill 904 the Americans went. Down the Hill 904 the Americans came. It all happened so quickly they did not have a chance to bring back their dead buddies with them. I wonder where the bodies went? The Americans did this again and again and again and again. Why? Because it was a habit now. The Americans were hooked on Hill 904. They climbed the mountain because the mountain was there. Hill 904 became the enemy. They called it the hairy ball, it was that tangled and twisted with jungle and the shit of war, the bodies and the shell holes, heads, arms, legs, coconuts, breadfruit, coffee cans, cocks, balls, C rations, rice, Winston cigarettes, letters from home, telegrams from the Hasbrouck Heights New Jersey Boosters Club congratulating them on their victory, beer cans, gin bottles, marijuana wrappers, Bibles, hymnbooks, a Guide to Better Living, autographs of Hubert Horatio Humphrey and the movie stars who visited the Hill on a calm day, millions of gallons of red blood as though it had been sprayed there by defoliation mission, all of a year's output of something from a chemical company for which the stockholders received a supplemental year's-end dividend and caused the stock to jump up three and five eighths, socks, condoms, letters from home, despair and pity and heartbreak and death and pity and heartbreak, that's what Hill 904 was made of.

So up the hill the Americans went, the same day the Unfriendlies decided to hold it, and the battle went on and on and on until the Americans had almost no dead to give. So General William Westmoreland, who had graduated from West Point fifteen years before Knightbridge and who was in charge of the whole show, decided that this was the time to make the statement that we were winning the war. That did not help. So General Westmoreland decided that this was the time to quit the field. For General Westmoreland to quit the field. So General Westmoreland got on an airplane with Ambassador Ellsworth Bunker and both of them went back to the United States of America and announced that they were winning the war. That did not help. Hill 904 was still held by the Unfriendlies. Then one fine day Clancy took it. It cost Clancy ninety-four men, but he took it when all had failed. General Westmoreland and Ambassador Bunker came back to Vietnam. Ambassador Bunker went back to doing whatever ambassadors do who walk a crooked mile to run a crowded country. General Westmoreland gave Clancy a medal.

That was nice, Knightbridge thought.

If Captain Clancy were on top of Hill 904 now, Knight-bridge thought, watching it, watching the hill, if he were up there now he could see where the remains of his company were, where Appelfinger was, the last remains of Clancy's company. The last remains of the outfit that took 904. Yvor was supposed to call me on the radio if they got into trouble. No one ever calls me on the radio. My radio never rings. I wonder what Clancy would think of the flower people, Bethany and Peter. Clancy never dreamed that the remains of his company would end up with the flower people, with the helpless and the hopeless. No, Clancy would not be able to see anything from the top of Hill 904. That is the problem of this war, you cannot see anything from anywhere. The jungle hides all. Excepting you can see the American base camps clearly from anywhere. The jungle hides all the rest. You can see the Americans by standing on a chair. Because the Americans clear the surrounding country. The Unfriend-lies cannot be seen from anywhere, from no matter how high up. The jungle is their protection. The jungle is the friend of the Unfriendlies. The jungle is the enemy of those that make it the enemy.

Knightbridge could see now by leaning backward so that he sighted over the radio that would not ring, and over the blue-green ridge that would not move, to the defoliation people in their C-123 transports going out to clear the forests so everyone could see better. Going out to get the rice paddies so the Unfriendlies could eat less. The defoliation people are very much misunderstood. "Nobody likes us. We tell our parents we are doing something else. If you tell people what you are doing, no one understands. It is basically the fault of the army public-relations people. They do a poor job. Then it could be the fault of the newspapers in the States. They do a poor job too. The TV are the worst, they pretend defoliation does not exist. That makes people awful suspicious."

The defoliation people are going out now to eliminate

another part of the forest, but they will also eliminate the monkeys, the deer, the water buffalo, the rubber trees, the birds, all the birds of bright noise and gay plumage, and the plants of this planet, and the people who eat the plants, some of them will go too because one of the many defoliations they work with—isn't that a nice word, Knightbridge thought— one of the nice words they spray with is a nice word called cyanide, and another called arsenic mixed with kerosene and sprayed from an airplane so that the arsenic drifts in great clouds all over this planet. You don't think man is smart? You don't think man will prevail? You should see him be- have in Asia. Yes, Knightbridge thought, watching the de- foliation planes of the 12th Air Command Squadron go out to get the jungle that was friendly to the Unfriendlies. That is what people do not realize about this war. They do not realize it is a war to end war. The end of man. My friend General William Westmoreland is encouraged about the progress man makes here. Everyone is encouraged. The birds and the beasts and the plants are encouraged. There is one awfully good defoliant that is flying over my head now with the 12th Air Squadron that kills by encouraging the plant to grow too fast. Most encouraging. Another kills by depriv- ing the plant of water. Everything is encouraging, but what is most encouraging is the spirit of men like Clancy. The man who got the men to take 904. Clancy wears his medal well. Clancy should be proud. Knightbridge watched Hill 904. The hill was vacant now. Clancy was dead.

Everyone was dead.

"Where are those planes going?" Nurse Jane asked.

"To win the war."

"They're not looking for Clancy?"

"No. They're going to win the war."

"Defoliation?"

"Yes."

"Isn't that awful?"

"No. Not if you don't think about it," Knightbridge said. "They don't think about it. Why should you?"

"Will they spray the whole country?"

"In time."

"The world?"

"Give them a little more time."

"Why?"

"Because they don't think about it," Knightbridge said. "They think about honor."

"Is there honor in killing everything?"

"Yes. There certainly is," Knightbridge said. "Honor, Family, Country, God and little fishes. If you don't think about it," Knightbridge said quietly.

"Where are the boys?"

"Gone to sell a bridge."

"Will that win the war?"

"Yes," Knightbridge said. "If you think about it."

"What happened to your project?"

"Of having sex at ten thousand feet? I am holding that in reserve."

"Your project of rescuing people down in the jungle."

"I have not made radio contact yet to get their position. Anyway the Bamboo Bed doesn't work. Nothing works. The problem of this war is that it is out of human control. Nothing works. Clancy was the last man alive who thought you could lose or win without a machine. He went up that hill with a sword."

"Pathetic," Janine said. "And sad."

"Yes," Knightbridge said, "it's the whole God damn history of the human race—pathetic and sad. But not us, Jane. Not you and me because we—"

"Have got the Bamboo Bed."

"Jesus no—and Jesus yes," Knightbridge said. "All right, yes. We have got each other. If there is anything I hate it's a buddy. You can't screw, the tension builds up and up and up until finally you want to kill the son of a bitch."

"What about Coneybeare and Weatherwax, Disraeli and Ozz, Batcheck and Lavender, Oliver and Elgar? Everybody in the Bamboo Bed?"

"They're screwing their country," Knightbridge said. "Any country."

"What about the people down in the jungle?"

"They're in trouble," Knightbridge said. "But they shouldn't be there."

"There's a war on."

"That's the trouble," Knightbridge said.

"Then you have no solution."

"The Bamboo Bed."

"It won't work."

"It will."

"Your radio won't even work."

"It will when they try to contact me."

"Why don't they?"

"I don't know why. People don't want to be rescued."

"Saved?"

"Yes," Knightbridge said. "Maybe they're trying and there's electrostatic interference."

"What's that mean?"

"That the military situation is normal," Knightbridge said. Then he said quietly, "Why don't you watch this thing for me? Listen to this radio and I'll go find out what the men are up to."

"They're selling a bridge."

"Then I want to find out how much they got for it," Knightbridge said. "If Appelfinger will not show, if Appelfinger will not call, the hell with Appelfinger."

Clancy to die. No, I guess he's not, Clancy thought. Tigers don't eat dead things. The tiger is curious. If I had my gun I would give him a burst. No, I wouldn't. That would alert the Unfriendlies. I would crawl back to all the dead men of Alpha Company. If I knew where they were. How far did Appelfinger take me? In which direction? Where has Appelfinger gone? Why did he leave me here? If a man must die, he should die in Vietnam. If you have to die someplace, sometime, why not now in Vietnam? Where did Appelfinger go, Tiger? Clancy asked the gay-striped, solemn cat silently. You must have seen Private Appelfinger carrying this load of fresh meat through the jungle and you must have followed us here. You must have waited here with the fresh meat when he propped me against this mahogany tree. You watched Private Appelfinger go away after he left his kill here. You probably figured he was coming back but in the meantime you would steal away with his kill. Well, there isn't going to be any meantime. I mean Appelfinger will be back any second now with Scott and the girl, and he will give you a burst. Ha ha, Iron Man Clancy told the cat, you didn't know that Appelfinger and I were buddies. You didn't know that I am going to be the next Senator from Montana. You didn't know you can't get elected to be dog catcher in the States without a good war record. I have the best. I took Hill 904. I had most of the medals. If my last battle had worked at Ridge Red Boy I would have had all of them. Why didn't it work? I made one mistake. I should have got further up the ridge to make my stand. Are you interested, Tiger? Or are you more interested in a meal? I will tell things to a tiger that I would not tell to anyone else. You can trust a tiger. A tiger will stick by you when you are abandoned by everyone else. At least it's true in a jungle in Vietnam. Hello, Tiger. What are you thinking now? That it's time to eat? Let's have a drink first. I bet that's where Appelfinger, the boy who brought me here, went. He went to get me a drink. Wasn't that nice of him, Tiger? I apologize for calling you Tiger but I don't know your name. We have not been introduced. My name is Captain Clancy. Iron Man Clancy. What is yours, Tiger? Don't tell me, let me guess. Is it Tyger, Tyger Burning Bright in the Forests of the Night? Well, that's one hell of a long name. Let's shorten it. If you're going to be in my outfit you'll have to cut your name. We can't have people wandering around the outfit with long names. Do I sound silly? Well, I have lost too much blood.

The tiger watched the silent bleeding Clancy and wondered whether it was the time to take him. Despite all the stories you hear, tigers do not eat man animals. Not very often. Until lately. Lately, all through Vietnam piles of man animals are strewn all over the jungle. The tigers have acquired a taste. I suppose the reason there are so few maneating tigers in Asia is that man is a dangerous animal. Until lately. Lately they have been generously (for tigers) killing each other for no reason, leaving the whole fresh kill for tigers. Perfect. Tigers have not only acquired a taste but a passion. Man is God damn good. A good young American male, fed on C Rations. Not too much fat. The meat well marbleized. Much better than any Vietcong meat, which is stringy and rice-fed. Still this male tiger, lying right here watching Clancy die, had eaten several VC near Hue on a bad day when the great American bombers had destroyed a village where the VC were hiding.

That's right, Clancy thought, People never think of all the reasons that people join the VC. I know of one Vietnamese Boy Scout Beaver Patrol that followed us in the Delta for three weeks hoping to catch us with our guard down, without our flankers out, with our point not functioning. Why would a Beaver Patrol desert to the VC? Adventure. Patriotism. George Orwell said that scoutmasters were homosexual to the man. What's that got to do with it? Nothing except, Tiger, I want you to know that I read books. Why in the hell am I trying to impress a tiger? Where is Appelfinger? I don't want to die in Vietnam and be eaten by a tiger. Why not? I want to assure you, Tiger boy, I have got no objection to being eaten by a tiger when I'm dead. I don't care what you do with me when I'm dead. Now that we have settled that point of etiquette and we have figured out why the Beaver Patrol joined the VC let's get to why the Americans are in Asia. What are the Americans doing in the jungle? We are helping you to be free. You don't believe it? Well, it's true. A tiger wouldn't understand anyway. Tigers are naturally stupid. My God, I'm getting cold. Why is it so cold? So awfully, awfully cold in the jungle? It's like when the leeches fall off you after they have sucked all of your blood they can drink. You don't know when they drop on you and you don't feel it when they are sucking you, but you know it when they leave you. You feel tired and cold. But I haven't been in leech country. I've been in bullet country. When a bullet hits you you damn well know it, but at the same time if you are busy, and in the last battle I was so damn busy trying to keep Alpha moving up the slope, at the same time you feel the bullet and you do not feel it. Does that make sense, Tiger boy? Well, it's the best sense I can make. I am feeling the bullet now. Weak. I feel very weak and very cold, Tiger boy. Appelfinger should have applied a tourniquet so I would not take such a blood loss. But you can't tie a tourniquet around the neck. I wonder if I can talk at all. I better not try. What is that? Who is that?

A man, an enemy man, was standing watching the captain and the tiger, an enemy man about ten meters away from Captain Clancy's mahogany tree and two clicks north. Standing watching Clancy and the tiger. The enemy man had a bicycle loaded with bags. About four hundred kilos of rice. The man was on enemy resupply. The enemy must eat too. They don't have any C rations so they eat rice and dried fish. Each man carries a ball of cooked rice in a waterproof silk package. The enemy doesn't have any helicopters for resupply so they use bicycles. Very primitive. But who ever heard of a bicycle being shot down?

The tiger did not move from his meal. The tiger stood his

ground. Good boy, tiger. Actually the peasant did not see the tiger. The tiger was perfectly adapted to the jungle with waving black stripes against a rufous coat. The tiger was about nine feet and would weigh in at close to five hundred, maybe 475 pounds. The tiger was big, heavy and silent, even the tiger tail was without any movement, guarding the kill silently.

The peasant had been assigned a resupply mission to the 324th North Vietnamese Regiment that were to hit the American 723rd Airborne Brigade bogged down in the monsoon mud outside of Dak To. He did not expect to meet any Americans on this part of the Sihanouk Trail. The peasant had a weapon slung on his back. The peasant unslung the weapon with haste. It was an old French army weapon, Clancy thought. The peasant threw a shell into the chamber and, still holding the bicycle that was loaded with four hundred kilos of rice up with his hip, aimed the gun at Clancy. Shoot straight, Clancy thought. Shoot straight. The peasant lowered the weapon. The peasant had been ordered never to shoot unless he was fired at. He was carefully instructed only to return enemy fire while on a resupply mission. Do not expose the operation to enemy reaction. Well, he is about dead anyway the peasant told himself. Look at all that blood. All down his tunic and into his shoes. He is drowning in his own blood. There must be five liters of blood. Even a white man doesn't have much more blood than that before it's all gone. He's a big man even for a white man. But even a big big man must die. I have got my machete with me, it is tied onto the rear of my bicycle. A machete is silent. I can take off his head in the wink of an eye. Even the wink of a round-eyed white man. The peasant reslung his rifle and with the same movement reached around with his free hand to extract the machete from the rear of the top-heavy, overloaded-with-rice bicycle, and the whole thing went down with a soft crash as the peasant struggled with everything.

Now everything was on the ground, including the peasant, and the tiger moved. It was only a faintly perceptible movement but the peasant saw it from the floor of the jungle and froze. Because—and now Clancy felt himself, not the victim but the ward of the tiger—because maybe, Clancy thought, because the little Viet bastard is scared shitless. And who wouldn't be? Only a person like myself. It is only a person who is going to be eaten by a tiger that can be rescued by one. It's like, Clancy thought, all those philosophers, all those God damned French philosophers who propound all this crap about man without ever having been one themselves. What does war do for you? Why does that Chinaman slither along in the jungle while you and the tiger watch, while you bleed to death, while the tiger drools? I tell you what war does for you. I never saw a man who spent a lot of time at the front line who was not a decent human being. But in this war there is no front line. So that is why Vietnam is full of sons of bitches. So you have ended up exactly where you started from, just like all those God damned French philosophers always do. Where did that Gook go? That nice Vietnamese gentleman that was going to shoot me? That Vietnamese Boy Scout who was going to get his first and ultimate merit badge by chopping off my head with a hysterical high flash of his machete. Where do all the young Gooks go? To kill the white guys every one. Tiger, boy, it's cold. It's cold in the jungle. If you have got something to do, Tiger boy, why don't you do it? I'm bored with dying and it hurts.

Captain Clancy began to say this aloud to the tiger but the blood gushed suddenly in his throat and he ceased. We all expect to be killed by an atom bomb, Clancy thought. It takes some getting used to the idea of being eaten by a tiger. Being eaten by a tiger is un-American. It's not the American way. Nevertheless this is the price I pay for the hill. For not making my stand higher up on Ridge Red Boy. And then Captain Clancy heard the blood gargle in his throat and he thought, the hill came high, and then again as he saw the mountain of tiger move in one great leap and incoming, then again Captain Clancy thought, the hill came high.

27

_____

"Captain Clancy's still alive," Elgar said to Oliver.

"Who says?"

"Nurse Jane."

"I thought Jane was screwing Tarzan."

"No, Nurse Jane was monitoring the radio. Tarzan and Ho Chi Minh, that is Captain Knightbridge and our Asian representative, decided on a search mission and they spotted Clancy near Dong Ho. They flew in very low and the tiger—"

"Tiger?"

"Yes. A tiger leaped up at the Bamboo Bed."

"Tiger?"

"Yes."

"What about Clancy?"

"There's too much ground fire to make a pickup on Clancy now but Knightbridge got rid of the tiger."

"Tiger?" Oliver said.

And Oliver and Elgar continued on toward the bridge and Elgar was telling Oliver that maybe Colonel Yvor who was with Billy Joe, or the body team who were in the vicinity too, and then there was Appelfinger, any of these might get Clancy. Excepting that now they were all tied up in separate fire fights.

"Golly gee," Oliver said. "Golly gee, there's a real war on."

"Yes," Elgar said.

"Golly gee," Oliver said, "Clancy sure can cause a lot of trouble."

"Even when dead," Elgar said.

"Is Clancy dead?"

"Radio doesn't know."

"It wouldn't seem like the same war without Clancy," Oliver said.

"They could find another Clancy."

"I thought they didn't make them like that any more."

"They got a lot more in the States."

"Clancy's one of a kind," Oliver said.

"I don't want to pull rank on you, Private Oliver," Private First Class Elgar said. "Don't make me pull rank."

"I won't. All you have to do is agree with me," Oliver said.

"I was just thinking," Elgar said, "with everyone off in the Bamboo Bed we're going to have to pull off this bridge deal ourselves."

"What's happened to the Intelligence man?"

"The Intelligence guy Whatsisname?"

"Mike. He's not our buddy."

"Yes." Oliver stood still. "Every man is my buddy under the skin. No man is not my buddy. That goes for the Gooks too. And the Russians and the Chinese. Everybody is my buddy under the skin."

"You're a Christian."

"No," Oliver said, "Christians believe in the brotherhood of man and all that baloney. Just baloney. Words that mean nothing. Words, words, words. Now, buddies mean something. We are all buddies under the skin."

"Some of your buddies are shooting the shit out of some of your other buddies."

"I know. They know not what they do," Oliver said.

"You're a pacifist."

"No," Oliver said, "I am a subjectivist. I think everyone associated with the Bamboo Bed is a subjectivist at heart whether he admits it or not. If you're on the Bamboo Bed you're a subjectivist."

"What are we subject to?"

"We are subjectively monitoring the war rather than objectively fighting it. That's important," Oliver said, taking a stalk of rice from the rice paddy and pulling through his front teeth to extract the sweet. "It's important," Oliver said, pointing the rice at Elgar, "because someone must leave a record that's meaningful and because if an important decision has to be made it must be made subjectively in the reflective cool of the rice paddy rather than in the twisted minds of a fighter in the jungle. Do you agree?"

"Yes."

"Another thing, if Appelfinger can be an evolutionist I can be a subjectivist."

"Yes. Is Appelfinger dead?"

"We simply don't know," Oliver said. "We were receiving him loud and clear after the hit on Operation Red Boy, then he went out ka-thunk."

"It sounds like he threw the radio in the river."

"Yes," Oliver said, pulling down on the limb of a mango tree.

"Why would he do that?"

"Spite? Bitterness? The frustrations of war. Unresolved sexual problems."

"How can you have unresolved sexual problems during a battle?"

"We simply don't know," Oliver said. "There is a great deal to be done in this. The literature is minimal."

"Yes."

"We suspect the American maybe is sexually excited by killing."

"You do?"

"Yes. There are no mangoes here."

"In other words you don't know why Appelfinger threw the radio in the river."

"There are many mysteries in life," Oliver said. "That's why the religions do such a good business. I think the VC got all the mangoes."

"Yes."

"Another thing," Oliver said, still looking for a mango.

"Another thing, it's a good thing everybody on the Bamboo Bed's not a WASP, a white Anglo-Saxon Protestant like you and me."

"Why is it good that the Bamboo Bed is not full of WASPs like you and me?"

"Because WASP is not a good image. You have to have a Batcheck and a Lavender. You notice that all the bad guys in the movies are WASPs."

"What about Disraeli and Ozz?"

"They're WASPs."

"Too bad."

"Disraeli's trying to pass as a Jew."

"Will he make it?"

"An American soldier can do anything."

"Yes." Oliver let the mango branch snap back to the mango tree. "I sure would like to get hold of those VC that stole all the mangoes."

"Let's forget the war and sell the bridge."

Shoot-em-up Bot, the village shoeshine boy who plasters your shoes with mud, owned the province's Coke concession, the GI laundry concession, the fire-insurance concession (not good if burned down by Americans), had got the contending parties to meet at the middle of the bridge. He had just got back from a running trip to his Coke concession and returned with six king-sized Cokes, bigger than he was, and passed them out to the contenders.

"We are only plenipotentiaries," Oliver said. "We do not have much leverage for bargaining."

Shoot-em-up Bot tried to get his Cokes back but it was too late.

Oliver and Elgar confronted the VC contingent in the middle of the bridge across their enormous Cokes. They were not really VC. They called themselves local guerrilla forces, but they only worked sometimes at night. Most of them worked in the local VC hand-grenade factory run by Shoot-em-up Bot.

"Let's be friends," Bot said. "If you all want to sell the bridge let's arrive at a price."

Bot had learned his English by servicing the GIs, but surprisingly enough most of his money was made from the hand-grenade factory. General William Westmoreland, who was commanding general of the Friendlies, liked to tell a long complicated story of how an ammunition bearer from North Vietnam took two months to carry one mortar shell to the Delta country. What did he do when he accomplished this feat? He turned around and went back to get a mortar. (Much laughter.) The laughter was because we like to think the Unfriendlies are only getting an occasional mortar shell to blast our balls off. Actually, except for some that come down the Sihanouk Trail and the Ho Chi Minh Trail by modern trucks, they make much ammunition right here and much is stolen from us. Our mortar shells will fit their mortar tubes. If we have some ammunition that won't fit their weapons, then they take our weapons along with our ammo. They complain frequently about the quality of our supplies but they make do. The price is right. There is a rumor and a joke making the rounds in Vietnam that the VC are complaining about the quality contract on our new TFX swept-wing fighter or the F1-11 and they want us to increase the air intake, up the manifold pressure and if possible without complete retooling, widen the landing gear for a shorter approach. The Unfriendlies have the knowledge or the illusion that they are going to take over most of our ordnance one day, and they don't want to be stuck with a lot of junk. Bot's hand-grenade factory was a free enterprise venture. Cost plus. His only customer was the VC. Like our army, the VC paid through the nose. The VC taxed the hell out of Bot, but Bot kept three sets of books.

"Lahk Ah see it," Bot said, "You-all Americans got foah thousands pee-astahs stuck into the adventure." (He had learned his English from the Texans in the 101st Airborne.) "And you would lahk to git it out, git shet of this bridge. May God bless you real good."

"I'd like a profit too," Elgar said. "Tell them that in Gook language."

"In Vietnamese," Oliver said.

"Ah cain't tell them that. These fellers know you damn stuck with this hyah bridge."

"This is the only bridge in the valley."

"Naw, there're two," Bot said. "This bridge is extree."

"We are planning to blow the other one up."

"Y'all know that ain't true."

"Try it anyway."

"They know that ain't true. They lived in this valley all their born days. Most of them worked for me since they was little tads. Ah cain't lie to them."

"Is that the way the 101st Airborne talks?" Oliver said.

"Ah reckon."

"Tell them anyway," Oliver said.

"Ah cain't."

"Are you getting a commission?"

"A little biddy commission," Bot said.

"Tell them we want out for what we got in the bridge plus twenty percent."

"Twenty percent?"

"For your commission."

"The buy-er pays the commission."

"Not in the States."

"You are not in the States, Biddyboy. The States is long gone," Bot said.

"We want the twenty percent for our trouble," Elgar said.

"Trouble?"

"We been guarding the bridge against the VC," Oliver said.

"You didn't have to, Biddyboy. All you had to do was pay the VC tax," Bot said.

"The people in the States don't like that."

"The people in the States are long gone, Biddyboy," Bot said.

"Tell them what we want for the bridge," Elgar said.

"Scooby do," Shoot-em-up Bot said. "All right." And he turned to the Vietnamese on the bridge and began to singsong to them in Vietnamese. Vietnamese is an ancient Chinese tongue and Bot spoke it as though he were playing all the big parts in a Mandarin opera. They sang back at him with feigned laughter, feigned horror and feigned contempt at such an outrageous proposition brought to them by one of their own flesh and blood.

"Okay, it's no dice," Bot said to Oliver and Elgar.

Oliver and Elgar were standing on the bridge in the manner of a pair of Napoleon's lieutenants at Austerlitz bargaining with the Mohammedans, as though they, with their arms akimbo, were deciding the future fate of many nations, many lives and much wampum because now Elgar anyway saw himself as some cavalry officer in a TV Western trying to sign an Indian treaty in the two minutes allotted the program between the two hours of commercials, and now maybe, both of them now, Oliver and Elgar, saw themselves ending the war in Asia at which everyone else had failed, not only failed but—and this is what appealed to Oliver and Elgar—had so entirely failed that they had given to Elgar and Oliver full power to say everything that had been said before.

"Okay," Oliver said. "If you don't do what we want you to do, then we will blow up the bridge and then we will blow up all of the bridges. We sure will blow up both bridges going into the ville."

"Yes siree bob," Elgar said.

"And if that doesn't work we will bomb China," Oliver said.

"And then Kansas City," Elgar said.

"Not Kansas City," Oliver said.

"What about St. Louis?"

"Noplace in the States."

"Why not?"

"Because that's where our loved ones abide."

"They drafted us, didn't they?"

"They thought they were being patriotic."

"How much will you give for the bridge?" Elgar said.

"Lookee, we don't want the bridge," Bot said.

"It's a fine bridge," Elgar said, patting the teak rail. "Why did you get us out here in the middle of the night if you don't want to buy the bridge?"

"Because we wanted to get you all out here and tell you where the tunnel is," Bot said.

"You mean the one where you're going to blow us up?" Elgar said.

"Yes."

"The very one?"

"Yes, sir."

"How much to tell us where the tunnel is?"

"Ten thousand piastres."

"I think the tunnel is apocryphal," Oliver said.

"The 101st Airborne never did talk like that," Bot said, and then Bot began to sing to the natives again in that gubble-gabble talk.

Oliver and Elgar waited to be blown up. That is the way it is in Vietnam. You spend most of your time waiting for the thing you are sitting on or standing next to to go up in flames and smoke. Now they waited for the bridge to collapse upward in one great Vietnamese explosion. But it probably wouldn't happen as long as the people who were talking gubble-gabble, the singers to each other, the hand-grenade workers, the tunnel diggers, were there. Because there would be better opportunities to get the white round-eyes, when asleep or in the incestuous pleasures of their beds, and that's not Airborne talk either, Oliver thought, and he said, "For Christ's sake stop talking gubble-gabble." And Bot pointed up and Oliver looked up and saw way up faint condensation trails. It would be the American bombers from Thailand come to bomb some bridges. This one? Of course, because we do not exist. And then the bombs began to fall.

"But why?"

Oliver and Elgar were safe in a VC tunnel. Safe with the VC.

"But why?"

"Because," Oliver said, "the American bombers didn't have time to wait for us to sell it. Didn't even know we were trying to sell it, because you see they don't even know we exist, don't even know anyone is down here."

"But Golly gee, they sure do know how to dig holes."

"Don't know anyone down here is alive. Because from way up there they're like God."

"Yes siree bob."

"Why don't they help Clancy, Yvor and Private Appelfinger?"

"Because they are the bombers, they have absolutely nothing to do with the war, any war. They are absolutely on their own. They are independent of the world. They are the bombers."

"I have figured out a way to end the war," Oliver said.

"Why do you want to end the war? Nobody else does."

"What about the dying and the dead?"

"It's too late to do anything about the dying and the dead. They know that."

"What about the people in the States who expect us to win the war?"

"They're crazy."

"What about all the Unfriendlies who expect to win the war?"

"They're crazy too."

"Then we people in the Bamboo Bed are the only people who are sane?"

"I wish those people in the States who talk about winning would come over here and do some of the fighting."

"Who would they fight?"

"The Unfriendlies."

"Finding them is the problem."

"They're all over the place."

"That's the problem."

"I like your idea that we're the only sane people here."

"Of course."

Oliver looked up and watched the great bombers disappear.

"The bombers will make it back in time to watch themselves on TV."

"Of course," Oliver said.

"Do you think, Oliver, that our being WASPs is why they drop bombs on us? That if this show appears on TV they can't maybe show minority groups getting bombed? That that's why they bomb WASPs?"

"Of course," Oliver said. And then Oliver said, "I don't know. Let me think about that. Let me sleep on that, will you, Elgar?"

And while the whole world slept the bombers sprinkled bombs near Clancy. Some country shot a rocket to the moon.

I have a dream.

There was a tiger.

A man lay dying.

There were some more commercials.

A man lay dying in a bamboo bed.

28

WE were a people, the dying Clancy thought. We were a people who had to make our world out of nothing, tigers and bullets, so we made it out of Roman helmets and toys. Do you understand, Mike? Try to understand. If you try to understand me I will try to understand you. I understand Madame Dieudonné. You would understand her. Anybody would. I believe I understand everyone in my outfit because we were all trying to make our world out of nothing.

Madame Dieudonné wanted to save her rubber plantation. We got to know each other very well. I never saw anything like it outside the newspapers. I mean you couldn't believe how the French lived in the middle of a war.

"Hello, Madame Dieudonné, has your son gone to Phnom Penh as usual?" Etienne Dieudonné would get in his car and drive to Cambodia every time the Americans threatened to bomb his hootch lines.

Madame Dieudonné had lost her husband at Dien Bien Phu when the French overran the Vietminh. After the French had overrun the Vietminh at Dien Bien Phu for the tenth time the French were defeated. And they all went back to France to live unhappily ever after. Excepting Colonel Dieudonné who was dead, and Madame Dieudonné who decided to stay on and run the second-largest rubber plantation in the world. It ran from horizon to horizon. It actually ran from Do Luc to Do Lin, one hundred square miles. With a swimming pool in the middle.

As Madame Dieudonné said, on Columbus' second voyage to America Columbus noticed the Indians playing ball with an odd globe of crude rubber, and now she quoted Colonel Dieudonné directly: "Columbus did not realize that this odd globe of crude rubber was worth more than all the gold in Mexico and Peru."

But Madame Dieudonné did. When Colonel Dieudonné got it at Dien Bien Phu Madame Dieudonné started to pick up her swimming pool and things and then she realized that she could not do this. It was physically impossible to take it all back to France. And as long as the war was on she couldn't get a plugged franc for it. And the VC implored her to stay on. They wanted everything kept in apple-pie order until they took it. It was a rich beautiful place running from Do Luc to Do Lin, with a swimming pool in the middle. Each tree planted ten feet apart in rows twenty feet apart running all the way to infinity, running all the way from the China Sea to Cambodia. It was a separate country that paid taxes to the VC.

That's what A for Alpha—that's what Clancy was there for, to stop all this.

Madame Dieudonné got used to the war too. Don't forget that if the Vietnamese had known war for generations, the French colons have fought forever too. Madame Dieudonné didn't know what it was like to go to bed without expecting to be blown up. That's why she always went to bed with someone. To be safe. Slept with Clancy now.

Madame Dieudonné's son Etienne slept outside her door to protect her. Protect her? So Madame Dieudonné had a secret door busted through in the rear that her son did not know about.

It was not true that the enemy, as the Americans claimed, were always regrouping and attacking from Cambodia. Sometimes they attack from under the bed. The point is that in Vietnam the Unfriendlies are everywhere, and there is no place and there is no time they will not hit you.

When Captain Clancy slept with Madame Dieudonné he

never slept. No one did. There is not much sleeping in Vietnam, not with all the Unfriendlies around. But the Unfriendlies were only one of the reasons why Captain Clancy did not sleep with Madame Dieudonné. She kept him awake. She would have considered it an insult if Clancy slept.

"Are you awake?"

"Yes."

"Why don't you stay on here and help me with the plantation?"

"Because I am in the United States Army."

"When you're finished."

"Ah, but when I'm finished I won't be any good to you."

Madame Dieudonné was silent, soft and silent somewhere close in the big bed. Madame Dieudonné was beautifully built. She was at the age that Balzac called the greatest achievement of women. Had Clancy read Balzac? Better not ask. Better not risk it. The danger with men is they are very sensitive. They can be put off making love very easily. With a word. Women are supposed to be the sensitive sex but Madame Dieudonné knew this was not true. One word from her about Balzac and Clancy could be put off. Balzac when there is a war on? Balzac when we are in bed?

No, Madame Dieudonné decided that there must be some other way found excepting Balzac to get Clancy to marry her and take over the rubber plantation. Although Balzac himself would be perfect, Madame Dieudonné thought. All his life Balzac had been looking for a rich widow. Madame Dieudonné was not only rich but owned the second-largest rubber plantation in the world. The only thing that stood between Madame Dieudonné and happiness was the Vietcong. A small matter of ten million Unfriendlies. Outside of that everything would be fine. But Balzac was dead. He had been dead a long time now. Madame Dieudonné would have to look elsewhere. Madame Dieudonné decided on Clancy because Clancy was here. And because Clancy seemed to have dedicated his life to fighting the Unfriendlies. And Clancy was good in bed. Clancy was handsome in an ugly way.

Clancy spoke French. Clancy spoke some Vietnamese. He would be able to direct her myriad workers, her hundreds of naked rubber slashers and bright insect-colored servants. And although Clancy did not hate the French, he had been stuck, as Madame Dieudonné had, with the remains of their colonialism. Although he does not hate the French now, he will in time, Madame Dieudonné hoped. Like most sensible Frenchwomen Madame Dieudonné did not think much of her countrymen. And like most colons she felt she had been abandoned by the French just because they had lost at Dien Bien Phu. That should only have been the beginning of the war. They had dropped her husband by parachute at Dien Bien Phu and then refused to supply reinforcements. The French had murdered her husband. She didn't even know where Colonel Dieudonné's body was. Clancy would rescue her husband. Clancy would fight the war the French never fought. Clancy would bring back the second-largest rubber plantation in the world. Clancy could be taught. The trouble with Americans was that they treated Asians as equals. The Vietnamese were children, bright insect-colored children, that need guidance and help. Clancy could be taught. Clancy did not have to be taught about how to perform in bed. Mon Dieu, are all Americans this good? Madame Dieudonné did not think so. Madame Dieudonné was not promiscuous. She did not know. Why take a chance? Better stick with Clancy. Like all Frenchwomen Madame Dieudonné knew love to be a practical business. Any other meaning of love was for men, foreigners and children. Where was her lover, Clancy, now? Lost somewhere here on the vast bed.

"Mon cher capitain."

"Yes?"

"Je ne suis pas encore fini avec toi. I have not finished with you."

"All right," Clancy said somewhere on the billowing ocean of bed. "But I am supposed to be doing something else here too."

"What else, mon chéri?"

"Stop you from paying taxes to the Vietcong for one thing."

"Who else is there to pay taxes to, mon coucou?"

"I don't know. No one else will leave Saigon to collect them."

"Tu vois, mon p'tit capitain?"

"And I am supposed to rout out the VC infrastructure here."

"Qu'est-ce que ça veut dire?"

"No one knows what the VC infrastructure means. But the army likes the word and it keeps us from having to learn English."

"Formidable."

"I think it means the local government."

"Mais dans ce cas-là, qui peut gouverner ce pays?"

"Who would run the country if the infrastructure is routed out? I don't know. We haven't figured that out yet."

"Viens ici. Come here."

"Where? What will you give me if I come over there? In English."

"In English I will give you all the gold in Mexico and Peru."

"A rubber plantation?"

"Yes."

"I'm coming."

"Where?"

"Here."

"Oh."

"I want something else."

"Quoi?"

"This."

"Oh."

"And this."

"Oh, mon capitain!"

Clancy held her naked body away from his naked body so he could look.

"Qu'est-ce que tu vois? What do you see?" she said.

"Heaven."

"What is this?" she said, looking at his nakedness.

"A man. Un homme."

"And this? Et ça?"

"My cock."

"Puis-je goûter?"

"Why not?"

"Ce n'est pas trop grand, mon chou. It's not the largest thing in the world."

"It is big enough to get the job done."

"Ah oui. Et qu'est-ce que c'est que ça?"

"Shrapnel scar."

"Et ça?"

"Bullet."

"Ceci?"

"Napalm."

"Triste. Et puis ceci encore? And what is this again?" she said, holding it.

"We are back to our favorite subject," Clancy said. "Where is Etienne?"

"Outside the door. Protecting me," she said in English.

"Will he hear the noise?"

"I have had the door, the wall, it sound-proof-ed."

"Why didn't you send Etienne to Cambodia?" Clancy said.

"I did. He return-ed."

"Why?"

"To protect me."

"From what?"

"From you. Like Hamelette he does not want anyone making love with me who is not his father."

"His father's dead."

"So was Hamelette's father. It makes no difference to Etienne."

"But the wall is sound-proof-ed?"

"Oui. Yes, mon coeur."

"Then we can ignore Hamlet," Clancy said.

have to answer that. This is a free country as long as the Americans are here. Did you know that a python has hips too? You have to cut one open to find them, but they are there. The remains of hips. The python once strode the world like a colossus, like an American. Excuse my calling you all these things, Python, but I am light in the head. Did you know that pythons don't drop on people from trees like in the movies? And pythons are not man-eaters. The man's shoulders are too wide; a python cannot get him down. I'm telling you this in case you get any ideas. A python could eat a child but that's about it. Americans are not children. A man could blunder on a python when the python is coiled sleeping. The python would strike him with his fangs, then coil around him and crush him and then, when it was all over, the python, looking at the mess in the somber light of the jungle, would wonder what he had done and why, what he had got. Can't eat a man. Too big. In spite of Walt Disney and all the movies and the Sunday supplements it is no dice. Remember that, Python. Americans are not children. Then you ask me what I'm doing way out here alone in the jungle? A good question, a fair question.

Clancy noticed that the blood seemed to have stopped running and was coagulating, dark red on his tunic, turning to an almost-black. How long would he live now? Will I stop dying now? And then Clancy remembered, don't cry, don't laugh, don't live. Who said that? Who's trying to tell me what to do? People are always trying to tell Americans what to do. We have got the world by the balls and people are always trying to tell us what to do with it. Or is it a tiger by the tail? You tell me, Python, you tell me what to do. I'm sorry. You asked another question. You asked what I was doing here in the jungle. It is the same question. I am the man who took Hill 904. Four outfits had tried to take it before we took it. Why did we take it? We took it because it was there. Hill 904 was there. That's why. It was because the Unfriendlies were on top. We took Hill 904 because the Unfriendlies were on top. Does that make sense? Well, a python doesn't make sense either. We crawled on our bellies to take it. Maybe a python can understand that.

Now, Clancy thought, what am I doing talking to a python? Pythons are the only ones who understand. Pythons are the only ones who understand why we took Hill 904. How about all the people who gave me medals? I believe now that the victory on Hill 904 led to the disaster at Red Boy. Do you know why?

Let me tell you the secret of the war. But first let me tell you how we took Hill 904. How we took the tallest hill in Nam. How Alpha Company crawled up the hill to victory and then marched on to Ridge Red Boy. Are you ready, Python? This is called The Hill Came High.

It was a good morning. It all began on a good morning in Vietnam.

Captain Clancy had noticed that the blood had started again. I'd better wait. No, I better not keep the python waiting. And I must tell someone the secret of 904 before I die.

We called it Hill 904 because that is how many meters high it was. The secret? I'm coming to that.

I did not call for an air strike because I wanted to blood the men properly. I wanted history to say Captain Clancy took 904, the toughest hill in Vietnam, without Air. That's a pretty good trick if you can pull it off. Air is getting all the credit in this war and I wanted to stop that nonsense. Air is useless in this war. Because of the jungle canopy they can't see what they're hitting and if you can see what you're supposed to be hitting it's buried so deep you can't hit it. I said I wanted the new men blooded properly and called off Air. Maybe it was because I just don't like useless noise. I also did not want to give the men the illusion that something was being accomplished for them.

Alpha went up 904 in three columns of platoons, 325 meters separating the left flank from the right. We did not use a point squad because we knew Charlie was home. I had sent a recondo out at 0500 and Victor Charlie killed half of it; it was a son of a bitch getting those men out.

The hill was a paradise. I never saw anything like it in Vietnam. No low vegetation and the forest canopy at ten meters and the canopy was all flowers and shit so that it was like moving up through a vast hothouse. It should have been photographed by the *National Geographic* or if we had somebody from *Life* that would have been good. Excepting that he would have been dead because nobody ever told us it was a whole regiment we were trying to take and no one told us they had bunkers five feet thick and they had artillery. I never heard of artillery this far south and I never heard of artillery in 2nd Corps. I never heard of guerrillas with artillery anyplace. We didn't have any artillery. We had mortars but because of the low canopy they were no good. Because we were in this paradise Charlie could fire straight through the wild bananas with their rifled straight-trajectory recoilless cannon and blow us all over the breadfruit and the palms and the orchids of Paradise 904. When you tried to dig in you dug into other Americans that had tried to take Paradise 904 yesterday. I dug right into one guy's face. But you dug around yesterday's people. There was room for bodies between if you poked around. The dirt was purple. Purple dirt. It must have been red earth, but then in that filtered light, filtered through the arcade of bougainvillea, Cambodian mimosa and bright tropic shit, it was purple. And the blood was purple. Everything became purple in paradise. We dug too shallow because we didn't want to dig up anybody. We didn't want to discover anything. And because that was all the time we had to dig before their artillery hit us like a busted world running over us. The train was whistling and shrieking and off the track and exploding and hissing monsoon steam and dying and coming apart all over us, shooting final fiery streams of burning oil and lead and pieces of eight, hissing burning coal and separate great explosions. Then its atomic reactors blew up in the burning banana trees. Then it entered all in on us, heavy, big, silent, and you were missing parts.

I said that we were dug in too shallow so that when the

rains came they flooded you out so that you had to fight to stay in. So that when you bailed you bailed into someone else's hole. It was like a flooded underwater real-estate boom where you bailed into your buddy's lot. So that finally you just kept the brim of your helmet above water and waited for the next explosion. The train was never late. I had my CP with Second Platoon. I was using First and Third as flankers with Heavy Weapons in reserve. Reserve? I didn't even know who the guy floating next to me was.

And now I'm going to tell you the secret. The big secret. Captain Clancy's secret secret. Iron Man Clancy's top secret. I am a coward. Clancy is a coward. Clancy never had it. Why do you think I volunteered to take paradise? Why did I ask, beg, to take 904? Because I must have known, felt, prayed, that Hill 904 was a way out. That's not true. Strike that. I knew, must have known by this time that there was no way out. Becoming a hero makes you feel a bigger coward than ever. I discovered that as a child. Nothing helps. I did not have to come all the way to Vietnam to make that discovery. I did not have to fight all the way from the Delta to the DMZ to recognize a coward each morning in the reflection of a rice paddy. I went up Hill 904 simply because by this time, by this long endless time, it had become a habit. Taking hills today that are lost, given away, tomorrow had become a habit. Ask any man in Vietnam. It had become a habit like the women who go each Sunday to church but only because they have gone all the preceding Sundays. Or the man who works in a coal mine but only because his father did and died there and that's what he's going down there for, for that same cave-in that killed his father. Don't you understand that anything else would be cowardice? That going up an idiot hill in a world of war is the only sanity? But the only order I want to establish, the only command I want to cherish and obey, the only thing I'm married to, is that I am a coward.

And so I jumped up and said, Follow me. Because no one enjoys being a coward. Because it was an old habit of mine.

Because everyone expected it from Iron Man, and because I was drowning in that bomb hole.

When I got up I got knocked right down again so I passed the word along to follow on their bellies. To follow the Roman hat. That's why I had this steel crest welded to my helmet so the farm boys would have something to follow. Up the hill the Roman Clancy went, followed by all the brave. Then we hit the instant swimming pools and we couldn't move back. The obstacle in front, the instant swimming pools, were caused by our B52 eggs. The preceding day they dug one thousand holes twenty feet deep and even when they are dry we call them instant swimming pools. No forward, no back. Just lie there in the flower arcade and die. That's when Air is good, when you're willing to kill everybody to save a few. We at least knew Air was coming. I told Appelfinger, my RTO man, who always followed my ass, to call Forward Air Command Bird Dog and give us a strike. I threw out red smoke and passed the word along to fall in a swimming pool.

The napalm came in almost before you could say the Lord's Prayer. The tunnel of jungle was consumed in a great flash. All the oxygen was sucked out and you could not breathe. There was nothing to breathe except a vacuum. Everyone died and then some came back again. Some came back to be eaten alive by the jellied gasoline that flew everywhere. It dripped from the wild burning banana trees and all the jungle turned into a dense red glow dripping with scalding deadly jellied gasoline. Some came alive again to be incinerated in the water. They have perfected the stuff now so that it will burn in water. Ask Chemical Warfare. Ask the man who drops it. No, don't. They don't want to know. Ask any man who was there in the Second Platoon. No, don't. There aren't any left. Excepting Appelfinger, Peter Scott and me. Why are Appelfinger, Peter Scott and me always the God damn survivors? Thank God the Unfriendlies did worse. I told Appelfinger to radio First and Third Platoons to move into our vacuum and continue the advance up Hill 904.

No one asked what happened to the Second Platoon. No one asked what we had done with it.

We assembled in the vacuum easily enough. It was like after an explosion in a fireworks factory. No more factory. No more jungle. Just a few breadfruits and palm sticks burning like dying Roman candles. The awful smell. It was easy enough to get the men to move out. The evil smell.

Victor Charlie had been exterminated in this sector. So the next hundred meters up 904 was easy. Then we reached paradise again and the Unfriendlies began to pour it on.

The hills in Vietnam look tall, smooth and undulating in the newspaper photographs and the picture magazines. Actually, when you are climbing them against the Unfriendlies they are a series of ledges. This is always concealed in the photographs because of necessity they are shot from above and the ledges or plateaus are camouflaged and ironed out by the waving top vegetation.

Charlie will always give you part of a hill in order to make a better stand on the next ledge. Charlie is cute. Old Charlie is smart.

Like I said, the next hundred meters were easy up, with my RTO Appelfinger hugging my ass, lugging the radio. The First and Third joined now, following my ass too, following my Roman helmet. I had that crest welded on at Ban Me Thuot. A Roman helmet helps. I was using a point now to find the hostiles and I still kept Heavy Weapons in reserve. Where was my Second Platoon? Ask the Air Force. Ask the friendly folk at public relations.

Where was I? Yes, the Unfriendlies up ahead. Like I said, Charlie will always give you part of a hill in order to make a tougher stand on the next ledge. Charlie is cute. Old Charlie is smart. When we got to that ledge Charlie rained down phosphorus grenades on us. We rained down CBUS on him. We don't use CBUS much in combat, it is too dangerous to use close to your own troops. CBUS is real murder against civilians. Remember a Vietcong is a dead Vietnamese. The Air Force says this in humor but I think they mean it. No, the Air Force doesn't mean anything. They just drop things.

CBUS is a canister filled with huge steel tennis balls, each containing hundreds of bomblets; the bomblets contain millions of minibombs and each thing goes off in turn like exploding firecrackers, shooting steel balls and sharp shit to all points of the compass. You can tell a civilian Gook who has been hit by CBUS because he looks sewn up like a football. The doctor slits him open with long strokes, takes his insides out, places the insides on a table, fingers through the insides for sharp shit and miniballs. Satisfied that he has got all the sharp shit and miniballs he can find he puts all the insides back and sews the Gook up like a football. You see them all over Vietnam. Women and children. Quite beautiful. I slept with one once. When I saw her I got up and vomited. Oh Clancy, oh Clancy, what are you doing here? I'm getting the shit kicked out of me by those Gooks. They're raining down phosphorus grenades.

But we will rain down CBUS on them. Air flashes in, Phantom jets. Brand-new bombers, steel fighters, the latest. The best. CBUS stream out their ass. Help prevent forests. Help prevent humans. Beautiful. The CBUS streaming out the stainless-steel ass of the fighters knocks down everything. Oh boy. Oh joy. Oh Clancy. Look at the world blow up. The world disappears this way. Do you want to see the world go? The world goes this way. It's quite beautiful if you're not in on it. For those who are in on it the world goes this way and that way and then makes a long slide to the wrong side before it goes back where it did not come from because you are standing on your ass. The world is flat and wrong side up and then burning again. The world is on fire. The world is fragmented by miniballs and sharp shit. The forest above is gone. All gone. There's plenty more where that came from. Where are the Gooks? Still there. Raining down phosphorus grenades. Must have been well dug in. Where are my First and Third Platoons? Some still here. Most missing. God is missing. Must have been not well dug in. The fucking Air Force. Should go back to bombing civilians.

I knew now that I would have to rout them out by hand.
I knew now that I had to take each Gook out of his hole
separately and strangle him by hand. Follow me, men. Where
are my followers? Killed by our miniballs and sharp shit
every one? No, here they come. America's finest. Following
my Roman hat. Up we go. Keep down, everyone, and keep
up. Keep up with Iron Man Clancy, the noblest Roman of
them all. The biggest bullshitter in Two Corps. The world.
A tinhorn Custer. A madman. A coward. The bravest of the
brave. They had all kinds of opinions, theories, wise and
contrariwise, about me. I knew. I knew because I know what
finally happened on Hill 904. The secret of 904. A key to
904 could be the key to every hill in Vietnam. Ask Clancy.
But wait. We are moving up 904. The boys are good. Well
trained. Well motivated. They are well motivated by the
Unfriendly phosphorus grenades raining down on them.

We have gained the ledge now without losing too many
more. How many more? How many have I got? They move
well and they are quick. They are quick because Charlie
makes them quick. Charlie is cute and old Charlie is smart
and his good position now is paying off. From his slitted
bunkers he is able to bring his awful firepower slightly down
slope because although we had gained the ledge the hill is
still up. Old Charlie knows every bump in the hill and he's
got compensator guns to cover the terrain not covered by
the flanker guns. Old Charlie has got us beat before we start
a million ways to Christmas. Excepting for one thing. Clancy's there. The Iron Man has arrived. I mean by that that
the only time Clancy thinks straight is when the battle is
lost. All comes into a sharp perspective in my mind as though
you are turning, turning, binoculars and suddenly you get
it clear and perfect. The picture is quite brilliant, in focus.
The problem with the hostiles was they had it too good. It
was all their own way. When you have got a perfect defensive
position you are finished because there is no perfect defensive
position. You are done. If this were a perfect defensive position there would be no more war. Charlie would sure win

this one. Charlie couldn't lose. Charlie lost. Charlie lost because I sent out flanker decoys from Heavy Weapons to shake the green bamboo, three clicks, fifty meters north, and while Charlie was shooting the shit out of Heavy Weapons I had Leroy and Dummy Dumphries encircle old Charlie's rear and give them two grenades each through their bunker slits. Silence.

Now you say, the day is done, the battle won. But you say that because you are a snake. A snake in elephant grass. What do people have against snakes? You seem a nice enough person. What you don't understand is we are only halfway up Hill 904. Another thing you don't understand is I would not tell this to everybody, anybody. The secret of 904. I am working up to that. It comes at the end. I want you to stay for the end. I'm going to die. Nobody wants to die alone. Nobody wants to die a hero. The trouble with heroes is that no one believes in them. The trouble with heroes is that we are born in the wrong century. Lonely is the hero. Let me be a coward. Let everyone else on Hill 904 be a hero. If that's the way they want it. But make sure it's the way they want it.

We would regroup right here at the VC bunkers and start up again. I now had about ninety ambulatory patients left to make it to the top. We had come four hundred meters up 904. Everyone had been hit by something. Those that were hit too bad I left along the way in perimeters. Old Charlie made it too hot to bring in a Medivac. The Bamboo Bed flew over a couple of times. She took heavy ground fire. She took so many holes we waved her off. When she came back we took a couple of shots at her ourselves. Everybody shoots at the Bamboo Bed. Both sides. Both sides shoot the shit out of her. Why? Because she's there. Because the Bamboo Bed always shows at a disaster. When you see the Bamboo Bed you know it's the end. Both sides.

Like I said before, we started up 904 again. I was leaving the too-bad wounded in perimeter. The dead could take care of themselves. I had three flesh wounds. None too bad. The thing that hurt like shit was the muscle of my left arm where I had taken napalm back there in paradise. The military call it infragel and that's what it feels like. They must have missed some of it. Leroy and Dummy Dumphries cut it out of my arm while Peter Scott sat on my head. But they must have missed some. It hurt like shit. No morphine. As long as you have command position there can be no morphine.

"Well, that's it, sir," Peter Scott said.

"Are we all set to go? Who's missing?"

"God is missing," Peter Scott said.

Up the hill we went. But slow now. I could see old Charlie was sucking us up. Old Charlie was going to have an ambush party. Old Charlie was smacking his lips watching us make it up. Old Charlie was happy happy happy. I could no longer stand Charlie's happiness. I could not take any more silence. I ordered our forward movement stopped. I had the word passed along for our line of skirmishers to dig in and the First and the Third were not to bunch up but maintain their line contact. I had Appelfinger call up to point on his crystal set. I questioned the point about any suspicious signs but they had detected nothing. I told them my arm hurt like shit and I would take the point. I told them they were no good. I told them from what I knew about terrain and from what I knew about old Charlie we were already in his ambush. Why hadn't Charlie sprung it? Because we weren't in good yet.

Charlie is cute.

I told them my arm hurt like shit and I was going to dig Charlie out. God is missing? I would take over the point. I took Weintraub, Tim O'Catlin, Leroy and Dummy Dumphries, and of course Appelfinger followed my ass. Peter Scott was missing. Leroy and Dummy Dumphries had signed over twice in Vietnam. They said they enjoyed killing people. No more, just that. They said they enjoyed killing people. I told them that that was not the correct thing to say, that it was negative. I told them that they meant that this was a dirty job that no one liked, but someone had to do it. They said everyone had their hangup, everyone had their thing. They said they liked killing people. I told them about love of country, honor and freedom. I told them about stopping the Communists. They said everyone had their bag, everyone had their thing. They said they liked killing people. They had not at first but now they liked killing people. I told them to get out. I told them I did not want dishonest people in A for Alpha. Transfer them to the Ghoulies, grave registration. Then I tore their transfer papers up, had them attached to my CP. I wanted to study them. I was curious. I guess every human being is curious about aberrant behavior. Aberrant? Aberrant means truth. By seeing them I wanted each morning to look into the mirror of myself.

"Look," I told Dummy Dumphries and Leroy in the ambush on 904. "Listen, I want you to understand me."

"We understand you perfectly," Leroy and Dummy Dumphries said.

"You can see we are walking into the neck of a funnel. It does not appear on my tactical map, but you can see the ridges narrowing in infinity."

"Infinity?"

"That's us."

"Does Charlie know we don't appear on any map?"

"Charlie knows."

"About this?"

"Charlie suspects nothing appears on our map."

"The little son of a bitch could be right too."

"Yes."

"Fuck me."

"Yes."

"We're in Charlie's ambush?"

"Yes."

"What do you reckon to do, sir?"

"Leave Heavy Weapons Platoon right here as a blocking force, then divide First Platoon into two recondo units and have them move up the ridge. First will jump off first. Second

Platoon will move up the valley on our right in the concealment of that wild rubber tree and then drop over above Charlie and cut his escape while the recondos from First are pushing Charlie off the ridge down into his own ambush."

"Then we'll all move in and kick ass on old Charlie."

"Yes."

"I'll go with the Second," Leroy said.

"And I'll go with the First Recondo."

The Bamboo Bed fluttered in now and hovered above the ambush just out of range.

Dummy Dumphries raised his automatic and gave them half a clip.

The Bamboo Bed jerked out and away.

"Don't. Don't, don't."

"I bet you'd like to do the same thing yourself, sir, wouldn't you?"

I set up my CP with Heavy Weapons and we started to push a little as soon as the Unfriendlies were pushed off the ridges by our recondos. As soon as Second Platoon had pushed up our flanking wild rubber valley and dropped into our valley way up to form the stopper at five hundred meters they were to give me red smoke. I didn't see any smoke yet but old Charlie panicking down into Charlie's ambush was too positive not to exploit, so Heavy Weapons moved up.

"If we move up too fast, sir, with the booby traps and all we'll get blown the fuck up our own selves."

"Yes."

But we moved up. Still no smoke from the Second Platoon that was supposed to form the stopper. Maybe the wild rubber trees were giving them a bad time. I didn't hear any shooting in the rubber valley. You don't need any Unfriendlies to make the Second Platoon shoot. Sometimes they will shoot at the rubber trees to make them come. They blast them with automatic fire until they come. White sticky stuff streams down their sides. A for Alpha called rubber trees "come trees." But now it was all silent in the rubber valley.

30

BUT now Clancy was looking for a way up Hill 904. The First Platoon recondos were forcing the enemy to bleed down the ridge into Heavy Weapons. Hooked in fire.

"You see anything, Weintraub?"

"Not yet, sir."

"If they can't filter through us here below they will try to swing through us over our heads. They will fly through as a band or in twos. There's one."

"There are two, sir, in the banyan tree." Weintraub clicked his M1 with telescopic sights off safety. Weintraub was fighting heavily bandaged. He could fight standing up or lying down. He could not get off shots from a sitting position because of the pain. Clancy had told Weintraub he would not have to go along on 904.

"Bullshit, sir."

Clancy asked Medic Oliphant what he thought.

"I think he'll hold together, sir."

"How long?"

"A few days."

"And then?"

"He'll come apart."

"Where?"

"At the seams."

"We don't need you, Weintraub."

"Bullshit, sir."

"How can a man with a Ph.D. in psychology talk like that?"

"Practice."

Weintraub, a tall slant-faced basketball-playing type from Brooklyn College, had marched in all the peace parades, burned all the draft cards and then had himself been drafted as a penalty.

"After a while you enjoy killing, don't you?" Clancy said. Silence.

"After you shoot a few it's easy, isn't it?"

"Yes."

"It's like shooting ducks."

"Yes."

"Monkeys?"

"Yes."

"After a while you enjoy it, don't you? It's like sex."

"Yes."

"If they hadn't drafted you you'd still be in the peace marches. You'd never know what a killer you are. That you're the best shooter in 2 Corps. Sometimes everything happens for the best. Sometimes when everything seems to be getting darker you discover new sex. The army is a whore. Love away from home. The army is a fucking good place."

"Yes."

"Weintraub, I'm not taking you on Hill 904."

"Bullshit, sir."

"No. I was thinking, Weintraub, what are you going to do after the war?"

"After the war?"

"That's a silly question all right. I'll take you on 904."

"Thanks."

"If you'll take it easy. I need someone badly who can hit from the outside. If you'll take it easy."

Now Captain Clancy watched Weintraub leaning against the sand rock, peering through the thornbrush up at the banyan trees.

"Anything?" Clancy said.

"They got good concealment."

"They wear that stuff."

"I know."

"Lead them good."

"I know."

"Any signal smoke from Second Platoon?"

"Not yet."

"They should have been in back of them now. Leroy must be letting his men shoot at the rubber trees to make them come. What's wrong with Leroy?"

Weintraub got off two sudden shots above Clancy.

"I got two."

"Good boy. Where are the bodies?"

"They're hung up. Here comes one."

A bundle from the giant banyan tree fifty meters forward cleared the vines and fell with a soft faint sock.

"Here comes his buddy down."

Another heavy thing, but not very large, fell off the banyan tree and landed near the first Unfriendly.

"Good boy. Why don't you try the next one prone."

"This is all right."

"What's happened to Lieutenant Leroy?" Clancy said.

"I don't think he's being permissive."

"What does that mean?"

"Stop playing soldier."

"Stop the peace-march talk. You hear, Weintraub? The peace is over."

"I know."

Something fluttered in and flickered out.

"What's that?"

"The Bamboo Bed."

"You want to try a shot?"

"No."

"What do you think it means?"

"Our conscience."

"Oh, God, Weintraub. My God. I never should have brought you on 904."

"I'm all right."

"You're coming apart at the head. Medic Oliphant forgot to sew you up in the head."

Weintraub leaned heavily on the sand rock, the M1 with the big telescopic sights at port. He wiped something off his face with his wrist.

"What do you see?" Clancy said.

"Nothing."

"I'll stand and draw fire," Clancy said.

"Okay."

Clancy struggled up and an abrupt burst like a door thrown open, the sudden tearing of cloth, an enemy automatic fusilade, sent him sprawling on his ass in the thornbush.

"Did you get him?" Clancy said.

"Yes. Did they get you?"

"No, I don't think so."

"Feel around."

"I'm all right. Where's the enemy's body?"

"In the rocks. The banana tree, three clicks north. See the blood dripping off the rim rock?"

"I see. I see. You never miss."

"You sure they didn't get you?"

"They never do."

"I know that, but why? Tell me why they never do."

"Maybe they taught you why at Brooklyn College."

"No they didn't."

"Maybe they taught you why Lieutenant Leroy hasn't closed the gap."

"No they taught me nothing."

"You're learning now."

"Yes."

"Good boy. I think we better move up." Clancy motioned to radio man Appelfinger who was hiding in the rocks and told him to get the squad leaders moving. While Appelfinger was busy on the radio Clancy looked for smoke from Leroy but he saw nothing. Forward Air Command swept over the battle and circled in a twin-engined push-pull Cessna. They wanted to drop something. Clancy told Appelfinger to tell Air Control to lay off. They always wanted to drop something. They thought the war could be won by dropping things. The Bamboo Bed from Search and Rescue was nowhere. Maybe they had learned their lesson. They did not want to drop things. But they wanted to stick their ass in things.

"Do you know what Weintraub said about the Bamboo Bed?" Clancy said to Appelfinger.

"No."

"Tell him, Weintraub."

"I don't remember."

"Weintraub got three hostiles. Confirmed kill," Captain Clancy said to Appelfinger.

"How did it feel?"

"It felt good," Weintraub said.

"Tell Appelfinger what you said about the Bamboo Bed."

"I said the Bamboo Bed was our consciences."

"Ha ha."

"Ho ho."

"Hee hee."

"Medic Oliphant forgot to sew up Weintraub's head," Clancy said.

Appelfinger stared up from his radio set at Weintraub's head. Weintraub was still leaning on the sand rock, still slant-faced and peering forward into the jungle for a target.

"I don't know," Appelfinger said.

"What do you think of the Bamboo Bed?"

"I would rather not say."

"Good boy. But you haven't shot at them lately?"

"Not lately," Appelfinger said.

"My arm burns like shit," Captain Clancy said. "Did you cut to the bone?"

"Yes."

"Get all the infragel out? That's a nice name for burning shit."

"Yes."

"All of it?"

"Yes."

"If I complain again shoot me, will you?"

"Yes."

"Thanks."

"That's what buddies are for," Appelfinger said.

There was a silence and then Clancy said, "Is Heavy Weapons moving up?"

"Yes, sir. Can I make a suggestion?" Appelfinger said.

"No."

"I wanted to suggest that if we are a blocking force we better not pursue."

"I want to suggest you stick with your crystal set," Captain Clancy said.

"Yes, sir."

"It's simply that I've given up on Leroy and I want to move into that patch of jungle ahead and exploit the clear field of fire on both flanks."

"You don't have to explain your strategy to a private, sir."

"When you're carrying napalm in your shoulder you can behave badly too," Clancy said.

"I understand. I tell you, sir, I God damn well understand."

"That's better," Clancy said. "Let's move the CP." And then Clancy did something that anyone who has lived through any war or any peace will never forget. Clancy's body had been leaning rearward in the thornbush. Now he swung his body forward so that it touched the sand rock in an attitude of prayer and now he pounded the sand rock with his fists, and now repeated in a high loud lament, each word coming across the soft jungle clear and separate: "Shoot me! Shoot me! Shoot me!"

Appelfinger leaned over Clancy as though he did not quite understand, as though the tongue were foreign. Then he pulled Weintraub's leg and Weintraub passed down his weapon with the big telescopic sights. Appelfinger received the weapon firmly in both hands, then he released one hand from the big semi-automatic weapon and removed Clancy's helmet. Then he took the weapon in both hands again as he knelt over Clancy. Clancy did not cease chanting "Shoot me! Shoot me! Shoot me!" Appelfinger reversed the weapon and tapped Clancy carefully on the skull with the heavy wood stock of the M1. Appelfinger did not swing the M1 like an ax or even a hatchet, but like an instrument used in some ceremony. Clancy went down all the way and ceased his chant. Weintraub came down off the sand rock and sat on him and Appelfinger took out his switchblade knife and clicked it open. Now he cut away Clancy's heavy shoulder bandage and now he said, "We missed some of the shit last time."

The wound was as big as a giant silver dollar and dark and deep, all the way to the white bone. And now Appelfinger shook his head like a priest, wiped the blade on Weintraub's leg like a butcher and began to peck away down there someplace in the huge silver-dollar wound like a hunter, and each time he found a piece of something he placed it like a hunter of gems on a stalk of nearby bamboo and then studied it, both studied it, to see if it was alive, whether it burned the bamboo. Then Appelfinger would go back again to his quest until he finally announced in a low voice to the yellowing Vietnamese sun, "I think I got all the burning shit," and Weintraub said, "Sure?" and Appelfinger studied the pocket, the hole in Clancy and said, "Until we see how he acts."

"See how he acts? Okay," Weintraub said, and got off Clancy.

Appelfinger got the clumsy bandage back on Clancy and the Roman helmet back on Clancy and they both sat and studied Clancy, waiting until Clancy came to, "to see how he acts."

The sun was a more yellowing evil as it hit into the late green day, the monsoon sky that was so wet it would rain if you coughed. It would rain if you whispered.

"Maybe you hit him too hard."

"No, I've hit him before. I hit him when he first caught the infragel."

"But maybe this time you hit him too hard."

"No, not this time. I didn't go to college."

"What's that got to do with it?"

"Plenty." Appelfinger looked up at Weintraub. "I heard you got drafted because you protested about the war."

"Yes."

"But now, even after a napalm you like it fine."

"Yes."

Appelfinger spit upon the ground, but it was a dry spit.

"That is why I want to check and see if I'm going crazy," Weintraub said.

"You're not going crazy, Weintraub," Appelfinger said.

"Sure?"

"Yes. I know enough about evolution to know that man adapts."

"You mean if he adapts to insanity he's not going crazy?"

"Yes." Appelfinger said.

"But he's crazy if he doesn't become crazy? If everyone else is crazy?"

"Yes."

"Why is that?"

"Because we have to set a norm," Appelfinger said. "Even if that norm is crazy. It's called a mean."

"And you never went to college?"

"No. I studied evolution on my own."

"It's an interesting theory. That I am not crazy."

"It's not a theory, it's a fact, Weintraub," Appelfinger said, touching Weintraub's jungle boot. "I promise you it's a fact."

"Why did everybody laugh when I said the Bamboo Bed was our conscience?"

"Because," Appelfinger said, "those guys in the Bamboo Bed are crazy. They are against both sides and they are for both sides. In any book that's crazy."

"Yes. I guess it is," Weintraub said.

Clancy stirred.

"He's moving."

Clancy got up to his knees. "Did you get all of it?"

"We think so."

"Then let's get the war on the road again," Clancy said.

31

Now do you want me to tell you the secret of Hill 904? The secret of Hill 904 is that it disappeared. Do you remember? I must have told you about that Forward Air Command Cessna that wanted to drop things. I hated that Cessna. The Forward Air Command Cessna could see that the Unfriendlies were escaping to the top of Hill 904. The Cessna could see that Leroy had not closed the gap. Do you know what happened to Leroy? Leroy was eaten by a tiger. Strange? The whole unit that was making its way secretly up-valley through the wild rubber trees was eaten by tigers. That's right. They got lost or something. Anyway we never saw them again. When a unit gets lost or destroyed and is missing in Vietnam we say they got eaten by tigers. They say they got eaten by tigers. Everybody says they got eaten by tigers. It's the simplest explanation. It makes everything easier. The Cessna saw that Second Platoon was being eaten by tigers. That they would never close the gap. That the Unfriendlies were escaping to the top. The Cessna decided to close the gap with Air. They overdid. They knocked down the whole mountain. Cloud after dark cloud of B52s came in. You could hear the explosions all the way to Kansas City. When they were all finished we looked up and there was no more mountain. The top was gone. It was a volcano now. More like a caldera, which is a volcano that has collapsed. That was the end of 904. That was the secret of 904. It disappeared. What about the Second Platoon? They disappeared too. We put the Second Platoon down as eaten by tigers. Everybody did. It's simpler that way. Everybody did except the Bamboo Bed. They are still looking for them because it's more complicated that way.

Let me tell you that if they find the Second Platoon they will find everything. Because I believe that the Second Platoon found a way out. I will find the Second Platoon, then I will know the way out. The Second Platoon exists. I believe that. They will show me the way out.

Let me tell you the rest about Madame Dieudonné because I haven't told you yet what happened while my A for Alpha was off chasing that pickup VC outfit in Cambodia, or was it Laos? That's the trouble with these countries, there are so God damn many of them.

And that's the trouble with dying, Captain Clancy thought. Everything gets as confused as hell. I don't even know, can't even see, whether there is a snake out there. Who does? I think I hear the Bamboo Bed. Yes, there is a snake out there. If I had my gun. If Appelfinger had left me a gun I would take a shot at the Bamboo Bed. Why? Everybody does. Everybody does because it's there. Because the Bamboo Bed is neutral. Because the Bamboo Bed has a sense of humor and because the people in the Bamboo Bed are out of it. They try to make us beasts. They have got us here living with tigers and snakes while they circle above us like God. While they circle and wheel above us like a bird. Decency and compassion are for the birds. During a war all these things are for the birds. The Bamboo Bed is a bird.

Snake, what do you think? Do you think we can let them get away with this? They are like Mike. Remember Mike? I hope Mike never sees what happened to Alpha. I hope Knightbridge doesn't see it either. Yes, I hope Mike sees it. I know what it looked like. I hope Mike saw it. I hope Mike sees what the hostiles placed in the mouth of Clinton and Dummy Dumphries, what Appelfinger and I saw from the bamboo. I hope Mike tells the world about that. I bet they wouldn't print it. Leroy and Dummy Dumphries signed on again because they like warm weather and got to like killing people. I bet they wouldn't print that either. It's in bad taste. It doesn't look nice. What the VC did to Clinton and Dummy Dumphries is in bad taste. And it doesn't look nice.

Well, Snake, what do you think about the Bamboo Bed now? If you think what Charlie did to us is bad let me tell you what we did to Charlie. How we got even with old Charlie. How we got even with Charlie even before Red Boy. In war you have to seize the target of opportunity. You have to do something to old Charlie before Charlie does something to you. Sound complicated? War is quite simple.

Take the time on the Delta we were on Search and Destroy with the gun ships and we shot up the hootch lines. Hootch lines are a single row of peasant houses along a dirt road or canal. There are two ways of hitting them, one is called recon by fire, the other is recon by smoke. Any way you slice it it ends up burning down the hootch lines and sometimes the hostiles inside. How do we know they're hostiles? War is simple. Because of their reaction. If they run, they're VC. It's that simple. They tell you we control the villages. Never at night. So we give them this trial by fire. It's okay for Knightbridge, it's okay for Tarzan and Jane, but who's going to fight the war? It's okay for Tarzan and Jane to be sanctimonious. It's okay for them to screw and all the rest of you to pass judgment at ten thousand feet, but who's going to fight the war? You're all screwing in your Bamboo Beds and every time A for Alpha does something you say, That's not nice. Well, to quote Colonel Yvor I say to all of you, Bullshit! Bullshit! and again, Bullshit!

Captain Clancy was not alone now. The snake had slithered off but a man had arrived. It was the same Vietnamese peasant who had decided to shoot Clancy, thought better of it because of the noise, then had fallen and lost his rice when he saw the animal. He ran as fast as he could go down the wrong trail and ran into a VC ambush. It was an ambush the VC had set up beautifully for the remains of Alpha, Clancy and Appelfinger, and the hostiles had got one of their own. You must be where you're supposed to be in this war or you're dead. Sometimes you are dead if you are where you are supposed to be. But if you are where you belong you will not be killed by your own side. If you are where you belong you will have the satisfaction of being killed by the enemy. It's not good to die by your own hands. The peasant running from the tiger in his goatee, pyramid hat and short black pants and American Army underwear had run into a VC ambush and been cut to pieces. The peasant had run into the crossfire of two Russian machine guns. He would never do it again. He would never do anything again. When he was hit he ran back up the trail and by the time he got back to Clancy he was dragging himself along, blood all over his American khaki underwear and black pants. He wasn't going back to Clancy. That was just as far as he got when he ran away from the fire of his own machine gun before he fell. The hostile peasant fell in the green bamboo where he could watch Clancy bleed while he could feel the faintness of his own life leaking into his bamboo bed.

And, as I was saying, Clancy thought, as I was saying before we were interrupted by that firing down the trail, as I was thinking before all that noise, we sure did good on 904.

But first I was going to tell you how we got even with Charlie, how we got even with Charlie for what he had not done to us yet on Red Boy.

It was on the plateau between Do Luc and Do Lin. That's where Madame Dieudonné had her French rubber plantation. The French? The French are still here. As soon as the French know which side is going to win the war they will know which side to be on. That's what Mike said the morning we hit the hootches on Madame Dieudonné's rubber plantation. Mike also said, "How does it feel to bomb the hootch lines, Clancy?"

"How does it feel to watch?"

"I can't believe it."

"You're an American."

"That's why I can't believe it," Mike said.

"You get used to it."

"No."

"What will you do? Will you do something intelligent for Intelligence?"

"I'll do something," Mike said.

"You'll write a book?"

"Everyone will write a book," Mike said. "What will you do with Madame Dieudonné?"

"I'm coming to that."

Captain Clancy looked over to where the snake was and there was a Vietnamese man sitting there in a pyramid hat bleeding to death in his GI underwear on a bamboo bed. Good, Clancy thought, that will teach you how to play war. And then he thought, that will teach me how to hold a ridge. Clancy thought he was seeing a mirror image of himself. Clancy thought the end was very near. That's all right, but let me tell you about Madame Dieudonné. Mike asked, didn't he? Someone wanted to know. Was it the snake? I want to tell everyone who thinks that Clancy made a mistake. I want to tell everyone who thinks the Americans are wrong. Before I die something must be saved for everyone who did it here, for everyone who died in a bamboo bed. That goes for you too, he said to the pyramid hat.

The Vietnamese peasant in the pyramid hat smiled when Clancy smiled. Outside of their mutual death that was the only communication they had. The Vietnamese peasant believed he was seeing a mirror image too. The only thing else they had in common was that they both had been shot by their own side. They were mutual victims of the Friendlies. But even if Clancy had said something coherent and aloud, instead of sometimes a babble, the Vietnamese would not have understood. But the enemies seemed to understand each other perfectly in death.

32

MADAME Dieudonné wanted to get married. That is, at first it was true. Then she had some other kind of idea. That is, she said she could not go through with any definite plans until Etienne had a marry-ing, until he was taken care of. I think it had something to do about the law in Vietnam, that I would get all the property. She wanted to give Etienne half the damn rubber plantation, one half of one hundred square miles. But not before he made a marry-ing.

"You can give Etienne the whole damn thing," I said. But she wasn't there, she was in the bedroom playing Tchaikovsky's 1812 Overture, and Clancy knew what that meant. It would be a wild night for everyone in Madame Dieudonné's bed.

The rubber from Colonel Dieudonné's rubber trees was all sold to the Paris-based firm of Rondeaux Frères through family connections and all made into rubber condoms. Colonel Dieudonné had used that very brand himself. He wore one at Dien Bien Phu against the Asian microorganism, the jungle rot. Madame Dieudonné insisted that Clancy wear one of the condoms. You would have thought that after having Etienne through the failure of Rondeaux Frères best brand, Scarlet Nonpareil, she would not trust one again ever. What other kinds are there? Rondeaux Frères made six different brands, eighteen different qualities, because each brand, Madame Dieudonné explained, carried three grades, Good, Better, Best—Bon, Meilleur, Le Meilleur. But the finest in the world was Rondeaux Frères Scarlet Nonpareil.

"That was some flying lesson, Jack. After a tough session like this how do you relax? With a Rondeaux Frères?"

"I've tried them all."

"Here, try a Rondeaux Frères."

"Do you save the coupons?"

"Sure. How do you think I got into the French Army?"

While Clancy was off inspecting the rubber trees Madame Dieudonné was playing the 1812 Overture, the simpleminded Etienne was listening at the wrong door, A for Alpha was off chasing the Unfriendlies in Cambodia.

When the rubber tree is seven years old and has reached a circumference of eighteen inches it is time to tap it. Starting three feet above the ground, the VC who worked for Madame Dieudonné cut a slanting incision. As he goes down the tree the worker keeps cutting at the rate of an inch a month till he reaches the bottom, then he does the same thing on the other side of the tree. It takes three years on each side for the cuts to reach the ground. In six years it's all healed up and you can start all over again.

In about six years, Clancy thought, the war will be over and we can start all over again.

Etienne was walking up under the rubber trees.

The milky latex oozes out and is collected in special cups.

"Yes?"

"The VC have return-ed," Etienne said.

"Tell them to go away. Tell them A for Alpha's not here. Tell them A for Alpha has not return-ed from Cambodia," Clancy said.

"The VC have come back to work."

"Good." Clancy let some of the dripping latex run over his finger. "Did they learn anything?"

"Yes."

"Good." Clancy tested the latex by allowing a drop of it to stretch between his thumb and forefinger. "Good. I could use boys like that in my outfit. There is a lot of combat talent around, but to perform well under pressure, that's what I look for. I could make them into a good team. Maybe I couldn't get them to be top contenders but I could make them pros."

"It's not a game."

"Of course it's a game," Clancy said. "It's not a war."

"It's not a game."

"All right, it's not a game. It's not a war. What is it? We keep getting back to a mutual insanity. It's strange that a simpleminded boy like you would have thought of that."

"You did."

"Then I take it back. We are in Asia to save the rubber trees. Can you imagine what the world would be like without the rubber trees?"

"Synthetic." Etienne pronounced it sin-tet-teek. "The world they have synthetic rubber now."

"Everything synthetic. The people. Everything."

"Sin-tet-teek," Etienne said.

"We are here then," Clancy said, "because we were invited here. We got an invitation. An engraved invitation."

"The Vietnamese cannot engrave."

"Whose side are you on?"

"Which are the sides?"

"I don't know which are the sides," Clancy said. "I will have to think about that."

"We did not invite you to the plantation."

"Madame Dieudonné did."

"No. Ma mère does not need protection. But what then does ma mère need?"

"Me," Clancy said.

Etienne was standing alongside a parapet-like stack of fertilizer. The bags of fertilizer were used as breastworks by both sides. When a bullet hit them, and particularly when automatic fire hit them, the stench would drive you underground. When a mortar hit them the smell would drive you to Laos.

"I wonder if my boys are in Laos."

"We were talking about ma mère."

You could hear the 1812 Overture coming out the tunnel. An overture is the part of the symphony that has nothing to do with the rest of it so the audience has time to get in their seats. It was to give Clancy time to get ready too.

"We were discussing ma mère."

"Were we?" Clancy said.

"Yes. I am concern-ed that you will be killed like Papa and she will again be all alone."

"We are all again all alone," Clancy said. "But the ass of life goes on. It's got to. That's what's left. We make a world out of nothing. Ask my bullshitters."

"Quoi?"

"My philosophers. Weintraub and Appelfinger. That's what I hired them for."

"Ma mère?"

The Vietnamese sun was descending into a fire fight somewhere out the hell and gone. Clancy could see a burning village erupting like a sudden torch. The flames and black smoke hit into the falling Asian sun and all together they turned the Vietnamese sky into a purple shroud on a horizon flag, a curtain gay with pennanting death, an effulgent storm of fire and sun for the ultimate act, awful and admonitory and theatrical too, as though the foreground, the curved proscenium of the world, might erupt with actors in fright wig and thundersheet to announce the end.

"Ma mère."

"I didn't hire her at all," Clancy said. "She just joined the outfit."

"But ma mère . . ."

"I know. But there is nothing I can do. Anyone can do." Clancy began to walk away. "Didn't I tell you?" Clancy stopped. "You weren't listening, Etienne, when I told you that every day, every second, we make our world from nothing. Do you understand? Rien. Rien. Rien. Nothing."

Clancy walked on into the blue-green gloom of rubber, the white tapping cups all hung up to catch the thick white blood that always dripped. No one knows what latex does for the tree.

No one knows why there is rubber in a rubber tree. No one knows what part it plays. Why it's there. Botanists have argued about it. It has got sugars and salts, alkaloids, enzymes and tannin, but none of this helps the tree. Rubber does not seem to belong in a rubber tree. It's just there. The white blood of the rubber tree makes no difference to the tree. If you remove the rubber blood the tree still does good. In a few years, except for the scars, the tree is the same. In a few years after the Americans have gone, except for the scars, Asia will be the same.

Yes, Clancy thought, except for the scars. And Asia is bleeding our white blood too, everybody's blood. All. And a thing about blood of importance, did any one of you realize that Madame Dieudonné is Vietnamese? You never bothered to ask. It's embarrassing. No one suspected it. Everyone suspected it. It's embarrassing to ask. If Madame Dieudonné was proud of her Vietnamese blood it would be easier to ask. But when the Americans are here the Vietnamese want to be French. Isn't that terrible? They think the Americans like the French. Americans hate the French. Why? Because the French quit Vietnam and they were right. We can excuse their quitting Vietnam but we cannot excuse their being right. Isn't that terrible?

Clancy hated the French but loved Madame Dieudonné. Isn't that beautiful? Clancy's love for Madame Dieudonné went back to the days of sex. Before love. Before love was invented and everybody got a divorce. Love is a lot of Christian shit that went on all over Germany while the Germans were burning people in ovens. And now love goes on all over America while the Americans are burning people in villages. Oh, what a lie, Clancy thought. What a lie. What then is the truth? The truth is you. The truth is Madame Dieudonné. The truth is what you do. I am a fucking philosopher. I mean it. All other philosophers talk about love. I am a fucking philosopher. I am proud of it. What do you do?

Clancy sat down on a bucket of rubber. I must have my buddy Appelfinger and my Brooklyn College Weintraub put this into English and read it back to me. See how it sounds. That's what I hired them for.

About Madame Dieudonné being Asiatic, that's all right. Most people in the world are Asiatic. Some of my best friends are Asiatic. Fuck the Asiatics. That's what I do. What do you do?

"Sir?"

It was O'Catlin back from Cambodia.

"With the captain's permission, sir."

"Please, no movie talk, Tim," Clancy said. "What have you got to say, Tim?"

"Over there at that ville, sir, Do Luc, coming back from Cambodia, we got caught in Harassment and Interdiction."

"You mean the villagers shot at you. Why didn't you say that?"

"I believe too, sir, that Lieutenant Dumphries is a W.I.A."

"You mean they hit Dummy Dumphries with something but he's not dead. I am going to teach everyone on my team to learn English before it kills me. It almost has. And I am going to teach everyone that K.I.A. means dead, and it's okay to say dead. That's why we're not doing so well in Vietnam, Tim. None of us can speak English anymore, and it's too late to learn another language."

"Yes, sir."

"You tell Dummy Dumphries to get his ass back here."

"Yes, sir."

"Where was he hit?"

"Where you said, sir."

"Well, you tell him to get his ass back here and stop playing burning villages."

"Shall I tell him to put the village out?"

"No, it's too late for that too," Clancy said. "Just get his busted ass back."

Clancy still sat on his rubber bucket, the music still wafted. Etienne still stared at the parapet. Madame Dieudonné could be impatient. You could not keep her waiting too long. Lately Madame Dieudonné admitted to being half Vietnamese. That was a start. If the future king of France kept giving her a bad time she might renounce all of her French blood. She was just the girl who could do it. Madame Dieudonné had Chinese blood too. She had something of everyone who had ever invaded the country. Most Vietnamese have some neighbor blood. Her grandmother had married a French officer. Her line had every kind of blood but American. Clancy would take care of that.

But now Clancy stood alien among the dripping rubber, watching Do Luc burn. If you were very quiet you could hear the rubber ooze. Would Clancy like to live forever in Vietnam within the rubber trees? There were worse places. But the war would never stop. The war would stutter but the war would never stop. That is the only thing certain in this world. The war will never stop. What else could Clancy count on? He could count on Madame Dieudonné. Everyone could count on Madame Dieudonné. Madame Dieudonné was the only Vietnamese in Vietnam that could be counted on by all sides. Madame Dieudonné stood like an odalisque in the rubber. Now she waited in the wings, waited for Clancy to make his entrance. Wait a second! There was another thing you could count on. A bamboo bed. Vietnam waits. The bamboo slithers in a quick clash in the monsoon wind. The bamboo waits.

Do Luc burned. Madame Dieudonné arranged things around the enormous bed. Do Luc burned. Madame Dieudonné looked quite Vietnamese in the dim and colored bedroom light. Her face wide and flat, the big and cat eyes shining in feline magic, the shoulders gently sloped. Good hips, tight ass, flat belly, and she moved like a Cambodian dance, and her room became a temple, a stage, around which the erotic perform.

Clancy made a wish. Standing there silent in the rubber trees he wanted the fire of Do Luc to go out. Do Luc would burn until dawn. That is the problem of the Vietnamese villages, they will not go out. Clancy wanted to say something. Clancy wanted to say he was the eternal warrior way back to the time when the first caveman picked up the first rock and hit the first used-car salesman. He wanted to say that he had participated in all wars, that he had been a captain in some good wars. The side he had been on most times had been a good side. That was the problem with those people in the Bamboo Bed. They were against both sides. They were against all war. They would sell a bridge to anybody. They would sell their chopper, the Bamboo Bed, to any side if need could be established. In the meantime they will screw at ten thousand feet and help anybody below who needs help. They were the eternal peacemakers. Fuck them. Have a drink. Who is right? Madame Dieudonné is right. Right for now. Clancy moved toward the swell of music.

Madame Dieudonné had laid out some French wine. By French wine she meant champagne. She said that at one time the ice to cool the wine had been brought from France by Messagerie Maritime, halfway around the world. Now it was made in the villa from electric wires that were cut by the VC when the payoff wasn't made. When the VC felt capricious. When everything else went wrong too.

The wine was good. The VC had checked the wires that made the ice before they left for Cambodia. That was nice of them, Clancy thought. I hope my boys did something useful before they left for Cambodia to chase them.

"I like the Cambodian look you have when you're naked," Clancy said. "You look like one of the friezes on the temples, one of those print rubbings they take from the bas-reliefs, when you are naked. Never be caught with your clothes on. I like your Vietnamese look."

Madame Dieudonné pulled back on the corners of her eyes to look more Vietnamese. "You like that?"

"Yes."

"Then we are happy. We can make a little love. Where is Etienne?"

"Near the fertilizer."

"I do not want to make a rush on you," Madame Dieudonné said. "Drink your wine."

Because, Clancy thought, people like you who move like you, who are naked like you, belong to a different world. You should start a different country. You did. You should live in a jungle. You do. That's what all your country is, a jungle that is foreboding and towering and solid, that goes on secretly forever so that the clearings are only a respite, only something they call a city now, but which will return to jungle. Because look at you, so unselfconscious and naked and natural, so that it is a joke and a contradiction that you call yourself a Frenchwoman and live like a Westerner when all the time and underneath you are a graceful and animal thing. You are this soft curved odalisque wild-assed this. Remember how a white woman looks? Clancy tried to remember and it must be something born to the city, born to the clothing and the gewgaws, bangles and baubles that conceal the awkward nakedness of sudden angles, that need the high heels to stumble down concrete as though throwing themselves forward and desperately trying to recover. And we call it a woman walking. They need the glass and steel and concrete called living to complement and conceal the tamed tits and straight hips we call women. And the poking faces and the no belly, abrupt shoulders and sudden angles and talk talk talking and we call this a woman in bed.

But it is not all that, Clancy thought, it is all this. How could a white man go back to that when he has had this? Habit. And because it's all good. And because the Vietnamese women only live in Vietnam. Only now in this room. Only now Clancy was naked and only now she was naked. Only now she slithered across the surface of that bed like a snake and propped herself up like a damn Spanish postage stamp, the Oriental Maja. The grip Clancy had on her was good. Clancy's grip. But she was gone again too, along his body somewhere and everywhere, the soft animal, graceful, a scintillant play of light, of body now against body, but light, symbiotic and light, so that it was a kaleidoscope, a titillating, shaking light within light, a hard warmth, and soft sounds, so that when the explosion of light came in a burst of sweetness and point it was a somnambulance of color, a something soft and hard that swept to infinity and back. The warrior now, no, not now. Now? No, never now, but sometime later. Now he would breathe hard into her soft color and wait, and linger and wait, and merge in warm light, and there would be nothing more, nothing—ever.

She said something in French. French? Clancy looked up and saw something different, saw Madame Dieudonné in her *position du Roi*, staring at the fake French photographs, still naked over him, but still not Vietnamese. She was two people. We are all a hundred people. Madame Dieudonné was two people. That's nice. Clancy ran his finger up her thigh and kissed her blackness and from her sitting position above him she ran her Vietnamese fingers through his hard hair, and some bangle, some Oriental bauble on the faint wrist, dangled free and swept his face, icelike and hard. Titillant.

Etienne quit the parapet and walked into the moonlit valley of rubber. The soaring, cooling moon had now mixed with the flames of Do Luc on the high distant rubber ridge and the moon mixed with fire threw a torrid maze of crazy lights on the arcades, the bowers, the streets of rubber, the fire-dabbled avenues of Vietnam, and even if, Etienne thought, even if, even if we are Vietnamese, that is a small price to pay for being the center of the world. And even if the Americans all go home, that will expose us, but get rid of Clancy. Will it expose us as collaborators with the Americans? Will it expose us to justice? Will it expose us to the tyranny of the mob? Everyone in Vietnam collaborated with the Americans during the daytime. Where will the mob come from? Everyone in Vietnam will conveniently forget the daytime. And even if the mob forgets what they did in the daytime and remembers what others did in the daytime, and only remembers what they themselves did in the nighttime, what they would have liked to have done in the nighttime, and even if this happens, there is still Cambodia to flee to and even if Cambodia disappears there is still Singapore and even if Singapore disappears there is still God.

Everyone thought Etienne was simpleminded because he saw all sides of the question and believed in God.

Even though, even though, and even if I hate my mother it is to protect her from being a whore. Everyone says my mother should make love. The doctor looks at her gravely and says, "Madame, my advice to you is to become a whore." The butcher, the baker, the candlestick maker, everybody says she should become a whore. That is, they want her to forget Papa. I must teach everyone a lesson. What lesson must I teach them? I must teach them to leave my mother alone. Clancy first. This is what I will do. I will go to America and teach. This is what I will do. I will go to France and buy a place in the country where Maman and I can live. Maman would like that. I hate Maman. Where is Maman now? This is what I will do. I will join the VC and kill Clancy. Then I would be a real hero. Then Maman and I could live in peace. Everybody would be happy.

Everyone thought Etienne was simpleminded because he thought anyone could be happy in Vietnam and live in peace.

But, Etienne thought, who can kill Clancy? Clancy is the eternal warrior and Maman is the eternal whore. They were bound to come together in Vietnam. There is nothing I can do. There is nothing anyone can do because all that is past and all that is to come has already happened and there is nothing I can do to change it. Everyone knows that Clancy has been fighting since the first caveman picked up the first rock and hit the first Papa. So he could have Maman.

Etienne paused in the rubber trees. I tell you what I will do. I will go to Do Luc and tell them Clancy started the fire. No, that would be the cowardly thing to do. I will do the only thing a man can do. I will break down the bedroom door and kill Clancy and kill Maman.

Everyone thought Etienne was simpleminded because at the great burning of Do Luc he seemed to be warming himself at the fire and to anyone who would listen he told how Clancy had done it. How Clancy told Lieutenant Dumphries to do it. Told Americans to burn the world down beginning

313

with Do Luc. Then he wandered back to the villa to listen.
To wait. To wait like everybody else.

Clancy felt the bangles on his face, then he pulled her
down until her heavy Vietnamese tits played against his face.
This is the way the world went. The male and the female fit
together nicely. They belong together. Everything fits. Everything fits in all kinds of strange positions. The best position
to be in during a war is the position Madame Dieudonné
found herself in now. Upside down. Downside up is good
too. It is all good. She loved everything, everyway, because
everything everyway was lovely, delicious, hard and sweet.
You take it as it comes. It comes as you take it. The world
is a soft sweet place for a straight cock. The world is a
dangling place for tits to be sucked, asses kissed, balls fondled.
The world is a myriad of asses and places and places for asses
to be. Take Clancy's ass. She did. Clancy was probably the
greatest cocksman the world has ever known. The eternal
cocksman. Clancy was probably . . . She turned him gently
over. Yes, he probably was. All things considered the world
was made for fucking. The fucking world. The male and the
female are known to each other in the known world. The
male and the female fit together perfectly all over the world.
In Vietnam too. It makes no difference whether they are
Friendlies or Unfriendlies. Everyone is fitted beautifully for
this. Beautifully fitted to make love in a bamboo bed.

"Come over here and I will wash you," she said.

"Wash me?"

"Rub me first," she said.

She was standing in the marble tub.

A marble tub in Vietnam surrounded by rubber trees.
Beneath a pool. Surrounded by Friendlies and Unfriendlies,
naked in a marble tub. Her skin glinted golden, Vietnamese.

Clancy got a huge towel. The towel was red and big like
a tent. He put the towel over her like a burnoose, then he
withdrew it suddenly like a magician who had put a rabbit
there and now revealed a naked woman.

"Voilà!" she said.

So she is becoming French again, but she cannot pull it off when she is naked. The Vietnamese body all shows.

"Hear me! Hear me!" Clancy announced to the assemblage of French furnishings. "What am I bid for this naked little French slave girl? As is. No trade-in. All in good working order. Do I hear a thousand piastres? Two piastres?"

Then over her sloping Vietnamese shoulder Clancy saw in his mind's eye Do Luc burning and the moon's mixed fire frightened him. And Clancy did not frighten easily. And he turned all cold.

33

OUTSIDE on the rubber plantation the VC were looking for some Americans to kill, and who should be sitting in the middle of all the rubber trees but Clancy's Alpha Company waiting to oblige. Until now Captain Clancy's outfit had fought mostly NVA, North Vietnamese Army units, that had come down the Ho Chi Minh or the Sihanouk trails through Laos and Cambodia looking for a war. These units would stop and have a look at McNamara's line which was being built to divide North and South Vietnam. They did not believe the line would work. The line meant that they would have to go over it or underneath it or bust a hole through the line, but it bothered them. The line bothered them because even the Unfriendlies hate to see us waste money. Oddly enough even the Unfriendlies knew the line was being built by the man who was responsible for the Edsel. The Edsel was an automobile that did not work either. The Unfriendlies do not have much to read so they look at the pictures in the American Army newspaper, *Stars and Stripes,* when they overrun a position. There was usually a picture of Mr. McNamara designing the Edsel. Actually there were pictures of Secretary of War McNamara in wire glasses in front of a blackboard with a pointer designing the line that would stop the infiltration from one part of Vietnam to the other part, or it would show our great Secretary of War demonstrating on the same blackboard how the war would be over in '64. The problem was that this was '68. Well, these were old newspapers. Another one, and this was a recent *Stars and Stripes*, showed General West-moreland demonstrating in front of the same map and the same intrepid newspaper correspondents, the boy correspondents, how the planned withdrawal of American troops would soon begin. Because the turning point had been reached. We have reached the beginning of the end. There were now fresh signs that the Unfriendlies were cracking. After all, how much longer could the enemy sustain such losses? That was the good part. The bad part was that none of the boy correspondents had the heart to tell General West-moreland that the Unfriendlies could sustain such losses from now till Kingdom Come. The Unfriendlies had about an even one billion men waiting their turn to come down the Sihanouk Trail. The intrepid boy correspondents did not tell the American general this because they did not want to upset him. Why bring up the obvious? Why be a wet blanket? And everything was going so well. Plenty of booze. No women permitted in the Caravelle Hotel but there are compensations. Church of your choice on Sunday. Those who can't get laid together can get prayed together. All in all the American correspondents are probably all Communists. Let us be fair and say strongly influenced by the Communists. Duped? Would you say that, Westy? No? What would you say, General? I would say that very soon we can begin our phased withdrawal, now that Tet New Year is coming up. We are beginning to see the light. The enemy is cracking.

The light he may have seen might have been the fire fight on Madam Dieudonné's rubber plantation.

Lieutenant Clinton and Lieutenant Dumphries of Captain Clancy's First Platoon Heavy Weapons were just back from detached service with Operation Hearts and Minds, and Second Platoon were all dead. They had been eliminated in an ambush, worse luck, near An Khe. That may have been part of the beginning light the general had seen. One part of the phased withdrawal Westy talked about already start-ing. Anyway, be that as it may, no comments, please, gentle-

men. Bethatasitmay here we are back at the rubber plantation. Rubber plantation?

Captain Clancy wiped blood off on the bamboo. Rubber
plantation? I should have said rubber plantation in the
beginning light. But I am never half so clear as I might be.
It spoils it. Boy, am I getting light in the head. Where are all
my animals I was talking to? Where is the Bamboo Bed? This
one will do.

Captain Clancy tried to remember what might have been
happening on the rubber plantation when he was so rudely
interrupted in his bout, in his liaison with Madame Dieudonné. Noise? Trouble? Etienne? No. Madame Dieudonné's
idiot child was off in Cambodia, I think. A fire fight? Who
knows?

"Listen to me, you all," Lieutenant Clinton said. "Listen
here to me now. I don't want no more firing at those little
rubber trees to make them come. Charlie could hit us and
we wouldn't know it."

Charlie had already hit them and they didn't know because it wasn't regular Unfriendlies that had hit Alpha in
the rubber trees. It was a pickup outfit of Unfriendlies from
the plantation itself. A newly organized bunch who had just
received a lot of American weapons stolen from the docks at
Saigon and thought they would give it a try. Actually they
had rehearsed this often. They were quite good. They had
sense enough to hit when replacements for Second Platoon
had not yet arrived. When Heavy Weapons was off on Hearts
and Minds. When Alpha's good captain was off having sex
with Madame Dieudonné, and at the beginning light.

"I think I hear something," Sergeant Pedernal said.

"That's us."

"No."

"Clancy?"

"No."

Now the roof of the rubber plantation fell in. That which
had been dark became light and that which was silent became pandemonium.

Several of the privates who were digging dug deeper and covered themselves over.

Hoping to be overlooked.

Two privates in the same squad ran toward the rockets.

Hoping to be killed.

But most looked toward Clinton and Pedernal, the commissioned and noncommissioned officers.

Hoping to be saved.

Captain Clancy did not show up. Captain Clancy did not show up for the rubber-plantation battle because he wanted Clinton and Pedernal blooded properly. They must learn command. They must learn not to depend on him. The United States of America and Clinton and Pedernal would one day have to get along without Clancy. Better start now. Start learning now while the Unfriendlies were practicing. Learn for Red Boy.

The battle swirled.

Without the two privates who had buried themselves, and without the two privates who had committed suicide. The battle swirled.

The thing to do would be to bend back a rubber tree, fill it full of rocks, and let it go like a catapult. But that idea fell in the profoundness of its own weight. Alpha was fighting it by the book. A for Alpha went into a half-zone full-press defense, which was in reality our offense. Charlie was allowed to believe by A for Alpha that their sudden mortar-and-rocket attack had knocked out Alpha. Each man in Alpha held his fire. Charlie moved into the Alpha zone. But Charlie was careful. Charlie suspected a rat. Charlie was timid. Then Charlie stepped up the attack.

Now Charlie came on like a flamethrower. Everywhere you looked there was black Charlie. Black Charlie blazing away in new black pajamas and black new M16s from every Middlesex village and farm, from in front of every rubber tree. Exposed, vulnerable, carefree, dashing. Victor Charlie was here. A for Alpha was silent. Commit some more men into the Alpha zone. Victor Charlie brought in two more squads for the cleanup. Now Alpha exploded. Grenade launchers first to stir Charlie up, then everything. Hit everything that moves. Because everything moving is Charlie. Full press. Charlie liked this. Charlie had found Alpha. Charlie fed more men into the zone. Alpha left a gap for Charlie to feed into the zone. That was enough. No more Charlies were allowed through. A for Alpha closed the gap. Victor Charlie's effectives were divided. Now Alpha went into a full-offensive half press. All Alphas, three clicks south, would fire first as Charlie moved to the opposite flank, then North Alpha opened up as South Alpha went silent. Charlie was moving exposed now from come tree to come tree and getting all knocked down. All red blood and white rubber come on the black pajamas. All dead now. All quiet. Half of Victor Charlie were K.I.A.s. The other half of Charlie had tried to break through to relieve but no luck. The first hour had gone badly for Victor Charlie. But what do you expect? It was a VC pickup team. They had tried to take wise A for Alpha. Clancy's Alpha. Clancy's boys. Clancy was there in spirit. In sickness and in health, in Delta and in DMZ, until death do us part. Clancy loves you. All. Every one. Clancy will die for us all. Clancy died for our sins.

Clancy placed his glass of formaldehyde beer on the diving board and sat on the end of the board himself, naked. Vietnamese beer tastes and smells like formaldehyde. It smells like the dead on both sides. Why? Ask both sides. Another smell came to the end of the diving board, caused by the soldiers practicing war in the rubber fields. It was the sharp, acrid, high stink of fertilizer. Colonel Dieudonné had been good to his rubber trees, and although not a religious man he had seen that his rubber trees were cared for and brought up properly. Particularly the young. Plenty of fertilizer. The young rubber tree takes four years to mature and in the meantime it must be nurtured and understood. There must be concern and love. Otherwise the young rubber tree will die. Colonel Dieudonné had thought about this much in his final days at Dien Bien Phu. He knew he had developed through selection and concern the finest rubber trees in the world, and no matter what happened to him at Dien Bien Phu he hoped, and it was an abiding consolation, that Etienne would carry on.

"Thanks for the flying lesson, Jack. Hey, let me have one of your condoms. Mine feels rough."

"Sure. Had the same problem myself until I switched to Rondeaux Frères."

No, it was only Etienne standing at the bare end of the diving board and he wasn't saying anything. Yes, he was saying, "Why are not you with your men?"

"Because I am sitting on the end of this diving board. Idiot."

"Are you going to marry with my mother?"

"No, because you already thought of that."

"I have not a marry-ing with my mother."

"I thought you left for Cambodia."

"Why should I leave for Cambodia? This is my country."

"No, it isn't."

"Would you like some wine?"

"No. I like formaldehyde. I'm getting myself ready."

"That's very chic. Americans are not all as stupid as one believes. That is very chic."

"Yes."

"When are you leaving?" Etienne said.

"When this war is over."

"I mean here. Here leaving?"

"Never."

"Nev-air?"

"When you get back from Cambodia."

Although Clancy did not want to make a marry-ing with Madame Dieudonné now he would later. Everything later. Now there was another hill to take—Red Boy. There was always another hill. Another thing a man can't, a man shouldn't . . . How can a man expect to live who has seen so many Friendlies dead? Unfriendlies too. Lately the Un-friendlies had become people. Isn't that a hell of a thing?

When did it start? When did the Unfriendlies become people? Someone should write a book—When the Enemy Became People.

It would be unfair to Madame Dieudonné to make a marry-ing with her because she had already lost one husband to the war. When the war was over, yes. Would the war ever be over? No. Not for Clancy. There would always be dreams. The dark shadows on the wall. The myriad dead. The Unfriendlies had become Friendlies and the war would never end.

One nice thing about marrying Madame Dieudonné was the underground villa. The reason that you never saw anything but a swimming pool in those hundred square miles of rubber plantation was that the villa was underneath. Underneath the swimming pool. It's safer to build that way in Vietnam. The house is not a target. The villa is cool. Any mansion with a pool on its head is pleasant. The villa with a pool on top. Tunnels led down from the side of the pool into the villa. The villa was on three floors, all underground. On the good days when there was no war you lived alongside the pool. When the war slowed down you could get a good tan.

Another excellent reason for marrying Madame Dieudonné was that she was the world's finest businesswoman. All women are, but she was the best. Women are able to sublimate their aggressions with business. A man needs the real thing. A man has got to go out and kill someone to prove that he is alive. When there are no more Unfriendlies, inventions in the world, man will sicken and die. That's what had happened to Clancy. The invention, the fantasy, the fairy tale had ended. The Unfriendlies had become Friendlies. The war was over. But the fighting went on. There's a problem for you. Clancy's dilemma.

Another genius of Madame Dieudonné was her ability in bed. But forget that if you can for a moment, dear reader, or dear Python, or dear Tiger, or that guy who was here in a pyramid hat, or whoever is listening. I promise you to get back to that, but for now consider the fact that she kept the munificent account with Rondeaux Frères after Dien Bien Phu despite the fact that the family connection was with the dead Colonel Dieudonné's side of the family. Colonel Dieudonné dead? It was hard to believe. After Dien Bien Phu he seemed to live forever through his splendid rubber trees. His spirit lived on through entering millions of women every evening through his rubber trees. The women of the world will always remember Colonel Dieudonné. And why shouldn't they? Colonel Dieudonné did not figure to live on after Dien Bien Phu through Etienne. Etienne had been a mistake. Etienne represented the failure of a Rondeaux Frères condom. Etienne represented the first failure. The second the colonel died with at Dien Bien Phu.

Madame Dieudonné told everyone. Women have no secrets. Women call anything a secret they tell to everyone. That's why men burst. Rondeaux Frères burst. Everything bursts excepting women, because they have no secrets. Madame Dieudonné remembered the Rondeaux Frères well that produced Etienne. It was scarlet. It had the usual company motto on it. What's the motto? Tell you later. No, that is not the company motto. Who wants to know? Tiger? Python? Reader? The guy who was listening in the pyramid hat? Let me finish about the scarlet condom. It had the motto on it because it was all class. Built for the carriage trade. Thin as a gossamer. Colonel Dieudonné raved about it. Raved about it those final seconds at Dien Bien Phu while dying into the bamboo.

Clancy could see from the end of the diving board that Etienne had disappeared. To Cambodia? Clancy could also hear the way the battle was going. He had heard too many battles. At one time Clancy believed the war could be won, as much as any war can be won. It would be simply a process of winning a series of battles. But that had already happened and even now A for Alpha was fighting a battle on a rubber plantation. A plantation of rubber that had been conquered one week before by B for Bravo.

Why not marry this rich French broad and cop out of the army? In time of war you cannot do this. But there was no war. War had never been declared. Congress in its wisdom had decided that there was no war. Madame Dieudonné would agree. Business was good. Taxes were high but the Vietcong left loopholes in the tax laws for the rich. For example, par exemple, as Madame Dieudonné said, you get tax deductions for the rubber trees the Americans shoot to make come. A tax depletion allowance for American defoliation. Amortization based on future continuous American operations Ranch Hand, Market Time and Hearts and Minds. No tax deductions for VC damage. The Vietcong were angels. What possible harm could little angels do saving their country?

A messenger came up to the plastic platform at the base of the diving board with a message from Lieutenant Clinton. Clinton wanted to know whether they should pursue the enemy into Cambodia. Hot pursuit?

"No."

"Begging your pardon, sir, but we could destroy them."

"Soldiers," Captain Clancy said, "only say 'Begging your pardon, sir' in books."

"Yes, sir."

Tim O'Catlin was the boy standing at the wrong end of the diving board. He had some old blood on his pants and some fresh stuff on his shoulder where stars would have been placed had he been a general. He was a pinch-faced Boston slum boy out of Charles Dickens who was somehow related to Brendan Behan, an Irish poet who died of drink, which made him interesting to Clancy. Made Tim interesting, not Brendan Behan.

"You'll get yourself killed in Cambodia, Tim," Clancy said.

"Yes, sir."

"That's just a pickup VC outfit, Tim, that tried to take us on for practice."

"But they had American weapons, sir."

"Imitation is the sincerest form of flattery, Tim. Stupidity. Still, maybe they'll get the bugs out of our ordnance."

"Yes, sir."

"You tell Clinton to come home."

"Begging your pardon, sir, but you mean we were only fighting peasants?"

"Yes. But if they suck you into Cambodia you'll get hit with the real thing."

"Yes, sir."

"How many of theirs did we get?"

"We got a confirmed body count on theirs of eleven."

Clancy moved the formaldehyde glass three inches to the left on the burlap pad of the diving board. The beer became a scintillant amber in the Vietnamese sun.

"Ours?"

"None."

"Good boy, Tim."

"We took no K.I.A.s, sir."

"I've got good boys," Clancy said.

"We took three wounded."

"Who?"

"Shaplan, Kerr and Weintraub."

"Bad?"

"Superficial."

"I've got good boys."

"Weintraub is gutted kind of bad."

"Again?" Clancy shook his formaldehyde. "I can't spare Weintraub."

"Medic Oliphant's got him patched up."

"Medic Oliphant is no good," Clancy said. "He should have been a doctor but not a medic. He's no fucking good."

"He's got the internal bleeding stopped. It's not coming out of his mouth no more."

"Not good enough. I can't spare Weintraub. He's the only good shooter I got. All my boys are good close in when the play is working, but I need someone who can hit from outside. You got to get those monkeys in the trees or they can hurt you very badly when you're in perimeter and they have the trees. Clinton should never have committed Weintraub in a pickup fight."

"Weintraub went into the full press on his own."

"Weintraub is stupid enough to play hero but Clinton should have been smart enough to stop him. That's what we're paying Clinton for. That's why we hired him. That's why we don't sell him to the hostiles." Clancy winked at Tim and put down the glass.

"Yes, sir."

"You tell Lieutenant Clinton to bring the boys home. Everybody wants to go to Cambodia. You tell Medic Oliphant to pull Weintraub through or I'll kick his ass."

"Yes, sir."

"Tell Oliphant he should have been a doctor."

"Yes, sir."

"Tell—no, don't bother. Tell me, Tim, what did you think of Brendan Behan?"

"I never knew him personally, sir."

"Where are you going?"

"To stop Lieutenant Clinton from going to Cambodia."

"Cambodia's a long way."

"Five thousand meters, sir."

"Five thousand meters is a long way. Tell me, what did your family think of Brendan Behan?"

"They never said, sir."

"Tim, did anyone in A for Alpha ever tell you what a great conversationalist you are?"

"Yes, sir."

"Crazy sons of bitches. They would. I got good boys. You tell Clinton to come home. Tell Medic Oliphant I'm going to kick his ass real good if he fails on Weintraub. I need that boy on Red Boy. I was saving him until I could bring another boy along to take his place. All right, Tim, go and tell Clinton to bring my boys home."

Tim disappeared into the rubber trees and a beginning monsoon seep.

Clancy sloshed the bitter remains of his formaldehyde around in his shell glass, then looked down at his cock, then up at where the sun was slicing through the big multiclouds. Yes, that's what the son of a bitch Medic Oliphant should have been, Clancy said to the Asian heaven. A fucking doctor.

34

MADAME Dieudonné often wrote to the King of France. Like all colons she treated the mother country not as it was but as it should be. She was writing to the pretender, the Duc de Paris, who lived in exile in Belgium. Sometimes he answered. When the now and future king answered she framed his letters and tacked them over her bed on picture hooks. When Madame Dieudonné was active in bed with Clancy she assumed *le position du Roi* so that she could communicate with the king while having Clancy. It was the only attitude in which she could achieve orgasm. She had assumed the same position with the late Colonel Dieudonné—la femme en dessus. Clancy claimed that when she achieved orgasm she shrieked Long live the King! This was not true. Pas vrai. But she thought the observation très chic. It was true that she played Tchaikovsky's 1812 Overture during intercourse. If you can call what Madame Dieudonné, any Frenchwoman, does in bed intercourse. Again Clancy's mot juste. Again Clancy was not complaining. Sometimes she played Beethoven's Ninth, on occasions Haydn's court music. You could tell, Clancy could tell now, what kind of performance she would put on by the tape she selected. When she played Stravinski's Fireworks, Feu d'Artifice, you knew everyone in bed was in for a wild night. If that be the case then it was equally true that when the party was over Madame Dieudonné was all biz. There was much paperwork to be done on the plantation. This was supposed to be the job of her stupid son Etienne but he spent most of his time listening at the door to learn whether she was being unfaithful to him. That is why she called him Hamelette. This is in part why she played the music. But Etienne was not that easily deceived by his mother's deceits—the soundproof-ed walls, the faint strains of the 1812 Overture. Etienne was stupid but he was still French. The problem, the business, that Madame Dieudonné faced this Vietnamese morning was that the pool leaked. They always will. You do not realize this unless you live under a swimming pool. Few of us do. Madame Dieudonné did. The three-story villa had been built entirely underground with the pool on top to protect the foreigners inside from the Unfriendlies outside. The people of Vietnam have been Unfriendlies ever since they were invaded by the first invader, the Chinese, three thousand years ago. That's a long time to be Unfriendlies. They were getting good at it. That is why the Dieudonnés built underground. The underground villa. They were not the first to think of living underground in Vietnam. Among others the Chinese tried it fifteen hundred years ago. But the Dieudonnés were the first to do it so God damn well.

Madame Dieudonné had first corresponded, again through her late husband's connections (the last to die at Dien Bien Phu) with the late great French architect Le Corbusier. But he "could not come." If you cannot come how can you call yourself a man? But Madame Dieudonné crossed that out and wrote to the architect Corbusier, "I will double your fee."

"I do not believe in houses underground."

"Then I do not believe in Corbusier." She crossed that out and wrote, "Then you do not believe in Vietnam."

When Madame Dieudonné crossed something out it was still readable. She wanted people to know how she felt without being rude.

Bien, bien. The pool was leaking. All of her bright-insect rubber-plantation workers were being pursued into Cambodia by the Americans. But today was another day. Tomorrow the workers would be back. It was their way of showing their mettle. They liked the Americans fine. They fought them because they were here. It was also an excuse to get more arms into Cambodia to be buried under a temple and used another day. They liked being chased by the Americans. It was a game. Draining rubber trees was a bore. It was the same with Colonel Dieudonné in the Garde Mobile. Before Dien Bien Phu the French used to chase the bright insects all the time. Then the insects gobbled the spider. Dien Bien Phu ended the game.

Bien, bien, but the roof is still leaking. The pool drips on the underground. The villa had been built without Corbusier by removing a hill in the middle of the rubber trees, then building the villa, then piling the hill back up over it, placing a pool on top to mark the spot. You could see the villa beautifully from the air. It refracted a blue mirror in the midst of one hundred square miles of green rubber. Coming back from bombing the north the Americans could always tell where they were by the blue mirror.

Now the mirror leaked. Madame Dieudonné told a boy to go up and pour a can of American Army radiator stop-leak into the pool. That usually stopped it. Everything in Asia is borrowed from the American Army. If the American Army quit Vietnam it would set the country back to the time before Christ, which would be fine with them. If that failed, if the American Army radiator stop-leak failed, there was always Elmer's Glue. Asia is held together with Elmer's Glue. You could not tell now until the pool got hot in the noon sun whether the radiator fluid would work. Elmer's Glue always worked but it took about a gallon. It looked like latex that came from the rubber trees but it came from the American Army too.

The Vietnamese who worked in the underground villa were never let out. Some were born there, some had died there. None tried to escape. There was a continuous war above them. They did not feel lucky or unlucky to be underground. It was simply where they lived. Some people lived in the mountains, some in the valleys. This is where they lived. Sometimes when the children got out of line the parents threatened to send them up and out where the fighting was, the napalm and the CBUSs. They threatened the children with the hell of the surface of the earth. The children of course did not believe them, but one day a child got out and came back and told them it was true. After that the underground children believed their parents. When the bombing on the surface of the earth was particularly bad and the underground shook like hell they would all gather in the communications chamber to listen to what was happening above.

Madame Dieudonné went into the communications room now. There were four Vietnamese in jungle uniforms working the radio telephones that were in contact with each part of the hundred square miles of the neat jungle of rubber above. This room was used in war and peace. There were tactical and topographical maps on the wall. These were map coordinates so that artillery could be brought to bear on any part of the plantation. There were huge maps with red, green, yellow and blue pins which the radio telephone people kept moving about. The pins represented various kinds of Friendlies and Unfriendlies and all their movements on the surface were monitored here below.

A for Alpha's radio man, PFC Appelfinger, was seated in a corner beneath a fluorescent that turned him blue, reading Charles Darwin's *Variations of Plants and Animals Under Domestication.*

"Did you know," Appelfinger said as Madame Dieudonné entered, "that Charles Darwin studied for the ministry?"

"No," Madame Dieudonné said. "I know the pool is leaking."

"Where do you keep the Elmer's Glue?"

Appelfinger went up top with the glue. While Appelfinger poured the white stuff into the pool he studied Captain Clancy seated naked and Buddha-like at the end of the diving board.

"Did you know, sir, that Charles Darwin never formally studied science?"

"I know that Clinton lost Weintraub. He won't make it to Red Boy."

"Medic Oliphant will pull him through, sir."

"Let's hope so, Appelfinger."

"Yes, sir."

"I told you that when we were alone not to sir me."

"Okay, Clancy."

"It gives me the creeps."

"This place gives me the creeps." Appelfinger put back the cap on the Elmer's Glue. "Wouldn't you say this place was bizarre?"

"Yes," Clancy said. "But so is the war."

"How long has it been going on?"

"Forever."

"How long ago was Dien Bien Phu?"

"That word is never supposed to be mentioned."

"How long ago was it?"

"Almost fifteen years."

"That's almost before some of us were born."

"Yes."

"It seems like everything is measured here before or after Dien Bien Phu."

"Yes."

"Where is it?"

Clancy pointed his arm. "Out thataway. Not far." Then he looked down.

"What's the matter?"

Clancy was staring into his formaldehyde beer. "I have had it."

"Dien Bien Phu? Did that scare you?"

"No. I am getting scared of myself."

"Everyone goes through that, Clancy. You'll pull out."

They looked at each other across the blue mirror.

"I hope so, Appelfinger."

"Medic Oliphant says it is the most common sickness in Vietnam."

"On both sides?"

"Yes."

"What's the treatment?"

"Death."

The Elmer's Glue penetrated, octopuslike, into the deep blue of the mirror.

"Come on now."

"He says they get themselves into a situation where they get killed."

"I see," Clancy said. "I see. But I can beat it. I see," Clancy said. "But—but I know a way out."

"Of course you do, Clancy."

"I will be all right."

"Of course you will, Clancy. They didn't call you Iron Man for nothing."

Clancy was silent. Then Clancy said, "They say she's death. They say she's living underground in a grave. They say we are visiting a grave."

"Who says? Nobody says. Madame Dieudonné is a very beautiful woman, a perfect woman. She lives underground because there is a war up here. It is perfectly logical. It makes sense."

"Does the surface make sense, Appelfinger? Does the war?"

"Yes, of course. There will always be war."

"Let's stop it."

"That's against regulations."

"Let's win it."

"That's against regulations too."

"Then we go back to fighting."

"Like everybody else."

"I see. I see," Clancy said. "It's normal, like everybody else. You have been a help, Appelfinger."

"That's what a buddy's for."

"Still?"

"Still nothing, Clancy. In a little bit you'll be perfectly

all right. You've helped a lot of boys from Alpha in the same fix."

"Maybe I am death."

"Shake it off, Clancy. You got to shake it off. Where is the Iron Man? Where is the old Clancy?"

Clancy looked out over all the rubber trees. Way out the Bamboo Bed flickered in and flickered out like a bird.

"I don't know where he is," Clancy said.

"You said before you were beginning to see a light."

"I didn't say that. General Westmoreland said that."

"You said you know a way out."

"Yes," Clancy said. "But it's a secret passage."

"You wouldn't even tell a buddy?"

"Not until I know whether it works."

"Then you'll tell me?"

"Then I'll tell everybody," Clancy said.

"Why do you want the boys back from Cambodia?"

"Red Boy."

"Are you going to take that one too?"

"Why not?" Clancy said.

"Because there are millions of hills in Nam. Why do we have to pick one with Unfriendlies on it?"

"The High Command."

"Who is the High Command?"

"Insanity," Clancy said.

"If that's all you have to say then you're not worth listening to," PFC Appelfinger said.

"Thank you," Clancy said taking the last of the formaldehyde beer and leaning forward staring across the blue mirror. "The captain wishes to thank the private for giving him the message."

"As Charles Darwin said, 'That's what buddies are for.'"

"Do we have a Charlie Darwin in the outfit?"

"We have now," Appelfinger said.

"Yes." Clancy looked around. He felt he was not taking part in the conversation. He was only saying words. Now he had something to say and he placed the glass in the Vietnamese sun next to his naked body, both warm in the sun, scintillant and alive in the morning dazzle. Hooked in sun.

"Does he know a way out?"

"No. No one does."

"I do. I swear to Christ I do, Appelfinger. I know a way out."

"Yes, sir, I'm afraid you do."

35

THE Bamboo Bed darted, danced above the Friendly and the Unfriendly in erratic flight, then paused, a great bright butterfly surprised at some flash movement below in the continuous jungle. The jungle that knew their alien fate. Solemn, somber and vast, the jungle remarked their presence, silent, serene, endless, indifferent.

Captain Clancy lay against the mahogany tree where Appelfinger had left him and thought of all the nice things that were coming to pass, all the good things that were going on around him. This was not ironic. The forest was growing back on Red Boy. The jungle did not take long to recover. There was an army of parasol ants, carrying building materials over their heads like umbrellas, in front of him now. Soon they would have the homes rebuilt that were destroyed at Red Boy. The peasant in the short black pants and pyramidal straw hat five meters to the right was crying from wounds inflicted by his own people. By people who were himself, Clancy thought. But he looked as though he had been a good breeder and in some part of the jungle kids were growing up that would take the place of people who were himself, that were dying in another part of the jungle. Appelfinger's moral evolution had failed. People were not getting any better, but there would always be plenty of them. If they did not evolve they would revolve. What the hell does that mean? Where is Appelfinger? Where is Madame Dieudonné? A man can use a woman when he is dying. Where is Colonel Yvor? And where is Captain Knightbridge and his gang and the Bamboo Bed? We have got our bamboo bed right here, he said to the enemy peasant, both of us, and dying in the same bamboo bed. Move over.

Stop bleeding. Do you want me to take your temperature? What were we fighting about? I don't remember.

Now Clancy remembered Madame Dieudonné. She was a good memory. He would have to get back to her underground villa. The bedroom underground. He would have to get back right away. "Peasant?" he said to the dying Vietnamese, "how do I get back to the Bamboo Bed, not the bamboo we're lying on now or the one flying around in the air, but the original. The one and only. You don't know? Well, you're not much help."

Can you see Ridge Red Boy? The one over there with the red top. There's where I will crawl to. If a man has got to be eaten by a tiger it should be in a place he knows. You agree? A place he lost something. That's where they were eaten by tigers. I must discover a way out. Everyone knows that only the Christians are eaten by tigers. They must have found a way out. Did Alpha escape to Tibet? Did they go out by way of Laos and India to Nepal? Every soldier on any side dreams of the great escape. Except Clancy. Clancy was the original Roman and Clancy had come to fight. But it would be interesting to know the way out. My boys must have left some message, some especial code for Clancy, something, some cipher that would be understood by another soldier. Yes, we must make it up Red Boy while we still have a little life left, he said to the peasant. Are you game? Want to try it? The peasant, dripping blood into the bamboo, seemed to shake his head yes. But I haven't said anything, Clancy thought. With this throat I can't say anything. But he seems to read me good. All the dying understand. The dying speak a universal unspoken language. Do you hear those shots? They must be my buddy Appelfinger. It must be near the end for Appelfinger because he's firing in very short bursts to conserve ammo.

*   ✿   ✿

Private First Class Appelfinger and Peter and Bethany had been found in their clearing in the jungle by Colonel Yvor and Billy Joe. They had been reinforced by Appelfinger at the bottom of the barrel. The incompetent had arrived to save the inept. The improbable to save the impossible. They were all the people in any war who will always find an indefensible position to defend. When they ran they should have been standing and when they stood they should have run.

"But on the other hand," Appelfinger said, "what about if you're lost in this jungle, I don't think either standing or running does any good. I think you end up right where you are no matter what you do, and where you are is where you die."

"I wouldn't say that," Bethany said.

Colonel Yvor and Billy Joe were not saying anything yet. They were both too tired and surprised to talk. They had found the way into Appelfinger's perimeter following the noise of the shooting. They had expected to find soldiers and instead they had found this. They had not recovered yet from their discovery.

When Colonel Yvor arrived at 0900 hours, thirty minutes ago, he whispered something to Sergeant Billy Joe and they had pulled in rotting palm logs to improve the perimeter so they all huddled now in back of an apex of palm. Each time the monsoon fog rolled in Colonel Yvor would have Billy Joe cut the grass. That is, he would send him out with his bayonet to cut down the high elephant grass that afforded cover for an enemy assault.

"What happened to Clancy?"

Appelfinger looked at the colonel. "I don't know."

The colonel winked at Sergeant Billy Joe and Sergeant Billy Joe shook his head.

"I don't know," Private Appelfinger said. "I left him over there someplace." He pointed. "And when I got back he was gone."

"I mean what happened to Alpha?"

"They're gone too."

"All?"

"Yes."

Billy Joe gave a low subsonic whistle and winked at the colonel.

"How?"

"They hit us."

"Why?"

"We were the Unfriendlies."

"But did Clancy ask for it?"

"You mean did he provoke an attack?"

"Yes."

"No."

"We heard different," Billy Joe said.

"Positive," Colonel Yvor said.

"We provoked the attack by being here instead of Jersey City, instead of our own country. Is that what you want me to say?"

"That's what we don't want you to say," Colonel Yvor said.

"It's the last thing we want you to say," Billy Joe said.

"What do you want me to say?"

"Say it was God's will."

"But it was Colonel Yvor's will," Appelfinger said.

"That's the same thing," Billy Joe said.

"Positive," Colonel Yvor said.

"You mean you're God?" Appelfinger said.

"God is everywhere," Billy Joe said.

"Think about that," Colonel Yvor said.

"Maybe Clancy asked for it a little bit," Appelfinger said.

"Tell us more."

"Maybe he wanted them to make a hit."

"More."

"Maybe he underestimated their strength."

"Are you trying to say—" Colonel Yvor said—"are you trying to say something?"

"What about this," Private Appelfinger said. "What if I tell you the truth?"

"That depends on what it is," Colonel Yvor said.

"There are all kinds of truths," Billy Joe said.

"I never knew that."

"Don't lie. You knew it," Billy Joe said.

"I will tell you the truth as I know it."

"Tell the truth as I know it," Colonel Yvor said.

It was Private Appelfinger's turn to whistle now. "I couldn't do that."

"Of course you could," Billy Joe said.

"You'll be doing it for your country," Colonel Yvor said.

"I couldn't do that to my buddy Clancy," Appelfinger said.

"Think about this," Colonel Yvor said. "How could Clancy be your buddy when he was a captain and you're a private?"

"They were buddies, sir," Billy Joe said.

"I'll be damned," Colonel Yvor said. "But what about your country?" Colonel Yvor said.

"Yes, what about your country?" Billy Joe said.

"What about my country?"

"If the Unfriendlies lie and cheat and steal do you want us to sit idly by?"

"Do you want us to just sit around on our ass?" Billy Joe said.

"If the other side, the Unfriendlies," Colonel Yvor said, "go in for lying and cheating and stealing, why can't we go in for mendacity?"

"By mendacity you want me to lie?"

Colonel Yvor said, "Why is it that everything we do is wrong and everything the Unfriendlies do is perfectly all right?"

"I want to know that too," Billy Joe said.

"Because of moral evolution."

"Repeat."

"Because of moral evolution."

"Is there such a thing?"

"I don't think there is such a thing," Billy Joe said.

"We can make moral evolution," Appelfinger said.

"Can you make evolution?"

"Evolution is everywhere."

"You still can't make evolution."

"Ah, but we can," Appelfinger said. "That's the secret."

"How?"

"Because we must."

"I didn't say why, I said how?"

"The chances of our getting out of here alive are pretty nil," Appelfinger said. "The private doesn't have to answer the colonel's question."

"Not correct."

"Yes, that's correct," Colonel Yvor said. "Answer me as a human being. How? How do we make moral evolution?"

"By starting it."

"There's a war on."

"That's why we should start it."

"I see now why the Romans fed the Christians to the tigers," Colonel Yvor said.

"I'm not a Christian."

"The colonel still wants to feed you to the tigers," Billy Joe said.

"Yes," Colonel Yvor said.

"I'm a mere evolutionist."

"The colonel still wants to feed you to the tigers."

"He fed Clancy to the tigers," Appelfinger said.

"Is that what you meant when you said you would tell the truth?"

"Yes."

Colonel Yvor looked at Sergeant Billy Joe and Sergeant Billy Joe looked at Colonel Yvor and they both at once winked. Then they both looked out into the jungle where the Unfriendlies were. The three-canopy jungle rose like an endless impenetrable wall of doom, a doom that not only knew and mocked but seemed to cherish the fate of men now, abide it. This is what Yvor thought and Billy Joe too, not thinking it but knowing that out of dark Asia, abiding; abiding and dark in the bright hurting sun, the saffron-robed priests, and even the triumphant and straw-hatted peasants, and the clearings and the alleys they have made are only for an hour and the cities too called Danang and Hue and Saigon are maybe for a minute, maybe only a second before the doom will do what it did to Angkor Wat, before the tiger of jungle swallows them all in some slow patient tangle of death which is its own life.

"And that is why I believe in moral evolution," Appelfinger said.

"Make sense, boy."

"Don't you see, it's all we can do?"

"No."

"Don't you see it's the only weapon we've got?"

"No."

"The only tool man ever discovered."

"No."

"That everything else is junk."

"No. Let me tell you, boy," Billy Joe said. "Listen to the colonel."

"Yes," Colonel Yvor said. "If I had a boy who was not a Socialist at fourteen I would think there was something wrong with him. But you're not fourteen, Appelfinger."

"I'm not a Socialist either."

"There's something wrong with you," Billy Joe said.

"Can I say something?" Bethany said.

"No," Colonel Yvor said. "You're not even supposed to be here."

"Are you supposed to be here?"

"The colonel is supposed to be any place he damn pleases," Billy Joe said. "If the colonel were not here the Communists would be here. Is that what you want to see happen?"

"Billy," Colonel Yvor said.

"Positive," Billy Joe said.

"I don't believe anything anybody says, including what you just said," Peter said.

"I thought you were dead," the colonel said.

"No," Bethany said. "Peter has got to the point of many

Americans where things get so bad he doesn't want to say any more."

"What I don't like," Colonel Yvor said, "is this silence."

"Silence?"

"The silence of the enemy," Colonel Yvor said.

"Positive," Billy Joe said. "We came to rescue Clancy and we got pinned down."

"No," Colonel Yvor said.

Appelfinger pointed over and into the jungle.

"So you pinned the remains of Alpha against a mahogany log?"

"I planned to go back."

"All of us do," Colonel Yvor said.

"Will you enlarge on that?"

"All of us do." Colonel Yvor said nothing more. He simply looked down to the side as though listening for the enemy to make their move. As though resting now before the last, the final fire fight. He had already said in the last few minutes more words than he had said in a lifetime. Until now, and certainly since he had arrived in Nam, he had confined himself, almost limited himself, to one word—bullshit. It had seemed to cover everything. Why had he talked so much now? Was it the civilians? Was it death? Yes, that was it. That must be it. Mai Li and Billy Joe never needed any talking to or with. Everything was understood perfectly without talking. That must be why he married Mai Li, so there would be nothing unseemly about not talking. They had no language to talk in, so they could communicate better. Talk is a defense against communication. With Sergeant Billy Joe there was no language they could talk in so the communication was perfect there too. Was there a language he could talk to the enemy in? Yes. Death. But why were they refusing to talk? Why were their guns so silent? Maybe they were getting up something good to tell us. And tell us all at once. That would be good. Anything would be good except this silence. Talk to me. And then Colonel Yvor said again, "Talk to me."

"What?"

"Not you," the colonel said. "They . . ." And then the colonel repeated the word "they" and then the colonel said, "I have still got my arms. My arms will be well soon again and I can take them out of this plaster cast across my chest. I have been in this attitude of permanent prayer now for four months. How can I function? How did I function without arms?" Colonel Yvor said. "It is simple. A man doesn't need them any more in this world. Arms. Arms are useless any more."

"I think, sir, they are making their move."

"When you stop thinking and actually see them making their move inform me."

"Positive."

The mission, Colonel Yvor thought. Clancy's mission. What would I do if I were the remains of Alpha? Everyone in the world is an Alpha survivor. But if you are the only one? Would I try to make it up Ridge Red Boy? That's what Clancy will do. He will try to make it home.

There was a twang. A guitar twang.

"Don't do that, Peter," Bethany said.

"It doesn't make any difference," Colonel Yvor said. "The Unfriendlies know we are here."

"Why don't they hit us then?"

"They want to get Clancy first. All of Alpha first. Then they will talk to us."

"That sign you've got on you," Colonel Yvor said, pointing to Bethany's button. 'I Have a Dream.' Do you still have it? The dream?"

"Yes," Bethany said.

"Are you sure you don't want a new button, 'I *Had* a Dream'?"

"No," Bethany said.

"Then you will make it out?"

"Yes. Yes," Bethany said. "Because they can only kill us."

There was no break in the steady terrific jungle silence, the jungle that waited and watched—listened.

344

Peter played a sweet ballad song. It was not a protest song, but melodious and sad. A lament. The survivors of Alpha sang. Soft. Softly. Then a 90-millimeter North Vietnamese rocket shrieked over and into their song perimeter and exploded with crashing of tympani and cymbals and drums and when the monsoon shifted there was nothing—the song had ended.

36

TYGER, Tyger burning bright in the jungle of the night, did He smile His work to see? Did He who made the lamb make thee?

And me, Tiger? Did He make the man who led Alpha? The ear collectors? That's not true, you know. That is, you tell a lie by only telling part of the truth. Both sides did it. Because a war is not a teaparty, Tiger. The jungle is cruel, Tiger. I hope Mike tells what both sides did when Alpha was hit. The evidence is all there on Ridge Red Boy. All of it. Mike, write out of this jungle. I hope to Christ he tells it all. I hope to Christ, Tiger, someone tells the battle. I hope to Christ Mike, or someone, frames Ridge Red Boy in all its fearful symmetry. Tiger, Mike, the Crip, has got to do it for Alpha. For all the Alphas yet to come.

Tiger, that could put me out of business.

Clancy could no longer see the tiger but he could see the tiger's eyes.

There comes a time in everyone's life, Tiger, when he must begin all over again. Knightbridge did it. But he had Nurse Bliss. Well, I had got Madame Dieudonné. A man must start from scratch. Starting from scratch is an untrue cliché, Tiger. A man has got to start from something. A woman. And if a man's any good he ends with a woman.

Tiger? Remember me. Try to make it right.

The survivor of Alpha, Clancy, watched the moon rise big. Watched the moon rise over Ridge Red Boy. Over Madame Dieudonné's underground villa. Over Vietnam. Come up all over Asia. Innocent. As though not a thing were happening. The problem is we are unable to understand the suffering of others. The moon started it. The indifference of the moon. The moon started it and it quickly spread to others. Now the light of the new moon was visiting all the problem places and seeing nothing. There is nothing to be seen in the light of the moon. Sad? No, it would be sadder still if the moon revealed, if the moon exposed Asia. Clancy was hidden from the new pale light by the overhang from the mahogany tree. About now Madame Dieudonné would emerge naked in the moon. Strange? Not if you have lived in Asia. The moon is warm. Particularly if you have to live in an underground villa. The moon is warm. The sun is cruel. The Asian sun is cruel because it discovers everything in the world. The moon is kind. The moon is gentle and hiding and as Madame Dieudonné glided through it naked the moon sat still. Why did Madame Dieudonné walk naked in the moon? Everyone had a theory. Clancy believed that she was going to join him on Red Boy. As Clancy started to crawl out he beckoned the peasant to follow and the peasant did. The peasant followed Clancy because people always did. Even without the Roman helmet. The helmet with the crest on top was back someplace with all the dead on A for Alpha's ridge, Ridge Red Boy, already twisted in vines, strangled by Asia.

Madame Dieudonné was simply taking a walk naked in the moon as was her custom. Hell, it was not her custom. Who said it was her custom? You can't have a custom of walking naked in the moon. Who says you can't? Madame Dieudonné did. If you do not believe this there is no poetry in your life. If there is no poetry in our lives there is no poetry in our deaths. Madame Dieudonné had learned about the trouble on Clancy's ridge over the French shortwave radio from Laos. Everyone knew. The whole world knew. Like Madame Dieudonné, when your whole world disappears on a ridge, you behave strangely. You revert. You walk naked in a new moon near Laos. But she had not behaved thus when Colonel Dieudonné got it. Because Colonel Dieudonné had been a business proposition, a business proposition with rubber connections in Paris. A business reverse is terrible, but not tragic. It makes for an advertisement but not for a poem, for suicide but not for a walk naked under a naked moon near Laos.

The moon that should be tired, rising so many times, came up out of Laos like a cause, as though it had something to say, to show you, to point out, like, There's where Victor Charlie lives, There's where he hides, and There's where he moves and There's where he hit Clancy. There—near Red Boy, where she walks naked.

The woman who walked alone. The woman who did not stay home in her villa. The woman who had no choice. It is so easy to say that she is corrupting all the distant youth in Asia. It is so easy to say. But there are no youth left in this part of Asia. They are all off giving their death for a cause that has got nothing to do with man or woman. Has got nothing to do with life. So it is easy to say. It is easy to say that she should not walk naked at moontime in the far fantastic jungle of the night. It is easy to say.

Clancy could hear the forest grow. You could hear the jungle breathe. Festooned with drooping and dripping vines, intestinal like a creature opened up. The forest quickly closed up to hide its insides. To hide Clancy. To hide tenderly Clancy and his new buddy, the peasant. A buddy is anybody you die with. Clancy was bound for home, Ridge Red Boy. The peasant followed. The Unfriendly followed. To keep an eye on him? Not necessarily. No man wants to die alone. Clancy was the peasant's property. The peasant had discovered Clancy. The peasant would not allow his property to wander off. How would you feel if your property wandered off in the direction of Ridge Red Boy? How would you feel if you were trying to keep your head when you had lost so much blood? That's the way the peasant felt. Light. Very light. How would you feel if you had been shot by your own people and someone you have been taught to shoot asked you to lie down in the bamboo bed and die beside him. That's the way the peasant felt. The peasant could not allow his discovery to get away. A man who would not defend himself. It was quite a discovery. They were tied together now against all the rest of life. One Friendly and one Unfriendly had joined together to constitute an army of two. It was quite an army. They would recapture Red Boy together and then make secret plans. They did not know what the plans were yet. One plan might be to discover a language, then everything might fall into place. It might not. Another plan would be to save something. Save what? Save something, that's all. Everything is not being saved and they would save something. They would be the great saviors. They would have many plans.

Now it was getting very dim in the bright moon. Madame Dieudonné, clothed in Vietnamese nakedness, caught up with Clancy. They would take a rest. They would lie down in the bamboo together. Nothing hurt any more now. There was no more pain.

The Bamboo Bed came in gently as death and quickly picked up Clancy and the peasant, and their hands were gripped together. The crew put their bodies on the Bamboo Bed leaving them with their hands together the way they found them together with their hands together because it seemed right. Exactly right.

Knightbridge and Jane were both looking good. Excellent. It was a good day for a pickup. The Bamboo Bed was a fine ship. It had come right through the jungle forest. The trees didn't stop it at all. The rotor blades cut through the crowded trees nicely as though they were not there. It was good to be on the Bamboo Bed with the Friendlies and the Unfriendlies. Everyone was on the Bamboo Bed. Madame Dieudonné was beautiful. No one wants to die in an underground villa. It is best to keep walking until it gets you. That is the best plan, until something gets you. She is beautiful and she is here. All are here. The Bamboo Bed was making a final trip. That was nice. The war must be over. Over for me. And Mike, my friend Mike, caught up with me at last. At the last. The end. Mike does not have to remove me from command. I removed myself. Who do you blame for Red Boy? They? Clancy? All. Everyone. Clancy and all. We were all on Ridge Red Boy. Did He who made the lamb make thee? All.

The Bamboo Bed was entering the monsoon. It got black-dark. Clancy tried to hold the Bamboo Bed together until it came out on the other side. It took everything he had left. When the Bamboo Bed came out the other side there was nothing left.

The copter soared up against the sun, aerial and light. The Vietnamese sun bore down with such a magnitude in the abiding Asian forest that the butterfly, the Bamboo Bed, the insect in the vastness, was for long seconds visible until it once again came into the long shadow of the monsoon and was forever lost, disappeared, eaten by tigers, enveloped in the gentle, tomblike Asian night.

Mike looked down past all the bodies, down to the peaceful and jewel-green and abiding jungle below. The assignation place. There was Hill 904. There was the villa. There was Ridge Red Boy. There was death—she was our captain's bride.

LANNAN SELECTIONS

The Lannan Foundation, located in Santa Fe, New Mexico, is a family foundation whose funding focuses on special cultural projects and ideas which promote and protect cultural freedom, diversity, and creativity.

The literary aspect of Lannan's cultural program supports the creation and presentation of exceptional English-language literature and develops a wider audience for poetry, fiction, and nonfiction.

Since 1990, the Lannan Foundation has supported Dalkey Archive Press projects in a variety of ways, including monetary support for authors, audience development programs, and direct funding for the publication of the Press's books.

In the year 2000, the Lannan Selections Series was established to promote both organizations' commitment to the highest expressions of literary creativity. The foundation supports the publication of this series of books each year, and works closely with the Press to ensure that these books will reach as many readers as possible and achieve a permanent place in literature. Authors whose works have been published as Lannan Selections include: Ishmael Reed, Stanley Elkin, Ann Quin, Nicholas Mosley, William Eastlake, and David Antin, among others.

SELECTED DALKEY ARCHIVE PAPERBACKS

FOR A FULL LIST OF PUBLICATIONS, VISIT:
www.dalkeyarchive.com